MIDLIFE MOUSE

by WAYNE FRANKLIN

Cover illustration and design by Wayne Franklin
with art direction by Nicklaus Louis
"The Last Drawing" illustration by Chris Garrison
Author photograph by Kris Wheeler

Printed in the United States of America

First Printing, 2013

ISBN 978-0-9888359-0-0 (hardcover)
ISBN 978-0-9888359-1-7 (paperback)
ISBN 978-0-9888359-2-4   (Kindle)
ISBN 978-0-9888359-3-1   (e-book)

Wannabe Books

www.midlifemouse.com

For Kelli, Savannah and Cooper

Contents

Midlife Mouse is a work of fiction. Given that it deals in prophecies, curses, benevolent intelligent machines, secret organizations designed to take over the world's largest media conglomerate and, strangest of all, a fully functional American family, that should be self-evident. However, the fictional events and fictional characters of this book dwell in a world very much like our own. (Now we're getting to what I like to call the "Please Don't Sue Me" section.) Any resemblance between fictional characters and actual, living, breathing human beings is purely a coincidence. In creating a mythology for the Walt Disney Company, the book weaves in strands of real Disney history and refers to a number of legendary Disney artists, executives and Imagineers -- and to Walt Disney himself. However, as they pertain to the mythology of the Prophecy of the New Son and the Council of the Nine and its constituent fan groups, these appearances should not be interpreted as factual events. Consider the versions of the Walt Disney Company, Walt Disney World and the various Disney legends here as existing in a parallel reality, one where Disney Magic is more than just a marketing slogan. Those who know the history of the company and its theme park properties well will note that certain attractions have been altered or removed completely from the Magic Kingdom since the time depicted in this book, while others have been added. Based on those and other clues, savvy readers will be able to pinpoint the events in this book as taking place in an alternate version of 2009 and 2010. My hope is that you will see this book as it is intended: a satirical look at the nature of fandom and an admiring tribute to the visionary spirit of one Walter Elias Disney.

Chapter One:
Skulking in the Shadows of a Giant Spaceman's Legs

"Hell of a thing." As he peered through the fractional slit between the curtains of the darkened hotel room, Bill Durmer spoke a little too loudly. The situation demanded more of an under-the-breath delivery, but he made a habit of never speaking in a manner that could be described as a murmur. He knew it unlikely, but on the off chance that someone should ever write a book about him, he would find it utterly embarrassing to read the phrase "Durmer murmured." Moreover, being overly empathetic (he could never bring himself to darken the doors of a karaoke bar without becoming physically ill), Bill could not bear the shame on behalf of the writer. Therefore, he always spoke loudly and distinctly out of an abundance of caution. He breathed deeply and tried to pierce the pitch to spot even the slightest hint of movement outside.

"Hell of a thing." Bill cast a sideways glance toward the small figure crouching next to him in the dark. Under ordinary circumstances, he would have chided his daughter for repeating his mild profanity. After all, for most of her nine years, "stupid" and "shut up" were deemed the foulest of language. These, however, were clearly not ordinary circumstances. "I don't think Mama's going to be very happy with us."

Bill sighed. "No, Cleary, I suspect she isn't." He half expected his wife to come bursting through the door at any moment: first, to scold them both for their pie-eyed foolishness, and second, to save them from their current predicament. The more he considered the former, the less he wanted the latter. He hoped he wouldn't see her for quite some time — at least not until he had found a way to explain his actions of the previous two weeks.

It wasn't that Bill was afraid of his wife. She wasn't shrewish or harsh in any way. He simply hated to disappoint her. By his estimation, he had disappointed her in grand fashion at least seven times in their marriage. All of those missteps combined now paled in comparison to this most recent adventure. He wondered if she would ever forgive him. Could she? Could anyone? He thought it best to start the process of making amends with the closest of his victims. "I'm sorry I got you into this, Sweetie."

"It's okay, Daddy. I wouldn't have missed it for the world."

Bill could hear the bittersweet smile in her voice. It reminded him of the time she voluntarily gave up her spot in the party scene in the Decent Chance Ballet Company's annual production of The Nutcracker. Although winning that role had been the proudest moment of her young life, she willingly, out of compassion and a preternatural selflessness, gave it up to her best friend, Dara Thompson.

***

Thompsons had been friends with Durmers for generations, dating back to the founding of Decent Chance as a Utopian experiment in the mid-1800s. At least the families told it that way. In truth, the Thompsons and Durmers were bitter rivals for decades, feuding over the privilege to serve as the town's official Jubilee Masters. The title was far more regal than the responsibility. In earlier generations, Jubilee Masters were little more than unpaid fishmongers, tasked with scooping up all the shrimp, blue crabs and fish that would mysteriously, spontaneously migrate into the shallows during a Jubilee and then distributing them to all the families in town. As the saying in Decent Chance went, "If the eyes are the windows to the soul, then fishy fingers are its rafters." Bill often joked that the town's poetic license was revoked before anyone could bother to define the metaphoric roof those pungent rafters supported.

It was only after 1900, when the city of Bay Minette stole the county seat under cover of darkness, that the rift was healed. Bay Minette's men had affected the state-mandated move by staging a murder. The idea was to lure the sheriff and his deputies away from the old county seat of Daphne so the county files could be smuggled out while they were away. According to the murder yarn weaved by the Bay Minette leaders, a Durmer was the victim and a Thompson the perpetrator. When the patriarchs of the two families got wind of the hoax, informed by an embarrassed and dead sleepy Sheriff wearing only pink, one-piece pajamas and a Colt revolver, they resolved to put the feud behind them and unite in defense against a common enemy: everyone not from Decent Chance.

Always more prosperous than neighboring towns, Decent Chance had failed to realize its full potential due to the bitter acrimony of the feud. From that fateful night, however, with the two wealthiest and most powerful of the founding families united in common cause, the town resolved to convince the world what they had long held as fact themselves: that the people of Decent Chance were vastly superior to everyone else. Recent polling data showed that as many as 14 people outside the city actually believed them.

✳✳✳

Bill had known Dara's father, Kenny, since birth. They were inseparable throughout grade school, once declaring themselves blood brothers after watching an episode of *The Andy Griffith Show*. They tried to recite the exact oath sworn by Andy and Opie, but could never get past the part about Boojum Snark. The name would send them into peals of laughter every time they said it until they couldn't utter more than "Boo" without rolling on the ground, convulsing together in fits of silent guffaws. Their friendship waned for a time in high school when Kenny joined the football team and Bill the marching band. Shortly after graduation, Bill left the state for college, but they picked up where they had left off when Bill moved back home. In the meantime, Kenny had married Bill's sister.

Cousins and best friends, Cleary Durmer and Dara Thompson were born only 16 hours apart in adjacent birthing suites at Mobile Infirmary. They took their first steps on the same day. Always the more verbal of the two, Cleary spoke her first words several months prior to her friend, but her first word was "Dara." Sure, it sounded like "Dada," but Cleary made her meaning known by always patting her friend on the head like a dog when she said it. In fact, she also said "Dada" when petting the family dog, but everyone wrote that off as coincidence. At three, the girls started pre-ballet classes under the tutelage of Nancy Durmer Thompson, Dara's mother and Bill's sister.

Nancy had taken the reins of the Decent Chance Ballet Company from her mother, who had founded it in the mid-1960s. From the girls' first lesson, it was clear to everyone Nancy was grooming Dara for future stardom. Maybe it was the way she glided into the studio the first day of class, picked up her daughter, spun the girl around and announced to all present, "and I'm grooming this one for future stardom." Nancy was renowned for her subtlety.

Once the girls were old enough to audition for roles in the company's productions, everyone assumed Nancy would simply wield her power to put Dara in a featured role. Then something unexpected happened. Dara froze up in her spurious audition. Though she eventually danced well, her initial trepidation cast doubts in the minds of the casting committee. For the first two minutes of her allotted five, Dara simply walked in circles, chewing her nails and murmuring to herself. (As a Thompson freed from the curse of her mother's maiden name, Dara was allowed to murmur with abandon.)

The audition disaster put Nancy in an untenable position. If she allowed the committee to have their way, come Christmas her only daughter would be watching from the audience while, as Nancy described them to her husband, "fatties and the spawn of mechanics" stole the spotlight. On the other hand, casting Dara would make Nancy look even worse. If there were one thing less appealing to Nancy than her daughter's humiliation, it was damage to her own reputation. So Nancy did the only thing a self-loving, image conscious Junior Leaguer could do: she resolved to treat her daughter as a pariah.

Mere hours after the cast list had been posted, Nancy sat on the deck at Bill's house, high atop the bluff overlooking Mobile Bay, sipping a mint julep and making a show of her disappointment. She alternately cried and fumed and dramatically reassured her daughter that it was okay to be untalented. Plenty of unremarkable people have led fulfilling lives, Nancy reminded her, though she couldn't name any off hand. For her part, Dara couldn't fathom the sudden flip-flop of her mother's affections. In all of her seven years, her mother had never uttered even the slightest criticism, forgiving mistakes and justifying failures with half-baked excuses and cleverly worded euphemisms: "she possesses so much beauty, it couldn't be contained in a normal-sized head," or "why should she use a potty when a planter is a more natural choice?" But this day, Nancy's euphemisms were wearing thin and occasionally giving way to unshielded insults. Dara could bear it no more. She ran weeping into the house and hid under Cleary's bed.

Cleary found her there, huddled up with a menagerie of bean-bag animals. She brushed her cousin's hair back with her fingers and simply said, "Don't worry. I'll take care of it."

Bill suspected something was up when he heard his daughter's call for help. The tone of her cry didn't quite ring true, but he ran for her nonetheless. He found her sprawled at the bottom of the stairs, clutching her ankle. He scooped her up and carried her to the sofa.

"Katherine!" Calling his wife was unnecessary, as she had already handed off the baby to Kenny and was collecting ice cubes in a dish towel. Before she could reach the sofa with the cold compress, Nancy had identified the loophole that would restore her dignity.

"Dara, dear! You're back in the show!" She called upstairs. "Isn't that wonderful news?"

"Your niece is in pain, here," Bill snapped at his sister. "Can't you save your gloating for later?"

"I'm sorry, sweetheart." Nancy feigned concern for Cleary, shoving her brother aside and taking the girl's hand with a well-rehearsed look of compassion. "But it's really a blessing this happened now, because as clumsy as you are this was just as likely to happen on stage. But you can't help it. You simply have too much of your mother in you."

"I don't think it's that serious," Katherine interrupted, ignoring the insult. She may have left her job as a nurse to focus on raising her children, but she had never stopped nursing. "Cleary, are you sure this hurts? I think this will heal up before you have to start rehearsals."

Cleary let out a pitiful moan and squeezed out a few tears. "I don't think so, Mama." She spied Dara sheepishly entering the room. "It's okay. I would want Dara to take my place." She smiled at her cousin. Real tears mixed with false ones.

❋❋❋

Sitting there in the dark of the hotel room, Bill realized this was the first time he had thought about "The Nutcracker Business," as it came to be known in the Durmer household, without his blood boiling a little. Perhaps the bizarre events of the past two weeks had brought him to a place of forgiveness toward his sister. Or maybe it was simply that the rush of adrenalin and the pounding of his pulse in his ears prevented him from feeling anything else.

"I can't see a thing," Bill said, peeking under the curtain. "You think they're still out there?"

"They're still out there."

"How do *you* know?" he asked with an incredulous tone.

"Because these situations never just end. They always come to a head."

Bill snickered, "And you've been in these situations how many times before?"

"Never," Cleary demurred. "But I watch a lot of TV."

"That's okay," he replied. "So do I. I am just a glorified TV repairman after all."

"No, you're not. You're a genius." Had Cleary been able to see her father's reaction, she would have seen a man humbled and grateful. At that moment, Bill felt at least one person in the world truly understood him. She didn't offer her praise with conditions or with scorn as his sister often did, nor did she temper it with talk of contentment and acceptance of one's circumstances, as would her mother. There was no talk of prophecies or destiny or secret councils or "word bearers" — words he had heard all too often over the last two weeks. She stated it simply as fact. For that, Bill would be eternally grateful.

Suddenly, it began to rain the hard rain of a central Florida summer thunderstorm. Now came the *tink-tink-tink* of tiny hailstones rapping on the window. Bill felt sorry for those outside in this mess, and for a moment he considered inviting them inside to get dry. He knew that would be a mistake. A flash of lightning illuminated the courtyard. In that instant, Bill could make out the shapes of men crouching behind huge alphabet blocks or skulking in the shadows of a giant spaceman's legs. Thunder rumbled and shook the window so hard that both Bill and Cleary jumped back clear of the glass, just in case.

They slowly crept back to their vantage point. With each flash of lightning, Bill tried to discern if any of the figures on the roof were actual snipers or only metal cutouts of toy soldiers. He saw one of the figures move slightly. Another flinched at a particularly bright flash of light. The lightning glinted off the front element of another's rifle scope.

Cleary sighed, "Yep. They're still out there."

"Yep." Bill tried to count them. Thanks to the lightning, he had made out at least two dozen, but he suspected many more. He and Cleary both started at the sound of footsteps from the roof above. Bill shifted his weight and collapsed back against the bed. They were surrounded. How had it come to this? All he wanted was a fresh start, to embrace a new dream — albeit a profoundly stupid one. How had he let it spin so far out of control? He wanted to offer his daughter words of comfort. He wanted to reassure her that it would all be okay, but he couldn't. When he tried to speak, the lies caught in his throat and would go no further.

All he could muster was this: "As God is my witness, I never knew Disney World had its own S.W.A.T. team."

Chapter Two:
The Mystery of the Towel Baby Couple

A white ibis glided down, snagged a chunk of leftover croissant from an abandoned tray of breakfast and swooped within arm's reach of Bill as he stumbled toward the food court. At home, Bill would routinely quip to his family that one should not be expected to do something so complex and essential as making coffee before they've actually *had* a cup of coffee. Katherine and Cleary would chastise him, reminding Bill that, of the four coffee pots they owned, only the French press wasn't programmable, and each time, Bill would resolve to use the feature. He never did. Instead, most late evenings found him dozing off in his workshop, trying to keep awake long enough to install one more actuator or servo, or fine-tune the control system on his geek project *du jour*.

To his left, splashes and squeals and giggles emanated from the resort's swimming pool. Without hearing a single accent, Bill knew instinctively every one of those guests was from the North. No Southerner would be caught dead swimming in 70-degree temperatures. Northerners may have considered the weather balmy, but Bill had lived through many a warmer Christmas than this back home in Decent Chance. The very thought shifted his mood from bad to worse, and his face reflected the change. No number of classic holiday songs by mid-century crooners booming over ingeniously camouflaged speakers, no cleverly themed trees decorated with motion picture film as garland and strands of tiny studio lights, no talk of "the magic of the holidays" could convince him that this was any way to spend his Christmas.

He muttered to himself, "Humbug," as he pushed open the door to the food court. He slipped deeper into his funk when he saw the line at the coffee dispenser. For years, he and Katherine had told the children, "You decide your mood." Today, he decided his mood would be Crabby Old Man. Without fail, he was less successful at following his own advice than were his children. He was just grateful they hadn't come along to call him out on it.

"Merry Christmas!" bellowed a voice ahead of Bill in the coffee line. Surely, this guy was not queuing up for his first cup. Bill, who had been lost in complete lack of thought, reacted slowly. His eyes followed the pale, pudgy legs up from their fleshy bases wrapped in black rubber garden togs, to emerald green Bermuda shorts whose waistband was straining and groaning under the burden of too many all-you-can-eat buffets, and beyond to a triple-extra-large Hawaiian shirt printed with Santa hat-wearing hula girls dancing under palm trees bedecked with Christmas lights. His eyes settled on a massive, grinning head topped with a lighted, foam Christmas tree masquerading as a hat. "Of course, it's not Christmas Day yet," the big man belted out jovially, "but every day's like Christmas when you're here, huh?"

Bill wondered what manner of escapist holiday fervor could reduce a man to this level of buffoonery. Just because people were on vacation didn't mean they had taken leave of their sense of sight. Or taste. But this man had seemingly taken leave of both. And of his sense of shame to boot.

Bill nodded politely. He had a rule against making small talk. Nevertheless, he felt compelled to indulge people's desire to make meaningless conversation ever since he was a boy, when he had heard Father Macerney speak on a verse in Philippians that said you should consider others better than yourself. Since that fateful day — a day marked by one of those embarrassing, life-altering nothings of a moment that only happen in childhood — Bill had tried his best to do exactly that. He mostly failed.

That being said, he simply couldn't bring himself to talk about nothing. Instead, when confronted with a bout of small talk, he would shoot for an inappropriately profound response, backing the person into a conversational corner.

A simple, "Some weather we're having" would yield a response like, "And to think one stray bit of space rock could rip away our atmosphere, leaving us gasping, helpless, metaphorically naked as the day we were born. We are so fragile, you and I. Let us silently revel in our fragility." This usually led to the other person backing away slowly and avoiding eye contact.

He tried to assuage his guilt over his tendency to ambush people in conversation by telling himself it was his way of being salt and light in a dark, flavorless world. But he was simply killing the conversation as quickly as possible. Surely, Paul would have reconsidered the idea of considering others more important than yourself had he lived today. There was no way any of the Philippians were as annoying as your average American.

In this instance, desperately in need of coffee and wanting to avoid deeper dialogue, he opted for the easy way out. "It is quite lovely," Bill replied.

"Yes, it is. Yes, *it is*." The big man with the Christmas tree on his head seemed satisfied, justified even, by Bill's response. Just then, the person at the head of the line finished preparing his coffee. It was the big man's turn to fuel up. Offering a parting bon mot to Bill, the man bellowed, "Enjoy your trip!"

Bill nodded and smiled. He glanced around and studied the room as Christmas Tree Head filled his oversized travel mug with Nescafé. World Premiere Food Court was, as with everything at Walt Disney World, themed to the hilt. Bill noted the design influences of early 20th century movie theatres: velvet ropes strung between brass stanchions, marquees above the service counters, posters for seemingly every Disney film ever created and an old single-reel projector on display amidst the tables. Bill thought the design overused the filmstrip motif. *Okay, we get it. It's a movie theme. Ease up on the sprocket holes.* Otherwise, he found it a whimsical delight. His mood lightened as he took it all in. The big man popped the top on his mug and gave Bill a mock salute.

"Have fun today," Bill offered. *Have fun today?* Like it or not, he was better at blather than he'd care to admit. Dispensing coffee into the first of his mugs, Bill thought again about Father Macerny's sermon some 27 years earlier.

✳✳✳

That morning, when he was 12, he and Kenny had been laughing and teasing a girl named Jenny Tillman. She was a year their junior and going through an awkward phase. Her hair was chopped a little too short. She was skinny with arms and legs that seemed too long for her body. A mouth already full of large teeth was packed to the brim with shiny metal braces and a half-dozen rubber bands. Because her single mother's real estate business was foundering in the recession of the early 1980s, Jenny's clothes were weathered hand-me-downs that didn't quite fit. In other words, she was perfect fodder for the cruelty of prepubescent boys. And, as 12-year-olds often do, the boys believed they were invisible to adults that morning.

"And you young people," Father Macerney intoned, "steel yourselves against the temptation to tease or to treat cruelly those less fortunate than you." Billy, as he was known before college, hadn't heard a single word of the priest's sermon until that point, and he didn't know what had suddenly grabbed his attention then. Over his 12 years, he had mastered the fine art of ignoring priests, to the point that he could stare directly at the speaker, nod at appropriate points, and glance away to maintain a sense of realism — all while reciting the entire script of Star Wars in his head. Looking back on that day through the filter of adult experience and wisdom, Bill could only explain his sudden awakening as being gifted "with ears to hear," but as a 12-year-old boy, he was sure someone had ratted him out. Either that, or the good Father had more going on spiritually than Bill would have cared to believe.

With trepidation, he looked up toward Father Macerney and found the priest staring directly at him. Macerney continued, "Recall the words of St. Paul when he wrote, 'Do nothing out of selfishness or out of vainglory; rather, humbly regard others as more important than yourselves.'"

What the? Bill's conscience was gripped. To that point, his spiritual life had consisted of doing whatever he wanted all week and wiping it away with a confession and a few Hail Mary's on the weekend. He wasn't a bad kid. He certainly wasn't "on the drugs" as his Maw-Maw Cleary would say. But this selflessness thing hit him like a ton of guilt bricks.

He struggled to fight back tears as guilt washed over him. In that moment, sitting in the rearmost pew of Our Lady of Superior Breeding, every arrogant action, every condescending thought came rushing back to him. He recalled giving his cousin Brenda the worst piece of cake (the piece with the least icing) at his 10th birthday party simply because he didn't like the way she smelled. Brenda's parents were hippies from Grayton Beach. The girl couldn't help it if her handmade hemp clothing reeked of patchouli oil and cannabis.

He thought about the time in gym class when a group of boys were picking on a new kid draped in dirty clothes, whose oily face was riddled with pimples and blemishes. Bill had said nothing. (The kid never suspected Bill later became the mysterious benefactor who kept his locker stocked with Clearasil.)

Offenses large and small rushed through his mind, culminating with poor, awkward Jenny Tillman sitting there in the pew in front of him. Out of the corner of his eye, he saw Kenny reaching forward to hand something to Jenny. Horrified, Bill realized it was the note they had been passing back and forth about the girl. He reached for the note, instead grabbing Kenny's hand and loosening his grip. The paper slipped out and landed on Jenny's mother's lap. Kenny caught his breath and buried his head in a hymnal. Bill froze, his arm still extended.

Jenny's mother picked up the paper, glanced at it briefly, and handed it back to Bill. "You should pay attention," was all she said to him. Bill, eyes full of tears, nodded and turned his gaze back to Father Macerney. He never knew whether Ms. Tillman read the note. If so, she never let on.

In the 10th grade, Bill heard from mutual friends that Jenny Tillman had a crush on him. By that time, she had grown out of her awkward phase into quite a beauty, but Bill, still burdened by the shame of that day and the fear that her mother had indeed read the note, could never muster the courage to ask her out.

Years later, Bill and Katherine were walking through Bel Air Mall in Mobile when a curious sight caught his eye. There before him, larger than life, was a poster of a familiar-looking, beautiful brunette dressed only in a lacy, black bra and panties. Jenny Tillman had become a Victoria's Secret model. Although Kenny would tease Bill about Jenny every few years, Bill would quickly change the subject, mostly for Katherine's sake. He wasn't concerned that she would be jealous, but rather that she would learn what a thoughtless jerk he could be.

∗∗∗

The memory lingered as he filled his two souvenir mugs and began to make his way back to the room. Along the way, he noticed details he hadn't seen when the family checked in the night before. The All-Star Movies Resort was a far cry from a resort in the usual sense of the word. It was nothing more than a collection of three-story motel buildings grouped around a series of courtyards adorned with giant sculptures based on classic Disney films. Strip away the enormous brooms from Fantasia, the cutouts of Dalmatians, the ubiquitous filmstrips as balcony rails, and the place was little more than a typical roadside motel. But theming was key. Bill knew it was all so much lipstick on a fairly attractive pig, but he liked it.

A little boy sat behind the wheel of a sculpture of RC, the remote-controlled car from *Toy Story*, posing as his mother snapped a photo. At first, Bill thought he would describe it as life-sized. Then it occurred to him that a life-sized RC car would be the size of, well, an RC car. The thing suddenly seemed freakish to him, and he gave it a wide berth. He could swear its cartoon eyes were following him.

He passed through an open door roughly 12 feet tall set in a free standing wall and into a courtyard bordered on the other three sides by another giant wall opposite him, an even larger statue of Woody the cowboy on his right and, towering above the building, an enormous statue of Buzz Lightyear rising on his left. Bill stopped to take it in. If he squinted his eyes just right and blocked out everything of normal size, he could imagine he was a toy in Andy's room.

But then the difference in scale between Buzz and Woody and the rest of the design killed the illusion. If the scale of the walls and other toys was designed to make him feel like a toy, then that made the films' two heroes giants by comparison — ten times the size of the kid that would occupy this room. The more he thought about it, what at first glance had seemed charming became downright menacing. What kind of mad scientist designed this? He looked at his feet, to avoid the gaze of his giant toy overlords, stepped over a checker the size of a manhole cover, weaved between two alphabet blocks nearly as tall him and made his way up the stairs to his room. By the time he got there, he had managed to purge himself of his sudden fear of toys and gotten into an unreasonably perky mood. It was probably the coffee.

"Okay, what's it going to be?" Bill bellowed as he entered the motel room. "Which park will we hit today?" The Durmers had, to a person, a bad family habit of barking out whatever was on their minds as they entered a room, without regard to any conversations that might be taking place, naps that may be in progress or elderly guests with sensitive constitutions who might soil the furniture if startled. Katherine and the kids, guilty bellowers themselves, were unfazed.

"Animal Kingdom!" Cleary shouted.

"Ammal Keendom!" repeated Clay, the Durmer's three-year-old middle child. Cleary changed her mind and interrupted her brother before he could finish the protracted "dommmm..."

"No! Magic Kingdom!" she shouted.

"Maja Keendommmm!" Clay bellowed, echoing his sister. Bill turned to Katherine, who looked like an octopus wrangler as she attempted to feed the baby. Her only goal was to get another spoonful of puréed sweet potatoes into the baby's mouth without looking like the victim of a tuber hate crime.

"What about you, honey?" Bill asked. She frowned at him, shoved the spoon in the baby's mouth and, in one continuous motion, scooped up ten sheets of paper — stapled and folded lengthwise — out of the nearby carry-on bag, handed it to her husband and scooped more sweet potatoes from the jar.

"Enjoy," she said as she handed him the documents.

"What's this?"

"Nancy," Katherine growled. Turning her attention back to the baby, she managed to combine sing-songy and sarcastic tones in a way only mothers can, "Clementine Durmer, you better stop trying to grab this spoon. Yes, you better, or I'm gonna drown you in the toilet." The baby cackled, spraying sweet potatoes in every direction. Clay rolled onto the floor laughing at the mere mention of the word "toilet."

"Please don't kill the little one," Bill offered dryly. "I actually like that one."

"I heard that," Cleary chimed in without looking away from the TV. She had almost gotten the hang of her parents' irony. Still, just to be sure, she added, "Mommy, please don't kill Clementine."

Bill winced every time he heard Clementine's name spoken. Not that there was anything wrong with the name itself, but he never wanted to be those people — the ones who name their children alliteratively. In fact, it had never been their plan to do so.

Cleary Elise Durmer was named, in fine Southern tradition, for Katherine's maiden name and for Bill's mother, Elise Durmer. There was quite a scandal in the family for several months over the choice to make Cleary the baby's first name, rather than the middle, which anyone of good breeding knows is the proper way to apply the tradition. That, combined with what

Nancy perceived as Katherine's influence in Bill leaving The Church, led Nancy to refer to her as "that woman" for the better part of a year. Even to her face.

William Claymoor Durmer II was named for his great-grandfather. Bill had a rule against using names with numerals in them, but after the Cleary scandal, he couldn't bear another family controversy. He got one regardless. Katherine had barely gotten out the phrase, "and we'll call him Clay," when Nancy butted in saying that only Communists and truck drivers go by their middle names. Bill refrained from pointing out their grandfather had, in fact, answered to his middle name of Claymoor his entire life. (He had recently made it a personal rule to enjoy the absurdity of Nancy's hypocrisy in silence. Everyone needs a hobby.) As a result of Bill's silence, Clay's room was littered with toys, blankets, piggy banks, picture frames and t-shirts emblazoned with the name William, every one a gift from his aunt Nancy.

With Clementine's birth, Bill and Katherine's contrary nature got the best of them. Though they justified themselves by explaining it was the name of Katherine's great-grandmother, the truth is they did it just to get under Nancy's skin. The baby's full name? Nancy Clementine Durmer. Adding insult to spite, neither Bill nor Katherine had ever called the baby Nancy.

Bill opened the document, glanced at it and sighed. "Why? Just ... why?"

"She's your sister. You tell me," Katherine retorted.

Cleary butted in, "I thought we weren't going to speak ill of Aunt Nancy in front of..." She pointed at her brother, shielding the offending finger with the palm of her other hand. Clay was oblivious, transfixed by an old Goofy cartoon on television.

"Adult conversation," Katherine sharply replied. Cleary caught the meaning of her mother's cryptic remark and feigned shifting her attention to the cartoon.

"An itinerary? Seriously?" Bill's emerging good mood was quashed. "Why does she think she can give us an itinerary?"

"Because she paid for the trip," Katherine matter-of-factly stated.

"She didn't pay for anything," Bill snapped.

"Try telling her that." Kenny had gotten the trip as a thank-you from one of his company's vendors. He had inherited his father's construction

company shortly after college and quickly turned it into one of the premiere developers of so-called "New Urbanism" communities along the
Gulf Coast.

New Urbanism was all about meticulously planned communities that
put schools, shopping and work spaces within walking distance of residents' homes. Porches, parks and other features encouraged interaction between neighbors. But the prices made anyone of moderate means wonder
if the floors were paved with diamond-studded gold tiles, hand-laid by the
Pope himself. Bill found the basic philosophy admirable, but he agreed
with the movement's detractors when it came to the expense. It seemed like
just another means of class segregation — or at least segregating those with
interest-only mortgages from those smart enough not to fall for such nonsense. For that reason and the movement's tendency to embrace a design
aesthetic grounded in nostalgia, Bill was ambivalent, at best, about his best
friend's business. Nancy, of course, was a fan.

"I knew I'd regret this," he huffed.

"Bill..." Katherine chided him, motioning toward Cleary with her eyes.
The chief reason the Durmers had agreed to come along was for the girls'
birthdays. Dara's was December 20th and Cleary's the 21st. Birthday parties were difficult for Bill and Katherine every year. With Christmas only
days later, they had always found it difficult to give Cleary a day of her own.
Nancy, however, had never let a little thing like celebrating the birth of the
Christ child get in her way. Every year, she would host an elaborate Christmas Ball in Dara's honor and invite every child in Decent Chance within
two years of Dara's age and whose father earned at least $250,000. And
every other year, she would even invite a child with two working parents.
(To think her brother thought her an elitist!)

This year, however, Kenny convinced her that hosting a ball in a slow
economy would be in poor taste. Nancy had embraced the fashion of the
new frugality as quickly as anyone, going so far as to have her maid purchase store-brand groceries for the church's annual Thanksgiving food
drive. Never one to buck the latest social trends, Nancy agreed to cancel
the ball. She immediately hired a graphic designer to create "free the date"
cards, which she had printed on the finest linen stock and sent to every
family of means in Decent Chance, informing them of her choice to fore-
go the celebration out of respect for "families of lesser means and those
who made poor career choices." She even sent regrets to families she had

refused to invite in previous years. Why shouldn't she send non-invitations to those with whom she shared a mutual animosity? It was Christmas, after all.

Bill and Katherine got the kids and themselves dressed, put on a good face, and caught the bus to the Grand Floridian Resort, where the Thompsons were staying. Upon entering the Grand Lobby of the Victorian resort, Cleary gasped.

"Why didn't we stay here?" she asked naively. "This place is awesome!"

"It is beautiful, isn't it?" Katherine added, matching Cleary's enthusiasm.

Clay nearly fell backward looking up through the five-story lobby. He tugged at his father's pants. "Daddy? It goes way high up high!"

"Very high up high." Bill scooped the boy up. "You know who's staying here?"

"Nope."

"Well..." Bill drew it out, trying to build the boy's anticipation, "why don't we just call upstairs and see who comes down to meet us?"

"Okay!" Clay didn't know what game his Daddy was playing, but he was all in.

Bill made a quick call to his sister while Katherine roamed the lobby with the children. Within a couple of minutes, Nancy, Kenny, Dara and Dara's four-year-old sister, Elise, emerged from the elevator. Cleary and Dara ran to embrace each other.

"I can't believe we're going to turn nine at Disney World!" Cleary said excitedly.

Clay started jumping up and down at the sight of the Thompsons. "Auntsy Nancy!" He ran to Nancy, who scooped him up in her arms. Despite all her faults, she genuinely loved the boy.

"Well, hello there, young William!" Her voice dripped of Old Money South. Her Rs came out as "ahs" and she broadened and flattened her tongue against the floor of her mouth, so her voice resonated with a warm, wet tone. "Are you ready to go see Mickey Mouse?"

"And Goofy and Minnie and Donahd and Puto and Mickey and Goofy and Daisy and... Who else?" He rattled the words out so quickly and with such an excited pant that Nancy could barely keep up.

"Who else? Who else? Only Dumbo and Beauty and the Beast and Cinderella and so many others." She kissed him on the nose and put him down.

Bill gave her a half-hug and a kiss on the cheek. "Hey, Sis. Nice digs."

"Oh, Billy, you have no idea! Breakfast was amazing! You should have joined us."

"We had Zone bars and orange juice in our room," Cleary volunteered.

Nancy playful slapped her brother's arm. "Why didn't you stay here? We could have had so much fun together."

"Because you booked the rooms, Nance. We stayed where you put us."

Nancy feigned ignorance. "Well, we could have upgraded you."

"I tried to upgrade the rooms myself. You told me I couldn't." He turned his attention to Kenny, shook his hand. "How was the flight?"

"Not bad." Kenny shrugged and tried to downplay what was coming next. "Those little corporate jets aren't all they're cracked up to be. How was your drive?"

"Good. We took back roads most of the way so we could see Old Florida." There was no hint of animosity in Bill's voice. He preferred road trips to flying. He had a rule against sitting in tubes.

"Katherine," Nancy rubbed her sister-in-law's upper arm as she spoke, "we will fix this whole room mix-up today. I insist we all stay together as a family. We shouldn't be separated, especially at this time of year."

Kenny butted in, "I thought the concierge said they're booked up through New Year's."

"He did?" Nancy asked incredulously. Bill had heard enough. He knew his sister well enough to know this was all an act. He tuned out the conversation and began to visually explore the room.

"Yeah, last night when we checked in."

"I don't remember that." She laughed, her expression intimating that Kenny was delusional.

"Yeah, you said it was a wonder anyone would stay here with as slow as the check-in procedure was," Kenny replied.

Nancy turned back to Katherine. "Well, we'll check into it today. I promise."

Bill wandered away from the group, captivated by a sight a few dozen yards across the lobby. He had spotted an aging woman wearing designer sportswear, cradling what appeared to be a swaddled infant in her arms. Her husband, dressed equally well, was talking to the concierge. Bill couldn't put his finger on it, but something was off. He slowly walked in their direction. He watched as the woman cooed and tickled the baby. The child didn't move. Bill could not actually see the child, only layers of blanket and a knit cap. He continued walking toward them. He felt compelled to see the child.

Nancy, Katherine and Kenny were deep in conversation about the itinerary when Katherine noticed her husband was missing. "Where's Bill?"

"Wandering off, I'm sure," Nancy offered. "Daddy was always bad about that, always lured away by some shiny object. I guess that's where he got it." Kenny spotted Bill growing closer to the couple with the baby and pointed him out. Nancy gasped.

As Bill drew closer, he saw the concierge awkwardly reach across the counter to rub the baby's foot, or at least where the baby's foot would be under the layers of swaddling. The child's parents seemed delighted at the attention, but the concierge quickly pulled his hand back ashamedly and looked around to see if any of his co-workers had seen. The baby didn't move.

"It's that couple," Nancy said, her voice a mixture of alarm and disgust.

"What couple?" Katherine's curiosity was piqued by Nancy's tone. Nancy leaned in to share her secret, making sure the children were out of earshot. Katherine and Kenny leaned in to hear.

"The staff call them the Towel Baby Couple," she whispered.

"Why?" Katherine asked.

Bill was within arm's reach of the woman now, but her back was turned. He craned his neck to try to see the baby. Just then, the woman turned to face him. Bill froze. His eyes widened as he stared at the bundle in the woman's arms.

"Because that's not a baby," Nancy explained. "It's just a towel wrapped in blankets with a knit cap on. But they make the staff treat it like a baby, even bring it milk and baby food in the restaurants."

"What!?" Kenny and Katherine said in unison.

"Goes to show that money can't buy sanity." Neither Katherine nor Kenny could discern whether Nancy was being judgmental or sympathetic.

A look of alarm swept across Katherine's face. "Oh, God. Bill!" The others knew immediately what she meant.

"He'll say something," Kenny added, half-grinning at the prospect, "You know he will."

Katherine turned and cupped her hands, calling for her husband. "Bill!'

"Hey, Bill!" Kenny joined in, but it was too late.

The woman with the towel baby stared at Bill, studying his face. Bill noticed her stare and met her eyes. "I'm sorry," he said softly, "I didn't know." The woman smiled gently at Bill. At that moment, her husband joined her, putting his arm around her as they both gazed at the bundle of cloth.

"He knows it's you," the woman said.

"He certainly does," the proud father added.

"I'm sorry?" Bill was far outside his element here.

"My baby," answered the woman. "He knows you're the one." Bill backed away slowly, unsure what to do.

"I ... um..."

Kenny grabbed his shoulder from behind. "Bill, come on, buddy," Kenny said casually. "These kids are about to bust to get on the monorail." Bill started to step away, unable to take his gaze off the Towel Baby. Kenny nodded to them, "Good day."

"Goodbye, Bill Durmer," said the man. Kenny turned Bill back toward their families and led him across the expansive lobby. As Bill and Kenny retreated, the man called out, "We'll meet again!"

Bill hoped not.

Chapter Three:
The Buffet Promise

Bill couldn't shake his encounter with the Towel Baby Couple. The alien quality of the woman's voice and the surety with which she spoke to Bill haunted him throughout the day. Who were they? How could they have possibly known his name?

"Come on, just tell me it was you," he would say to Kenny every couple of hours, "I promise I won't get mad." Sometimes he would be lost in thought, unaware of his surroundings, of the hectic goings-on at the Most Magical Place on Earth. Then he would bust out laughing without provocation. "This is classic," he would say to no one particular in the group, "You outdid yourself this time." Kenny would protest vehemently, laughing nervously all the while. The more Kenny protested, the more Bill believed him. Yet he would accuse Kenny anew a few minutes or hours later — not because he thought Kenny would confess, but because it was easier for him to hope it was all a prank than to embrace a more mysterious or, for all he knew, more ominous explanation.

There were moments when Bill would forget, ever so briefly, about the couple. He hadn't been to Walt Disney World since he was 16 and only once before that. Checking in at The Magic Kingdom, he glanced up at Main Street Station, admiring the detail of the craftsmanship, the whimsical nature of Walt Disney's interpretation of Americana. As he did, he heard Cleary at his right hand.

"Wowwww..." She dragged the word out as if to savor its resonance. She slowly spun, wide-eyed with wonder, taking in every sight and sound: the narrow gauge steam locomotive tooting its whistle upon departing the station, ferry boats blowing their horns as they passed one another on Seven Seas Lagoon, the monorail they had disembarked only moments before now whooshing overhead, the whine and *shoosh* of brakes from a caravan of buses bringing guests from all points around the World, and the mass of people moving toward them like modern-day land grabbers, eager to lay claim to their parcel of the vaunted Disney magic. Bill saw the look in her eyes and was immediately taken back to his first visit in 1978, when he was eight years old. He recalled standing roughly where Cleary stood now, turning in circles and gawking with the same awed expression that had taken hold of her face. For the briefest moment, he could see life through eight-year-old eyes. It wouldn't be the last time he had that sensation.

He zipped up all the pockets of his backpack once the security guard had inspected it, slung it over his shoulder. He leaned down toward Cleary's ear. "And we're not even inside yet," he said slyly. She flashed a grin the Cheshire Cat would envy and hugged her father's waist tight.

Once inside, Nancy immediately took charge of the outing. She snapped her itinerary open with a crack. "Now then," she started. The adults and even the eight-year-olds knew that when Nancy started a sentence with "now then," it meant trouble. Nancy continued, "if we start out straight ahead at the castle, then ride Dumbo before the crowds get out of control, we can systematically work our way through Fantasyland before our lunch reservation at Crystal Palace."

Bill perked up. "Crystal Palace? Really?"

"What?" Nancy was indignant. Bill smirked coyly.

"Nothing. It's just that..." He glanced at Kenny, who turned away to keep from laughing at his wife. "Crystal Palace is a *buffet*. You know that, right?"

"So? I eat at buffets." She grew a little pale and her stomach convulsed ever so slightly as she said it.

"Since when?" Bill laughed.

"I eat at them all the time!" she protested.

"You do not!"

"I eat at the Gift Horse in Foley at least once a month with the girls from the Garden Club." Nancy's arguments were weakening, as was her resolve.

"You order off the menu!" Bill protested.

"Kenny, tell him," she demanded of her husband. Kenny only grinned and raised his hands in mock surrender.

"Okay!" Nancy broke under the pressure. "Elise loves Winnie the Pooh, alright?"

Bill put an arm around her shoulder. "It's a very brave thing you're doing, Sis," he said in sham sincerity. "You're an inspiration to generations of women. I'm proud of you."

She shoved him away. "Oh, shut up."

"Mommy!" Dara gasped in shock. Cleary joined in.

"Aunt Naaancyyy..." she said in her best condescending, parental voice.

"Now please," Nancy pleaded, "just don't say anything about boogers or scabs or puss while we're in there, or I'll throw up." This elicited revulsion from the older girls and hysterical laughter from the adults. Elise and Clay didn't know why, but they joined in the laughter, too.

"Boogers or scabs or puss?" Katherine's incredulous tone barely crept through the laughter. "I've never heard you say one of those words, let alone all three in one sentence."

Nancy turned sixteen different shades of red while her family attempted to regain their composure. Bill was grateful to see a more human side of his sister for a change. Since she had married and become a mother, Nancy had developed into a person he didn't recognize. At least he didn't recognize her as his sister. She had become their mother, and that was the one thing Bill had hoped would never happen to his little sister.

"Okay, fun's over," Nancy declared, the normal color slowly returning to her cheeks. "We need to keep to our schedule."

"You heard the lady," Kenny said, scooping up Elise and putting her next to Clay in the rented double stroller. "The fun's over."

"There will be no fun today at Disney World," Bill said in a mock announcer voice.

"Y'all quit it! You know what I meant." Nancy took Kenny's arm as he walked past, pushing the double stroller. Cleary and Dara followed close behind, skipping excitedly. Katherine handed off Clementine's stroller to Bill and playfully wagged a finger in his face.

"Be nice to your sister." She gave him a quick kiss on the lips.

"I'll think about it," he said with a wink. "But it really is so much more fun when I'm not." They double-timed it to catch up to the others.

The girls oohed and ahhed at Cinderella Castle from the moment they set foot on Main Street. They craned their necks back until it seemed they would topple over backward as they entered through its brightly hued gates. Dara rubbed her fingertips across the surface of the mosaics depicting the story of Cinderella. Cleary, who had watched seemingly every Walt Disney World television special ever aired, regaled her cousin with trivia about the castle: the mosaics took almost two years to complete and feature more than 500 colors of glass; the castle is not built of brick or stone but with a steel frame and 10-inch thick concrete walls; the castle suite was originally intended as an apartment for the Disney family, but was left incomplete for years following Roy Disney's death. This last fact was met by a dubious look from Dara.

"Who's Roy Disney?"

"Walt Disney's brother," Cleary replied.

"But Walt Disney isn't a real person," Dara protested.

Cleary's jaw dropped.

"You have got to be kidding me!" She flagged her father down in the crowd. "Dad!" Turning to her cousin, she demanded, "Tell my dad what you just said." Dara shrugged.

"Walt Disney isn't a real person." Bill stared at her blankly for a moment, unwilling to believe what he had just heard. His mind raced, wondering what historical figures could be more slanderously maligned by such a statement and could only come up with three: George Washington, Coach Paul "Bear" Bryant and Elvis. For an instant, he was awash in guilt for not including Jesus in his top three. However, he justified the slight to himself by arguing that Jesus was too controversial, whereas the others were unassailable.

"Come with me," he finally answered. He took them each by the hand and led them back the way they had come. As he passed Katherine, she gave him a puzzled look. "I'll be right back. Meet you at Dumbo!" He led the girls down the ramp at the front of the castle, against the flow of traffic and into a circular garden at the foot of Main Street. He led the girls around a large bronze statue of a smiling man, gazing up Main Street, one arm outstretched and gesturing with his hand as if to indicate where the next wondrous attraction would go, the other hand grasping that of Mickey Mouse, who stood grinning at his side. The statue was titled "Partners."

"Now Dara," Bill said as he pointed emphatically at the statue, "*that* is Walt Disney."

"You're telling me he's a real person," Dara retorted.

"Yes. That's what he looked like."

"Well, if he's a real person," she put a hand on her hip as she formulated her argument, self-assured of a satisfactory outcome, "why is he holding hands with Mickey Mouse? Are you telling me Mickey Mouse is real, too?" Bill gritted his teeth. He had no patience for children who lacked imagination.

Cleary buried her face in her hands, ashamed to be seen in public with someone so literal. "Aiyiyi," she murmured, risking her father's ire.

Taking a deep breath, Bill tried again. "It's called 'artistic license,' sweetheart. The sculptor chose to depict him holding hands with Mickey, because a Mickey Mouse cartoon a long time ago is what started all of this."

Dara thought about this, studying the lines of Walt's face in the sculpture. If he weren't a real man, she thought, surely they wouldn't have made him look so old. "He may have been real, but" she turned and faced her uncle, "what did he do?" Bill smiled.

"Let's catch up with everybody. I'll tell you on the way." Bill explained to Dara that the Mickey Mouse cartoon "Steamboat Willie" was one of the first to feature characters talking and playing music to a synchronized soundtrack. He told her about Disney's early history as a creator of cartoon shorts, about the release of Snow White and how no one thought a full-length animated movie would ever work, about how the company grew to produce non-animated fare like nature documentaries and live-action films such as 20,000 Leagues Under the Sea.

It was at just that moment he realized something was missing beyond the carousel behind Cinderella Castle. "20,000 Leagues Under the Sea used to be right there. That looks weird." Bill's memory baffled even him. He had been to this place only twice before in all of his 39 years, but certain sights were indelibly written deep in the recesses of his mind. He almost remarked that he couldn't fathom why the ride was gone, but then he realized the word "fathom," itself a nautical measurement, could be interpreted as a pun. And he had a rule against that kind of thing.

He shook it off and continued his recount of Walt Disney's achievements as he and the girls joined the queue for the Dumbo ride. The more he talked about Disney, the more he realized how much he truly admired the man. And that surprised him.

He was never much of a Disney fan as a kid, at least no more than any other kid. Being a bit of a contrarian, Bill had always considered himself more a Looney Tunes devotee, identifying with the subversive, ironic humor. However, once he had children, he re-discovered the Disney films. Because that's what red-blooded American parents do. It was then he realized the Warner shorts needed Disney, that without the Disney aesthetic he had so often mocked when he was younger, the Looney Tunes shorts would have never existed. Action and reaction.

Bill and the girls watched and waved as Katherine, Nancy, Clay and Elise circled around in their elephant. The Dumbo ride consisted of 16 vehicles, shaped like their namesake flying hero, and mounted on articulated arms connected to a central, rotating hub. It was, in concept, no different than the cheap airplane rides at any county fair. But, as with all things at Walt Disney World, the execution and theming took it to a different level. Clay flipped a small lever up and down rapidly, causing the elephant to climb and dive as quickly as the ride would allow. Nancy held tightly to Elise, but smiled and cheered with her as the elephant sank and rose. Bill told the girls the Dumbo ride was one of the original rides at Disneyland when the park opened over 50 years earlier.

"Where did people go before Disneyland?" Dara asked.

"What do you mean 'where did they go?'" Bill thought he knew her meaning, but wanted to hear her explanation.

"I mean," Dara searched for the words, "like, where did they go for fun, like what other park?"

"You mean theme parks?" Bill asked.

"Yeah."

"Well…" Bill thought about his answer, not wanting to mislead the girls. He had a rule against giving anyone incorrect information, for fear of them sharing it and being humiliated at some later date. That same fear of vicarious shame often led him to correct the slightest error in casual conversation. He called it spontaneous fact-checking. Katherine called it being a know-it-all and a jackass.

"There weren't any theme parks, really. I mean, not like this." He remembered something in a documentary about Walt drawing influences from amusement parks in Europe and Knott's Berry Farm in California, but he couldn't recall the specifics. So he chose not to mention it. Besides, it was time to fly an elephant.

As he led the girls onto the ride, Bill was unaware of the Towel Baby Couple watching him from the shade of a nearby tree. Or of the small lady with the rubber doll spying on him from near the carousel. Or of the fact that every costumed character within sight would turn occasionally to catch a glimpse of him and the girls, as though they were tracking his movements.

"I want to sit with Uncle Billy," Dara declared as they made their way to an empty elephant. Since Nancy still called her brother Billy rather than Bill, Dara had picked up on the habit. This irritated Cleary, whose own mother had only ever called her father Bill. She was also jealous that Dara was commanding so much of her father's attention. Even though she had heard all the stories about Disney history herself on the drive down, she envied the fact that so much of the lesson was for Dara's benefit.

"I get to drive, then." Cleary had to claim some ground for herself. The ride started and they heard little voices calling to them above the din of the crowd.

"Ceawy! Daddy! Daewa!" Clay called, jumping up and down and waving his arms. Elise mimicked him as best she could. Bill and Dara waved down to them. Bill had fretted for more than a year over Clay being slow to speak and his inability to pronounce certain sounds. Cleary had talked early and often, as had he. Bill had often quipped that the Durmers may not be athletes, great thinkers, barons of industry or leaders of men, but if nothing else, they could talk with the best of them. It never occurred to him what an idol he had made of being well spoken until faced with Clay's limitations. Sure, it was a stupid thing to worship, but way better than that whole golden calf affair.

He turned his back on that particular sin and chose to love his son through the challenge. At least that's what he told himself. But every month or so, he found himself sneaking the kid peanut butter sandwiches on dry white bread. He would coax Clay to lick the sticky goo from the roof of his mouth. Meanwhile, Bill would say L-words to the boy, hoping he would associate the action with the sound. The problem, they later learned, was that the boy was tongue-tied and couldn't physically do that. So Bill's little speech therapy sessions would often end in abject frustration, with him yelling, "You can't say 'lollipop' by scraping the roof of your mouth with your fingers!" (Katherine could never figure out why the boy had an irrational fear of suckers.)

"Uncle Billy?" Dara's voice snapped him back into the moment. "Tell me more about Walt Disney." Bill smiled and happily indulged her curiosity.

"Well…" Again, he dragged it out as long as he could to determine which way to go with his little history lesson. He defaulted back to what he remembered from the documentaries he had made the kids endure on the drive down. "Even though a few amusement parks had taken to using themes, Disney had a grander vision for his park." Bill spoke even louder and more distinctly than normal to be heard over the hullabaloo. Cleary pretended not to listen. "And he had something no one else had."

"What's that?"

"Thirty years of cartoons and movies to base his attractions on. He was brilliant about it. He used the movies and his name recognition to promote the park. He even created a TV show that would run the movies and cartoons. At that time, all the movie studios were afraid of TV. Not Disney. You know what he called the show?"

"What?" Dara was drawn in.

"Disneyland. And the stories on the show were themed around the lands in the park: Fantasyland, Frontierland, Tomorrowland…"

"So the TV show was themed around the park, and the park was themed around the movies?"

"Exactly! Each thing was drawing from and promoting the others," Bill's tone became more melancholy, "but not like the way it's done today, with characters just thrown in where they don't really belong." He couldn't figure out why he thought the cross-promotion Walt employed in the 1950s was somehow nobler than that used by the modern corporation that bore his name. Maybe it was because the company had become so large and impersonal. Maybe it was just naïve nostalgia.

The ride quieted, and its rotation began to slow. With a hiss, the hydraulic pistons slowly lowered the ride vehicle. Cleary leaned forward, interjecting herself into the conversation.

"He wanted the experience of visiting the parks to be *immersive*," Cleary delivered the line as if it were well rehearsed. In fact, she had been thinking for several minutes about the exact phrasing she would use.

"What does immersive mean?" Dara asked. Cleary leaned back with a self-satisfied, smug grin. Bill knew what his daughter was up to, and his scowl let her know he knew. It was time to get off. As they made their way around the ride and toward the exit, Bill answered Dara.

"It means he wanted a trip to Disneyland to feel like you were entering the world of the movies, like you were living them right along with the characters."

"I thought everybody knew what immersive meant," Cleary grumbled with a snide tone. Dara had already trotted ahead to reach her parents, and so did not hear her. Bill heard her perfectly well and spun around to confront his daughter. He took her by the arm and led her aside.

"I'm not sure what has upset you, but I will not have you treat anyone, especially Dara, that way. Do you understand?" He was firm but controlled. He tried to connote his love and concern for Cleary in his tone, but feared he had only come off sounding like one of those people who threaten their kids in the check-out lines at Walmart with phrases like, "I'll tear yer butt up!" You know the kind.

"Yes, sir," Cleary said, dropping her head to study her shoes.

"She's not just your cousin," Bill continued. "She's your best friend. And even if she weren't, that's no way to treat anyone. Remember, 'in humility...'"

Cleary picked up where he left off, "'regard others as more important than yourself.' I know, Dad." He smiled and cupped her face in his hands.

"It's hard to do, almost impossible. Just remember that none of us are who we say we are, nor are we what we do. We are what is done for us." He kissed her forehead, took her by the hand and led her to rejoin the family. He wasn't sure she understood the meaning of what he had said. He could only pray that someday she would.

The rest of the morning found the Durmers and Thompsons visiting the Hundred Acre Wood, following the second star to the right and flying straight on 'til morning, riding along on a scary adventure with Snow White and reminding themselves that it is, after all, a small, small world. The adults lamented the loss of Mr. Toad's Wild Ride (the defunct ride based on Disney's take on *The Wind and the Willows*) and 20,000 Leagues Under the Sea, but the children were delighted with what met them around each new corner. Watching them reminded the adults how to approach everything as a new experience and how to imbue those experiences with child-like wonder. *If only*, each of them thought without mentioning it to the others, *this feeling could last when we get back home.*

The temperature pushed past 80 by midday. The women fanned themselves with park maps as they waited for their name to be called for lunch seating at the Crystal Palace. The restaurant, like many of the buildings along Main Street, was inspired by turn-of-the-century architecture. Though named for the colossal steel and glass structure built for London's

Great Exhibition of 1851, the designed was inspired by San Francisco's Conservatory of Flowers, a Victorian green house built in the 1870s. None of that mattered to Nancy, who had become ill tempered as her hypoglycemia took hold. Four children constantly reminding everyone they were hungry didn't help.

"I don't understand why they can't have an air-conditioned waiting area. This is Central Florida," she griped.

"At least we didn't come in the summer," Katherine said, trying to offer some perspective. "If this were July, it'd be 100 degrees."

"If they don't call our names soon, we won't be coming back at all." In fact, an employee of the restaurant (or "cast member" as Disney referred to their employees, even those working retail in shopping malls) had been calling the name Thompson for a couple of minutes at that point, but the meek young girl was simply too shy and insecure to project her voice and couldn't be heard more than ten feet away. Bill eventually recognized this fact and suggested Kenny approach the hostess. Soon, he had the family seated and ordering drinks.

After several visits to the buffet and many posed pictures with the denizens of Pooh Corner, everyone was in a better mood. Kenny needled his wife.

"Now," he started, stretching as he spoke, "that wasn't so terrible. Was it?"

"No," Nancy admitted, "it wasn't. It was actually quite adequate."

"So you've never eaten at a buffet?" a dubious Katherine asked, "Ever?"

Nancy looked to Bill with a mischievous squint. "You haven't told her?" Bill shrugged innocently. Nancy answered, "The last time I ate at a buffet was twenty-three years ago."

"Twenty-two," Bill interrupted.

"That's right, twenty-two. Right here. At this restaurant."

Katherine was captivated by this revelation. She hadn't learned anything new about Bill and Nancy's childhood in years. "Did you get sick?"

Nancy shook her head and pointed at her brother.

"Guilty." Bill demurred.

"We ate here for lunch the last day of our trip." Nancy explained the trip was with a large group from their church. After eating at Crystal Palace, the group had piled into the chartered tour bus and headed northwest toward Alabama. Somewhere beyond Ocala, Bill suffered severe stomach

cramps, but he refused to go to the bus's restroom. The bus driver had neglected to empty the "honey tank" before departing Orlando. The stench
had been palpable throughout the bus, and Bill couldn't imagine actually
entering the inner sanctum of stink. Talk about immersive. Kenny cringed
and squirmed as Nancy described it, even though he had heard the story
many times before.

"What did you do?" Katherine asked her husband.

"Let's just say staying out of the bathroom wasn't an option." Bill picked
up where Nancy left off. He had gone into the bus's privy. Hot air from the
engine and the road rose up through the toilet, pushing a fetid reek directly
into Bill's nostrils. And mouth. The air was so hot and uncomfortable that
Bill couldn't do anything, but every time he tried to get up, the cramps and
urge to go would return with a vengeance. So he sat, broiling his bottom,
his face plastered against the window so he could get the benefit of the cold,
fresh breeze blowing up from the air conditioning vents.

Katherine and Kenny couldn't help but laugh at the mental picture Bill
painted. Bill showed no hint of shame, instead embracing the tale as merely
a part of his overall story. He continued without missing a beat.

"Then we stopped at some mall in Tallahassee for dinner. It was Sunday, so the only thing open was Morrison's Café."

"Another buffet," Katherine commented. Nancy nodded and picked up
the story.

"I never understood why we were traveling on a Sunday in the first
place. Maybe somebody bought a dispensation," she quipped. Bill burst
forth a laugh. It wasn't so much that what she said was all that funny, but he
had never heard his sister make even the slightest joke about the Catholic
Church before. Of course, had he made the same comment, he would have
caused a schism the likes of which hadn't been seen since 1054.

Nancy continued, "Billy rushed off the bus, knocking over old people
and babies, and made a beeline for the bathroom. I thought I was going to
have lunch with everyone else."

Katherine interrupted, "I was about to ask, because you said this," she
tapped the table firmly with her finger, "was the last buffet you ate."

"As I'm walking past the restrooms, I hear a weak little voice moan-
ing, 'Nancy... Nancy...' I cracked the men's room door, and it was Billy. He
sounded so pitiful." She looked at her brother with an adoring look as she
spoke, then reached over and rubbed his hand. Katherine hadn't seen this

kind of affection between them in years. Maybe this really was a magic kingdom. Nancy continued, "So instead of eating dinner, I spent the whole two hours in the men's room, handing Billy rolls of paper under the stall." Nancy used the abbreviated euphemism "paper," because she couldn't bring herself to say the word "toilet" while sitting at a dining table.

"Awwwww..." Katherine was bowled over by the act of devotion, especially from Nancy. "I can't believe you guys have never told me this."

"So, it was just the experience of sitting in the men's room for two hours that turned you against buffets?" Bill asked. Nancy looked at him incredulously.

"You mean you don't remember? You honestly don't remember the promise?"

Bill, clueless of her meaning, shrugged and shook his head. He hadn't thought about that day in years.

"I handed you a fresh roll of paper under the stall door, and you said..." Bill leaned in, wondering if this was a set-up for a joke at his expense. He honestly could not remember the moment. Nancy affected a pitiful, sickly voice, imitating her big brother's of that day, "You said, 'Nancy you have to promise me you'll never eat at a buffet ever again. I never want this to happen to you.' And I did. So there. I've kept my promise."

"Until today," Bill said. He smiled sweetly at his sister.

"Until today," Nancy repeated. Kenny rubbed his hand across the back of his wife's shoulders proudly.

Nancy, feeling too vulnerable, quickly snapped back into character. "Besides, you were right. Buffets are disgusting. Sneeze guards my eye. That's making some awfully big assumptions about the way *those people* wipe their noses. When they invent people guards, then we'll talk. Oh, that's right. They have. They're called 'waiters.'"

"And she's back," Bill quipped.

Nancy cracked open her itinerary, ignoring her brother. "We've got to get moving if we're going to get all of Frontierland in this afternoon." She rose and started corralling her children toward the door. Katherine looked at Bill and rubbed the hair back over his temples.

"Your sister's not completely evil after all." She kissed Bill on the forehead and joined Nancy in gathering up children.

"Just mostly evil," he replied to no one in particular.

As the Durmers exited, a group at a table in the far corner of the restaurant shifted to watch them go. The Towel Baby Couple, the small lady with the rubber doll and a large man in a business suit watched them intently.

"The sister could be a problem," the large man grunted. "The Mechanism warned us about her." The small, old lady patted his arm.

"I have it on good authority that she's not that bad," she reassured him. "She was a child too, once — quite an imaginative one from what I hear. She has only forgotten. Besides, you heard her story."

The large man grunted his disapproval. "She's a wild card."

"I think we're going to need some help," the male half of the Towel Baby Couple said, nodding in agreement.

His wife chimed in, "I think we're going to need a miracle."

Chapter Four:
According to the Bus Driver

Late that evening, Bill held a limp, snoring toddler in his arms outside the door of the family's room at All-Star Movies. He waited for a staggering, exhausted Cleary to catch up with him. Because of his height, long stride and restless impatience, Bill routinely left his family behind. They could be strolling through the mall or weaving through crowds at Mobile's Mardi Gras; it didn't matter. Inevitably, Katherine would call out, "You have a family, you know!" Bill would then oblige by stopping to wait for them, at least what Bill defined as stopping. It was more of a stationary march that made him look like a cross between a marching band drum major and a grade school kid who was waiting desperately for the next available stall in the restroom. Within minutes, however, he would be thirty yards ahead again. He would sometimes try to match the glacial pace of Cleary or Clay and find it almost physically impossible. The inertia of his lanky frame would pull against his slow, small steps, almost causing him to trip over his own feet and fall flat on his face. The end result was a teetering shift of his weight from foot to foot, an awkward compromise between walking and standing still.

He repositioned Clay in his arms. Cleary shuffled up to her dad and buried her forehead in his gut, leaning all her weight against him. Soon after came Katherine, who was pushing a snoozing Clementine. Katherine's feet were sore, and she winced with every slow step. She looked at her husband as if he were insane for keeping the kids out on the sidewalk rather than taking them inside.

"My key's not working," he answered her unspoken question. Katherine let out an exasperated sigh and started digging in her purse, which dangled from the stroller's handle. She produced a key card bearing her name, swiped it through the door lock to the same end. She tried again. No luck. Again and again Katherine swiped the card through the reader, growing angrier at each try.

"It works on magnetism, not friction," Bill quipped. Katherine was exhausted and incapable of euphemism. Sensing an impending torrent of obscenities, Bill quickly plugged Cleary's ears while balancing Clay on his forearm.

Cleary watched her mother pound the door and mutter an angry string of words she couldn't make out. She thought for a moment she discerned at least one phrase when her father's finger slipped to the side, allowing a few choices sound waves to tease her tympanic membrane. However, she couldn't reconcile why her mother would be ranting about muddy truckers, so she wrote it off to imagination.

Tantrum complete, Katherine took Clay from Bill's arms, freeing her husband to march off toward the resort's office. Bill, who was originally apathetic toward the key malfunction, now found himself matching Katherine's mood expletive-for-expletive, much to his dismay. On occasion, after a particularly stressful day, the two lamented their inability to extricate their emotions one from the other. He envied other couples whose moods were complementary, where one partner's emotional weakness was the other's strength. Even his sister and Kenny seemed to balance each other this way. Kenny's levelheaded calm came with the downside of an ineffectual passivity, which was a perfect counter-balance to Nancy being crazy, mean and aggressive. In the best way possible. He and Katherine, however, were so empathetic toward one another that the one couldn't help but feel what the other felt. While perhaps less effective than other pairings in some ways, it at least meant they were always in emotional lockstep.

Bill strode past the pool area, around a few night owls tying one on at the outdoor bar that jutted from the dining hall, through the cafeteria, between Christmas trees and into the lobby. He stopped short of the queue area. Lurking there, at the other end of the lobby, stood Christmas Tree Head talking with the concierge. Bill noticed a difference in the big man's demeanor, a gravitas he hadn't noticed at the Nescafé dispenser that morning. The concierge, noticing Bill, gestured toward him. Christmas Tree Head turned. Upon spotting Bill, he transformed into the same buffoonish character Bill had met earlier. He waved wildly, motioning for Bill to come over.

Hesitating, Bill wondered if he could pretend to have not seen the man, but his own good manners betrayed him. Reflexively, he raised his right hand and sort of half-waved back. Now he was committed. Bill hung his head and shuffled over.

"Mr. Coffee!" Christmas Tree Head bellowed. He jutted a meaty paw forward, grasping Bill's hand before he could even respond. Bill hated being dog-pawed, as he called it when someone grabbed and squeezed his hand before he could execute a proper grip, rendering his hand deformed and limp and about as much a participant in the exchange as a dog's paw rising to a shake command.

All he could think was, "I have opposable thumbs; let me use them! It's the only thing I've got over the dolphins!" What he said, however, was, "Ha! Coffee!" Sometimes Bill lamented that he was even given the power of speech.

Christmas Tree Head turned Bill's hand over, inspecting his long, slender fingers. "Got some dexterous digits, there." Bill was uncomfortable, yet he let the man study his hand for reasons he himself couldn't even understand.

"Pianist's hands, my mother always called them." Bill sighed, "Probably broke her heart that I quit my lessons to play in a rock band."

"No..." Christmas Tree Head protested. "Around here, these are Imagineer's hands — quick, nimble, steady, precise. Yes, sir." He released Bill's hands and stared into his eyes. Bill saw a spark of mischief there, one that belied an unexpected wisdom. Clearly, he had judged the big man too hastily. "Some say you can learn a lot about a man by looking into his eyes. The eyes may very well be the window to the soul, but the hands... They reveal the intellect." He gave Bill a knowing wink, then turned back toward the concierge. "Young lady, I believe you have something for Mr. Durmer here."

"Yes, I do." She slid a manila envelope across the counter. Bill glanced at it but turned back to the big man with a quizzical glance.

"How did you know my name?"

Christmas Tree Head chuckled and pointed to Bill's left hand. "You're still holding your key card." He slapped Bill on the shoulder and burst into a belly laugh. The large man with the larger head topped with a foam

Christmas tree strode away across the lobby, still laughing. "Goodnight, Miss Ramona!" he called.

"Goodnight," the concierge replied. Bill got the sense that, in this place, Christmas Tree Head was like a regular in a neighborhood bar.

"And Mr. Durmer," Christmas Tree Head stopped to deliver his parting words, "find yourself before others find you." Bill was speechless. "Merry Christmas!" The big man exited with a grand wave and activated the blinking lights on his hat.

Bill reached for the envelope. "I'm not sure—"

"Your card's not working?" The concierge interrupted him.

"That's right." Bill opened the envelope and out slid new key cards for his family and some folded pages. "Seems everyone knows an awful lot about me tonight." He flipped open the papers and became even more perplexed than before. "Something's wrong here. This says I have a suite at the Grand Floridian. I can't afford that." She pointed to the bottom line.

"Fully paid. We hate to see you go, but the Grand Floridian..." She raised her eyebrows, and envy crept across her smile. Bill knew her unfinished argument was right. Why turn away such a gift? Then it hit him.

"Nancy."

"I'm sorry?" the concierge queried.

"Nothing." Bill snapped up the cards and shoved everything back in the envelope. He slid a five across the counter to her. "Thanks." She noticed Bill's hint of irritation but didn't understand it.

As Bill was walking away, she grabbed her iPhone and updated her Facebook status: "Some people don't know how to be grateful."

Twenty minutes later, Bill, Katherine and the kids found themselves on board a shuttle bus headed north toward the Victorian themed resort on the shores of Seven Seas Lagoon. All of the kids slept, Clementine in her stroller, Cleary sitting upright and leaning against her mother, Clay stretched out across two bus seats.

"I still don't think it was Nancy," Katherine whispered.

"It was. Our key cards were disabled, the reservations made, *our luggage* moved," Bill put special emphasis on this offense, "all without our knowledge, let alone our approval. Who else would do that?"

Katherine protested, "But it's too much, Bill. A suite? At the Grand Floridian? Even she wouldn't spend that much money just to belittle you. Or control you. Or whatever reason she has for treating you the way she does."

"Oh, come on," Bill was firm in his assertion. "We get there, she meets us in the lobby. We protest it's too much. She says, 'No, I want to do this for my big brother.' Eventually she gives in and agrees to take the suite for herself. Then there we are, in the middle of the night, swapping rooms and moving luggage all to satisfy her need to believe the world really does revolve around her." Katherine shrugged. Bill had her.

"Yeah. Sadly, I'd believe that." She sighed.

Bill closed his eyes, hoping to doze off for the duration of their ride. The bus driver, silent until that moment, snickered. Bill glanced up at him.

"I'm sure you hear this kind of craziness all the time."

The driver laughed, "No. I can honestly say this is a new one." He glanced in his mirror, making eye contact with Bill's reflection. With a jovial wave, he said, "Name's Red, by the way." Bill studied the thinning grey hair and freckle-free complexion to quickly surmise that the old man had never been a redhead.

"Red? Pleasure to meet you, Red." Bill carefully walked across the swaying bus and offered the man his hand, "Bill." Red took Bill's hand in a shake that allowed Bill to maintain his dignity. "Let me ask you something, Red."

"I can't promise you I'll know the answer, but I'll sure make something up."

"Fair enough," Bill replied. He crouched next to the older man. "Have you ever heard anything about an older couple that carry around a towel baby?"

Red recoiled, befuddled. "Towel baby?"

"Yeah. It's a towel that they have swaddled, with a little cap on it, and they carry it around like it's a real baby. And the baby has ... some kind of psychic powers or something." Bill couldn't help but laugh as he heard himself say it. Red, sensing Bill's discomfort, laughed along with him.

"You haven't been drinking the water in the Jungle Cruise, have you, Bill?"

"Not that I know of," Bill replied sheepishly. Red took a deep breath and exhaled slowly.

"I am aware of the couple. The Robinsons." Red swept back the hair at his temple as he contemplated each word. He unspooled a tale about Mr. Robinson, a talented chemist-turned-corporate tycoon who had "invented some kind of a solvent or something that they use in crime scenes." He looked at Bill and shrugged. "I don't pretend to understand what it is or what it does, but I do know it made him a very wealthy man."

Bill grabbed a handhold as Red took the bus through the sweeping turn of an on-ramp. Red continued, seemingly without even shifting his weight to compensate for the turn. He explained what the Robinsons wanted more than anything was a child, but for years that dream evaded them. Instead, they gave generously to children in need, buying clothes and school supplies for dozens of kids every fall, providing food and presents every Christmas. They would even host a Christmas party for hundreds of children each year at the headquarters of Robinson Corporate Systems (or RobinCorpSys) with Mr. Robinson playing the jolly old elf himself.

"The Robinsons met in college," Red continued. "They saw Uncle Walt's last picture on their first date."

"*The Jungle Book*," Bill confirmed. Red nodded, impressed. Bill admired the charming way Red referred to Walt Disney as "Uncle." He wondered if that was something all the cast members of his generation did, or if that particular appellation was unique to Red himself.

"You know your Disneyana, young man."

Bill shrugged, "A bit."

"Anyhow," Red picked up with his tale, "the two fell in love. They planned to marry, but delayed the wedding for two years. Told the family it was so he could get his Master's degree. Truth is, they wanted to wait until '71, because of their honeymoon." Bill chuckled, understanding what Red meant: the Robinsons had put off their wedding for two years so they could honeymoon at Walt Disney World. "Needless to say, they were fans."

Red went on to explain that as the Robinsons' fortune grew, so did their philanthropy. They combined their generosity with their love for all things Disney by annually bringing a large group of needy children on a trip to Walt Disney World during the holidays. It was the highlight of their year.

After years of disappointment, the couple finally had a child of their own. "And they lavished everything on that child." Red made broad gestures with his right hand as he spoke, describing Robinson's hand-carved sleigh bed crib, the pram designed by freelancing Imagineers, the elaborate nursery murals painted by Disney animation directors John Musker and Ron Clements in a brief work hiatus following the flop of *The Black Cauldron.*

Red stopped the bus at a traffic light and leaned in close to Bill as if sharing secrets with a long-time confidant. "They say that Robinson gave Clements a book of Hans Christian Andersen. You see, the Robinsons wanted the room to be themed around one of Andersen's tales."

"*The Little Mermaid*?"

Red winked at him. "Two weeks after they finished the mural, Musker and Clements got a green-light from Katzenburg to make the film. No one on the production knew that Mermaid had been one of Uncle Walt's favorites. Heck he started developing a version right after Snow White." Red shifted the bus into gear and eased away as the light turned green. "But Robinson knew."

"So what happened?" Bill had moved on from what many fans would consider a prized bit of Disney trivia. He was now emotionally invested in the Robinsons. "What happened to the boy?"

Red sighed. "Crib death. They lost him two days before his first birthday." Red leaned forward on the steering wheel as if the telling of this part of the story were a physical drain. "One day before they were going to bring him down here for his birthday party."

"Wow." Bill shook his head.

Red explained that the Robinsons couldn't bring themselves to come back for years after the baby's death. "Until they showed up in my bus one day about ten years ago. It would have been their son's 18th birthday."

"Did they have the towel with them?" Bill asked.

"No." Red shook his head. "Not yet." Red opined that the Robinsons had made a mistake on that first trip back by coming alone. Without the throng of children and chaperones surrounding them, they were left only with painful meditations on what could have been. He thought at the time it would be their last trip to the parks. To his surprise they returned the next year. "I thought they had adopted a baby at first, but then I got a good look."

"How does that happen?" Bill asked rhetorically. "Did they just come unhinged or what?"

"I honestly don't know. I've heard that, in their daily life, everything is as right as rain, but when they come here..." Red allowed the thought to hang in the air palpably before continuing. "I guess folks are capable of just about anything when their hearts' fondest desires are shattered." He offered Bill a fatherly smile, "Makes you realize we need to be careful what we set our hearts on, doesn't it?"

"What's your heart set on, Red?"

Red smiled and pulled the bus up to the front of the Grand Floridian.

"That's a question for another day." He punched a button, and with the whoosh of hydraulics and the whir of servos, the side doors swung open, and one side of the bus lowered to curb height. "And this is your stop."

Bill glanced out the window to see that they were indeed at the Grand Floridian. He stood, stretched the kinks out of his legs and ambled back to scoop up Clay. Katherine roused Cleary. The girl grunted something incoherent and stumbled toward the door. Before departing, Bill offered Red his hand. "Red, it was a real pleasure."

Red studied Bill's hand as he shook it. "Hmm..." He left the thought unfinished. Bill looked at him quizzically. He, too, showed a spark of recognition.

"Red, you look awfully familiar. Have we met before?"

"I can assure you we haven't," Red said, smiling. "That I would remember."

"Bill?" Katherine called from the sidewalk, "These kids are ready for bed." Bill offered his final goodbyes and shuffled out to join them. "Get your nap out?" Katherine jibed. Bill had no idea what she meant at the time. He furrowed his brow and gave her a quizzical look.

"Nooo..." he drew it out slowly, offering her a chance to recant her nonsensical question. "But I think you need to." He pushed past her and lead the family toward the entrance. Within minutes, they found themselves in an elaborate two-bedroom suite. The older children slept in their own queen size beds, while Clem enjoyed an ornate Victorian bassinet. With the kids down for the count, Bill and Katherine poured themselves a drink from the wet bar and stepped out onto one of the suite's three balconies. Bill exhaled deeply.

"This is not Nancy." His gazed reached out, far across Seven Seas Lagoon. A cool December wind blew his hair back from his face. "It's too much. Even for her." Katherine snuggled up to her husband for warmth. He wrapped his arm around her.

"Let's worry about who did this tomorrow," she cooed. "Tonight, let's just enjoy the fact they did." Neither of them said another word for the balance of the evening.

Chapter Five:
Beware the Cartoon Future That Never Was

The setting sun was evident only in a hint of an orange glow atop the west-facing side of Space Mountain. Tomorrowland was awash in a blue and green neon glow. Faint strains of Christmas carols could be heard emanating from hidden speakers but only between the shrieks and squeals of delighted children, the overhead hiss and whoosh of the Astro Orbiter, and the noisy clank and roar of the track-constrained go-karts of the Tomorrowland Speedway.

Bill marveled at how little of this place he recognized from his childhood. Much of the whitewashed, streamlined future as seen through the eyes of 1960s designers had been replaced by a more millennial aesthetic: brushed metal, exposed faux girders and what seemed like miles of neon. It was no longer a vision of a utopian possible future, but rather a cartoonish pastiche of science fantasy clichés earmarked with the requisite character tie-ins to help push product. He didn't like it.

As he turned the corner toward the noisy Speedway – an attraction that he never felt represented any kind of future and now only seemed more anachronistic in a world at war over oil – he was suddenly and most unexpectedly stricken by an overwhelming sense of déjà vu. In an instant, he was eight years old again, holding his father's hand and begging to go inside the Tomorrowland Terrace for a burger. The restaurant, now called Cosmic Ray's Starlight Café, looked remarkably similar to the way he remembered it. Even the planters in the concrete courtyard seemed familiar in a way he could have never anticipated.

"Let's grab a bite," he called back to Katherine, hoping to sustain the

wave of nostalgia that had swept over him just a bit longer. Katherine nodded, red in the face from the abnormally hot day and from willing her
pores to hold back even the slightest hint of perspiration. She may have
been no Azalea Trail Maid, but even the most radicalized of Southern girls
knew sweating in public was tantamount to heresy. She struggled to push
Clem and Clay uphill in the rented double stroller.

"Yes. Awesome. Absolutely," she panted. Bill, recognizing her exhaus-
tion, doubled back and took hold of the stroller handle himself and strode
away at a brisker than usual pace toward the entrance of the space-themed
fast food joint.

"Thank you, girls!" The cartoon-y voice bellowed over the din of a
hundred or more diners, most of them over-tired infants or older children
cackling madly at the top end of a sugar high or whining their way down
to a spectacular crash on the backside of one. Not one diner — neither
adult nor child — was paying any heed to the animatronic space lizard
at the head of the room, Sonny Eclipse. "Anybody out there celebrating a
birthday today?"

Bill watched from his vantage point in the ordering queue for the
slightest hint of any response from the crowd. Nothing. If the idea were
to recreate the uncomfortable experience of watching a bad lounge singer
who everyone in the room goes out of their way to ignore, the Imagineers
had succeeded.

Bill's plan to prolong the euphoric sense of déjà vu he experienced in
the courtyard had gone horribly awry. While he was mildly entertained
by this new Tomorrowland, he couldn't help but wonder what had happened to the idealistic futurism, naïve though it may have been, espoused
by park designers three decades earlier. It wasn't that the new version was
inherently bad, but it paled in comparison to the place Bill remembered.
He stopped just short of complaining about the retrograde design in the
"land," for fear of becoming The Old Guy. Ever since an offhand remark
about the decline in American animation resulted in him being described
as "prematurely curmudgeonly" in his college's newspaper, the *Technique*,
Bill had made a concerted effort not to evoke "the good old days." That,
and Katherine had made it abundantly clear that he was to keep his varied,
sanctimonious opinions in check while they were on vacation. Once they
were home, he was free to grouse about the use of outdated and noisy servos in the park's animatronics or lament the overuse of the word "magic" to

describe every little experience, but not while they were on vacation.

As he reached the head of the queue, Bill quickly rattled off their dinner order. He had rehearsed it several times over in his head while he waited, because Cleary, no doubt taking a cue from her hypoglycemic mother, had cautioned him against "flaking out." Bill was notorious amongst family and friends for allowing his mind to race away — pondering topics as myriad as the best method to achieve sustainable manned space flight, concern over how the Crimson Tide's policy of not offering scholarships to place-kickers could cost them a championship and attempting to mentally calculate the flow rate of the nearest water fountain — resulting in him completely forgetting the task at hand. This time, despite Sonny Eclipse's best attempts at distraction, Bill managed to stay on task: "Two rib and half-chicken combos with Dr Peppers and carrot cakes for dessert." Thank you, Imagineers, for saving marriages through your lame, easy-to-ignore lounge lizard.

Bill deftly balanced the two trays filled edge to edge with their fast-food feast as he weaved through the dining room to a far corner table which Katherine was now cleaning with bottled water and a fistful of napkins. "I thought you said one of the reasons Walt Disney created these parks was specifically to have a place that was 'as clean as anything could be.'"

"Walt's dead, honey," Bill replied matter-of-factly. He chose not to point out that her complaining sounded exactly like the kind of thing she didn't want to hear from him, because he agreed with her. And he was content with his current number of orifices.

"Well, he's rolling over in his grave right now," she grunted as she worked on a stubborn, gooey mix of ketchup and barbeque sauce. "Or spinning around in his cryonic head tube."

"That's a myth," Cleary pointed out as she gingerly plucked a Dr Pepper from the tray without warning. The tray was thrown suddenly off-balance, nearly causing a Rube Goldbergian chain reaction of plummeting food and wanton cursing from his wife. Bill quickly adjusted his grip and slid the tray onto the table before it toppled over.

"I was cleaning that," Katherine protested.

"And I was dropping that." Bill set the other tray down, positioned himself between Cleary and Clay and began to slice off chicken and ribs for them.

"I wish Dara could have come with us," Cleary pouted as she awaited her portion of the dinner. "If I were going to a restaurant with no kids allowed, I would want my kids to be with family instead of some stranger they hired at the hotel."

"She's not a stranger. She's with the babysitting service the resorts offer," Bill clarified. He couldn't decide if he was prouder of his daughter's views on parenting or her correct use of the subjunctive tense.

"Besides," Katherine chimed in between delicate bites of a rib, "Aunt Nancy thought if the kids came with us, they'd eat nothing but 'garbage.'"

"Which is what?" Cleary queried, "What we're eating now?"

"Exactly," her parents answered in unison. Bill glanced at Katherine and caught her eye. He gave her a wink. She slid her hand across the table and took hold of his pinky. The petty squabbles faded away in an instant.

Sonny finished warbling a cheesy number about gravity and was rewarded with canned applause. Save a rapt toddler or two, the flesh and blood audience was oblivious. "What a crowd!" the lounge lizard exclaimed before launching into a series of lame jokes about needing to loosen the asteroid belt due to universe expansion. Bill scanned the crowd again. The few kids who were actually paying attention weren't old enough to have any idea what an asteroid belt was.

"I wish somebody would tell me exactly what a keyboard-playing space lizard has to do with the world of tomorrow," a man's voice exclaimed from behind Bill. Bill spotted in Katherine's eyes a mixture of amusement and awe. She had already seen the man, and the sight was apparently a thing to behold. Her eyes widened, and she motioned with them for Bill to have a look for himself.

What Bill saw when he looked back was a sixty-something man, a little paunchy around the middle and sporting a wave of Brylcreemed, Reagan-esque black hair — an oil slick tsunami permanently frozen in a gravity-defying peak. But it wasn't the hair that had most of the diners in the café turning to point out the man, but his garb: a spaceman suit that made him look as if he had walked out of a 1950s B-movie. It was made of silvery-white rayon with exaggerated, puffy rings just below the knees, just above the wrists and an even more exaggerated set forming the collar. Atop the collar rings sat a huge fishbowl helmet with a swath of silver shielding "protecting" the top and back of his head. A sort of antenna spanned laterally across the helmet and supported a vertical antenna rising at least eighteen inches from the apex.

Despite his best efforts not to, Bill made eye contact. All he could think was, *Oh, crap. He's going to talk to me.* He was right.

"How about you, sport?" the spaceman blurted out toward Bill. "Can you explain these animatronic hijinks?"

Bill did his best to contain his laughter, but the man's baritone voice and uber-earnest delivery evoked memories of Gary Owens on *Laugh-In* and Ted Knight as the narrator of *Super Friends.*

"I take it you're not a fan," Bill said, chuckling through a broad smile. He hoped he came off as laughing more with the man himself than at him.

"Where are my manners?" The man offered Bill his hand. "Your name, son?"

Bill sighed and shook the spaceman's hand. "Bill Dur—" Before he could even finish his name, the man interrupted.

"Bill Durmer, it is my honor." His grip was freakishly strong for a man of his age. Bill could feel the eyes of everyone in the restaurant training on him. "I am..." The aging spaceman paused for dramatic effect. His eyes drifted far afield and dimmed a bit. His grip weakened slightly, and Bill feared the old man would die before he could reveal his name. Just then, the man gripped tighter as he broke the pause. "Tomorrow Man."

Katherine let out the slightest hint of a snort, and Bill felt a piece of a half-chewed rib stick to the back of his neck. *Philippians 2:3, Philippians 2:3, Philippians 2:3.* Bill repeated it over and over in his head. *Humility, humility. Regard others as more important than yourself.* He was so focused on trying to respect the man that the only response he could muster was a sing-songy, "Mmmmmm..."

"Bill Durmer, may I sit?" The man was already drawing a chair alongside Bill. "Thank you." He sat bolt upright in his chair with a posture that would make a pageant queen weep with envy. He carefully smoothed out the curves of his collar rings.

"That's some suit," Bill commented in an attempt to break the awkward silence. Small talk may have been Bill's nemesis, but if employing it would unlock the truth behind this walking enigma, Bill was willing to wear the mantle of hypocrite.

"These money grubbers have been trying to get their paws on it for years," Tomorrow Man said, motioning generally toward Cinderella Castle. "But they can retire that notion." He leaned closer to Bill and lowered his voice. "It's not so much the suit itself, Sport, but it what it represents."

Bill instinctively leaned in as well. "And what is that, exactly?"

"Vision." Tomorrow Man was more earnest in his one-word answer than he had been to that point, and the man oozed earnestness.

"Vision?" Bill puzzled over this answer. Noticing Bill's befuddled gaze, Tomorrow Man slapped Bill on the shoulder and spun him around toward the opposite window.

"Do you see that, Bill Durmer?" Bill correctly guessed he was pointing toward Space Mountain. Tomorrow Man explained Walt's fascination with futurism, including manned space exploration. He elaborated that Walt had originally conceived of Space Mountain for Disneyland a full decade before it finally took shape in Florida. Tomorrow Man enunciated every syllable as if life and death hung in its balance and added dramatic flourishes to his delivery at every opportunity. Bill thought the man was not so much preachy as passionate.

"Walt's vision extended out to other areas," Tomorrow Man continued as if delivering a keynote, "like transportation, urban planning and home automation." He looked into Bill's eyes. "It was a real vision of tomorrow — not just cartoon characters from space."

"And the suit?" Bill queried, pushing for a more definitive answer. Tomorrow Man studied his costume with new eyes, carefully pulled away tiny specs of lint and hair, and answered Bill with a soft, self-effacing tone of which the younger man hadn't thought him capable.

"I know I look a fool, Bill Durmer," he sighed. "But this suit means as much to me today as it did when I first donned it in 1961, possibly more." Waxing nostalgic, Tomorrow Man explained he had worked at Disneyland that summer, nearly 50 years earlier. As Tomorrowland's space man — paired with a mini-skirted space girl — he acted as a park host, posing for photos with visitors and welcoming all to the world of tomorrow. He reprised the role over the next four summers until Tomorrowland was completely revamped in 1966. "With the coming of attractions like Uncle Walt's Carousel of Progress and the WEDway People Mover, the focus of Tomorrowland had become decidedly more terrestrial. And besides, those were the days of Alan Shephard, John Glenn and the Mercury Seven. A college kid in a goofy space man costume has no place in a world with real astronauts." Bill could swear he saw a tear roll down the man's cheek. Either that or his verbosity had reacted with the cool surface of the plastic bubble on his head to create a tiny rain storm.

"So you got the suit when they retired it?" Bill had long since forgotten about his lunch, his family and the room full of gawkers — most of whom were now ignoring Tomorrow Man as fervently as they had ignored Sonny Eclipse earlier.

"Oh, no," Tomorrow Man chuckled, "not yet." After graduating from CalArts, the art institute co-founded by Walt, the man had gotten his dream job as a designer at WED Enterprises, the home of Disney Imagineers. Under the tutelage of John Hench, a longtime Disney animator and pioneer of theme park design, the man had worked on a wide variety of projects. "And then in the Seventies, I helped to design and build that big, white weenie over there," he said, pointing again to Space Mountain.

Bill was familiar with the term "weenie" from some of the Disney documentaries. Walt's theory was that each "land" should have a large, iconic attraction that drew the visitor forward. He likened these landmarks to using a frankfurter to lead a dog where you wished him to go. Not exactly the most flattering analogy for visitors, especially coming from America's favorite uncle, but it worked nonetheless.

"The day before we opened Space Mountain here in Florida," Tomorrow Man continued, "I was telling Hench about my days as the space man in Anaheim. I didn't think any more of it, but that must've hit Hench in a certain way. When I returned home to California, I found a package waiting for me. Hench had sent me the suit. It was the last one." Bill got the impression that the man rarely let down the façade of Tomorrow Man while wearing the suit, revealing the introspective, thoughtful designer within. The older man brushed and straightened his sleeves in what seemed to Bill a well-rehearsed ritual. Apparently, OCD is still a problem in the world of tomorrow. "I don't wear this old thing as a reminder, Bill Durmer."

Tomorrow Man then did something quite unexpected: he removed his helmet, placed it carefully in his lap and stared right into Bill's eyes. "I wear it as a caution, a warning to Imagineers and company leadership that when you design a place called Tomorrowland, you'd better deliver on the promise of the name. Don't rely on pop culture to drive your aesthetic — like this old thing or our animatronic friend over there. Build your attractions based on real science and with real vision."

Bill smiled at the old man, recognizing the soul of a dreamer, beaten but not defeated. He leaned back in his chair a bit and stared out the window at the big white weenie. "I remember my dad taking me on Space

Mountain when I was a kid. We rode it over and over again. He didn't really care much for roller coasters, but he loved the post-show." He glanced at Tomorrow Man to gauge his reaction. The old man was smiling, nodding his approval, almost as if he had been waiting for Bill to tell this story. "He was an unapologetic futurist, my dad. The whole futuristic home thing—"

"RCA's Home of Future Living," Tomorrow Man interrupted.

"Right," Bill continued. "He loved that, as cheesy as it had become by the early eighties. I guess that's what inspired me to—"

"Go to Georgia Tech and MIT?" Tomorrow Man interrupted again. Bill was perplexed. He was fairly certain he hadn't mentioned his college pedigree. Had he flaked out again, mid-conversation? Rather than paint himself an idiot, he chose to go along.

"Yeah, exactly."

"And what became of that vision of the future, Bill Durmer?" Tomorrow Man's eyes blazed intensely as if an old fire within had been freshly stoked. "What have you done, since donning the Grad Rat and leaving the hallowed halls of the Institute, to make it a reality?"

This question came like a punch in the gut to Bill. He hated talking about MIT, not so much because of the place itself, but because of his own failure.

"Actually, I never finished my graduate degree," Bill replied. "It's a long story."

"Of course," Tomorrow Man said in a way that suggested he already knew this. "But you still have your degree from Ma Tech. Besides, a vision doesn't require degrees."

"I guess not."

"Well!" The Space Ghost-channeling Tomorrow Man was back, bellowing forth his words with the forcefulness of a retrorocket. He slapped Bill on the knee, donned his helmet and stood, drawing the attention of any newcomers to the dining room. "I trust you'll recapture that vision in due time, Bill Durmer." He turned to Bill's family, whom he had utterly ignored to this point. "Good children, dear lady, I bid you farewell." Placing his right fist against his heart in earnest salute, he bowed to the table and then turned to the crowd of on-looking diners. He pointed at Sonny Eclipse, now singing an ode to his invisible back-up singers, the Space Angels, and commanded, "Beware the cartoon future that never was!" He beat a hasty retreat up the stairs, past the order line and out into the plaza.

Bill sat speechless for a second. Katherine stared at her husband with the same look of disbelief. Cleary craned her neck to try to see where Tomorrow Man had gone. The other diners slowly resumed their conversations until the din of the crowd had returned to normal. Clay finally broke the silence at the Durmer table.

"I want padamas wike that!" he cried out.

"I want pajamas like that, too," Bill said, rubbing his son's shoulders.

Katherine sighed, "Bill, did you get a tattoo that I don't know about?" Bill looked perplexed by the question. "Because I swear there's a sign on your forehead that reads 'weirdoes welcome.'"

Bill nodded, "Yeah, maybe so." Under normal circumstances, he would have taken the bait and dived off into some world-class self-deprecation. But Tomorrow Man had forced him to do the one thing he promised himself he wouldn't on this vacation: think about the current state of his life.

✳✳✳

For all the freaky occurrences of their first few days in town, the Durmers managed to enjoy the rest of their trip uninterrupted by spacemen and psychos. The girls celebrated their birthday with a lavish party at the Grand Floridian, complete with a huge cake that read "Happy Birthday, Dara!" and a cupcake that read "and Cleary." Nancy spared no expense. Except the cupcake. Bill paid for that.

Though he had only been there once before, Bill lamented the loss of the EPCOT Center of old, just as he had done with Tomorrowland. He never noticed that, during each of his tirades about the park's lost purpose, an older man in sport clothes and with a wave of jet black, Brylcreemed hair watched him from a distance. And smiled.

Chapter Six:
All Because of a Yard Sign

Katherine rubbed her knees in a vain attempt to return the blood flow to her lower legs. She had never been in the backseat of a police cruiser before, and she prayed this would be the last time. In her right hand, she clutched an old, tear-stained handkerchief. Holding it up to catch flashes of reflected blue light, she studied the monogram. A-B-C, it read.

Arthur Benedictine Cleary had been Katherine's father. As she traced out the letters with her fingertip, she considered how much he had always hated his name. His mother's stubborn insistence on clinging to the last vestiges of her Catholicism saddled him with the most unwieldy middle name he could imagine. Worse yet, she claimed ignorance of the fact that she had given him initials better suited to a Kindergarten bulletin board than a successful man.

In college, he embraced the taunts of his classmates, adopting the nickname of Alph. The name had served him well. An entire generation of college kids across the Gulf Coast region could slur every note of the Alph Cleary Wine and Beer jingle:

> *"There's no need for acting dreary.*
> *Happy hour is drawing near-y.*
> *When it's time for spirit lifting,*
> *It's Alph Cleary Wine & Beer-y."*

At least once a semester, some student would take the "spirit lifting" line literally and try to shoplift a few bottles. Alph figured he had heard at least a hundred students whistling the jingle as they browsed the stores for each one who took advantage of the five-finger discount. So he'd pretend not to see rather than change the infectious tune.

Katherine had always promised herself she would never use gimmicky names for her own children. She also promised herself she would never experience the cramped quarters and shameful view from the back of a police car. Chalk both up as examples of the typical self-betrayal of an American adulthood.

She sighed as the darkened Central Florida landscape whizzed by her window. She saw citrus groves hung artfully with fruit like rows of summertime Christmas trees. She noted how greenish-brown the ripe, plump oranges appeared in the flashing blue light. She saw cars awkwardly pulling to the sides of the turnpike, making way for the caravan of law enforcement vehicles in which she rode. She noted the curious, judgmental faces glaring at her as if she were Public Enemy Number One.

"All because of a yard sign," she muttered.

"What's that?" the female officer riding shotgun — and packing one — asked.

"Nothing," Katherine replied. She was reluctant to go into the whole absurd business. Then again, she desperately needed to talk to someone. Ever since she received the alarming message from law enforcement officials requesting her presence to "resolve a crisis involving her husband," she felt increasingly isolated and never knew whom to trust. So she let her guard down. "I was just saying this whole thing started with a yard sign."

The officer tried to be understanding and compassionate, but she was clearly too far outside the loop on this one. "I'm sorry; I don't understand."

"Neither do I," Katherine cryptically replied, continuing to stare out the window.

"I'm Jaimee." The officer did her best to sound friendly. Katherine noted the long, curly blonde locks peeking out from under the woman's hat. She envied her smooth, blemish-free skin, perfectly white teeth and stunning blue eyes. Katherine suspected the woman was new to police work, not only because of her youthful appearance, but also her seeming lack of cynicism. Nancy, she thought, would suspect the officer of having a very different sort of job on the side, based on appearance alone.

"Nice to meet you, Jaimee." Katherine extended two fingers through the metal grate separating her from the officers. Jaimee chuckled and shook

Katherine's fingers.

"I'm sorry you have to ride like this," she demurred. "These things aren't exactly made for carpooling."

Katherine tightly smiled her gratitude while trying to fight back tears. Welling up at such a banal pleasantry caught her by surprise. Perhaps it was the sincerity in the young officer's voice or the genuine look of concern in her eyes. Since this bizarre ordeal began, she had not once allowed herself to cry. But now, cramped into the back of a police cruiser, escorted by an atonal chorus of sirens and a strobing illuminage of red and blue, she found herself unexpectedly moved by the awkward kindness of a stranger. She couldn't hold it back. Her chest convulsed violently as she fought against the wash of emotion. She gripped her mouth to muffle her cries. Jaimee turned away before she, too, lost her composure.

Suddenly, the sirens went silent, and the strobes went dark. Katherine wiped her eyes and peered out the window as best she could. The car passed under a large gate supported by massive, square, segmented red columns. To the right of one column, was a large figure of Mickey Mouse. Katherine caught a brief glimpse of him as they sped past. She resented his fixed, unchanging grin. She felt mocked by his look of eternal optimism.

Seeing the smiling, anthropomorphized rodent reminded her of Bill. He often complained that, in turning Mickey into an icon, Disney (the company, not the man) robbed him of the more mischievous traits that endeared him to fans in the first place. But thinking of Bill only made her angry, so she stopped.

Jaimee's partner turned toward Katherine with a wry grin. "Welcome to Disney World!" he joked. Katherine burst into laughter despite herself. Jaimee, at first mortified by the ironic joke, joined her.

"The most magical place on Earth!" Katherine belted out through her tears, eliciting more laughs from the officers. Jaimee reached through the grate with her finger. Katherine took it as if they were old friends sharing a secret handshake. The three rode in silence for a few minutes. The monotonous drone of tires on asphalt was periodically broken by a staticky call over the radio. Katherine couldn't for the life of her figure out how these people could understand one another over those things. To her, it was nothing more than broken squawks and croaks, like the adults in a Charlie Brown cartoon filtered through an old CB radio.

As the procession drew nearer to Bill's hotel, she thought about what she would say to him, how she might talk some sense into him. Saying a quick prayer to herself, clutching Jaimee's finger ever tighter, she allowed a peace about the situation to wash away her anger. She put herself in her husband's shoes. After all, apart from the ill-considered decision to shave his head in his late twenties — hoping it would make him more menacing — he had never been an impulsive man. And he had just lost his family's business. Maybe it was nothing more than an overblown midlife crisis. Heck, the stress of being Nancy's brother alone would be enough to wreck anyone's sanity.

Images of their life together washed across her mind: Bill holding an infant Cleary in his arms and hauling her down to the bay in the middle of the night for her first Jubilee, the kids turning him into a human jungle gym every time he dared fall asleep on the living room floor, Clementine dozing on his chest only hours after she was born. No matter what the rest of the world might think of Bill, he was her husband. When she said "for better or for worse" in her vows, she meant it.

"Almost there," Jaimee's partner called out from the front. Jaimee released the single-finger grip she had on Katherine and started loading and cocking firearms as if she were in some trite action movie. A squawk on the radio sent the driver scrambling for something on the floorboard. He doffed his hat and replaced it with an odd-looking headgear with what appeared to be a monocular mounted on it. One by one, the cars in the procession shut off their lights. When the car in front of them did so, the driver pulled the eyepiece of the monocular over his eyes, flipped off the headlights and pushed a button on the headset.

Once the headlights of the cars behind them were all off, Katherine couldn't see a thing. She heard a splat. Then another. And another. Then a tintinnabulation of splats, plops and dings rang out all over the vehicle. Growing up along the Gulf Coast, she knew immediately it was the sound of a heavy tropical rainstorm unleashing its fury. There was a quick flash of lightning, and Jaimee's partner cried out, ripping the night vision goggles off his head. "I hate these things." Katherine couldn't see if he put them back on or not.

Through the pouring rain, Katherine could barely make out the shapes of hotel buildings each time the lightning flashed, first All-Star Sports, then All-Star Music. The resorts were eerily dark — no brightly lit exterior signs, no streetlights, no room lights. All she saw was complete darkness.

"What are you gonna say?" Jaimee inquired from somewhere in the dark in front of her.

"I'm sorry?"

"To your husband," Jaimee clarified. "What are you gonna say to him when you get there?"

That was the question of the hour. She had wondered the same thing since she left Decent Chance early that morning. She thought about it as she drove the Bayway across Mobile Bay, faintly hoping the rippling waters might whisper the answer. She pondered it again as she sat on the tarmac in a private jet as its lone passenger, awaiting takeoff. And she thought about it for the entire duration of the flight.

"I'm going to tell him," Katherine answered serenely, "that I love him." To her surprise, she actually meant it. Despite everything she had been through in the last few weeks, she meant it.

"Well, good for you," Jaimee replied. Despite the darkness, Katherine could hear her sincerity, and she found it refreshing.

The car slowed to a stop. The storm was in full swing now. Lightning crashed so frequently Katherine thought for a second that someone in one of the squad cars might have reactivated their strobes. She tried to make out what was going on ahead of them, but could only see each time lightning struck. She could, however, hear voices shouting over the rain and thunder. They were coming closer. They were coming for her.

A tap at Jaimee's door and she sprang into action. She bolted out and opened Katherine's door for her. Katherine tried to shield her head and ambled out into the pouring rain. Jaimee draped a raincoat over Katherine's shoulders and pulled the hood up over her head. A man in a black rain slicker drew close to Katherine.

"Mrs. Durmer?" he shouted.

"Yes?" Katherine replied loudly, her voice quavering only slightly. Not bad, given the circumstances.

"I'm Battalion Chief Mortimer of the Reedy Creek Critical Action Response." He bellowed out every word with precision and force. Lightning illuminated his steely gaze. "I've got two hundred men out here in the mother of all thunderstorms," he continued, "all because of your husband." Katherine felt a knot growing in her gut. The Chief concluded, "I'd appreciate the hell out of it if you would talk some sense into him." The Chief turned and stormed away.

"Come on, Katherine," Jaimee said softly. She took Katherine's arm and lead her the way the Chief had gone.

All Katherine could think as she slogged through puddles was "two hundred men." The Chief's words echoed in her head. What had Bill done? What in the world was he thinking, letting his hare-brained scheme get this out of hand? This was no midlife crisis. It was more like a terror crisis. "Jaimee," she grunted through gritted teeth, "I changed my mind. I'm going to kill him."

Chapter Seven:
Everything's Disposable

"Oh, it's just an electronics store."

Bill pegged the tourist's accent as being from either Wisconsin or Minnesota. For all he knew, confusing the two might be the most egregious insult to citizens of those two states. So, he chose not to say anything. Not that there was time to do so. No sooner than she had stuck her head inside the front door, she was ducking back out again on a quest for something more "authentic." (Authentic in this case meant hand-carved, nautically themed knick-knacks from China featuring the saying: "There's a decent chance I'll go back to Decent Chance, AL.")

"Come back again!" Bill yelled in irony after the woman and her party. They paid him no heed. He returned to his laptop in a mock home office in the far left corner of the showroom. Working in Photoshop, he pasted images of flat screen TVs onto a vintage newspaper ad for Durmer Radio and Television. He placed a stock shot of a 55-inch LCD TV over an old ArvinTV ad that read, "Here's the greatest TV news in years! Get all 82 present and future channels at the turn of a knob." Bill applied a halftone effect to the newer image and adjusted colors and levels to make it blend into the older ad. He chuckled at the juxtaposition of words and images, and then scrolled back to the top. He sighed heavily, and his shoulders drooped as he read the ad's headline.

The bell above the door tinkled as someone entered. "Whatcha got for me?" Nancy called out in a playful tone. She had used this same greeting when entering the store since she'd been old enough to speak, first addressing her grandfather and father, and for the last seventeen years, her brother.

Bill found it charming the first few times Nancy said it to him, when he had taken over the store following their father's death, but now it grated on him.

"Hey, Sis." He didn't even bother to turn around to greet her.

"Is that how you talk to a paying customer?" she chided him.

He spun around to take her on, "Since when have you paid for..." He stopped short when he saw that Nancy was not alone. Standing at her side was a tall, leggy brunette. Bill blinked to adjust his eyes to the light pouring through the storefront and leapt to his feet when he recognized the woman. It was Jenny Tillman, awkward pre-teen-turned-supermodel, victim of his adolescent cruelty.

"Jenny?" Bill asked incredulously. She smiled warmly and glided across the floor in his direction. He hadn't seen her in more than 20 years. Was she going to slap him? Punch him? Bruise his fragile ego and suddenly shaky body image? Unsure of what to do, he nervously outstretched a hand. She promptly brushed it aside to embrace him. He was hugging a supermodel. He was hugging a supermodel, and no one had a camera. This day was most definitely on an uptick.

She held him longer than he expected, forcing him to relax into the hug and actually return it. Over Jenny's shoulder, he saw Nancy's eyes grow wide. He shrugged as the longest hug in the history of the world lingered.

Jenny finally pulled away, but held fast to Bill's shoulders, studying his face. "Bill Durmer. It has been too long."

"What the he—" he started, but then shifted gears, "What brings you back to Decent Chance? I thought your mother had moved up north to be closer to you."

"She did, but we're looking for a change of pace." She gestured toward her own face and body. "These aren't exactly affording the Manhattan lifestyle the way they once did." Bill was shocked. He would have paid a couple hundred bucks for just a glimpse of her walking down the sidewalk. Staring closer, he did notice, however, the slightest hints of time's unflagging march: crow's feet struggling to appear at the corners of her eyes, the fractional widening of the hips from carrying two children, hints of gravity's effects on her jaw line. Compared to the average 38-year-old woman, these tell-tale signs of age were hardly noticeable. But modeling was a young woman's game, dominated by girls with million-dollar salaries who weren't old enough to rent a car.

"You're moving back?"

"Not exactly." She gestured toward Nancy. "I'm talking to Kenny about a new multi-use development on some property I bought near Week's Bay."

"Wow. That sounds..." Bill searched for the right word. "Ambitious." That wasn't right. "Exciting. I meant to say, 'exciting.'"

"It is, thanks." She had now slid her hands down his arms and was holding both of his hands. Too familiar. Bill pulled away and sat on the edge of his desk.

"But what brings you *here*?" Bill wiped his hands together reflexively as if trying to wash away the evidence of her touch. Nancy stepped forward to usurp the conversation.

"Jen bought one of the new units at Exclusion and her TV is on the fritz." Exclusion by the Bay was Nancy's pet project, a condo development that had landed Kenny in hot water with historical preservationists when "hippies and do-gooders" caught wind of his plan to build atop one of the town's most sacred sites, Louisville Mashgill Hill.

✳✳✳

Louisville Mashgill, or Big Lou, was a legendary redfish in Mobile Bay, rumored by sport fisherman to be "as broad as Eleanor Roosevelt and as long as her memory." For the better part of two decades, anglers from the world over flocked to Decent Chance hoping to land the big red.

Joseph Jackson, a drunken keeper at Middle Bay Light discovered the fish, accidentally snaring the beast while using a treble hook to wash his underwear in the bay. He was so enraged at the thought of losing three precious pair of his best Sunday boxers that he jumped aboard his small wooden boat and chased the fish in circles around the offshore lighthouse for hours, beating it furiously about the right side of its head with a Louisville Slugger whenever it would near the surface. Legend has it that, after three hours of this routine, the fish finally tired of the keeper's antics, leapt over the boat, grabbed the bat and sawed the boat in half with 100-pound test before snapping the line and escaping – bat, hook, boxers and all. At least that's the story the keeper told when his replacement found him passed out and naked from the waist down, his boat curiously missing.

The story, originally intended as a humorous column on the sports page of the Sunday Press-Register, was printed as a news article instead, and the legend of Louisville Mashgill was born. In the mid-fifties, after suffering years of humiliation, Joseph Jackson (now known as "Pantsless Joe") admitted that the story was a fabrication. Tourism officials in Decent Chance tried desperately to keep the legend alive, but to no avail.

Then, on the morning of August 18, 1969, while surveying damage from Hurricane Camille, the people of Decent Chance discovered the carcass of a redfish washed ashore on the hill overlooking the city pier. Measuring more than eight feet in length and estimated at over 200 pounds, the fish bore the rusty remnants of a treble hook in its mouth ... and the gills on its right side were battered flat. Louisville Mashgill was dead. Long live Big Lou.

On Founders' Day 1970, the hill where his body was found was renamed in his honor. Original plans had called for a plaque to be placed at the site, but budget reallocations meant the money earmarked for the plaque was instead spent on the oversized ribbon and giant scissors used in the dedication ceremony.

∗∗

Now, some four decades later, Kenny and Nancy agreed to incorporate a public park atop the hill, adorned not only with the long-delayed plaque but a fountain bearing a life-size bronze statue of Big Lou. Actually, that was Kenny's plan. Nancy's plan was to call the INS, the DEA and whoever else was necessary to send "those people" back to where they belonged.

Between the park and Nancy's constant design upgrades and revisions, the development had gone over budget by nearly four million dollars. Now, in a down economy, they were sitting on 62 empty units of the most finely appointed bay view condominiums along the Gulf Coast. Such a debacle was Exclusion by the Bay that the locals had taken to calling it Nancy's Folly.

Bill bristled at the thought of even setting foot inside Exclusion. Kenny had intended to hire Bill to design state-of-the-art interactive media and communication systems for each unit and a delivery hub for the entire complex. Bill's design would combine off-the-shelf components with his own proprietary hardware and software designs to create a ubiquitous computing system capable of recognizing users and tailoring their entertainment choices, information and home automation preferences based upon usage history. Utilizing that data, the hub system would then aid in programming entertainment in the community's club room and digital theatre to suit the tastes of residents, even sending personalized invitations and encouraging social networking between those residents with similar interests. Allowing himself to dream of a new career path for the first time in years, Bill envisioned licensing his system to high-end condos, luxury hotels and cruise ships around the world. Durmer Electronics would finally break out beyond the town limits of Decent Chance, and Bill would at last have a project worthy of his pedigree.

Kenny, well connected within the world of architects and developers, agreed to plug Bill into his network for a small finder's fee. But the dream came crashing down when Kenny jokingly remarked to Nancy that Bill stood to make ten times the profit off Exclusion they did. Couching her argument within economic concerns, Nancy convinced Kenny to scale back plans for the systems to the point that Bill could no longer afford to even design them. In the end, they bought only discount-grade flat screens, those just barely above cost, and only half of them through Bill. Bill had invested tens of thousands of dollars in attorney's fees, trademarks and patent applications. With 80 percent of the units pre-sold, Kenny confidently assured Bill he would repay him for those costs. When the market tanked, and most buyers simply walked away from their mortgages, Kenny's promises became worthless.

"Is it one of the units we supplied," Bill asked his sister, "or one of the cheapies you picked up at that fire sale?"

"It's mine," Jenny offered. I drove it down here in my trunk. Do you think that could have damaged it?" Bill shrugged.

"Hard to say. I'll have to check it out." He sighed and hesitated a bit, "But to be honest with you, unless it's a top-of-the-line set, you can probably replace it cheaper than you can have it fixed."

"Seriously?" Jenny balked. "That's insane."

"I know, but the prices on these things are artificially low because of cheap components and even cheaper overseas labor." Bill offered his well-worn lament with a tinge of resignation. "One little thing breaks, and suddenly you're looking at hundreds of dollars in labor to replace a fifty-cent part." Jenny shook her head in dismay.

"But it's a TV; it's not supposed to be disposable," she protested. Bill looked around the little store, studying each nook and cranny.

"I know, but these days," he looked into her eyes with a deadened gaze, "everything's disposable." Jenny's eyes moistened, reacting to Bill's defeatist tone. Nancy perked up again to break the silence.

"Wellll... You'll have to forgive my brother's sales pitch." She leaned on Bill's shoulder. "He may be a whiz with gadgets, but he's not much of a businessman." Bill chose not to lash out at her. He was too exhausted for that. Nancy read his silence as acceptance and kept going. "Did you know he wouldn't even put up a yard sign to protest the Walmart coming to town?"

"Ugh..." Jenny groaned. "I hate that place." The model gave him a sly wink and smile when she noticed Nancy wasn't looking. "How could you do that, Bill?"

"Probably wouldn't have made a difference anyway," Nancy shrugged. A quick "society hug" for Jenny, and she was making her way for the door. "I'll leave you two here to talk business." A quick glance at her watch induced a groaned: "Ballet." She swung the door open dramatically, nearly knocking the decades-old bell from its mount. "It's a good thing I love dance, because I loathe other people's children." The door slammed behind her.

"My little sister, ladies and gentlemen," Bill deadpanned. "Improving the world one condescension at a time." Jenny burst forth in a laugh of relief and took a big breath.

"Oh, my God!" she exclaimed. "I forgot how exhausting she could be. Worst part is she was just as bad when I used to babysit her. At least back then she had a little imagination. Now she's kind of a b—" She slapped her hand over her mouth with a sudden realization. She slipped the hand down just enough to say, "I'm so sorry. I shouldn't talk about your sister that way."

"Yes, you should," Bill half-joked. "Everyone should." He had forgotten that Jenny would watch his sister on occasion. Babysitting was a loose definition. Jenny was only three years Nancy's senior. She would stay with the younger girl when Bill and his mom, Elise, were helping out at the store. Jenny never knew Elise Durmer had hired her only to ease the financial burdens of Jenny's single mother. Standing up, Bill slapped his hands together and rubbed them excitedly. "Let's look at some TVs!"

For the better part of an hour, Bill and Jenny explored every minute feature of every television in the store. They did so in relative privacy, as during that time not one other customer darkened the doors; only the mailwoman came in, bearing the daily crop of mounting bills. When

Jenny's indecision got the better of the both of them, they collapsed into the cushy auditorium-style seats in the home theatre room with sodas and popcorn. They reminisced about old high school friends. They laughed about the travails of parenthood. Jenny lamented the failure of her marriage. Bill spoke of his religious faith (violating yet another of his personal rules), boldly reaffirming his belief in God's grace and sufficiency even in life's darkest hours. He wasn't sure if he said it for her or for himself.

"I have to say, I'm a little disappointed in you, Bill Durmer." The use of his full name struck Bill as odd, reminding him of his strange encounters at Walt Disney World some six months earlier.

"The Walmart thing?" He relented, "I know; I should have put up the sign. I guess I'm paying for it now."

"No," she turned toward him and fixed him with a solemn stare. "When I heard you got into grad school at MIT, I just knew you were going off to change the world. My only regret..." she trailed off and looked away. Bill could swear he saw her blush in the dim light. "...was it meant I'd never have the chance to tell you how I felt about you." Flattered, taken aback, Bill took a deep, long breath and slowly blew it out. "When I got my first modeling contract, I thought maybe we'd run into each other in New York or someplace in Europe. It's a small world, after all."

Disney again. At this rate, Bill half expected Annette Funicello and Fess Parker to come bouncing through the door, in all their 1950s glory, at any moment. If Jenny were in on some elaborate joke at Bill's expense, she wasn't letting on. She continued, "I thought about you often. I almost called you once when I was passing through Boston."

"I guess you're glad you didn't make that mistake," he remarked with a forced grin. His attempt at self-deprecation fell short. His eyes revealed a gloomy sincerity, which she met with a look of reproof.

"Look, I think it's very noble what you did, taking over this store when your dad died, but you have so much more talent than that. You could still have a bright future. A great, big beautiful tomorrow." She maintained eye contact and spoke with an earnestness he hadn't seen from her before. "Share your talent with the world." Bill tried his best to match her seriousness, but couldn't. He started to laugh.

"A great, big beautiful tomorrow? It's a small world after all?" He nudged her playfully. "You're a Disney nerd!"

She was definitely blushing this time. "I just do this thing," she fumbled for words, more blood rushing to her cheeks. Finally, she blurted out, "Yes! I'm a Disney geek! I admit it. I just have this thing for the Sherman Brothers..." Her Manhattan-cool façade melted away in a fit of unselfconscious laughter, until it almost stifled her ability to speak. It occurred to Bill that she likely hadn't let anyone see her true self in more than 20 years, that her laughter might actually be the sense of relief from finally letting her guard down. Jenny gamely attempted to compose herself. "I just think you should, you know..." Bill cut her off.

"Can we go back to the part where you're a supermodel who's a Disney geek?" he kidded. "Because I love that part." She laughed even harder now. Wiping tears from her eyes, she playfully slapped at his arm but missed, slapping him square across the face.

"Ow!" Bill recoiled into the fetal position and matched her laughter in intensity and volume. She tried several times to apologize, but simply couldn't muster the will to stop laughing and get the words out. Bill got it together first, rubbing his reddened cheek for effect. "See if I give you a discount on a TV now!"

She took several deep breaths to calm herself. "I was getting a discount?"

"Don't think you're special," he said in mock irritation. "This week everybody gets a discount." His laughter and smile melted away. "It's a going-out-of-business sale." That was enough to chase away Jenny's smile, too. She took his hand and squeezed.

"This is an opportunity." One glance at her face would prove these weren't token words of comfort, not a moment of cheap grace, but of genuine conviction. "You will recapture your vision, Bill Durmer." Shock and perplexity swept across his countenance. Why did she choose those words, the same words Tomorrow Man had used? Did she know what Tomorrow Man had said? Was this a gag? Maybe someone actually was playing a six-month-long practical joke at his expense. But who? All valid questions, but the most troubling question to Bill was this: what vision?

Jenny bought a 55-inch LED TV and a surround sound system. She refused to accept the sale price, insisting instead on paying Bill not only full price, but also a bonus for spending so much time helping her decide. Bill couldn't help but feel it was a pity purchase. But she was a supermodel who quoted the Sherman Brothers, and that eased the pain. When he delivered the gear to her condo the next day, the building manager had to let him in.

Jenny had packed up and caught a flight to New York immediately after leaving the store. He didn't know why, but Bill had the distinct feeling he would see her again. And soon.

Chapter Eight:
One-Eyed Jack and All of His Trades

Claymoor Durmer stood proudly in front of the simple brick store-front, wearing parade dress, his Purple Heart displayed prominently on his chest. At the behest of the photographer, he crouched down, resting one elbow atop the small, wooden cabinet of an RCA 630TS 10-inch television set, which was perched on its own custom stand. A crowd of onlookers gathered on the sidewalk, hoping to catch a glimpse of the device. Claymoor beamed as the photographer's flashbulbs fired. A reporter from the *Weekly Fishwrapper* elbowed in beside the photographer.

"How much you gonna charge for that electric fish tank, Clay?" the reporter yelled over the murmurs of the crowd.

"RCA has authorized me to sacrifice this technological wonder at a low price of only 435 dollars." Gasps emanated from the crowd. Claymoor, a tall, good-looking man in his late twenties, had a youthful exuberance untempered by his time in the Army Air Corps but a countenance that bore the lines and creases of an older, more experienced man. These features combined to make him a cunning salesman. He stood to his full height, careful to wince ever so slightly and clutch at his right knee as he did. Everyone loved the old war hero bit. He looked the reporter square in the eye and flashed a toothy grin. "You wanna be the first man in town to own a piece of the future?" The reporter laughed and waved him off.

"Why in the world would anyone pay car prices for a big box of tubes that can't even pick up a radio station?" he fired back. "There's not a television station within two hundred miles."

"An historical inevitability!" Claymoor had been preparing for this question since he lay recovering in a British hospital from a blast of shrapnel in the skies above France as communications officer in a B-17. It was in that hospital where his dream took shape. "Why, over in Europe, all the big mucky-mucks were talking about how television stations were gonna sweep the nation as soon as the war was over." He favored his left leg slightly and rubbed his right knee. "Don't know if you got the word, but Hitler's dead, boys, and old Tojo's locked up and waiting for the hangman. It's an American world now. The old ways are over. Time for the new way, the American way. And that new way is television."

The crowd, many of whom had been questioning his sanity, disparaging his family name, even suggesting his parents had never been married only seconds before, now burst into fits of spontaneous patriotic fervor, clapping and cheering for their local war hero. They began to push beyond the press perimeter and make for the door. Clay put up his hands to halt them.

"Now before y'all go rushing inside, we got us a ribbon to cut." With Mayor Kerwin Thomas standing alongside him to his left, his parents standing on the other side of the RCA and his pregnant wife, Betsy, in front of him, Claymoor cut the ceremonial ribbon. Flashbulbs lit up the overcast afternoon. In the resulting photo, the Durmers were immortalized, glowing in their post-war idyll. Above them, a bright, new electric sign shone nearly as brightly as their faces: "Durmer Radio and Television."

∗∗∗

Bill carefully removed the old photo from above the store's original sales counter, which he had preserved out of sheer nostalgia. No employee had stood behind it nor had any transaction taken place upon its surface in over a decade. Instead, it served more as a living museum to the Durmer's that was: vintage radios spanning more than four decades, a 50s Bakelite toaster, a 60s portable reel-to-reel recorder, a 70s CB radio and an 80s Walkman. There were Super 8 cameras and early camcorders of all sizes — all in mint condition. And in the center of it all, under preservation glass and dim lighting, seated on velvet and surrounded by a lush curtain, was the 1946 RCA 630TS.

His grandfather could never part with that original TV, at least not in the later years. He had actually sold it at least seven times, and each time the owner would return it for the same reason: there was no TV station within 100 miles. The set had graced the parlors and living rooms of the most notable families in Decent Chance, belonging in turns to doctors, lawyers, politicians and one shrimp boat captain who had a lucky night at the poker table. And every one of them found his way back to Claymoor's door.

In 1952, WKAB went on the air as Mobile's first station, but it was on the UHF band, and the old RCA was a VHF-only model. Within three years, two more stations had begun to broadcast in Mobile. With the sudden growth of the TV market, Durmer's diversified their stock of televisions with bigger, more full-featured models, but the old 630 was Claymoor's favorite. It was the only set in the store he allowed to stay on from open to close, even when the fashion at other stores was to have every set on and tuned to the same station. He eventually built a special display for it. (Betsy would refer to it derisively as "The Shrine.") Above it, he hung the framed photo from opening day with a plaque that read, "Durmer's 1946 RCA 630TS. Alabama's first television."

It was that same photo that Bill now dusted with a chamois. Constant polishing by Claymoor in his latter years had worn thin the etching in the brass plaque. Long after the old man had turned over the reins of his store to Bill's dad, William, he would continue to come into the store as he had six days a week since 1946. He no longer kept pace with the technology the store sold, but would spend his days regaling customers and old friends with stories of his many exploits: his experiences deep sea fishing in Cuba with Hemingway, hunting big game in Africa with Jon Huston, testing out some new frogman gear called SCUBA with a "funny little French guy" named Cousteau and racing stock cars on the Florida beaches outside Daytona. The one common element in all his stories was that, to a word, they were complete fabrications. From the day Claymoor opened the store on Founder's Day 1946, he had taken only Sundays off and only six days of vacation a year, always used for a family trip.

Staring reticently at the photo, Bill said, "Sorry, Grandpa." He wrapped it in bubble wrap and placed it in a box marked "Keapsakes." Cleary had insisted on correcting her spelling error on the box, but Katherine suggested it would be a good object lesson for learning how to let some things go. After wrapping and packing the smaller electronics from the old sales counter and more old photos (of the store, his parents and some notable customers), Bill sealed up boxes until he exhausted his tape supply. He then shuffled out onto the store's front walk, plopped himself in one of the rocking chairs his grandfather bought for "jawin' time," and fired up a dried-out Cohiba knock-off (labeled "Hociba") he had found in the back of a desk drawer.

Looking across Establishment Street and down Fisherman's Way toward the bay, Bill could just make out, between the outstretched branches of ancient live oaks bedecked with Spanish Moss and faded Mardi Gras beads, the last sliver of the sun setting over the water. For at least thirty seconds, he didn't have a single thought — a new record for Bill. The peace was broken by the familiar ring of the bell above the door of the adjacent store.

"Tough day." The man's high tenor voice always made Bill smile.

"Evening, Jack," Bill said, not taking his eyes off the setting sun. Jack was a small man, no more than five-foot-one, who walked with an almost mechanical gait. He had a shock of perfectly symmetrical jet black hair atop his head that, as far as Bill could recall, had never been one millimeter shorter or longer in the seventeen years the two men had shared adjacent storefronts. Likewise, his hair had never grayed, nor had he shown any signs of growing old whatsoever. He was ageless. Whenever Bill broached the topic of Jack's hair or age with others, none had ever taken notice. That's because they were focused on the eye. Or the patch. It was one of the two.

Jack lost his left eye sometime before arriving in Decent Chance, and he always wore a black leather patch over the socket. Actually, no one had ever seen the socket, so it was conceivable that he had a fully functioning eye under there. When asked about it, he always laughed and made up some new, outlandish tale to account for the missing orb. Stranger than the patch, however, was his one extant eye. The iris was silver grey, almost metallic. Local conspiracy theorists swore they could hear his pupils dilate, describing it as a cross between the sound of the autofocus mechanism in a Canon EF 24-70mm L-series zoom lens and the slightly worn front breaks of a '68 Chevelle. Decent Chancers were nothing if not specific.

For the first few weeks Jack lived in town, everyone would refer to him mockingly as the Monocular Bionic Man, but the awkward lack of internal rhyme, alliteration or regular meter doomed that moniker from the start. Soon they took to calling him, predictably enough, One-Eyed Jack, even to his face. No one thought this inappropriate since his store was named

One-Eyed Jack's Sundries and Miscellany. He kind of had it coming to him.

Jack handed Bill a glass of something amber colored poured over ice. Without asking what it was and before Jack could even sit, Bill downed the drink. "Got any more of that?" he growled. Jack handed Bill his own glass. Bill chose to savor this one. "Macallan 12," Bill observed.

"Eighteen, actually," Jack corrected him. He studied Bill's face, trying to read his exact mood.

Bill took another sip. Impressed, he said, "Store must be doing okay if you're bringing me 18."

"Well..." Jack exhaled and relaxed into his chair, and searched for the exact point in the horizon that had Bill so transfixed. "Don't be too impressed. I didn't think you were worth the 21." Bill chuckled, took another sip.

"I prefer mine neat."

"I know," Jack replied manner-of-factly. "I was hoping the ice cubes would slow your roll." As if on cue, Bill finished the second glass at that exact second.

"I'd offer you a cigar, but I don't have any more." Bill took a long drag. "Tastes like feet anyway."

"The smoke would only foul up my circuitry," Jack said with a knowing grin. He had long since embraced the Bionic Man jokes and would allude to them in subtle ways, but only when talking to Bill. Bill could never ferret out how Jack knew about the failed nickname, and Jack wasn't telling. "Have you started taping up boxes, yet?" Bill nodded and grunted an affirmative. "That's the worst part. A store closing is never easy, believe you me."

No man on Earth could speak more definitively on the experience of closing a small store than Jack. He had shown up in town shortly after Bill took over Durmer's. Sundries and Miscellany was Jack's attempt to recreate the look and feel of a small-town general store from the early 1900s, but with kitschy found items and retro products that evoked mid-century hep. Despite how eclectic Decent Chance had grown in recent decades, and despite the cosmopolitan mix of tourists, summer residents and snowbirds who frequented the town, there just wasn't enough of a demand for tinsel Christmas trees, antique coin-operated horses, collectable lunch boxes and stationery featuring the cast of *Gidget*. The store closed after only a year of operation.

Most figured Jack would turn tail and run right out of town. The founding families, like the Thompsons and Durmers, had seen it time and again: carpet-bagging Yankees showing up, thinking they were smarter than the locals and on a mission to bring some "culture" to the hamlet. Kenny's father, Frank Thompson — a third generation mayor — once remarked of a restaurateur who hailed from Connecticut, "They think we Southerners are dumb, but they can't seem to get it through their thick skulls that sugar don't dissolve in cold tea." That particular restaurant closed within two months of its opening. Nothing dooms an eatery to failure in the South quicker than the refusal to serve sweet tea.

Jack, however, was a different breed of Yankee. Truthfully, no one knew anything about Jack's origins. His accent could best be described as "California neutral," the sort of non-regional accent used by news anchors, voice-over artists and those TV hucksters who claim to have made millions in something called the cash-flow business. He had alluded to living in both Southern California and Florida, but no one was sure where he was born; as any good Southerner knows, where you were born is where you're "from."

Within six months of the closing of the sundries store, Jack had completely remade the place into a turn-of-the-century ice cream parlor and soda fountain. Figuring his theming had gotten too convoluted in the store's previous incarnation, he was careful not to include any conflicting elements or styles into his new venture. He searched the entire country to find vintage striped wallpaper for the shop, bought an authentic soda fountain and bar from Salt Lake City, tin ceiling tiles from an old hardware store-turned-storage facility in Bay Minette and a collection of wrapped-wire chairs and tables scoured from junk stores and flea markets across the Southeast. The shop would serve hard ice cream, malts, shakes, hand-mixed sodas, floats and good, old-fashioned cold milk.

Jack named the establishment the Marceline Dairy Bar, leading many to suspect it was named for his mother. Jack shot down that speculation, but never acknowledged the inspiration for the name, insisting instead that anyone who wanted to learn the origins could do so easily enough. No one bothered, because the shop only survived for 20 months. An uncharacteristically cold spring and the introduction of a Dippin' Dots stand at the city pier ultimately spelled the shop's doom. After all, who wants to eat the ice cream of a hundred years ago when they can have the Ice Cream of the Future?

In the years that followed, Jack opened and closed the store no less than eight times, trying his hand at trades as varied as an after-hours day spa, a high-end unicycle shop, an organic junk food store, an Arctic-themed night spot with the unfortunate name Seal Club, a preschool boxing gym and a dry cleaner that specialized in whites only — and advertised itself as such.

After rebuilding from the opening day fire of the dry cleaner, he opened a Kosher market. That was followed, ironically enough, by Snooty McOinker's All-Bacon Emporium. Each iteration he elaborately themed and decorated, sparing no expense to get every detail precisely right. Bill could never figure from whence the money came, but watching the perennial reinvention became a favored source of entertainment.

With the store's most recent incarnation, Bill felt that Jack had finally found his true calling. In four short years, One-Eyed Jack's Toy Store had become a fixture in town — so much so that tourists who would otherwise have stayed closer to the beach were now choosing to stay in Decent Chance instead.

As with his previous business, the toy store was themed from floor to ceiling. The entrance was a replica of Winnie the Pooh's home, complete with a Mr. Sanders sign over the door and a bell labeled "RNIG ONLY." Once inside, visitors encountered a yellow brick road that wound back through the store to the various "lands" within.

First up was the Land of Letters, a mini-bookstore. Then came Jungle Land, a room filled top to bottom with plush animals and featuring a massive banyan tree kids could climb up into and explore a tree house outpost before sliding back down to the floor. The Milky Way was a space-themed room filled with every imaginable astronaut figure and spaceship. HomeLand offered everything kids could want for overlaying their own rules onto the mundane of everyday life: whimsical kitchen play sets, ride-on toy mowers, baby dolls, costumes and dozens of other toy versions of "grown up" items. A sign over the door read, "HomeLand Security, replacing locked doors with open ears, open arms and an open heart."

The Land of Possibility was a room dedicated to creativity and imagination, offering everything from LEGO and Tinker Toys to arts and crafts supplies. Child-sized drafting tables in the center of the room allowed for hands-on exploration of drawing, painting, sculpting and building. Finally, at the back of the store was the Barnyard, a party room and theatre hosted by a monocle-wearing, animatronic pig named Snooty McOinker — the one holdover from his ill-fated, eponymous restaurant.

Jack was more dedicated to his work than even Bill's grandfather had been. He had no wife, no family, no romantic entanglements. Curiously, he would sometimes leave, for up to two weeks at a time, unexpectedly and without warning. He neither told anyone where he was going nor where he had been. After the third or fourth such disappearance, Bill noticed that Jack always returned a little spryer, more fluid in his movements and with slight improvements in his social graces. At first, he thought Jack could be a member of a cult and his mysterious excursions were for reprogramming. As the pressures of running his own small business mounted, he realized Jack was probably just getting away to someplace quiet for the sake of his own sanity. It was the one aspect of Jack's life that Bill truly envied.

For several long minutes, the two men sat and watched the sun disappear behind the horizon, the only sounds being the occasional passing car, the creaking of their rocking chairs and Bill attempting (unsuccessfully) to blow smoke rings. Jack was first to break the silence.

"What now?" Jack didn't bother to further define the question. There was no need.

"I have no idea." Bill snuffed out the cigar on the sidewalk. "I thought I was going to conquer the world, Jack."

"Every young man does," Jack astutely pointed out. "Yet I only see old men pulling the strings."

"Yeah, but the worst part is everyone actually expected me to do it." Bill had never expressed this feeling to anyone before, but it had been building in him for years. Every milestone, every clever idea, every unique turn of phrase, good grade or academic achievement led to increasingly heightened expectations of his future success. Depending upon whom you talked to in Decent Chance, Bill Durmer was destined to cure cancer, erase the national deficit, invent water-powered hovercraft or be the first man on Mars. Now here he sat, on the doorstep of forty, unemployed, sharing expensive Scotch and a cheap cigar with a one-eyed Muppet.

"You still can," Jack replied. "Your destiny is still out there waiting for you, Bill Durmer." What was it about him that caused people to call Bill by his full name? Half the time he felt like a child in trouble with his mother, and the other half he swore they were doing to remind themselves who he was. As far as Bill could remember, Jack had never done it before that day.

Why now?

Bill chose to humor the little man, "Maybe so, Jack. Maybe so." Then he turned the tables. "What about you? You're a Jack of all trades — pardon the pun. Why don't you go save the world?" Jack snickered at the thought.

"Not me. I'm not wired that way." Jack observed wealthy tourists window shopping across the street. As they passed a shopkeeper sweeping his front stoop, they didn't even acknowledge him. Jack commented, "Every man has a purpose. For most, that purpose is small — like owning a little store or whatever paper pushing has paid our tourist friend there so well." He turned in his chair to face Bill. "But for some people, special people, that purpose is grander. You have a grander purpose, Bill Durmer. It's time to find it." Bill sighed heavily and stood up, handing Jack the empty glass. He offered the little man his hand and they shook in that casual way old friends do.

"Thanks a lot, Jack." What he thought, but did not say, was, *Thanks for ratcheting up the pressure.* Bill stepped inside, locked the door and flipped the window sign over to read "We are closed." Forever.

Chapter Nine:
The Night of the Black Jubilee

Two in the morning. A Northerly wind created a staccato *lap lap lap* of small, choppy waves. A dark night under a cloud-smothered moon, it was lit only by tiny pinpricks of light piercing the horizon from somewhere across the bay. Bill walked barefoot along the narrow beach below the bluff behind his house. He carried an old-fashioned kerosene lantern passed down from his grandfather to illuminate his path. So far, there was nothing much to see.

Inherited from his father, the title of Jubilee Master, once the subject of a decades-long feud, held very little weight in the community anymore. Part of the reason for that was a town ordinance that allowed citizens not only to keep all Jubilee spoils from their own property, but also opened up public beaches to anyone with "a strong back, a gunny sack and a weak gag reflex." Modern Jubilee Masters had virtually no power, but all the responsibility of rising every hour on the hour, all summer long, to walk the beaches looking for signs of a free seafood frenzy.

The Eastern shore of Mobile Bay was unique in the world for this late-night seafood party. A combination of low oxygen levels in the deeper waters of the bay and just the right parameters of wind, salinity, tide and temperature would send a multitude of crab, flounder, stingrays and other fish into the shallows and practically onto dry land. The resulting ad hoc celebration could last until well after sun-up with everyone from Daphne to Week's Bay scrambling out to the shoreline in their housecoats, Underoos and swimsuits to scoop up truckloads of free food.

A disputed Durmer family legend was that Decent Chance experienced the largest Jubilee in history on Founder's Day 1946 — the same day Clay-moor first opened his store. (Bill's grandmother, Betsy, recalled that it was actually 1947, on the first anniversary of the store's opening.) The unspoken suggestion was that Durmer's Electronics was good luck for the city, and that, so long as the store stayed open, the city would flourish. Now, only hours after closing the store's doors to the public for the final time, here was Bill, combing the beaches on the lookout for a Jubilee. Never one for superstition, he now secretly feared that his failure would put a halt to the events forever.

Bill had been out for nearly an hour on his watch. Closing the store had left his mind racing, trying to determine the course of his future. As much as he recognized that the store had put his planned career path on hold, he had come to depend upon the place. It was his refuge. At night, he would often sneak out of the house after Katherine was asleep and walk the seven blocks to the store. He would hole up in his workshop in the back of the store and noodle around with his latest pet project, whether that be experimenting with robotics or sculpting new float designs for the Mystic Krewe of Crabs. (Bill had been the chief float designer for the town's first and oldest Mardi Gras parading society for more than a decade. His 2003 parade theme, "Scandals of Papacy," nearly resulted in him being banned from both the town and all family functions. Since then, he had played it close to the vest, sticking to pop culture and mythology — the clean stuff, not all that nonsense with Zeus and his shenanigans.)

He had actually designed and constructed Snooty McOinker in that workshop as a favor to Jack. Jack had insisted he was well connected at Walt Disney Imagineering and could get a friend deal there, but Bill relished the challenge. After three months of tweaking the pig in an effort to create what Jack called "a more sympathetic upper lip," Bill began to second-guess his own generosity.

Two-oh-five. Not a fish in sight. He could have gone back inside and slept for an hour before coming back out, but his mind was racing. In all likelihood, he would end up on the sofa watching reruns of Mythbusters and drinking Green Russians — ice cream floats made with Vodka, Sprite and mint chocolate chip. Instead, he settled down at the foot of the steep, winding stairs that descended the bluff from his back lawn to the strip of sand some 30 feet below. Sipping on a watered down glass of sweet tea, he studied the movement of the water within the pool of light cast by his lantern. The smell of kerosene and salt water was a comfort to his soul. It reminded him of his father.

**

Though not a devout man, William Durmer would often use his Jubilee watch to share the tenets of faith with his son. Bill recalled more than once his father pointing to the Jubilee as an example of God's sufficiency and grace. He likened the event to a miracle, often comparing it to the feeding of the five thousand. William's faith was what Bill described as drive-by Catholicism: he would cross himself and say a Hail Mary or two as he drove by the cathedral on Sunday mornings, headed toward more earthly pursuits. Bill's mother, however, was the very picture of a good Catholic girl right up until the day she died.

Elise Durmer was born Elise Claire Pomeroy. She hailed from one of the oldest families in Mobile, able to trace her lineage back to the earliest French settlers in the region. Her grandparents had relocated to Baldwin county following World War I, when her grandfather, August Pomeroy, invested in farm land just inland from Decent Chance. She and William had grown up together, sharing classes throughout twelve years of school and attending Mass together every Sunday. For years, he had balked at attending. William's mother's response was always, "Now, don't you want to meet a nice Catholic girl and settle down? How're you going to do that, if you don't go to Mass?" William and Elise married the day after they graduated college. Mission accomplished. Clearly, the church had given him all it had to offer. Apart from Christmas, Easter and the occasional first communion, he was done.

Elise, on the other hand, only grew more involved in the church. Bill figured she was doubling up to compensate for her husband's impiety. She had the kids at Our Lady of Superior Breeding whenever the doors were open — for Mass, Sunday School, choir, bake sales, bible study, communion class, Saturday vigil and confession. And if for any reason they had to miss one of those, she threw in an extra confession for good measure.

The bay, however, was William's cathedral. Sundays, when the store was closed, he would rise before the sun, gather his cast nets and walk the narrow beach south, down to the city pier. He would cast out for two hours or more, hauling in mullet, shrimp, crabs, hard-head catfish, small sharks — whatever dared stray within his sight. Most he threw back. He wasn't there for the fish, but for the fishing. Once, Bill awoke early to join his father. With each cast, he heard his father whispering something to himself. Bill slowly eased closer and was barely able to make out what his father was saying.

"Put out into the deep and let your nets down for a catch." Over and again, William repeated the verse and crossed himself almost imperceptibly with one finger. Bill smiled, recognizing it immediately as being from Luke chapter six. He eased back to his own spot on the pier. He never let his father know that he had seen. Come the following Saturday, William asked his son if he intended to join him again. Bill declined. Far be it from him to interrupt the only real worship his father ever had.

***

Bill thought about his father's version of Sunday Mass as he stared into the shallows, and it still made him smile. Noting a school of minnows rushing into his pool of light, Bill felt his pulse quicken and hoped it the start of a Jubilee. No sooner than the fish had arrived, they were gone again. His heart sank. He wanted, no *needed* a Jubilee — on this night of all nights. Bill closed his eyes and began to pray.

Prayer had never been Bill's strong suit. Somewhere between scoffing at his mother's stilted Catholic verse, with all of its repetition and ceremony, and discomfort with the casual, nearly conversational prayers of his Calvinist wife, Bill found himself hung somewhere in the balance and unable to pray at all. However, suppliants are born of desperation, and this night Bill became one as the words flowed freely from his lips.

His prayer began honestly enough as he muttered repeatedly, "I don't know what to do. I don't know what to do." Recalling the Lord's Prayer, he used that as a template, beginning first with praise. For Bill, praise was the easy part. If one believed, as he did, that the God of the bible not only created everything, but was the very definition of the infinite — unbounded and unconstrained by the limitations of both time and space, possessing love, knowledge, justice, mercy and wisdom far beyond the scope of human comprehension — then praise came easily enough. What came next was the phrase Bill found most difficult: "Thy will be done." He was the first to admit that the height of hubris and hypocrisy was to, with one breath, exalt

God for his ultimate wisdom and knowledge, and with the next breath, refuse to accept any counsel but his own. Nevertheless, Bill did so religiously.

In the deepest, innermost chambers of his proverbial heart, Bill blamed God for his perceived failures in life. Why would God give him such diverse and unique talents, but deny him the opportunity to properly use them? One answer was that God simply didn't exist. For a time, Bill flirted with an atheistic point of view, but he felt the evidence of the divine was too great to embrace a belief in unbelief. The second answer was that God didn't care, or worse yet, actually wanted him to suffer. Between the guilt complex of his Catholic upbringing and his Calvinistic view of grace as being gifts for those deserving of nothing, he knew this could be the case. However, he couldn't will himself to like it or even accept it. No, he didn't deserve God's grace, but he could name at least 367 people he personally knew who deserved it less. And he did. He kept the list in his desk at the store.

Once he and Katherine were discussing the topic, and she reminded him of the verse that said they should be thankful for their suffering, because suffering produced perseverance, then character, then hope. Bill argued, "I have perseverance. When do I get to move on to hope?" Then, without a shred of irony, he followed that with, "I've had the worst headache for the last couple of minutes, and if it doesn't let up, I swear I'll die."

Sitting there on the steps, he prayed, "God, I don't know what your will is, but I guess I'm open to considering it. Just give me some kind of a sign." At that very moment, the winds shifted to blow steadily in his face. The moon peeked out from behind its thick, grey shroud. Bill opened his eyes and stared into the shallows. There he saw a curious sight: a field mouse swimming toward the shore. Reaching the sands, the mouse shook off as much brackish bay water as it could, skittered toward the bluff and stopped. Bill watch amazed as the mouse turned toward him, stood on its hind legs and stared, it seemed, directly at him. The mouse squeaked something and appeared to bow toward Bill, then darted into the shadows beneath the bluff and disappeared.

Sounds of churning water spurred Bill to refocus his light upon the shallows. A single crab crawled into the light. Then another. Then four more. Two flounder swam up, followed by a stingray. A saltwater catfish joined them. The number of fish doubled and doubled again before Bill could even stand. It was a Jubilee!

Bill's heart raced as he sprinted up the steep stairs to his gazebo atop the bluff. He reached into its rafters and took hold of a cobweb-covered rope dangling above his head. Hardened and brittle from exposure to the salt air, the rope's fibers cut into his palms. He ignored the granddaddy longlegs scampering down his arm and rang the Jubilee bell with an almost violent enthusiasm. "Jubilee! Jubilee!" He yelled the word over and over again until he thought he might lose his voice. His bicep cramped from his incessant ringing of the bell. Each year, on the occasion of the first Jubilee, he swore he would move the bell to a more manageable location. He never did.

Lights blinked on in the windows of one house; the deck lights of another followed. Flood lights, landscape lights, decorative paper lanterns, strings of party lights adorned with plastic globes shaped like chili peppers or beer bottles or sea turtles — every imaginable shape, size and color of light blazed forth until the entire Eastern Shore was aglow.

Within minutes of Bill's initial alarm, a spontaneous, miles-long carillon had come to life up and down the coast, comprised of chimes, bells, buckets, bottles and washtubs. Jubilee was a late-night party par excellence, an impromptu holiday — Christmas, New Year's and Mardi Gras all rolled together in a fishy bundle. Everyone got a present, and no one ever sent theirs back.

"Evenin' neighbor!" a voice cried out of the darkness. Bill gave his arms a break from ringing the bell and peered next door. He could just make out the form of Roland Turnipseed, his elderly neighbor.

"Got your nets ready, Mr. Turnipseed?" Bill called out.

"Yep. *Nnnnh...*" The old man puffed every word as if it were his last, grunting and pausing to catch his breath after each phrase. "Nets are fine. *Nnnnh...*" He wheezed a long, slow inhale. "Just hoping I can get down ... *nnnnh* ... these daggum stairs ... *nnnnh* ... afore this thing is over." He burst into deep, raspy laughter, a glass-gargling, bone-quaking cackle that seemed impossible for a man of his diminished lung capacity. The octogenarian hobbled out to a concrete picnic table where he retrieved a rusty old hand bell and joined the clanging chorus. "Jubi ... *nnnnh* ... lee!" It took him a good ten seconds to get the word out. Bill couldn't help but laugh at the old man's enthusiasm.

The Turnipseeds and Durmers built their homes on the bluff together when Bill was still a toddler. Bill could not recall living anywhere else as a child. The bluff had been infinite, immutable to his juvenile imagination, a source of comfort and inspiration, a refuge from the worries of life and a sanctuary for world-weary souls. Now, although he loved it still, the place was emblematic of his heartbreak and frustration. One warm November day, 17 years earlier, heartbreak had spoiled his sanctuary.

***

William awakened early that day to take Claymoor fishing as a gift for his 76th birthday. Claymoor had been unable to get out in his own boat for several years since undergoing a triple bypass. Claymoor, unlike his son, never missed a Sunday Mass, and given that neither man would leave the store without the other there, a simple fishing trip was a luxury. However, that morning Bill was home from college for his Thanksgiving break and took over the store for the day.

For days leading up to the trip, Claymoor had bragged about the multitude of redfish, drum and flounder he would catch, taunting his son interminably. He invoked his fabricated stories of fishing with Hemingway as proof of his mastery over the seas. The very elements were at his command. "You're gonna need a bigger boat," he would say. William suggested the unintentional *Jaws* reference might not be a good idea, considering what happened to the boat in that film. Claymoor would call him superstitious and return to his taunting.

The morning of the big trip, William stocked his boat, the *Nancy Elise*, with enough food, drinks and bait to last them well into the evening. He planned a complete tour of Mobile Bay: heading north along the Eastern Shore, fishing the marshes and rivers north of the causeway as they worked their way west toward Mobile, heading south to fish and have lunch anchored at Middle Bay Light, then continuing further south to fish the estuaries north of Dauphin Island. Finally, they would make their way east across the mouth of the bay to Mullet Point and have a leisurely cruise north along the Eastern Shore as the sun set.

A few hours into the trip, a cold front pushed in from the West sooner than forecast. A pop-up thunderstorm ahead of the main front whipped the bay into a frenzy, sending smaller boats scrambling for their landings and boathouses. Roland Turnipseed came into the store as the sky began to darken over Decent Chance, expecting to see William. When Bill informed him that his father and grandfather were still on the water, Turnipseed's face went pale. "That ain't good. Ain't good at all." He had just come off the bay himself and counted himself blessed to get back to his boathouse in one piece. After checking with Elise at home to confirm the men hadn't returned, Bill called a family friend with the Coast Guard.

Katherine, then Bill's fiancée, joined him at the store as they awaited news. Meanwhile, Nancy came home from her apartment in Mobile to stand watch with her mother and grandmother. Sky darkened. Wind raged. Every crack of thunder elicited a scream from Nancy, tears from Betsy and sent Elise into another round of praying the rosary. Nancy thought her mother would rub the beads clean through before the day ended.

As word got around town that the men were missing, dozens of friends and family gathered at both the Durmer home and store. The first storm passed without word. Plans to assemble an ad hoc flotilla to search the bay were quickly scrapped as the storm front bore down. After hours of rain, lightning, water spouts, tornadoes and straight-line winds, an ominous quiet fell upon Decent Chance.

When Bill spotted a Coast Guard vehicle driving up Fisherman's Way, he knew. An anxious confusion of fear and anticipation filled the store as one person after another saw the truck approaching. The closer the truck came, the more the crowd backed away from the door, leaving an aisle for young Bill. He paused before opening it. Katherine laid her hand atop his, and together they slowly swung the door open. The crowd watched in silence as the Captain removed his hat, hung his head and delivered the news to Bill and Katherine. Despite her efforts to remain strong, the young woman burst into tears, eliciting a miserable wail from the gathered friends and family. Through it all, Bill stood strong, stoic. He politely shook the Captain's hand, pulled Katherine closer and stepped inside. "I have to go home," he said to no one in particular. Fishing in his pocket, he retrieved the keys to the store, placed the proper key in the lock and left without looking back to determine what anyone else would do or who would lock up after him.

Bill was similarly stoic throughout the funeral planning, memorial services, wake and funeral. Katherine watched him carefully, concerned for his emotional well-being. Nancy, on the other hand, jealously monopolized her brother's time and attention, viewing Katherine as an interloper invading their private mourning. The two nearly came to blows the day after the funeral. During a quiet breakfast on the patio, Katherine confided in Nancy that she was concerned about Bill's dearth of tears. Nancy, then a college freshman, was a psychology major at the time. She tapped into her limited knowledge and began to excoriate Katherine, accusing her of trying to feminize Bill in order to compensate for her own overly masculine qualities. The discussion escalated to a shouting match in short order.

Hearing the din from inside, Bill stepped out onto the patio. After watching a few seconds of their exchange, he marched out across the back yard, directly between the two young women and to the tool shed. Nancy and Katherine, now silenced, watched as he disappeared inside the shed only to return a few seconds later wielding a chainsaw. He cranked it and scrambled down the stairs toward the beach, revving the engine as he went. The women ran after him, fearing what he might do. They reached the top of the stairs and looked down to see Bill take the chainsaw to the family's boathouse. He swung the saw wildly, randomly cutting down rafters, handrails, whatever was within his reach.

Reaching the bottom of the stairs, the women carefully approached Bill. They yelled over the sound of the revving engine, pleading for him to stop. Tears streamed down both of their faces as fear and concern whipped into a heady mixture. Bill sliced through a vertical support, and the bayside end of the roof collapsed downward. He darted back out of the way, slinging the saw into the water as he did. Before the women could reach him, he collapsed onto the beach and curled into the fetal position. He wept.

Still frightened, and mortified at her brother's behavior, Nancy climbed the stairs to seek out her mother. Conversely, Katherine lay in the sand beside her fiancé and held him for more than an hour. Elise ensured that neither Nancy nor anyone else disturbed them. Later that day, William's younger brothers, Albert and Daniel, arrived to finish the job Bill had begun with the boat house.

Within a week, Bill had dropped out of grad school and returned home to run the store. He and Katherine married the next spring and moved in with Elise. It was more than a year before Bill would even allow himself to look at the bay. Seventeen years hence, he had still never set foot on another boat.

∗∗∗

"Nice work, Master Durmer," Katherine's sleepy voice called from behind him, snapping him out of his dark remembrance. He turned and smiled at her, throwing his arms wide as if welcoming an ovation.

"I may not be able to run a business," he joked, "but damn it, I can see a fish and ring a bell!" She wrapped her arms around his neck and kissed him warmly. He moaned appreciatively. "Where are the kids?"

"The baby's sleeping. Cleary's helping Clay get dressed. They'll be along in a second." She took hold of his hand and led him toward the bluff. "I wanna see." They stood on the deck overhanging the bluff and peered down to the beach. Something was amiss. Rather than scooping up the fish and crustaceans, their neighbors were scratching their heads, poking at some of the fish with their net handles, holding fish up at a distance from their bodies to study them, or simply standing there, hands over mouths, with looks of utter dismay.

"Oh, no." Bill released His wife's hand. "I better get down there. Wait here for the kids." Midway down the stairs, he noted an acrid smell emanating from the beach. He had hoped against hope that his neighbors' behavior was the result of either lack of sleep or abundance of drink. But when he caught wind of that smell...

"They done rurnt it. *Nnnnh...*" Mr. Turnipseed grunted as he threw fish into a wheelbarrow. His arms were stained brown-black from the elbows down. Bill pulled a small LED flashlight from his pocket and trained it on the next fish Mr. Turnipseed lifted from the water. A brown, syrupy goo coated the fish, dripping in dollops onto the sand below. The fish itself seemed dispirited, weak. It was dying.

"It's oil," Bill commented, stating the obvious. The real world had invaded their storybook celebration. Two months prior, a deep sea oil platform had exploded and sunk in the Western Gulf of Mexico. For weeks, the town's collective anxiety had grown about how the resulting multi-million gallon spill would affect the bay, but thus far there had been no landfall. Now the oil was coming to their shores in a cruel and ironic fashion.

"Oh, God!" Katherine cried out from behind him as she and the kids reached the beach. Bill quickly met her.

"You guys don't need to breathe this stuff. You should get them back inside." She was too devastated by the sight to argue. "I'll be up..." he trailed off as his gaze stretched down the narrow beach. He sighed and finished his thought, "...sometime." Without saying another word to his family, he shuffled away to help Mr. Turnipseed scoop the oil-covered fish onto the beach.

Katherine watched her husband help the old man for a few seconds. In better times, he would have risen to the occasion, she thought. He would have rallied the citizens of the town with a plan to remove the fish and clean the beach, but not today. Scooping crab and flounder and tar balls and sand with an old, rusty oyster shovel, his shoulders drooped not so much from the labor, but from the weight of a long series of defeats. Before Katherine turned to ascend the long, winding stairs, she noticed several of their neighbors approaching Bill.

"What do we do, Bill? What's the plan? How do we fix this?" they variously called out. All Bill could do was keep shoveling and shake his head. Words would only bring tears, and Bill was not about to add public weeping to his days-long list of indignities. Katherine saw, and she knew. There was nothing more she could do. She gathered the children and retreated to the house.

"It'll never be the same again," Cleary asked as they climbed the stairs, "will it, Mama?"

"The bay?" Katherine asked. Cleary nodded. "Not for a long time. But it'll bounce back someday."

"What about Daddy? Will he ever be the same?" Cleary's prescient follow-up question left Katherine speechless for a long while. Cleary was impatient for an answer, but she had heard her parents argue often enough to know that her mother would rather remain silent than offer a hasty, ill-considered response. As they reached the top of the stairs, Katherine let Clay down onto the deck and looked back down to the beach where Bill steadily shoveled up the fishy, oily mess.

"I don't know." She lied. In her heart, she knew that there was no way Bill would ever be the same again. The only question that remained was: would he be changed for ill or for good?

With the weary, crestfallen kids back in their rooms, Katherine fixed herself a warm cup of tea and sat on the patio. And she waited. Slowly the shouts, cries and occasional screams of frustration faded with the night. Behind her, the sun's light began to creep over the treetops. With the warming air, the stench of rotting fish and the jet fuel smell of the weathered oil became overwhelming. Yet she stayed.

When at last Bill appeared atop the bluff — weary and stained with

mud and oil and blood and algae, barely able to walk — she rose and retrieved him a towel and a cold beer. He collapsed into an Adirondack chair
and turned back the bottle. She sat beside him and studied his expression-
less face. "How bad is it?" Bill took another swig of beer. His bloodshot eyes
filled with tears, and he struggled to speak.

"It's um..." No more words would come, but tears flowed freely down
his face. His resolve broken, he doubled over in the chair and sobbed open-
ly, his muddy, bloody, oil-stained body heaving with his cries. Katherine
watched him dispassionately. It had been seventeen years since she'd seen
him cry like this — since the day he destroyed the boat dock. Although
he was a sensitive man, he was prone to cry more out of sentimentality
than out of sorrow. He could shed a tear over Jessie's abandonment in *Toy
Story 2*, over Darth Vader's redemption at the end of *Jedi*, at the sight of an
American flag on the Fourth of July or at the first chorus of "Yea Alabama"
at the start of football season, but over something real? Not on your life.
This Bill was a bit of a curiosity. Katherine's inability to empathize with him
shocked even her.

Wiping his face with the towel, Bill finally found the strength to speak.
"It's all my fault." Her dispassion gave way to annoyance.

"Bill, don't be dramatic." If twelve years as Mrs. Bill Durmer had taught
her anything, it was that her husband's first reaction to adversity was defeatist hyperbole. Still, she knew she should tread carefully. "You didn't sink
that rig. I know this is a tough time for you, but you've got to give yourself
a break."

"You know the story," he protested. "Claymoor opened the store, and
that night they had The Great Jubilee. He used to sit in his rocking chair
and tell everyone who'd listen," he mimicked his late grandfather's accent
and cadence perfectly, "'*As long as Durmer's is open, we'll have bountiful
Jubilees. By God, this store is the city's good luck charm.*' I close the place and
look what happens." He wiped his eyes again, smearing oil across his face.

"That's just superstition. You can't actually believe that," Katherine implored.

"It doesn't matter if I do or not, Kat. Everyone else does. I'm done in
this town." Sipping his beer, he grimaced, "Which is fine. Because I've been
done with it for a long time." Rather than argue the point any further, Katherine tried to defuse him.

"You should shower and get some sleep," she gently urged. He looked at himself and grinned.

"Shower, really? I'm pretty tired. I thought I might skip that part."

"Not unless you want to buy me a new mattress and new linens," she joked, then took it too far, "and seeing as how you're unemployed…" Seeing the wounded look on his face, she stopped herself before she did any more damage. He stood and slammed his beer bottle down on a side table, sending beer flying.

"Thanks a lot, Katherine." He kicked off his boots and stormed through the door. Katherine watched and waited for him to climb the stairs inside before she followed.

"It's gonna be a long day," she sighed.

Chapter Ten:
There Goes the Baker

For the better part of the next day, Bill slept. Katherine, on the other hand, hadn't slept at all during the night. And the kids had awakened shortly after she had finally found the bed that morning. Cleary and Clay were cranky from a poor night's sleep — and full of questions about the oil, the fish and why they couldn't play outside. After fielding several dozen phone calls from the mayor's office, council members, business owners and family looking to Bill for answers on how to deal with the aftermath of the Black Jubilee, Katherine silenced all the phones. She was in no mood to deal with other people's desperation.

Sometime after three that afternoon, Bill finally roused to find Clementine and Clay napping in their rooms, Cleary asleep on the floor in front of the TV and Katherine sacked out on the sofa in the den. For a moment, he considered waking them. After all, he couldn't be expected to wallow in misery alone, could he? Wisdom prevailed, and he chose to pour himself a cold cup of coffee and head outside.

Opening the French doors onto the patio, he was nearly bowled over by the stench flowing in from the beach. He hurried outside and closed the door behind him to prevent as much of the air from getting inside as possible. With his t-shirt collar pulled over his nose as a makeshift breather mask, he staggered out to the deck overlooking the bay. He leaned out over the rail to survey the situation below.

Coast Guard cutters were anchored at several of his neighbors' docks. Dozens of people were scooping oily dead fish into piles on the narrow strip of sand. In fact, the sand itself was largely unseen now as the receding tide had left the ground littered with carcasses and tar balls between the man-made piles. As far as he could see, only one small fishing boat was making an attempt to haul the piles of fish away from the shore. At least ten boats, however, were ferrying media up and down the coast. There were even more cameras along the beach in both directions. It seemed many of his neighbors had decided to cash in their fifteen minutes of fame.

"Bill! Bill Durmer!" he heard a voice cry from somewhere below. He spotted the mayor, August Pomeroy IV, (Auggie as he was known to friends and family). Auggie was Bill's second cousin on his mother's side, but the two had never been particularly close. Bill assumed it had something to do with his and his father's lack of devotion to the church. Unbeknownst to him, it all stemmed from a family reunion when Bill was seven and Auggie five. Auggie had always been a rotund child and was the first to make fat jokes at his own expense. (He had dressed as Augustus Gloop every Halloween until well after college.) However, on that particular summer Saturday thirty-three years earlier, Bill had led a group of his other cousins in chants of "Auggie, Auggie, smells like a froggie," and the younger boy had never forgiven him.

Bill, for his part, always went out of his way to help his cousin, even going so far as to bend his own rule about no political yard signs. (He didn't fully break the rule as the sign was one inch across the property line in Mr. Turnipseed's yard, but it was close enough to be construed as an endorsement nonetheless.) Today, however, Bill was not inclined to help anyone. He acted as if he hadn't heard Auggie and retreated inside, confident his portly cousin wouldn't endeavor to climb the stairs to come after him.

Bill's bare feet made little sound as he tiptoed through the house, but the old wooden floors creaked as he entered a small, dark den. Katherine stirred slightly on the worn leather sofa. Bill froze in his tracks until he could determine by the rhythm of her breathing that she was sleeping soundly. He carefully sat in a rolling executive chair behind a large mahogany desk. The leather on the chair matched the sofa and love seat in the room, and the mahogany of the desk echoed the dark mahogany built-in bookshelves. This had been Bill's father's study, and it was the one room he and Katherine couldn't bring themselves to make over.

They alternately referred to it as the Dead Cow Room or the Rainforest Killer. Spring cleaning in the room was known as "slash and burn season." When they purged a leather side chair to make room for a big screen TV, they were "thinning the herd." For all their ironic jokes, the two saw this room as their mutual retreat from the world. After the kids went to bed at night, they would retire to the large leather sofa, snuggle up and watch TV while Bill played with Katherine's hair until well after midnight.

Bill jiggled a mouse to wake up the iMac on the big, old desk. He navigated to several news sites, both local and national. It seemed the Black Jubilee was the talk of the nation. Everywhere he looked, he saw images of heaps of oil-covered sea creatures and the alternately disgusted and saddened faces of Eastern Shore residents from Daphne to Bon Secour. Decent Chance was on the map for all the wrong reasons. "What have I done?" he whispered to himself.

Navigating away from the news sites, he checked his email. There were numerous messages from friends offering condolences on closing the store, a barrage of notes excitedly announcing the arrival of the Jubilee, then hundreds of emails from friends, family and random citizens expressing their outrage, heartbreak or pleading for his help in solving the crisis. He glanced over a few, but couldn't bring himself to dive into answering any. Occasionally in the mix he would come across interview requests from local and national media outlets including the *Press-Register*, WKRG, CNN, *USA Today* and Huffington Post. Then a curious one. It was from something called mouseblogger.com. His interest piqued, he opened it.

> *Mr. Durmer,*
>
> *I am currently investigating the influence of the Council of The Nine on day-to-day company policy. I was told you have had some dealings with this secret organization and lived to tell about it. I was wondering if you might agree to an interview.*
>
> *As I am sure you are well aware, this matter is of the utmost sensitivity and will require your complete discretion. I await your response with fear, anticipation and the bated breath of hope.*
>
> *Please heed this call of destiny, Bill Durmer.*

Regards,
Gaston

"What the?" Bill laughed out loud at the ridiculous nature of the cryptic email. He had no idea what a Council of the Nine was or what company they were supposedly influencing in regard to policy. And the more he wondered at these things and the man's earnest concern about them, the more he felt it difficult to restrain his laughter. Katherine stirred. He struggled to quiet himself and began crafting a reply.

Mr. Gaston,

(I am unclear; is that your given name or sur-name?)
I regret to inform you that I must decline your request for an interview. I am certain the reasons for this decision are clear to you. Be careful.

Bill Durmer

He smiled as he typed his response, imagining how his message would push the already paranoid mind of the mysterious Gaston to new heights of paranoia. The keys slapped down loudly.

"You suck at being quiet," Katherine groaned from the sofa. Bill clicked "send" then looked around the screen toward his wife.

"I'm sorry, Honey. Got carried away, I guess." Bill motioned for her. "You've got to see this crazy email I got."

"I don't have to do anything," she grunted. "Now, shush." She carried out her shushing until she dozed off again. In slow, deliberate moves, Bill rose from his chair and crept out of the room. Finding the rest of the house still silent, and dreading the thought of sitting alone with no company but his own, he climbed the stairs and went back to bed. He lay there for a few minutes staring at the ceiling. In his entire adult life, only twice had he slept late then taken an afternoon nap. Once was when he had walking pneumonia in both lungs, and the doctor had suggested that, if he didn't leave the store and get some rest, he might die — a suggestion purchased by Katherine with their tickets to that year's Iron Bowl. The second time was the day Katherine confessed to him that she had given away their Iron Bowl tickets. That time, Bill did it simply out of spite. But these were extraordinary circumstances. Middle-aged, unemployed pariahs can sleep as much they as they wish. It's one of the perks of being a scourge upon humanity. In fact, it's the only perk.

Hours later, Bill awakened to Katherine sitting beside him on the bed, caressing his shoulder. He cleared eyes and checked the window; it was dark out. He had literally slept the day away.

"Dinner's ready." Katherine spoke softly to ease him awake. "You should eat something." Bill nodded and stretched. She kissed him on the temple and took his hand. "Come on, sleepyhead." His arms and legs seemed to have doubled in weight while he slept. A slow rise to his feet resolved in a dizzy rocking back and forth as he attempted to find his balance. Katherine led him to the door. "You've got another message from Gaston, too."

"You read my email?" he replied in mock indignation. "I feel so violated."

"You said I had to," her playful tone indicated she was ready to leave the ugly exchange of that morning behind them. "Apparently, it was so important you had to wake me up to tell me about it."

"What do you think? Is the guy nuts, or what?" he asked. Katherine laughed, nodding in agreement.

"Just read the new message." As they reached the bottom of the stairs, she split off to the back of the house. Bill shuffled into the den and plopped behind the desk. Another sixty-some messages about the disaster unfolding in his backyard surrounded the reply from mouseblogger. Bill ignored the others, focusing only on Gaston.

> *Bill,*
>
> *I understand fully your position. It seems as though the powers of The Nine and their far-reaching tentacles into the upper levels of the corporatocracy are more than two windmill chasers like ourselves can conquer. Sadly, I must set aside my Quixotic quest for a time while I retreat to wither in the wilderness.*
>
> *If I may be so bold, allow me to offer some sage*

advice: this is no time for curious beauties or heroic beasts. Be like the baker.

Respectfully yours,
Gaston

Bill was amused and slightly disturbed by the message. Who was this person, and why had he or she contacted Bill in the first place? The temptation was strong to write this off simply as a case of mistaken identity, to believe that the verifiably paranoid Gaston had simply emailed the wrong man, but Bill's gut told him it was something more. He put the computer to sleep.

Upon entering the family room, Bill was mobbed by his children. Clay wrapped himself around Bill's right leg, while Cleary hugged him tightly around the waist.

"Daddy, you sept and sept and sept and sept," Clay showed no signs of ending his repetitive commentary on Bill's uncharacteristic hypersomnia, "and sept and sept and—" Bill interrupted.

"Okay, Clay. I got it. Daddy slept all day." Clay smiled at his father, gave Bill's leg a tourniquet-like squeeze, then returned to his dinner. Katherine had laid out a blanket in front of the TV and let the kids have their dinner on bed trays set on the floor.

"We're having a movie night!" Cleary announced with excitement.

"Nice," Bill replied. "What's the movie?"

"*Beauty and the Beast,*" She replied. "Mommy picked it." Katherine smirked as Bill caught her eye.

"Daddy's a big fan of Gaston," she quipped.

"You're very funny," Bill snapped sarcastically. Katherine laughed and kissed his cheek as she handed him his dinner. He chuckled. Cleary knew this was one of those inside joke moments between her parents, and they would likely keep her on the outside. Still, it was worth a try.

"What're you guys laughing about?"

"It's nothing, Sweetie." Katherine rubbed the girl's head. "Just a little joke between your father and me." Cleary sighed, expecting exactly that response. She'd heard those words hundreds of times, it seemed. She vowed someday to have inside jokes of her own, and when she did, she would make a point of flaunting them before her confused parents.

The family watched the movie in relative quiet. Clementine banged her rattle on the tray of her highchair in time with the music of "Gaston" and "Be Our Guest." Clay grew bored during the montage showing the growing love between Belle and the Beast and wandered upstairs to don his Darth Vader costume. Until the climactic battle sequence, he largely ignored the film while having light saber duels with inanimate objects. Cleary was fully engrossed in the film, mimicking the hand motions, dance moves and facial expressions of the characters.

As Belle and the Prince shared their dance at film's end, Bill queried his daughter, "Cleary, now that he's not a Beast anymore, what does Belle call him?" Cleary sighed.

"I know what you're going to say, Daddy," she groaned. "His name is not Will."

"Sure it is," he quipped. "Will da Beast."

"Not funny, Daddy." She turned her back to him and began navigating the film's special features.

"It's really not funny, you know," Katherine chimed in.

"You guys laughed," Bill protested.

"Sure the first ten times you said it." She wrapped her arms around his shoulders. "The last 490 times? Not so much."

"You just don't appreciate good humor." He kissed her gently.

"Sure I do." Her smile was mischievous. "I saw the humor in someone like me marrying someone like you."

"Ohhh ... Touché." Another soft kiss.

"You guys aren't going to be all kissy all night are you?" Cleary asked in disgust.

"Maybe," Katherine cooed. She sprang to her feet and picked up Clementine. "But you little heathens will never know, because it's time for bed."

"Awww, man," Cleary protested. Clay, not even paying attention to what was happening, parroted his sister. Katherine herded them toward the stairs, but not until each had gotten hugs and kisses from Bill. Katherine and the baby lagged behind for a moment.

"I'm spent. I don't see me staying up much longer." Her free hand tousled his hair. "I guess you'll be up a while."

"Yeah." He kissed her wrist. Katherine held the baby down for him to kiss, then made her way upstairs, leaving Bill alone. Having only been awake for a grand total of two hours since going to bed early that morning,

Bill prepared himself for a long night. He despised getting his internal clock out of sync. There were many nights he had closed the store only to stay up until three or four working on float designs, tinkering with robotics or building sets. In such cases, he would force himself to get up in time to open the store at ten and suffer the consequences of pulling the all-nighter. But as he got older, those nights took a more significant toll on his overall well-being, manifesting as baggy eyes, crow's feet, an ever-growing paunch and the occasional sinus infection that would take hold for a week or two. Bill's annual resolution to work more normal hours had become something of a running joke within the Durmer house, with Katherine going so far as to set up a betting pool between herself and the kids trying to peg the date on which he would first break the resolution. (Cleary had been the most recent winner, picking January 4.) Nancy chided Katherine for initiating her children into gambling culture. She then convinced Cleary to spend all of her winnings on raffle tickets she was selling for the church.

Bill brewed a fresh pot of coffee and parked himself, remote in hand, in front of the TV. He was careful to skirt the news channels to avoid seeing coverage of the Jubilee. After reading the channel guide no less than eight times and blindly surfing the channels twice, he switched the set's input and navigated the DVD menus to play *Beauty* again. He watched the opening prologue explaining the origin of the Beast and recalled seeing recreations of the stained glass windows from that sequence in the France pavilion at EPCOT.

Marveling at the beauty of layers of hand-painted images coming to life through the use of the digital multiplane camera (which replaced the half-century-old physical multiplane cameras the studio had used for decades), he tried to imagine what a revelation it must have been to audiences in the 1930s when they saw the opening shot of *Snow White*. Despite his utter admiration for the work of PIXAR, there was still something more innocent and charming about the old ways of analog.

Belle exited the charming ramshackle cottage inhabited by herself and her father and strolled into the little town, singing a song about the same. Where was her mother? Bill speculated that she was actually the old hag-turned-beautiful enchantress who had cast a spell on Will. (It was a fine name, and Bill was sticking to it.) Perhaps it was her way of creating a worthy suitor for her daughter's hand, a long con perpetrated by an unnaturally prescient and controlling mother — like Nancy all hopped up on pixie dust.

Bill had always enjoyed the moment when the animation ramped up its pace to match the music of Ashman and Menken. As the little town came to life with the bustling daily activities of its denizens, he began to wonder what exactly Belle was complaining about. The more he thought about it, the more she seemed like a spoiled brat who didn't appreciate the simple beauty of her home. Who wouldn't want to live in a quaint village in the French countryside? What was so wrong with this place that she felt the need to escape it? These were good, hard-working people. Sure maybe they were prone to gossip, were poorly read and deified traditional brute masculinity, but that sounds like pretty much every small town in America. He began to think it wasn't a quaint French village she was railing against at all, but America herself! And to think he'd been allowing this subversive tripe to infect the minds of his children for all this time!

After a chorus of "bon jours" from the villagers, Belle sang about the village baker, carrying his tray like always. Bill snapped out of his jingoistic fever dream and paused the movie. He stared at the fat, little baker with his bushy red beard and long red hair, inexplicably carrying a tray of bread *back* to the *boulangerie* to retrieve more baguettes from that slacker Marie. Bill backed up the film slightly and played the scene again. He sang along under his breath.

"The baker." He paused and rewound the film again. "The baker and his tray." Repeatedly, Bill played the scene, focusing on the baker, Belle singing the one line over and over again. After nearly an hour of looping the scene, he paused and zoomed in on a freeze frame of the baker. "Gaston. I get it now." Bill smiled broadly, clapped his hands together and blurted out, "Be like the baker!" He leapt up from the sofa and nearly sprinted to the den to retrieve his iPad. "Be like the baker!" he cried again, bellowing the phrase more as battle cry than mantra.

Returning to the family room, he resumed the film and began swiping and tapping away on the tablet. "Now what does it all mean, Gaston? What does it all mean?" Bill watched the film in its entirety four more times, all the while trying to piece together the cryptic clues he'd received from his mysterious digital pen pal. He felt certain they were the keys to unlocking the next phase of his life. By morning, he was convinced he knew what that next phase would be. He couldn't have been more wrong.

Chapter Eleven:
The Hyper-Caffeinated Delusion

When Katherine awoke the following morning, she found Bill at the stove, cooking omelets and bacon for the family. She noticed his hands jittering violently as he turned the omelets. She wrapped her arms around his shoulders and hugged him from behind. "Morning. Did you sleep?"

"Nope!" he said cheerfully, "Not a wink!" Hyperactive and excitable, Bill's demeanor struck Katherine as odd, but she wrote it off as the product of sleep deprivation. A crash was inevitable. Bill hastily slung the omelets onto plates, slinging bits of egg and cheese about the kitchen in the process. "Kids! Breakfast!" Katherine started at his yell. Cleary and Clay came bounding down the stairs. All flailing arms and matted eyes and cowlicks, they scrambled atop barstools at the bar dividing the kitchen from the family room. Neither said a word, only grunted, smacked and slurped as they systematically devoured their breakfasts.

Katherine took her plate to the dinette and pulled Clementine alongside her in the highchair. Bill followed her, setting his plate across from hers, but he didn't sit, instead pacing back and forth in the bay window in which the table was set, snatching bites of omelet with his fingers as he talked.

"I think I've got it, Kat. I think I figured it out." His finger tapped on the table as if he were a telegraph operator.

"Figured out ... what?" She was half afraid to hear the answer.

"My next move. Our future. Our destiny." Mischievous grin became triumphant smile. Triumphant smile became crazed laugh. Katherine was officially freaked out.

"How much coffee have you had?" Her tone was cautious, patronizing. He waved her off.

"Two, three. I don't know." Pacing again, he impatiently awaited his next move.

"Cups?" Katherine's concern grew with Bill's every paced step.

"Pots." He breathed deep and jumped right back into his diatribe. "It was the message, Gaston's message. Not the first one, but the second one. You know, the weird one."

"Yeah," her voice dripped with sarcasm, "*that* one was weird." He was undeterred.

"I started to suspect that the message had to be related to all the weird stuff that happened to us at Disney World. It had to be, right? Of course it did." Katherine began to wonder if she were even necessary for this conversation, if it could be called a conversation at all. Bill marshaled on, "And everyone's been telling me I need to 'recapture my vision' or something like that. 'But what vision?' I would ask myself. 'I don't know,' I would say." Katherine interrupted.

"You can leave out the internal dialogue."

"Right," he nodded, pointing his finger like a gun at her and clicking his tongue, which took Katherine aback because Bill had a rule that he would never adopt any mannerism that evoked used car salesmen. "So I started thinking about all of those things and thinking that maybe my vision had something to do with Disney. Then I watched the movie again, looking for clues. I mean, the guy has to call himself Gaston for a reason. And then ... there it was." He beamed.

"There what was?" Katherine was only barely keeping up at this point.

"The baker. Gaston said in his message, 'Be like the baker.' He meant the baker with his tray like always. You see?" Bill waited for her response.

"Ummm..." Katherine really wanted to meet him halfway, but short of discovering a portal to a parallel universe, that seemed impossible at the moment.

He led her, "What do we know about the baker in *Beauty and the Beast?*"

"Nothing."

"Exactly!" He clapped his hands and pointed at her with both hands then resumed pacing. "For all my life, people have said that I was special, that I would do great things. Then Dad and Grandpa died, and I had to take over the store. Next thing you know, all those hopes and expectations become pressure. And the pressure becomes bitterness. And I really started to resent everything — the store, the kids, this stupid little town."

Cleary butted in, "You resented us?"

"Yes, dear," was Katherine's droll response. "It's a parent thing. You'll understand someday." Cleary snickered and took another bite of her omelet.

"You guys couldn't live without us," she snapped.

"Don't talk with your mouth full." Katherine turned back to Bill and winked at him, "You may resume your insane rant now." Bill finally took a seat opposite his wife, bouncing his legs wildly under the table.

"I watched the movie over and over, like six times. I kept looking for something else, some other meaning, but I always came back to the baker. I have to be like the baker."

"Let me get this straight," Katherine rearranged the bits of omelet on her plate. "You drank several pots of coffee and watched *Beauty and the Beast* six times?"

Bill shrugged. "I wanted to stop it after four times, but my hands were shaking too violently to push the button. Anyway, that's not the point."

"What *is* the point, then Bill? Because I'm not hearing one." Her patience had worn thin.

"We don't know anything about the baker because he just ... blends in. He's part of the background." Bill reached for Katherine's hands and stared into her eyes. "Gaston, whoever he or she is, opened my eyes. Maybe I was never supposed to be special. Maybe I was never supposed to be great. Maybe I was just supposed to blend in."

Katherine couldn't help but laugh. "You've spent the last seventeen years running a small electronics store in an even smaller town. I don't think you can blend in any more than that. You already are the baker."

Bill scrambled back to his feet and began pacing again, flustered by her reaction. "Yeah, but I'm done here. This town, this place with all its pressure of family history and expectations, it just has too much baggage for me to blend in fully. You saw my inbox yesterday. Do you think everyone was calling the baker for advice or peppering him with hate mail when they discovered the Beast?"

"Nobody sent you hate mail," Katherine protested.

"You don't know that. You didn't read them. They may not be doing it now, but they'll blame me sooner or later. I know these people." He brushed aside the frustration and switched the crazed visionary switch back to *ON*. "But none of that matters, because we're not going to stay here."

"Oh, we're not?" Katherine crossed her arms in defiance. Bill softened his tone.

"When was the last time you were happy, Kat? When was the last time all of us were truly happy?" She shrugged. He answered for her with utmost certitude. "Disney World."

"That was a vacation, Bill," she explained condescendingly.

"But it doesn't have to be just a vacation," he struggled to make her understand. "It could be our life."

"So you want to work for Disney?" The idea wasn't abhorrent to her. "I mean, I don't really want to leave our home, but it's worth exploring."

"No." She wasn't getting it. "I don't want to just work for Disney. I want to live at Disney World."

"Oooh! Me, too!" Cleary piped up.

"Disney Erld!" Clay chimed in. Katherine endeavored to ignore the children and ferret out the meaning of Bill's hare-brained scheme.

"Bill, you're going to have to back up a little bit, because I'm having a hard time keeping up with your particular brand of crazy right now." Bill leaned forward, palms down on the table, unaware of how intimidating his posture might be at that moment.

"Walt Disney created the parks to be an immersive experience. He wanted people to experience, if only for a few hours, what it would be like to live within the world of his movies. With EPCOT, his original idea was to create an entire city where people would work and live — right there on the property. Then he died, and the company, well ... they lacked his vision, and EPCOT became just another theme park. But I think they both missed the mark. I think what people really want, what people need, is to immerse themselves in the world of Disney movies on a daily basis." Katherine sighed. He had lost her, and he knew it, yet he pressed on. "Look, the world has given up too much of its innocence. Even the idealists have become cynics. If we could all just embrace that kind of simplicity..." He trailed off, unsure of where to go from there.

Katherine eased off a bit. She uncrossed her arms and caressed his hand. "Listen," she looked back over her shoulder to see the kids hanging on their every word and lowered her voice to a whisper as she continued.

"Go. Go deal with this mid-life crisis or nervous breakdown or whatever it is. You deserve a little time to find yourself. But don't drag our children into your delusions. And when you've figured out what your real vision for our life is, I'd appreciate you consulting me before uprooting our family." She rose, kissed him on the forehead and stared into his eyes. "And no more coffee for you." Gathering her dishes and his untouched cup of coffee, she retreated to the kitchen and herded the older kids upstairs to get dressed, leaving Bill alone with the baby.

"At least she still trusts me with you," Bill said to Clementine, who giggled at her Daddy. "That's a good sign." He picked her up and tickled her abdomen with his nose. "You like my idea, don't you? Don't you?" Feeling a little woozy, Bill cradled the infant and sat in the chair to hold her. He rocked her in his arms and stared out the bay window toward the water. "Be like the baker, Bill," he said to himself. "Just blend in."

✳✳✳

That evening, Bill began to pack for his journey. Despite her taciturn expression of support, Katherine had not actually spoken to Bill since that morning. The two carefully avoided one another all day — while going out of their way to make it look as if they weren't. It was a time-honored technique Bill had learned by example from his parents. That day, he became an expert in it.

In packing his suitcase, Bill's awareness of the symbolic significance of each item he chose was heightened. Pack too much, and it may appear as if he were running away for good. Pack too little, and it might belie a lack of confidence in his idea. Resolving to treat the journey as a business trip, Bill packed accordingly, focusing on the pragmatic over the sentimental.

"Hey, Daddy." Cleary had entered so quietly that Bill jumped at the sound of her voice.

"You scared the snot out of me!" He wound and snapped a t-shirt at her, deliberately missing her by at least a yard. "Don't do that to an old man." Cleary hugged him around his waist. Bill brushed her hair back from her face.

"You're not old," she corrected him. "You're just not young."

"Wow." Bill folded the t-shirt badly and tossed it in the suitcase. "Thanks for the pep talk." Cleary pulled the shirt out and folded it more precisely and replaced it. Bill continued to pack as she rearranged the suitcase.

"I like your idea," she remarked. Bill noted how business-like she was in her tone, neither effusive nor emotional, simply matter-of-fact. Unfortunately for her, she had not yet become aware of her own tells. Whenever she desperately wanted something, this was her modus operandi: be helpful, don't be overly emotional, woo the mark with compliments, dull those compliments with reproach to throw off suspicion, present a rational argument (her version of rational was far more mature than that of a typical nine-year-old) and don't make eye contact until closing the deal. He didn't know what she was selling this time, but he decided to play along to find out.

"Thanks." Should he say more or just leave it at that? If he sounded too terse, she might anticipate a rejection and go to Plan B, which was typically to use both ends (Katherine and him) against the middle. But if he were over-the-top in his gratitude, she might see right through him and skip straight to the sales pitch. He wasn't as skilled at this as she. He finally settled on, "I kind of like it myself." Well played. Next should come the reproach.

"Although you haven't really thought it through," she said, casually re-folding his clothes and avoiding eye contact as expected.

"Oh no?" Bill couldn't wait to hear where this was going. Although even he had to admit that inspiration borne of self-loathing, sleep deprivation and hyper-caffeination was suspect at best. "How do you mean?"

"Well..." Filling her dramatic pause with a patronizing sigh only heightened Bill's anticipation. If she weren't his offspring, he'd be mortified by how overmatched he was. "Disney World doesn't really have a program in place for you to live and work on site as a background character. So in order to fulfill your dream, you'd have to both educate them and sell them on the concept."

"Right." Bill began to second-guess his decision to even tell his family the idea. Why couldn't he have simply gone out for bread and never returned? Sure it was a cliché, but it had worked for middle-aged men for centuries.

"And if you actually succeed," Cleary continued, "they'll probably expect you to head up the program yourself. So much for blending in." That one stung. The reproach phase had gone on longer than Bill expected and was more pointed than usual. Could it be she didn't actually want anything, but was there only to reprove him? If this was a sales job, what was she sell-ing? "But I don't think those are issues we couldn't work out on the drive down." There it was. Bill couldn't believe he hadn't seen this coming. Cleary had fallen in love with Walt Disney World on the trip and embraced all of the history and trivia of the place more than anyone in the family, save Bill himself. Plus, the two had a level of simpatico that exceeded the typical father-daughter bond. She shared many of Bill's interests: stagecraft, art, design, cinema, technology, futurism. He hated to shoot her down so soon into her pitch, but he couldn't allow her to get over-inflated expectations.

"Baby, I'm sorry." He sat on the bed opposite her to look her in the eyes. She focused on her task. "I promised your mom that I wouldn't involve you guys in this. I'm afraid I have to go it alone." Cleary stopped folding and stared at her father. She was not to be denied.

"Daddy," she said in a condescending tone, "you don't think I didn't know you would say that, do you?" Bill didn't know how to answer, because he wasn't entirely sure what she had said. Lack of sleep was catching up with him. "I know Mama doesn't want me to go with you, but you're my parent, too. You have as much to say about what I do as she does."

"Cleary, I promised her." Bill implored her to understand. Even when their relationship was at its worst, Bill and Katherine understood their roles in the family, and his first loyalty was not to the children but to her. But Cleary had a secret weapon.

"Probably doesn't matter anyway." Little fingers unbuttoned and re-buttoned a shirt, folded it with perfection. "She said you're not going."

"What?" Disappointment and betrayal swirled through Bill's mind. "When did she say that?"

"Just a few minutes ago at dinner." Cleary played it cool. "Clay asked when we were going to Disney World. Mama said we weren't, that you were just talking crazy, and you'd change your mind once you calmed down and got some sleep."

Bill fumed. Being perceived as delusional, paranoid and potentially in-sane was one thing, but he was not about to be called a quitter.

"Thank you for your help, Sweetie," Bill said, taking a shirt from her. "You should probably head back downstairs." Cleary leaned across the suit-case to give her father a hug.

"You're welcome, Daddy." Bill noted her sense of disappointment as she slouched out of the room. She had no indication that she had actually won. He isolated himself in the bedroom, packing his bags until Katherine came to bed. Apart from telling one another "Goodnight" and "I love you," the two didn't speak.

When Katherine awoke the next morning, Bill wasn't in the bed. She noted that his bags were no longer in the room. She ran downstairs to find Clay watching TV alone. "Where's Daddy?"

"Him went bye-bye," the boy answered without looking away from the TV. Then he turned and corrected himself. "No, him and Ceawy went bye-bye."

"What!?" Katherine shrieked. She rushed outside to see that Bill's Expedition was indeed gone. She scrambled back inside and up the stairs to Cleary's room. Dresser drawers hung open and empty clothes hangers were strewn about the bed. "Bill Durmer!" she yelled through clenched teeth. Spotting a folded note on the bed, Katherine snapped it up and read it.

> *Kat,*
>
> *I know you'll be upset with me, but Cleary will be fine. I need you to trust me.*
>
> *I love you,*
>
> *B*

Katherine slumped onto the bed and began to cry. She couldn't think. What should she do? Calling the police seemed like an overreaction, and she knew the disgrace that would follow might just push Bill over the edge ... assuming he hadn't already tumbled over it. For the moment, she resolved to take Bill at his word and trust him. That would not, however, save him from a full-on dog-cussing as soon as she could make the call. But now she had to be Mommy. Clementine was calling from the nursery. She wiped her eyes with her pajama sleeves and left the room, gently closing the door behind her.

Chapter Twelve:
A Case of Mistaken Affinity

"I'm sorry. You want to do what?" Marc Oerlander didn't sign up for this. The chubby fifty-two year old had been at his current job for exactly one month, and already he'd dealt with three accusations of harassment, two claims of discrimination, an executive chef who falsified his résumé to hide a six-year prison stint and a server who threatened to sue because he was commanded to bring a bottle for a couple's "baby," which was actually a towel wrapped in a blanket. But this one might prove to be the strangest yet.

When he took the job, he hoped that, as the senior human relations executive for the largest single-site employer in the world, he could delegate the task of dealing with all the weirdoes to his underlings. Somehow, this one had gotten past at least five levels of bureaucracy designed to insulate him from actually doing any real work.

Mark had never imagined himself working his way up the corporate ladder. He hailed from the small desert town of Cave Creek, Arizona, a haven for cowboys and artists. His father was the former, his mother the latter. Inheriting his mother's passion, he had dreamed of a career in art. After high school, he moved to California and enrolled in CalArts, the school Walt Disney himself had helped build. Though he had inherited his mother's passion for art, he had not, unfortunately, inherited her talent.

Thinking animators simply frustrated fine artists, he transferred from the school of arts to the character animation department near the end of his first year. When a classmate got a summer job as a skipper on Disneyland's Jungle Cruise, Mark joined him. Serious and driven, Mark quickly advanced to a supervisory position within Adventureland. The power went to his head, and he transferred from CalArts to UCLA to enroll in business school, dismissing animation as "kids' stuff." (The friend, a round-faced devotee of Chuck Jones and early Disney work named John Lasseter, chose to stick with the kids' stuff.)

When a colleague, an affable monorail driver named Dick Cook, made the jump from the park to a management position at Disney Studios, the competition was on; Mark wanted to beat them all to become the youngest CEO in Disney history, save Walt himself. There was only one obstacle: Mark really didn't like people.

Thirty years hence, after bouncing around the parks division, from Anaheim to Orlando to Paris to Hong Kong to Tokyo, Mark now found himself back in Central Florida and holding the most unlikely position for a misanthrope. As a matter of professional survival, Mark had learned to withhold his opinions of people many years earlier. Disinterest he masked with a well-rehearsed repertoire of silence, eye contact and thoughtful nods. He never asked questions about anyone and never volunteered information about himself. Ironically, every effort he made to insulate himself from others was mistaken for genuine interest. When the top HR position opened at Lake Buena Vista, company leaders could think of no better man for the job than Mark Oerlander. He was in Hell.

"I'm not entirely clear on what you want, Mr. Turner." No matter what the man said next, Mark was prepared to slip into stare-and-nod mode. And as soon as he got rid of this nut job, he was going to fire everyone who passed him higher up the food chain.

"It's Durmer, actually," Bill replied politely, "with a D." Mark's mind was reeling. How could he make such a rookie mistake? Now he'd have to talk again.

"Durmer, yes," he conceded. "Apologies." That's all Bill was getting. Mark stared at Bill, angrily he thought, but the man's pudgy face and down turned eyes made him appear profoundly sorry for his mistake. Bill, of course, believed this to be the case and relaxed, feeling as if he could share his every burden with the man.

"It's okay. I get that all the time." Bill relaxed into the chair and crossed his legs. Mark nodded.

"Mmm-hmm." He hadn't heard what Bill said and was instead thinking about chicken marinades.

"Let me explain this another way," Bill resumed his pitch. "You know how Walt Disney created the parks so people could be fully immersed in the worlds of his films?" Mark nodded at just the right moment, maintaining constant eye contact so as not to betray his complete inattention. "And how EPCOT was supposed to be a company-owned community?" More thoughtful nods, this time with a hint of a grunt. "Imagine combining the two so that people could extend the experience of visiting the parks, so they could feel some ownership over the experience. Do you see?" Bill waited patiently for Mark's response. The older man nodded off for a moment, but when he closed his eyes, Bill saw it as thoughtful consideration of his question. Snapping awake, Mark improvised a response.

"DVC. Disney Vacation Club. That'll let you stay longer in the parks." He was even boring himself. Mark had learned long ago that parroting the company line on any given topic would avoid deeper conversation. "And you are purchasing a piece of the magic." Bill respectfully disagreed.

"I'm not talking about a time-share. I mean actually living here." More nods.

"You'll want to check out Celebration, then," Mark offered. "I know someone who—" Bill interrupted.

"Celebration, right." Bill knew of the development, a Disney-owned New Urbanism community across I-4 from the main Walt Disney World property. Kenny had driven him around the development on their trip six months earlier. As with most New Urbanism, the planned community was criticized for its backward-looking architectural style — in this case, neo-traditional versions of styles common in the America of the 1930s, accented by more whimsical designs in the town center — and for its high cost of entry. "I'm talking about actually living *in* the park, working and living in the Magic Kingdom." Going back to his favorite illustration, he added, "like the baker." Mark only caught the last couple of words.

"Baker?" Mark typed something on his computer, pretending to be helpful. In fact, he was searching for articles about sinking of the *Lucitania*. He couldn't recall whether it was a ship or a dirigible. It was a ship. "So you have a culinary background?"

This was proving harder than even Cleary had imagined. Still, Bill was not to be deterred. "No, the baker with the tray." Nothing. "Like always? You know, *Beauty and the Beast*." Bill had opened with this odd request. Mark was irritated that he had come back around to it. His irritation, of course, read as sympathy.

"I'm afraid the baker is not a character we typically cast." Mark thought about pontoon boats. Maybe he should buy one. Then again, they were designed for large groups of people. But he liked the idea of a boat built on top of pontoons. *Pontoons. Pontoons. Pon-toons.* He batted the word around in his mind like a cat with a ball of yarn.

"The baker is just an example of what I'm talking about. It could be the baker or the Pizza Planet delivery guy or a Tortuga bartender." Bill leaned forward in his chair. "It's all about living a simple life as a minor Disney character, a life..." he paused for effect, "in the background."

Mark, yanked out of his pontoon boat fever dream, was growing weary of Bill's earnestness. It was time for the coup de grace: false hope. He quickly stood to intimate to Bill that it was time to leave. It came off as enthusiasm for Bill's idea.

"Give your information to my assistant, Mr. Durmer." He offered his hand — anything to get this guy to leave. "We'll have an answer for you by the end of the week." Bill smiled broadly and shook Mark's hand with vigor.

"Thank you, Mr. Overlander." Bill spotted the man's nameplate on the desk as he said it and realized his mistake. Before he could even apologize for his error, Mark had ushered him to the door.

"The pleasure's all mine," Mark said more out of habit than with a deliberate will to mislead. He attempted to push Bill out the door, but missed his upper back and inadvertently squeezed his shoulder instead. Bill was certain they would be best of friends. "We'll be in touch." He closed the door behind Bill before the applicant could get another word in.

Cleary was engrossed in conversation with Oerlander's assistant, Patricia, a voluptuous multi-ethic woman of about thirty, when Bill stepped into the outer office. They both froze and stared at Bill anxiously.

"Well?" Cleary asked. Bill winked and gave her a thumbs-up. He was becoming more of a used car salesman every day. Cleary smiled at Patricia. "I told you."

"Isn't Mr. Oerlander the kindest man?" Patricia swooned.

"Yes," Bill replied in unfettered admiration, "yes, he is."

✳✳✳

For the remainder of the week, Bill busied himself reading up on Walt

Disney, the history of the company, the parks, whatever he could get his hands on. Cleary spent her time in the pool. It never ceased to amaze Bill at how easily kids that age could make "friends," or how they could apply that word to someone whose name they hadn't even bothered to learn. But what was a friend, really? Based on the betrayals, broken promises and faded friendships he'd seen, perhaps adults had no better grasp of the word than their children.

As he read more, he learned that betrayals had shaped much of Walt Disney's career, from distributors who stole his lead animators in order to establish rival studios to union organizers who bullied the company through strikes, protests and threats. Then again, Walt was not always a candidate for employer of the year. He was often irascible and demanding of his employees, holding them to the same sky-high standards he set for himself — especially in his younger years, before the Disneyland TV series made him everyone's Uncle Walt. One Disney biographer believed the betrayals only exacerbated Walt's natural desire to control, even create, his own reality. He theorized that Disney's success in all arenas, from animation to live action to television to the pioneering of theme parks to the planned Experimental Prototype Community Of Tomorrow, was a direct result of his desire to create a world of wish-fulfillment realized. Bill thought it wasn't even that complicated. He figured Walt's quest for wish-fulfillment in the here-and-now, much like his own, was simply a longing for peaceful perfection in a noisy, imperfect world.

Upon finishing the biographies, he then quickly read *Team Rodent: How Disney Devours the World*, an angry, expletive-laden screed by satirist Carl Hiaasen. While Bill could relate to some critiques of the company's methods — not least of which was their ability to coerce the Florida legislature to incorporate Walt Disney World property as Reedy Creek Improvement District, a self-governing entity that put the company outside the reach of most zoning laws — he thought it ludicrous to blame Disney for the seedy tourist economy that had grown up in Orlando around the periphery of Walt Disney World. He felt doing so was like blaming the Gulf of Mexico for the debauchery of a Panama City spring break or blaming the football for the abomination that was the Super Bowl Shuffle. The more books he read, the more Bill came to believe there were two types of people in the world: those who liked Disney and those who hated it. Soon he would learn that was far too simple a classification.

Each day for Bill and Cleary was largely the same. He and Katherine had agreed he wouldn't spend money on tickets to the parks, so he made it his mission to find cheap or free things for them to do. They took in a rocket launch at the cape, explored the shops at Downtown Disney and Boardwalk, picnicked in a state park and swam in crystal clear spring waters. In the evenings, they would find vantage points outside the parks to watch fireworks. One night, they paid to park at EPCOT and rode the monorail over to explore the Contemporary and Polynesian resorts, then watched the fireworks show across Seven Seas Lagoon from the ferry dock. First thing every morning and last thing each evening, Bill would check in with the concierge to see if he had any messages. He was obsessive about checking his voicemail and email. A week passed and nothing. Every passing hour made him feel more foolish. Then came The Message.

Upon returning from an afternoon tubing on the Rainbow River in Dunellon, Cleary watched a video about the top "must-do's" at Walt Disney World for at least the fortieth time. She mimicked the perky host word-for-word. She turned off the TV and listened to the sound of the shower. Bored, she went to the door of the bathroom and called out to her father. "They used to have a channel that only showed old cartoons. I wonder why they don't have that anymore."

"I'm in the shower," came the chiding response. Cleary shuffled away, knowing she had struck a nerve. Her parents had three basic rules about privacy in the house: don't bother them in the shower, don't bother them while they were using the bathroom and don't knock on their locked bedroom door unless there were blood or broken bones involved ... preferably both. She flopped onto her back on the bed. A faint swishing sound grabbed her attention. Rolling toward it, she spied a note near the door. The small, white envelope was addressed simply "Bill Durmer." She carefully lifted it from the floor. Rushing to the window, she looked out for some glimpse of whoever may have left the note. There was no one in sight.

Bill emerged from the bathroom in a t-shirt and boxers, drying his hair with a towel. "Dad," she showed him the note, "I think this is for you." Bill turned it over in his hands, exploring the texture of the paper, searching for any indication of its origins.

"Who brought this?" he asked. Cleary shrugged.

"I just found it on the floor." She pointed to the spot where the note had been.

"What should I do?" Bill asked. Cleary wasn't sure if he was being rhetorical. She wasn't even entirely sure what rhetorical meant.

"I don't know," came her incredulous reply. "You're the adult."

"Let's see," Bill recounted the evidence against him, "I flaked out, drank too much coffee and imagined that the answers to my life's problems were hidden in a movie about a cursed prince with no name. Then I ran away to Disney World, taking my nine-year-old daughter with me and applied for a job that doesn't even exist." He turned to Cleary. "Does that sound like an adult to you?" Cleary was tempted to answer that it sounded exactly like an adult, but thought better of it. Instead, she snatched the note away from her dad.

"Good point!" She ran across the beds to the far corner of the room and ripped the envelope open before he could stop her. With the tips of her fingers, she slowly slid the note out. It was a single-fold card, red on the outside, white inside. The letter D was embossed on the front in gold, using the signature Disney font. After glancing quickly inside the note, Cleary folded it over and tossed it to her father. Bill opened it and found two words inside: "Accept it."

"Accept what?" Before Bill or Cleary could even begin to ponder the question, Bill's phone rang. A quick check of the screen found an Orlando area code. What to do? Bill had been awaiting a call all week, but the mysterious note had heightened his caution. Unconsciously, he gave the note back to Cleary. Taking a deep breath, he answered. "Hello?" Cleary listened to her father's half of the conversation with great anxiety. She only heard generic responses: "I understand," "I see" and "Yes, it certainly would."

Putting the caller on hold, he turned to Cleary. "They're still considering my proposal, but they've offered me a job in the meantime," he paused, dubious of the words he was about to say, "as a bus driver." He laughed at the ridiculous notion. "I have no idea how to drive a bus!"

Cleary, too, found the very idea funny. "No, you don't."

"What should I do?" Bill searched Cleary's face for the slightest hint of an answer. A mischievous grin crept across her face. She handed the note back to him. Bill read the two words again, mouthing the words to himself, "Accept it." He nodded and put the phone back to his ear. "Okay. When do I start?"

✳✳✳

No sooner than he had hung up, the phone rang again. Without looking at the incoming number, he answered, opting for the speaker phone so Cleary could listen in. He motioned for her to be quiet. "Hello?" Bill answered in an almost sing-songy tone.

"Bill Durmer," began the man on the other end in a robotic baritone. As soon as the deep, electronically-modulated voice emitted from the speaker, Cleary could see the look of distress on her father's face. "I'm not sure what you know or what you think you know, but I'm telling you to forget it. You are being used by some..." The voice paused long enough that Bill wondered if he had hung up, "By some very deluded people."

"Who is this?" Bill demanded. "How did you get this number?"

"I am a representative of the powers. You are in too deep, Bill Durmer, and my advice to you is to simply go home. Walk away now, and no one will get hurt." Cleary, at first amused, began to grow concerned. "Will they, Cleary?" the voice asked. That was too far. Bill switched the phone off speaker mode and stepped outside the room. Cleary could hear only muffled yells through the closed door, but peeking through the window, she saw Bill gesturing wildly and pointing his finger at no one in particular. He violently pressed the button to hang up and came back into the room.

"Daddy?" Tears filled her eyes. "Who was that man?"

"I don't know, but I'm going to find out."

Chapter Thirteen:
It Takes an Army to Fight a Closed Head Injury

Rattling glass and the interminable rumble of thunder served as harsh reminders that nature was undaunted by the cares of men. Neither Bill nor Cleary could determine how many officers surrounded them, but they suspected by the sounds of scuffling feet and barked orders in the distance that the number was growing.

"If they want us out of here," Cleary wondered aloud, "why don't they just come and get us?" Bill sighed. Cleary knew by the sound of it his answer was one he would rather she didn't hear.

"Because they think I'm armed." He was reticent to say more.

"Like with guns?" Despite all the weirdness of the previous month, she retained her unique balance of innocence and wisdom.

"Yeah." Bill withheld his suspicion that the most likely reason police hadn't yet employed tear gas and battering rams was they believed he was holding a hostage: Cleary. That someone might think him capable of deliberately placing his own child in harm's way sickened him, perhaps not as much if he were mistaken for an Auburn fan, but sickened him nonetheless. "You hungry?" he asked, trying in vain to mask his anxiety.

"Not sure it's a good time for a snack, Daddy."

"Just as well..." Bill spoke with the same distracted detachment Cleary had heard hundreds of times when he was working on a project in the back room of the store. "I don't think we could find the food anyway." Really, food was the farthest thing from Bill's mind. He was merely attempting to comfort her. With darkness so overwhelming, he hadn't a prayer of offering her solace in a look. Words were all he had. But the night had been talked out.

What was the point of discussing any further the legitimacy of the Council of the Nine? Or in speculating how things might have turned out if the bears hadn't said what they did? Or wondering what would have happened if the Powers had simply abided by the rules? To Cleary's credit, she had never once questioned his decision to interpret Gaston's email as a sign. They had both seen enough to know there was more to this situation than the hare-brained schemes of one man's mid-life crisis.

A flash-crack of nearby lightning coincided with the ringing of the room phone. "That was weird." Bill kept his eyes trained on the darkness outside rather than trying to locate the phone in the darkness inside.

"Aren't you going to answer that?" Cleary asked.

"Nope." The shuffling sound of the drapes told Cleary that her father was checking every angle for an oncoming assault. The phone continued to ring.

"That's going to be their commander," Cleary stated with the certainty of one with decades of law enforcement experience behind her, "or maybe a negotiator. Probably want to know your demands."

"Where in the world did you learn that? TV?"

"Dunno." Her voice even sounded like a nonchalant shrug. "TV, I guess." Hearing this, Bill resolved to keep better tabs on her viewing habits. More rings. "You really should answer it," she said. "They won't stop." Cleary knew she teetered on the edge of inappropriate behavior by telling her father what to do.

If she'd heard it from her parents once, she'd heard it a thousand times: "You must treat others with respect, especially your parents. I will not have you become one of *those* people." Cleary wasn't certain who "those people" were, but based on the evidence, she imagined them as a race of half-human creatures with unkempt hair, dirty faces, saggy pants and no shoes, who sassed their elders, snatched things away from small children and survived only on chicken nuggets and French fries.

Katherine would then not-so-subtly remind them of the first three verses of Ephesians 6, which promises that if children respect their parents, life will go well for them. To which she would add, "because we'll let you live."

Bill would then chime in with, "And if you don't respect your parents, the Yankees have already won." What usually followed was a series of eye rolls from his family. He had never bothered to notice that the next verse of Ephesians 6 warned fathers against exasperating their children.

"I'm not leaving this window," Bill answered. "If you can get to the phone, feel free." Bill felt Cleary brush past him as she scrambled up and onto the nearest bed. He heard the clatter of the plastic receiver against the phone as Cleary fumbled with it.

He began to question himself. Why was he letting a child handle the call for him? It's not like maintaining his watch would actually protect them. He tried to assuage his guilt by reminding himself of his rule against talking to telemarketers. Hostage negotiators were, after all, just a type of telemarketer, right? Using the phone to sell surrender to the desperate and the sociopathic. It was a stretch, but stretching was good. Except yoga. He had a rule against yoga. (It was the pants.)

"Hello?" Cleary answered with timidity. Bill inclined his ear, hoping to hear the voice on the receiver. It didn't take much effort.

"Miss Durmer, my name is Battalion Chief Mortimer of the Reedy Creek Critical Action Response," the man's voice bellowed forth from the handset. Bill marveled at the bass response of the receiver. "Can I speak to your daddy, sweetheart?"

"Daddy, it's for you," Cleary said as innocently as if it were a church elder calling to ask her father to fill in as an usher.

"I know. I heard," Bill grunted. "I'm surprised the guy didn't get feedback at that volume," he said to himself. "Try to reach the phone over here." Cleary scrambled to stretch the receiver closer toward her father's voice but to no avail. Bill leaned back as far as he could while still watching the window. He contorted his body and craned his neck back, calling toward the phone, "Hello? Hello?" There was no response. "What happened?" he asked his daughter.

"I don't know." Cleary was quiet for a moment, save some shuffling sounds. Finally, she piped up with, "Uh oh."

"What!?" he barked. Bill wasn't normally a barker, but now, cornered in a dark hotel room and surrounded by Mickey-eared commandos, barking seemed like the right reaction.

The phone began to ring again. It rang several times with no attempt by Cleary to answer. "What did you do, Cleary Elise?" Bill demanded in his best fatherly tone. The girl immediately went on the defensive.

"It wasn't my fault! You told me to stretch it!" The girl had put up with a lot from her father and his increasingly bizarre life over the last few weeks, but she was not taking the fall for this one. "The cord thingy snapped."

"Well, what are you going to do?" he demanded of her.

"I don't know. It just snapped off!"

"Well answer it!" The ringing phone was ratcheting Bill's anxiety higher and higher.

"How!?" Why hadn't she just gone to church camp with Dara? This was not what she had in mind when her father said they were going to Disney World.

Bill took a deep breath and calmly instructed her, "Use the speakerphone. It's one of the buttons." After numerous failed attempts, Cleary located the correct button.

"Hello!" Her voice dripped with snarky frustration.

"Cleary?" Mortimer's boisterous tone caused the entire phone to rattle. "You alright, sweetheart? What happened?"

"I'm fine," she sighed. "We had a phone issue."

"Tell me something," Mortimer dropped his voice to a whisper, which was slightly louder than the full-throated yells of four normal men. "Is your father hurting you?"

Cleary was offended at the suggestion. "No!"

"I can hear you, you know," Bill yelled back toward the phone.

"Mr. Durmer," Mortimer shifted into his "official" tone, which meant loud and threatening. "I'm Battalion Chief Mortimer of—" Bill interrupted him.

"I know. I heard you before." Bill was weary of this whole ordeal. He was not as respectful as would normally be the case. "What can I do for you, Chief?"

"You could start by taking me off speakerphone." Bill tried to explain why that wouldn't be possible. Mortimer wasn't buying it. He complained that he could hardly hear over the poor connection. This prompted Bill to make the critical mistake of referring to the hotel's phone system as being "Mickey Mouse." They could practically hear the chief's blood pressure rising.

"Mr. Durmer," Mortimer started into him with a vitriol that convinced Bill he'd never want to be on the receiving end of the chief's half of the old good cop/bad cop routine. "You may insult me. You may even insult my mother. But two things I will not tolerate: blaspheming the good Lord and speaking ill of the Mouse! I'll remind you that there is a fine assortment of firearms of every imaginable caliber surrounding you. And none of the itchy trigger fingers holding them would respond well to your little sense of humor. Leave. The Mouse. Alone."

Bill thought for a moment about challenging Mortimer on this point by insulting both the man and his mother. But the desire to maintain the appropriate number of holes in his body prevailed, and he remained silent. Cleary stepped in to diffuse the situation.

"Why don't you call us back on Daddy's cell phone?" she asked. Both men were reticent to admit how foolish they felt for not thinking of it themselves, let alone that they had been out-thought by a little girl.

"Okay," Mortimer simply replied, "give us a minute." And with that, he hung up. Bill and Cleary sat silently for a few seconds, waiting for the sound of Bill's phone. No call came.

"Hey, Cleary?" Bill called to her in the dark.

"Yes, sir?" Cleary politely answered.

"Don't insult the Mouse," Bill said dryly. Cleary burst into laughter, the sound of which allowed Bill to relax at least three muscles in his body, maybe four. Responding in kind, she did her best to mimic Mortimer's coarse bellow herself.

"*We've got all manner of calipers surrounding you,*" she grunted in her attempt at a *basso profundo*. Bill couldn't help but laugh at her misinterpretation. She could sense he was laughing *at* her and not *with* her. "What?"

"It's caliber, with a B," he explained. "It means the size of the bullet." At least, he thought that's what it meant. He wasn't entirely certain.

"Well, what's a caliper, then?" Cleary demanded. She had him. He knew he'd once been pinched with a fat caliper by a particularly cruel female trainer at the YMCA. Immediately after that particular workout, he had driven all the way to Mobile to buy a dozen Krispy Kremes — just to spite the woman. He had also been told by a mechanic once that his Expedition needed, among other things, brake calipers. That repair cost him over a thousand dollars — and also resulted in the consumption of a dozen original glazed.

He grasped for a definition that sounded plausible, but could only manage, "It's a squeezy thingy," which elicited peals of laughter from his daughter. Nothing made him happier. But his bliss was short-lived. A realization struck him. "I don't know where my phone is."

Bill re-checked each of his pockets at least three times, hoping with each fumbling search that a little Disney magic would make the phone suddenly appear. No luck, but he checked once more. Just in case. He groped around the floor within arm's reach. Cleary unmade and remade both beds, as best she could in the pitch dark, searching for the device. In the midst of this fumbling, bumbling chaos, the room phone rang again. Cleary quickly located the button. "Hello, Mr. Mortimer."

"Cleary, why in the h—" He stopped short of using expletives with the girl. "Why haven't you answered your father's phone?"

"We can't find it." Cleary stated plainly. Neither she nor their father had any problem hearing the exasperated sigh from the chief.

"Well, couldn't you follow the sound of the ringing to find it?"

"We never heard it. I swear! Are you sure you have the right number?" Cleary sounded like she was arguing with her little brother, not a S.W.A.T. commander who held their lives in his hand.

"Respect, Cleary?" Bill chided. He needn't say anymore.

"Yes, sir..."

"I guess the battery's dead, chief," Bill yelled to the phone.

"Well how about you charge it up for a few minutes, then?" Mortimer was beyond impatient.

Bill gently reminded him that they hadn't had power in the building for some time now. They couldn't be sure, but Cleary and Bill both could swear they heard the man banging his head on something large and metallic. Mortimer finally came back to the phone with, "We'll figure something out." He hung up.

"That went well," Bill said with no small hint of irony.

***

The phone whizzed just over Jaimee's head, flew out the door of the mobile command vehicle and sailed into the parking lot, eventually skidding across the pavement. The officers surrounding Mortimer exited the vehicle or busied themselves pretending to address the crisis. Driving rain, lightning and thunder continued its assault outside the truck. The chief rubbed the new, bright red sore on his forehead and turned to Katherine, whose eyes were saucer-like at the man's tantrum. "Mrs. Durmer, does your husband have a closed head injury I need to know about?" Katherine was unsure how to answer, but didn't want to be the target of his next improvised missile.

"Not that I know of," she offered hesitantly, "but he's been away a few weeks."

Mortimer lit a cigarette and inhaled deeply. "I quit a week ago," he said to no one in particular. "Twenty-third time I've tried to quit. Every time I try, some nonsense like this happens. Then I'm right back where I was." He took another long drag. "Wife says I just don't want to quit. Fact is, she's the one who doesn't want it. To quit smoking, gotta quit the job. Quit the job, quit getting the paychecks." He flashed Katherine a smile, "And she likes the paychecks." One more drag before tossing the cigarette to the floor and snuffing it out under his boot. "Yep, picked a bad day to stop sniffing glue." He caught Katherine's quizzical stare and replied to her unspoken question. "Lloyd Bridges? *Airplane*?"

"I know where it's from," Katherine acknowledged. "I just had no idea you had a sense of humor."

"Me either," Jaimee chimed in. Mortimer shrugged.

"I could see that." He snapped his fingers and pointed at the cigarette butt on the steel plated floor. A uniformed officer ran over and picked it up, scooping as much ash into his palm as he could.

"Cleanliness," Mortimer commented. "The big man liked his parks clean. Cast members take care of the literal trash. We take care of the figurative." For a moment, it seemed as if he were posing for a portrait. Like George C. Scott backed by an enormous American flag, he stood — proud, patriotic and slightly unhinged. He snapped out of it and shifted his attention toward Katherine again. "We'll get your little girl back for you, Mrs. Durmer." He tried to comfort her with a cliché hand to the shoulder. "Don't you worry." Katherine was perplexed.

"What do you mean get her back?" she asked, her mind racing, trying to piece together this absurd puzzle of circumstances. "I *let* her come here with her father."

"Are you telling me she wasn't kidnapped?" Mortimer asked, his incredulity mixing with a slow-boiling anger. Katherine answered in the negative. Mortimer pressed, "but what about the guns?"

"What guns?" Katherine realized what he was asking and was amused at the suggestion. "You don't think Bill has guns up there?" Mortimer nodded slowly, but was a bit embarrassed to do so. Katherine broke into full-on laughter. "No, no way. Bill has a rule about guns."

"A rule?" Mortimer asked. Katherine rolled her eyes as she began to explain.

"Bill has rules about everything. It's like a thing with him." She spoke as only wives can about their husbands, blending aggravation, admiration and amusement. "Of course he never actually follows any of them." She said it before she could stop herself. Looking up, she saw the steely look in Mortimer's eyes and knew what he was thinking. She quickly back-pedaled. "But not this one. He obeys the big rules. 'No guns, no drugs, no cheating...'" She couldn't think of any more big ones. Time to reach. "Keep your oil changed..." she was foundering, "'Reduce, reuse, recycle.' You know."

Mortimer was not convinced. "Then tell me, Mrs. Durmer," he asked, leading her, "what are the 'little ones' he doesn't follow?" Katherine was back on comfortable ground. Bill's self-imposed rules were both a pet peeve and a constant source of entertainment.

"Let's see," she began to run down her mental top ten list, "'Don't express your political opinion.' An offshoot of that is, 'no yard signs.'"

"Yard signs?" Mortimer asked.

"Yeah. That's a sore spot right now," she cautioned. "I wouldn't bring it up. Then there's 'don't talk to telemarketers. Don't make small talk.' That one's a big deal with him," she offered as an aside. "Don't drink anything yellow. Don't eat anything with sprinkles. Don't work in the bathroom. Always shake with the right hand unless the person you're greeting is missing their right hand. In that case, use the left. If the other person is missing both hands, pat them on the shoulder to avoid an awkward nub groping." She showed no signs of stopping until Mortimer interrupted.

"Okay, I get it." He called to a subordinate stationed outside the truck, "Sergeant!" His attention turning back to Katherine, he asked, "Why didn't you join your husband on this vacation?"

"Oh, it's not a vacation," she answered, "He's trying to get a job. He wants to be the baker with his tray like always. You know, *Beauty and the Beast*?"

"I'm serious about that head injury. Get him checked out."

The female sergeant entered, her rain gear soaked from the thunderstorm. "Sir?"

Shifting his gaze back to the sergeant, and his mind back to full-on commander mode, Mortimer's ire boiled up. "Get on the horn to HQ and find out why I have a damn D-Day invasion out here for a man who is armed only with his neuroses!" The sergeant doffed her rain gear and hunkered down before the truck's communication center. Katherine snickered. "Problem, Mrs. Durmer?"

She tried to wave it off as if it were nothing, but couldn't resist the urge to call him out. "'Get on the horn to HQ?' Seriously?" She chided him, "You just did that for my benefit, didn't you? You don't really talk that way." He showed no hint of breaking. Big mistake, Katherine.

"Let me tell you something about rules, Mrs. Durmer." Now came the lecture. "I have a rule to maintain order and safety. I have a rule to protect the guests of this resort. I have a rule to keep my people out of harm's way, if at all possible. I have a rule to follow a chain of command. And I have a rule to protect the great name of Walt Disney." He leaned in closer to her and lowered his voice, "And the only way I can do that effectively is to utilize a certain vernacular. It may sound like bad movie dialogue to you, but it is an absolute necessity to those of us out here with our necks on the line." Katherine wondered how long it would be before he told her she couldn't handle the truth. Instead, he lightened up a bit and smirked, "Plus, I like how cool it sounds." Katherine let out the breath she had been holding and returned the smile.

The sergeant returned and handed Mortimer a note. He read it, his breath catching about midway through. He removed his hat and ran his hands through his hair. "I should have known," he grumbled to himself. Folding the note, he returned it to the sergeant. "Destroy that." Mortimer donned his hat and looked to Katherine. "Mrs. Durmer, what do you know about the Council of the Nine?" Katherine's jaw dropped. In the previous week, she had learned quite a lot, thanks to Bill. What in the world had Bill gotten himself into?

Chapter Fourteen:
All the Best Storytellers Have Their CDLs

Bill climbed up and got himself into the driver's seat of bus number 3141. He'd been through a marathon two-day training course and a fast-tracking of his commercial driver's license test. (Bill joked that it all took less time than his last visit to the DMV.) He was ready to begin his career as a Disney Transit bus driver.

"You look good up there, Bill Durmer." The voice of the older driver climbing the stairs sounded familiar, but Bill couldn't place it. The man lifted his head to face Bill. The long nose, narrow chin and pronounced ears, when combined with his beaming smile, immediately put Bill at ease.

"Red?" Bill hoped he was remembering the right man. Quickly calculating the odds, he determined he was 68 percent certain this was the driver he met back in December. Another of his rules was to never call anyone by name until he was at least 97 percent sure, but he was feeling lucky.

Red extended a hand. "I'm surprised you remembered me." Red explained he would be riding along with Bill for a couple of days as he learned the routes and flow of the transit system. No passengers, no pressure. It would be just the two of them, master and apprentice, exploring the open roads of the Reedy Creek Improvement District.

As they pulled away from the transit station for the first time, Red began to introduce Bill to his new world. "This is the Gillig LF, the finest bus in the Disney fleet. As you may have guessed, the LF stands for low floor. So low, in fact, that you can drop that right side right down to the level of the curb and roll a wheelchair or stroller right on in." He patted Bill on the shoulder. "We'll practice that later today." Red was full of knowledge of the bus fleet and shared those factoids with Bill between giving him route directions. The size of the fleet: 230 buses. The average mileage between repairs: 5,000. He waxed poetic about the other bus models in the fleet: the Nova Bus, which many drivers preferred for its quick acceleration and smooth deceleration, and the older RTS, built in Roswell, New Mexico. "You can bet we had some fun with the guests with that one," he recalled.

Over the long hours of driving the roads and freeways of the resort, Bill learned this to be one of the key functions of the drivers: storytelling. "All Disney fans want a scoop," Red explained. "They want to know something few other people know, typically about the future of the parks." Over the years, it had become something of a competition between drivers to one-up each other. At shift changes, they would recount their most outlandish tales. Certain drivers would then scour the message boards of fan websites to determine whether the false rumors had taken hold.

"The key to a good yarn is the detail," Red instructed. "And it has to make sense within a world that the guest understands. And delivery is paramount. As Uncle Walt used to say, 'When you believe in a thing, believe in it all the way.' If you believe the story, the guest will certainly follow along."

"Do you ever feel bad," Bill asked, "deceiving people that way?" Bill often felt guilty for simply telling his children a bedtime story, fearing it might technically be defined as a lie. It was a Commandment, after all — one of the big ones. Though theologians could debate endlessly the true meaning of "bearing false witness," Bill had already defined it for himself: "knowingly speaking, writing, performing or implying any information that is false, contrived, manipulated or fictitious, whether for ill or good." It was one of his longer rules and one he found impossible to follow. But one must have standards to betray.

"It's not deception, my boy," Red explained, "anymore than a beautiful young woman dressing up in a blue ball gown and blonde wig and calling herself Cinderella is deception. The guests don't think she's the real Cinderella. And they don't think a bus driver is the ultimate source of insider information on the world's largest media conglomerate." Stopping at the intersection of Western Way and Buena Vista, Bill cast the older man a cockeyed glance. "Well, at least they shouldn't think that." The bus lurched forward a bit as Bill turned right. "Watch that accelerator," Red cautioned him before resuming his previous topic. "We're a part of the show, Bill Durmer, storytellers, raconteurs. Whether the guests believe us or not is beside the point. I think, if they're playing their part, they do believe us for a time."

"What exactly is their part?" Bill asked.

"Same thing that has gotten many a politician elected and made the movies a multi-billion dollar business," Red answered. "Willing suspension of disbelief."

Red began to recount some of the all-time great yarn spinners in Disney Transit. He started with Cyril Proud — Old Proudbottom, as the other drivers knew him. Cyril had worked at the resort since its opening, first as a tram driver, then driving the first RTS models ordered for the opening of EPCOT. He retired after more than thirty years on the job. Old Proudbottom had become the patron saint of bus-driving storytellers. He had suggested to management that bus drivers should be entertainers every bit as much as the skippers on Jungle Cruise or the cast members in character costumes. When transportation officials determined that finding capable drivers who were also entertaining was an improbable task, Cyril's idea was soundly rejected. So he took it upon himself.

He worked subtly, so as not to draw attention to his "performances." It started simply enough. Prior to arriving at a resort, of which there were only a handful at the time, or one of the two parks, he would announce their impending arrival and pepper the announcement with a bit of trivia about the place. Soon, guests began asking him questions about rumors they had heard. Initially, fearing that these were "ghost riders" (cast members paid to act as guests in order to gauge a driver's performance), he would shoot down the more outlandish rumors or feign ignorance about those that hit too close to the truth.

Growing bored with toeing the company line, and irritated with an especially loquacious know-it-all of a guest, he chose to silence the man (who boasted of knowing everything about Walt Disney) by telling him that company officials had been acquiring property in the guest's home state of Texas. He went so far as to mention a specific area around Dallas where the man might consider investing in property. Cyril claimed that Texas' Disney World would be at least twice the size of the Florida property and that Walt's original plan for EPCOT, known as Progress City, would finally be brought to fruition there.

"And that particular rumor is still going around," Red explained, "in some form or another to this very day. Longest running rumor in the history of the park. If they had a Hall of Fame for bus drivers, it would be named for Old Proudbottom." He went on to explain that Cyril's reputation as a storyteller and rumorsmith grew rapidly. Once, legendary animator Ward Kimball was visiting the park and sought out Cyril, seeking a good rumor he could share at parties. "Cyril took a sip of iced tea, clinked the ice around in the glass and shrugged, 'I heard Walt had his head frozen until medical science could revive him.' Kimball loved it and ran with the story."

"So that's where that started?" Bill was impressed.

"Hall of Fame, kid," was Red's response. "Hall of Fame."

"What about you, Red?" Bill inquired. "What stories are gonna get you in the Hall of Fame?" Red demurred.

"I don't know that I'm all that good." He rubbed his chin as he pondered the question. "I guess I'd have to put one particular story at the top of my list."

"What's that?"

"I told this internet writer — what's it called, a blogger?" Red asked. Bill nodded. "I told this blogger that there was a secret society that controlled everything the company does. Poor guy's just about gone mad trying to prove it."

It couldn't be. Bill was afraid to ask, but he had no choice. "What was his name?" He nervously awaited the answer.

"I never got his real name," Red admitted, "but he writes under the name of Gaston." Bill doubled over as if punched in the gut. He righted himself and began to laugh.

"What is it?" Red asked, carefully watching Bill's reaction.

"Nothing. I just had an epiphany. That's all." He couldn't believe he had turned his entire life upside down on the basis of a rumor started by an octogenarian with a CDL. Should he head back for the transportation hub and quit now, or at least finish his shift? He decided that pressing on was the best course of action. "Go on, Red. Let's hear some more of your greatest hits."

"Well..." Red took a deep breath and paused long enough that Bill began to worry about the old man's well-being. "I once told a couple, back in the Eisner days, that we were planning a fourth park that would take on Busch Gardens head-on by mixing live animal exhibits with Disney theming and attractions." He chuckled. "Guess I can't really take credit for that one. Funny thing is, they didn't even believe me."

"I'll let that one slide," Bill said. "Try again."

"Alright then." Red's voice seemed to deepen as he spoke. "I once said that Bob Iger becoming the CEO was the best way to salvage the Pixar relationship, and if it did happen, the two companies would merge and put John Lasseter in charge of all company creative."

"Red," Bill cajoled him, "you may be psychic, but I don't think you're going to win any contests for creative storytelling."

"No," Red confessed, "I suppose not. *All* of my stories tend to be true." The way he emphasized the word "all" caught Bill's attention. Bill pulled the bus into the parking lot of the All-Star Movies Resort and shifted into park. He spun around to face Red.

"Are you telling me the Council of the Nine is real?" Bill asked with considerable anxiety.

Red answered simply, "Yes." Bill's mind raced, his thoughts quickened by the revelation. Which question to ask first? As a student of pop culture, he had always been frustrated by characters in film and television that didn't ask the obvious questions or share pertinent information. Intellectually, he understood the narrative necessity of moving the action forward, but still he thought it was lazy writing. Now, here he sat, a character within the unfolding absurdity that was the story of his life, and he couldn't think what to say ... or ask ... or do.

If his life were a fiction (which he often suspected during existential bouts of self-loathing), it must be the work of a hack writer. Then again, maybe those writers he had harangued when talking back to his television over the years had truly tapped into the human psyche. Maybe, when faced with extraordinary circumstances, ordinary people simply weren't capable of getting to the heart of the matter. Perhaps the best course was to start with his own story.

"Last week," he began, "just after I was offered this job, I was called by someone who threatened me and my daughter. Was that them?"

"No," Red offered reassuringly then backtracked. "Well, maybe. But not exactly." That was helpful. Seeing the bewilderment of the younger man, Red knew he should elaborate. "You know Trekkies? Star Trek fans?"

"Trekkers," Bill nodded. "Trekkies is the pejorative." Red continued, nonplussed and undeterred.

"These are the Disney equivalent. No," he halted. Red furrowed his brow, struggling with how much to reveal. "No. They are so much more..."

He trailed off.

"More what?" Bill inquired.

"More everything," Red smiled with fear and admiration, "more fanatical, more fractious, more influential. Most of all, they are more exclusive. They don't advertise. They don't have a website. You can't sign up for a fan club, pay your membership and get a t-shirt. They are like a vapor — ever-present and invisible, amorphous and always changing. They're the Mickey Masons, if you will."

Bill explored the old man's face for a tell, any hints that this was merely another tall tale, a quest to earn a spot next to Old Proudbottom in the Hall of Fame. There were none. He needed more information. "So are they dangerous, or aren't they?"

Red sniffed and smirked the way old men do when they must deign to explain themselves to the young and foolish. "Yes. But they are not a single unified group. The Council of the Nine is a sort of ... well ... council representing nine very different groups, each with its own agenda."

"Does this have anything to do with the Nine Old Men?" Bill knew it was a long shot. The Nine Old Men were a key group of animators working for Disney during their golden age. As Bill understood it, they were all key contributors to the Disney style and to the medium as a whole, but not the only masters of the trade. What they were, without a doubt, were the animators Walt trusted most.

"In a sense." Red's words were a degree more measured and circumspect now. "They began as groups of devotees to each of the nine, shortly after Walt died, each rallying behind their man to be the 'new Walt.'" Red made a point of looking directly into Bill's eyes, "A ridiculous notion, don't you think? Could there even be such a person?" Bill, thinking the question rhetorical, stared blankly back. Red sighed, "Of course, corporations don't work that way. Walt's brother Roy took the reins until his death, and other members of the family were in the upper levels of management for many years, but..." Red gazed at himself in the mirror as if looking on the face of a stranger. He continued, "they just weren't Walt." He rubbed his eyes and settled back into his seat. "We should get back on schedule."

Bill obliged and eased the bus forward, continuing to follow his training route. As Bill drove, Red explained that the original nine factions of Disney fans grew and evolved over the decades. Alliances formed and were betrayed, some groups nearly died off only to be reformed with new members and new purpose. "Fans are a funny thing," Red observed. "Any entertainment business needs them to survive, but there's a tipping point. They become too loyal, and they develop feelings of ownership, a sense of entitlement." The nine groups took their feelings of ownership to heart and refined them into a plan. Each group recruited promising young animators, Imagineers, story men and women, and anyone else they hoped might be both sympathetic to their respective causes and capable of climbing the corporate ladder, giving the groups real power within the company.

"Fans setting policy," Bill noted. "That can't be good."

"Fortunately, they never managed to quite crack the alchemy necessary to reach those upper echelons of power," Red replied. "Not that certain members didn't get there, mind you. But once you get to that level, well, old loyalties are tested and typically fail."

Bill had so many more questions on the topic, but only one mattered: "What does any of this have to do with me?"

"Remember what I said to you when we first met?" Red asked, "When I first shook your hand?"

"Imagineer's hands," Bill answered.

"Right." Red explained, "Apparently one or more of the groups noticed you, too and has taken a shine to you. They see your potential, and they want to win you over to their side."

"And the threats?" Bill questioned.

"Where one group takes interest, another is bound to create opposition." Red stated it matter-of-factly, as if this were common knowledge.

None of it made any sense to Bill. He protested, "I'm just a bus driver, a-lousy-businessman-who-possibly-killed-his-entire-hometown-with-his-failure-and-then-ran-away bus driver. I have potential the way a nuclear bomb has potential." Red placed a reassuring hand on Bill's shoulder.

"Remember, 'all your dreams can come true if you have the courage to pursue them.'"

"Walt Disney," Bill confirmed. It was one of his favorite quotes and had been ever since Jenny Tillman had used it during an oral report on Walt in high school. "But Walt never met me," Bill joked, attempting to add some levity to the moment, "or it would have been more like, 'All your dreams can come true if you're only willing to compromise your standards.'" Taking visual note of his current standing, he added, "A lot." Red only chuckled at the well-rehearsed self-deprecation. "Tell me something, Red," Bill said, shifting gears both figuratively and literally, "how do you know so much about the inner workings of the company?"

Red shrugged, "I'm a bus driver." The two men rode quietly save route instructions from Red as needed. Over lunch, the conversation was limited to discussing family, and then only Bill's. For the balance of the day, they both saw fit to table the topic of the Council of the Nine. Back at the transit hub, as they were stepping off to end their day, Red cautioned Bill, "They will be coming for you at some point. They're harmless — most of them anyway. Others…" He offered Bill a smile, "Just keep your eyes open." Bill nodded and stepped off the bus. He was concerned at how common the cryptic warnings and bizarre coincidences were becoming in his life.

A few paces from the bus, he remembered the mysterious "D" card. Hoping the old man might have some insight, he turned back toward the bus. "Red?" But it was too late. Red was nowhere to be seen. "You're a spry old cuss, Red!" Bill called out to the night air. "I'll give you that!" He turned, the setting sun at his back, and walked toward his car. His first day as a Disney cast member had come to a close.

Chapter Fifteen:
Duct Taped and Stuffed in a Pig

A fiery orange-red glow filled the ice cave, followed a split second later by roars of impending doom. Outside the cave, fire burst forth, and meteors streaked across the false sky. Cleary smiled as the baby wooly mammoth to her right raised its trunk and trumpeted. Throughout the restaurant, animatronic dinosaurs, mammoths and even a giant squid — creatures that had no business being in the same diorama – thrashed and wailed at their impending bi-hourly fate. Of the diners, Bill could easily discern the regulars from the first-timers. Newcomers stopped eating, stared in wide-eyed wonder and attempted to capture the moment in stills or video. The regulars looked annoyed and tried to talk over the noise. Once the show was complete, the walls of the ice cave returned to their normal, soothing blue tint.

The Durmers had planned to eat at T-Rex Cafe on their previous trip in December, but the weirdness of that vacation had thwarted those plans. Bill munched on his bronto burger and imagined for a moment that he was Fred Flintstone. It wasn't much of a stretch, given that Fred was an adaptation of Ralph Kramden from *The Honeymooners,* a character who was, of course, a bus driver. Bill thought for a moment about the shabby, small apartment in which the old sitcom was set and found himself growing increasingly disgusted with his life. He would take the "mid-century prehistoric" architecture of the Flintstone's suburban home any day compared to the prospect of living in the Kramden's Bronx hovel. It never occurred to Bill that debating the merits of fictional characters' lifestyles might not be the best use of his intellect.

"This is way better than PB&Js in the hotel," Cleary noted.

"I thought my first day on the job deserved a celebration," Bill replied, trying to convince himself that this meal was anything other than a consolation prize, a parting gift for losing in the game of life. "It may not be the job I came to get, but hey, I got my foot in the door. Right?"

"Are you kidding? You spent the whole day driving around Disney World!" Cleary enthused, "That's amazing!" Bill loved her innocent optimism and allowed to it buoy his own flagging spirits.

"I guess it is," he replied, "when you come to think about it." He raised his glass of beer to toast her. She met his gesture with her souvenir cup of lemonade.

"Cheers!" she cried.

"Cheers, indeed, Sweet Pea." The plastic cup and the beer mug faintly tapped as they came together. They took big, celebratory swigs of their respective drinks. "Now, tell me about your day." Cleary began to recount her day with her Disney sitter. She tried to downplay the fun as she talked of hours playing in the resort pool, retreating into the room when a thunderstorm threatened and searching for Easter eggs on a stack of Disney DVDs.

Bill struggled to pay attention to her, but his thoughts crept repeatedly back to the Council of the Nine and Red's cryptic warning to him. He thought about the world of fanatical devotees out there: Trekkers and Losties, the 501st Legion of Star Wars fans, Elvis fans, Deadheads, Cheeseheads and Cameron Crazies. None of them could hold a candle to the sheer hubris of what Red had described to him. Only die-hard Crimson Tide loyalists came close in his mind, but even they had learned their lesson about trying too hard to control the thing they loved. If a loose confederacy of squabbling fan groups could be patient enough to take decades to gain influence in the company, what methods might they employ to bend him to their will? They had fashioned of the company a religion. Now they were striving to install their own self-made god.

"So, what color do you think I should get?" Cleary asked. Bill was apoplectic. He had no idea what she was asking.

"I'm sorry, sweetie." He begged her forgiveness and saw the faint wince of betrayal in her eyes. Fathers, do not exasperate your children indeed. "I zoned out for a second there. What were you saying?"

"Nothing," she mumbled. It was too late. He took her hand.

"Look, I'm sorry." He tried to look in her eyes, but she avoided his gaze. "Now, we're here to celebrate tonight, and let's do that. When do you ever get me all to yourself like this? No baby? No little brother interjecting the word 'poopy' into every conversation?" Bill's course correction worked, and she relaxed with a laugh. "Now hurry up and tell me about the rest of your day, because we've only got," he checked his naked wrist where a watch would be if he didn't have a rule against wearing watches in the summer, "about fifteen minutes before the world ends in a horrific meteor storm!" He delivered the line loudly, with the conviction and intensity of the most self-serious of community theatre players.

"Daddy!" Cleary said under her breath, her cheeks turning a deep crimson. She took a deep breath and started over with her story, such as it was: rambling, disjointed and completely lacking in narrative through lines. And Bill hung on every word with rapt attention. It was one thing to exasperate his child once in an evening. Doing so again might be a sin that he couldn't forgive himself.

They finished off dinner by sharing a dessert. Bill then took Cleary to the Lego Store. He was just like another kid, constructing brightly hued cars and buildings with his daughter for as long as she wished. When they had clicked together colored bricks until their thumbs hurt, they climbed aboard a launch for a leisurely round-trip boat ride to Old Key West and Saratoga Springs Resorts. That gave him some time to tell her an edited version of the story of the Council of the Nine, leaving out the more threatening elements and playing up the humor.

Arriving back at their room for the evening, Cleary was the first to notice the envelope just inside the door. "It's another one of those weird D-notes," she said, using the moniker they had adopted for the mysterious note of days earlier. "I wonder what this one says." Bill took it from her and tossed in on the small dinette table.

"Don't know and don't care. It can wait 'til morning." He slipped off his shoes and collapsed onto his bed. "Now show me some of those Easter eggs."

"Okay!" She darted across the room to retrieve her portable DVD player. Bill spent the rest of the evening trying not to think about the Council of the Nine. He was largely successful until Cleary went to bed. Then he was left alone with his thoughts. Finding them, as he had feared, unbearable company, he sneaked over and retrieved the D-note.

Sliding it out of the envelope, he found it was on the same paper, red on the outside with the gold embossed D on the cover. He opened it and read quietly aloud to himself. "Go with it." He folded the note, slid it back into the envelope and set it aside. "Cryptic, mysterious," he said to himself. "That's about right. And so it begins."

He lay awake most of the night awaiting the "it" of which the note spoke. For those fitful few hours, he alternated prayer with bouts of dreadful worry. Each twinge of anxiety was followed by the guilt for his lack of faith. He would then pray some more to seek forgiveness for the anxiety. Following the prayer, he would question whether he was really sincere in asking for forgiveness, which would then lead to further anxiety. Thus, the cycle would begin again. After more than four hours of this, he finally fell asleep and dreamt of being anxious about his lack of guilt for falling asleep during prayer. Then he dreamt of being swallowed by a giant pig.

***

Cleary roused him with just enough time to get dressed prior to the sitter's arrival. He tucked the D-note in his pocket and staggered, bleary-eyed and irritable, out the door. Under normal circumstances, he would take the stairs. Feeling too weak for stairs, he chose the elevator instead. He turned the corner toward the elevators and pushed the button. As he waited, he thought about how his father and grandfather never pushed a button in their lives; they "mashed" them, as all good Southern men do. He was lost deep in those memories when several unseen persons grabbed his arms from behind and pulled him quickly backward into the elevator. Just as quickly, they bound his wrists, blindfolded him and sealed his mouth with duct tape. A girl whispered up into his ear, "Just go with it." Her voice was impossibly high-pitched and sing-songy. Yet it seemed so familiar.

His abductors placed something over his head. It was like a helmet, but larger. And sort of furry. Before he could determine what exactly the head covering was, his captors lifted him off his feet and quickly fitted him into some sort of large suit. Like fuzzy coveralls, it slid easily over his shoes and clothes. His arms remained bound, and at least two people held him in place. He couldn't see, couldn't wriggle loose, nor could he cry out. So, he heeded the advice of the D-note and went with it.

When the elevator doors opened, Bill found himself being escorted swiftly out. He had heard anecdotally of the Secret Service not allowing the president's feet to even touch the ground under threat conditions, but he never believed that possible. Especially for Taft. But now, he knew all too well how plausible it was. Carted like a fleshy, fur-covered marionette out the door to who-knows-where, he heard children and their parents reacting to the sight of his abduction with curious delight.

"Oh look, Mommy! Look! Look!" a little girl called out.

"Wow! I wonder what they're all doing here together," said a woman Bill assumed to be the girl's mother. Other voices joined and blended together until he couldn't make out what any of them were saying. All he heard was a chorus of elated greetings. The next thing he knew, their forward movement had halted and he heard camera shutters clicking all around them. A few friendly farewells later, they were on the move again.

The unseen captors threw him into a vehicle of some kind. He could only assume it was a cargo van. Kidnappers pretty much cornered the market on cargo vans. The car sped off, flinging Bill against a wall, then another. Someone righted him and set him against what felt like the back of the driver's seat. And all of this before he'd had a single drop of coffee.

When at last he arrived at his destination, the headpiece was removed, his eyes uncovered and the headpiece replaced. Bill struggled to adjust to the light bursting through the small, dark screen set into the headpiece. Once he had regained his vision, Bill tried to get some idea of his surroundings. It was a long, dark corridor of a room. There was no one in sight. In every direction, he saw long racks of clothing in dry cleaning bags. He couldn't discern the ends of the room, and the racks appeared to converge at a vanishing point in each direction. His back was against one of the racks. Looking closer, he realized what he saw was not ordinary clothing, but costumes. The details were obscured by the plastic bags, but Bill thought he could make out a tattered 18th century sailor's coat in one, golden yellow fur in another and a sky blue Romantic ball gown in yet another.

Blinding light emanated from an array of bulbs arranged in a rectangle and suspended above a small desk across the way. He squinted to see past the glare of the light. Bill started as he made out a strange, pink figure staring back at him from some distance behind the lights. It had large, unblinking eyes and a stupefied grin. Its skin had a polished gleam to it. He leaned forward for a better look and realized the pink creature did the same. Bill moved his head left. The creature went right. Bill moved right, and it went left. Bill shook his head wildly, and the creature matched his move with mirrored perfection. The desk across from him was, in fact, a theatrical dressing table. And the void between the lights was not an opening, but a mirror. He was a pig! He had been duct taped and stuffed in a pig — a pig costume, to be precise. That explained the dream. Bill closed his eyes for a moment, hoping to fall asleep and dream of being buried under a billion one-dollar bills only to break free by flexing his monstrous six-pack abs. Alas, he was too alive with adrenalin to sleep.

With a clang and a screech, a heavy, metal door opened, far to Bill's left. Light streamed in for a moment, but disappeared when the door slammed shut. Footsteps echoed against the hard, concrete floor and high ceiling. They got louder as the person neared. A dark figure grew larger in his sight. Bill craned his neck as best he could to see out through the pig's mouth. His jaw would have dropped, if not for the duct tape, at what he saw: a young woman with pale skin, sporting a short, jet black wig with a red bow in it and wearing a dress with a high, white collar, blue bodice and a long, yellow skirt. He had been kidnapped by Snow White.

"Oh my!" she gasped in a spot-on Adriana Caselotti impersonation. The humiliation of his life was boundless. "Aren't you a funny sight?" she cooed. Then she giggled. Really. It was the same voice from the elevator. Based on what Bill could tell of their respective heights, odds were her henchmen were the prince and one of the dwarfs. Most people would have assumed Grumpy fit the profile, but Bill believed Happy the more likely culprit. He had always been suspicious of Happy. No one is that jovial.

"Mmmmuh-mmmmmuhh-muh," Bill grunted.

"Oh! Where are my manners?" Snow White removed the pig's head and set it aside, all the while talking in that high-pitched voice of hers. "I am so sorry that we had to bring you in like this, but we couldn't have you making a fuss around the guests. The customer always comes first, you know!" This chick was way too perky. She must've had her coffee and Bill's share as well. "I'm Snow White," she said as an ironic counterpoint to her next action, which was to swiftly rip the tape from Bill's mouth. Bill reacted appropriately, which is to say he screamed like a little girl.

"Oh dear!" Snow White covered her mouth with both hands in faux innocence. "I know that must have been dreadfully painful. It always hurts when I have my—" Bill cut her off right there.

"Why am I here?" Bill asked curtly. He may have been going with it, but no one said he had to be nice about it. Snow White was as chipper and apologetic in her reply as ever.

"Mr. Durmer, you may not realize it, but you're a very important man. Very important, indeed." Though she never broke character, Bill could sense that these were not the words of an actress playing a role. She meant it.

"And who are you?" He glanced up and down and wagged his head to indicate her costume, "besides the obvious."

"We are the Cast of Thousands, of course," she replied in the same chipper voice.

"No offense," Bill wryly noted, "but you're about 999 cast members short. Actually 1,999 if we're talking thousands plural." Snow White smiled politely, but with a hint of menace.

"Friends?" she called out to the room. On her cue, costumed characters stepped forward from behind the racks. Bill saw dozens, hundreds perhaps. Each one acted in character, waving at, being shy toward or haughtily ignoring Bill.

"Okay," Bill said, a little nervous about the sheer numbers surrounding him. "I stand corrected. Why am I here? I'm just a bus driver." A thin man in a candy-striped suit and straw hat stepped forward.

"We lot have got to watch out for ourselves, guvnah," the man said in a horrendous Cockney accent that helped Bill to recognize the character.

"Ahhh... Bert, the chimney sweep from *Mary Poppins*, right?" Bill asked to no avail. Bert marshalled on with his agenda.

"We know 'oo you are, too, Mr. Bill Durmah," Bert said, "and we 'ear rumahs about 'oo 'as been bending your eah. We just want you to know that we lot, we are not to be trifled wif." Bert crouched down in front of Bill, coming between him and Snow White. "These ovah blokes in the suits fink we just show up and put on a funny suit. But we've got brains, we 'ave."

"You might want to be careful, there," Bill offered as his sarcastic reproach. "You were slipping over into a Guy Ritchie film with that accent. Don't want to scare the children." Bill looked them over. "Let me guess: Council of the Nine. Am I right? You're one of the nine crazy fan groups?" The characters reacted nervously to his question, unsure how to respond.

Snow White stepped in. "Mr. Durmer, we may seem ever so silly to you with our costumes and our voices, but I assure you this is a most serious matter." She began, with Bert's occasional interjection, to lay out the group's agenda. Given the fact that Bill was bound and completely surrounded, it sounded more like a list of demands to him.

She explained that their group was comprised entirely of current and former costumed cast members from the Disney parks. Their belief was that they, more than anyone — more than executives or animators or television personalities — represented the true face of Disney. She also claimed that, to a lesser extent, they represented the rank-and-file cast member. Bill doubted that, however, noting the lack of non-costumed employees present.

Snow White bemoaned, with a theatrical display of grief, the relegation of certain characters only to holiday or parade appearances. She argued that all characters, no matter how obscure or minor, deserved to appear in "meet and greets" or be allowed to simply roam the parks. She lobbied for more so-called character meals in the restaurants. Her diatribe then ventured into an area better suited for a labor dispute than a cartoon kidnapping: talk of actor's equity, royalties for appearance in other media and bargaining rights agreements. Bill found it ironic that people so devoted to their respective characters behaved nothing like those characters and everything like the worst stereotypes of actors: self-absorbed and self-promoting. He almost pointed this out, but thought it best not to provoke the furry masses. (Bill had a thing against actors ever since he was passed over for the role of Joseph in the 6th grade Christmas pageant in favor of a boy with "more heroic cheekbones.") Truth be told, Bill found their concerns fascinating, but was bewildered as to why they were telling them to him.

"I know you must be confused, Mr. Durmer," Snow White said noting his puzzled look. She turned to her left and called down the corridor, "Marie?" Someone dressed as a giant, white kitten waddled forward, miming shyness as she neared Bill. Marie handed Snow White a manila folder. "Thank you, Marie." Snow White delicately petted the kitten costume on the head. Marie mimed a giggle and then returned to her spot in the lineup.

As Snow White opened the folder, Bill noticed his own name on the cover. "The baker with his tray like always. Oh, that is a most intriguing idea, Mr. Durmer." Her face grew uncharacteristically grim. "But we are concerned that if your plan were to be implemented, company officials might begin to require all costumed cast members to live on property."

"And that would be bad?" Bill asked, unsure where this was going.

"Ooooh!" she cried as if given a fright. "It would be dreadful. We love this place, but we would feel pressured to stay in character at all times. I have to drink tea with lemon and honey every night as it is, just to rehab my voice. It's not so easy to talk like this, you know."

"Oy! I don't want to live 'ere," Bert chimed in. "I 'ave an offer on a beach condo, I 'ave."

"Look, I wasn't trying to create a program or anything," Bill argued. "I'm in no position to set policy. I just wanted to..." Now that he heard himself saying it, he was a bit embarrassed to go on. "I just wanted to live in the magic. I know that sounds stupid, but there's something about this place that..." He was unsure how to finish.

"Speaks to your heart?" Snow White asked. Bill smiled.

"Exactly." He didn't feel so foolish anymore. If these people could embrace their passion for the place so shamelessly, why couldn't he? Bert placed a hand on Bill's shoulder.

"The time is coming when you will understand, Bill Durmer." Bert spoke in his own voice, eliciting gasps from Snow White and most of the other characters within earshot. "And if we're right about you, you'll have more of an opportunity to live in the magic than any man ever has."

"Except one," Snow White corrected him. She, too, used her own voice. It was deeper even than Bill had expected, smoky and full of character.

"Right, except one," Bert answered. He and Snow White smiled at each other, gazing deep into one another's eyes. Bill knew that look, and it made him long for Katherine more than he had in months.

"I wish I had the faintest clue what you people are talking about," he said.

"If you are indeed the New Son," Snow White said, "you will know soon enough. Bill wondered what she meant by "new son," but couldn't bring himself to ask. Hack writer. "Now, we must return you to where you belong. You'll understand if we place you back inside the pig?"

Bill nodded, "But no tape, please. I'll be quiet."

"Remember us, Bill Durmer," said Bert, blindfolding Bill and replacing the pig head. There was not much chance Bill would forget. "And beware others who may lead you astray."

Snow White leaned down and kissed the pig on the cheek, then spoke into the opening in its mouth. She resumed her character voice. "Goodbye, until we meet again." Unseen hands lifted Bill to his feet. No doubt Bert was one of them, but Bill was still suspicious of Happy. Snow White burst forth in another of her characteristic giggles. "Oh my, but you do look ever so funny!"

A long walk, a van ride and an unceremonious removal of the costume in the elevator left Bill right back where he had been abducted earlier that day. His foot slipped on something slick on the concrete floor. It was another D-note. It read, "Take it."

"Cryptic much!?" Bill yelled into thin air. Just then, his phone rang. On the other end was his supervisor at Disney Transit apologizing to Bill for calling him on his day off, which perplexed Bill, because he had been certain he was on the schedule to work. Apparently Red was right about the groups in the Council of the Nine having influence. The supervisor offered Bill an evening shift. Hoping Red would be there to shed some light on the morning's events and heeding the advice of the D-note, Bill accepted. Until the time came for him to leave, he shared lunch and a swim with Cleary and Tiffney, the 23-year-old Disney sitter. Other than the sting of chlorine hitting the sensitive, duct tape-exfoliated skin on his wrists and mouth, it was a perfectly glorious and uneventful afternoon. And that very fact made Bill a nervous wreck. Somewhere the great, cosmic hand of fate was dangling an absurdly large shoe. Bill was just waiting for it to drop, and with his luck it would be spiked. And it would drop on his head.

Chapter Sixteen:
It's a Big Bus After All

Bill's hopes for a debriefing session with Red that evening were dashed. In fact, not only could he not find Red, but no other drivers on duty even knew who he was. For someone who seemed to be such a fixture within the resort, Red was proving to be more mysterious than Bill would have suspected. Most of the early evening Bill spent alone in his bus, driving training routes. Three hours into his shift, dispatch called to send him to the Grand Floridian to pick up a VIP. A handful of buses were used daily for transporting VIPs and cast members, but Bill assumed only the best and most experienced drivers received those assignments. He switched on his LED sign indicating "VIP / Cast Member" and made his way to the Grand Floridian.

Upon arriving, he was greeted under the bus stop portico by an army of doormen and bell hops. Each cast member carried a plastic storage bin. Bill opened the door. The hotel staff formed a processional entering the bus, depositing the contents of their respective bins and exiting again. Bill scrutinized his overhead mirror to determine what exactly the staff were bringing on board, but the flurry of activity obscured his view.

Finally, when the last cast member had exited, a small, older woman entered, wearing a tartan plaid dress that looked more appropriate for Christmas than a typically balmy Orlando June. Under each arm, she carried a doll. The dolls were neither babies nor of the hyper-realistic American Girl or Madame Alexander types. (As the father of two daughters, Bill was all too familiar with the particulars of dolls.) He had never seen dolls like these in any toy store, catalog or boutique. Yet, they were eerily familiar. The dolls had large, round heads and compact bodies. One had long, silky black hair and was wearing traditional Hawaiian dress, including a grass skirt and a white lei. The other was a boy dressed in a white shirt, red serape and a tall sombrero. Bill noticed that the faces of the two dolls were identical. Glancing into his mirror again, he saw that every seat in the bus was filled with similar-looking dolls, each dressed to reflect a different region, nation or culture. And all with the same face. Bill shuddered at the creepy sight.

The woman paused as she stepped aboard the bus. "Hello, Bill Durmer. I'm so looking forward to our talk." Bill could only sigh. He had already reached his crazy quota for the day. He closed the door behind her. She took up residence in the seat directly behind Bill, the one he had hoped Red would occupy for the evening.

"Where are we headed, Miss..." Bill waited for her to fill in her name.

"You may call me the Doll Lady," she said in her kindly old voice.

"Of course I may," he replied dryly.

"Most people do. And I think I would like to simply drive around for a time — if you'll indulge me in conversation, that is."

"Yes, ma'am," Bill replied politely. She may have been crazy, but that was no call to be rude. He was still a Southern man, after all. Besides, he suspected she could illuminate some of the mysteries surrounding the Nine. "I'd love to talk," he said. He shifted the bus into gear and slowly pulled away.

"Could you play this for me, dear?" Doll Lady handed him a CD. Bill obliged and popped it into the player. A whimsical, bouncy melody emerged from the sound system, soon joined by a chorus of children singing about a world of laughter and a world of tears.

"I knew I had seen your dolls somewhere before!" Bill exclaimed.

"I would have thought someone with your enthusiasm for Disneyana would have recognized my little rubberheads on first sight," she admonished him. Bill couldn't explain it, but he was ashamed. Here was a woman who needed an entire city bus to haul her "friends" around, and he was the one ashamed.

"Sorry I needed a little reminder," he demurred. "It's been a weird day." He spun the big steering wheel of the bus and turned left out of the resort. He had hoped when he took the job that he would be awkward and perhaps even a little incompetent as a driver, not to the point of putting anyone in danger, but enough that no one would think him a natural. Much to his disappointment, he actually was a natural. He feared this might actually be his life's calling. Sure, he was only a couple of weeks removed from his coffee-fueled obsession with being a background character. However, that vision of his future was just quirky enough to convince himself he was not — perish the thought — ordinary. It wasn't that he was a classist like Nancy. In fact, he had no problem with other people being ordinary. It simply wasn't good enough for him.

"Any areas in particular you'd like to see?" Bill asked as he pulled onto Floridian Way.

"It's not so much about the destination as the journey," she answered. Bill was disappointed in her cliché. Surely someone this eccentric could come up with something more original. He realized he was projecting his admiration for Red onto the Doll Lady due simply to her age. Age didn't necessarily equate to wisdom, but there was no reason to believe she lacked it. Then again, there was no reason to believe she possessed it, either. In the absence of conversation, Bill continued this internal debate for several minutes as he drove. Lost in his own thoughts, he made the mistake of opening his mouth.

"I mean, you could be fruity as a nut cake for all I know." Upon realizing his complete breach of propriety, he clamped his mouth shut, but it was too late. The damage had already been done. To his relief, the Doll Lady chuckled at his non sequitur.

"True enough," she replied. "Although I wonder that I shouldn't say the same of you at the moment." Bill was mortified.

"I am so sorry."

"No apology necessary. I know how I must look to you — me and my friends," she said. It was the second time that day he had heard those words from someone most people would believe had taken leave of their senses entirely. Yet the fact that she had even spoken them revealed a certain self-awareness. He wondered what levels of passion for (or obsession with) a particular subject could result in such an unabashed display of nuttiness. For all his varied interests, nothing had ever inspired him that completely. Bill couldn't decide whether to admire them or pity them, though he knew they deserved more than dispassionate mockery.

The Doll Lady continued, "I should hope you see my methods as gentler than, say," pausing for effect, "duct taping you and stuffing you into a pig costume?" Bill couldn't help but laugh.

"I would say so," he admitted. "So, do you all know what the other groups are up to?" Before allowing her to answer, he thought to ask, "And which group do you represent, anyway?"

"Good questions both," she commented. "I belong to the Small World Society, and my friends here are not merely the affectations of a senescent mind. Each of them represents one member of our little group." She stroked the hula girl's hair. "I keep them with me to remind myself that I'm not here to act on my own interests." She leaned forward, close to Bill's ear, and adopted a darker, almost sinister tone, "Some may not take their role on the council seriously. And some are in it solely for their own good. You would be wise to tread carefully, Bill Durmer." Her tone made the hairs on Bill's neck stand on end.

Her warning issued, she returned to her previous posture and affable disposition. "Now, as far as knowing what shenanigans the other groups are up to, let's just say we all have our spies."

"Spies?" Bill was incredulous. "Seriously?"

"Oh, yes. Some are worse than others," she noted. "The Powers are the worst, ironically enough." Bill glanced back upon her mention of the Powers, recalling the threats of a week earlier. Doll Lady realized she had said too much and began to backtrack, "Oh, but I'm getting ahead of myself. There are rules about these sorts of things, you know."

"What rules? Why can't you say more?" Bill began to sweat as he faced more riddles and obfuscations. "Couldn't you bend the rules," he asked, "just this once?" He never held to his many self-imposed rules. Why should anyone else?

"When a new candidate emerges, each group must reveal themselves to him of their own accord," Doll Lady explained. "So you'll forgive me if I seem abstruse." Bill was uncertain if he was willing to forgive her, especially considering he had no idea what abstruse meant. "However, since the Powers handled themselves in such an uncouth manner, they have forfeited the right to stand on principal." Maybe abstruse meant swollen. No, that wouldn't make any sense. "And given your run-in with the Princess Brigade this morning, it's safe to say they're fair game," she said dismissively. "Everyone else, however, will remain anonymous ... for the moment." Bill was growing more confused by the second.

"Forgive me for interrupting your..." He searched for the right word, "abstrusity." It wasn't the right word. In fact, it wasn't a word at all. Nevertheless, he was undeterred. "But I really have no idea what you're talking about."

She gave him a patronizing pat on the shoulder. "Of course you don't, dear." She laughed, "If you did, you would either head for the hills or become completely unbearable." Bill liked hills. In fact, hills were sounding really good at that moment.

He attempted to piece it together. "So you represent the Small World Association."

"Society," she corrected him.

"Right. The Small World Society. And your group, the Cast of Thousands, the Powers and six other groups that you aren't allowed to even mentioned by name comprise the Council of the Nine?"

"Yes, sort of," she replied.

"And the purpose of the Nine is to identify candidates for ... something ... and at least a few of you think I'm a candidate?" He waited for her again.

"Go on," was her only reply.

"And whatever it is I'm a candidate for was triggered by my proposal to be the baker with his tray like always?" Doll Lady laughed at the notion.

"Oh, heavens no!" She leaned close to his face again. "We've had our eyes on you for a very long time, Bill Durmer." Bill had no reply. Sensing that he needed time to mull over such a revelation, Doll Lady continued, "Perhaps a bit of a history lesson would help," she said. She began to recount her own story.

"When I was a young woman, I studied to be an artist. I had no illusions of actually pursuing art as a long-term career, of course. It was the early 60's; things hadn't changed that much, yet. I—" She halted mid-sentence and turned around toward the back of the bus. "Stop interrupting!" she yelled at the rows of dolls. "I'll get to that!" Bill watched her warily in the mirror. He began to think of an exit strategy. Maybe he could stop at a resort and push her out. But no, he couldn't do that to an old lady, no mattered how unhinged she might be. Plus, that would leave him with a bus full of the dolls, and the dolls creeped him out. A lot. "Now where was I?" she asked of Bill, returning to her more genteel demeanor.

"You were saying you needed to get off at the next stop?" Bill goaded her. She laughed.

"They told me you were funny, Bill Durmer." She picked up where she had left off, "Oh yes, after college! I thought I might work as a graphic designer for a few years, meet a nice man, settle down and have children." She chuckled at the recollection of her own naivety. "I knew painting would be something to keep me sane when domestic life became a dreadful bore."

"Is domestic life ever a bore?" Bill asked rhetorically.

"Not if you do it well," she replied. "Not if you have vision."

"Which one happened?" Bill inquired, "The career or the dreadful bore?"

"Both," she answered, "and neither. I got a job doing illustrations for a small magazine. There I met a charming young editor. Boy meets girl, they fall in love, storybook wedding — the works. The publisher had a policy against married couples in the workplace. He claimed it a 'distraction.'" From the way she emphasized the word, Bill suspected there might be more of a story behind that policy, but he thought it best not to interrupt. She continued, "So I quit. After six months of setting up house, volunteering and being the dutiful wife, I knew I had to get another job. I prepared a fabulous dinner one Friday night. I had a brand new dress on, his favorite wine, his favorite dessert. I lit the candles and waited for my husband to come home so I could charm him and make my sales pitch."

"What happened?" Bill asked. "Please tell me he didn't shoot you down." Doll Lady was silent for a moment. Her voice cracked as she spoke.

"No. No, he didn't shoot me down." She picked up the Mexican boy doll, straightening his clothes as she continued. "Actually, I had asked him to stop and pick up some flowers for the table. He didn't want to. He was tired and, of course, had no idea what I was up to. But he stopped anyway." She halted, staring at the doll. She took a deep breath and carried on. "There was a robbery. He fancied himself such a tough guy," she laughed, "and he was such a tiny thing, really. He thought he could stop it." The Doll Lady couldn't go on.

"I'm so sorry," Bill offered gently. She sniffled so quietly Bill wondered whether he had heard it at all. After a few long minutes of riding in silence, she placed the doll back into the seat beside her and marshaled on with her story.

"I had no intention of marrying again. I had married my one true love. Why would I ever try to replace him? So I enrolled in graduate school. No sooner than I had, I found myself dropping out to take an apprenticeship with a very talented woman whom I hoped would become my mentor." Bill could hear the smile had returned to the Doll Lady's face as she recounted this, "You see, she had this whimsical little project she was working on for the World's Fair."

"It's a small world," Bill confirmed.

"Precisely."

"Mary Blair or Alice Davis?" Bill asked.

"It was Mary," she answered, leaning forward to observe Bill's reaction.

"Wow! You were mentored by THE Mary Blair?" Bill was thoroughly impressed. "What was she like?"

"Oh, she was a lovely woman," Doll Lady enthused, "so generous in spirit. And she had arguably the best sense of color of any artist who ever lived." Bill knew this was not hyperbole. Though very little of her signature style of drawing ever made it into the Disney films, her color designs filled the animated features of the early 1950s. She was brought back into the Disney fold after a period of freelancing to bring her unique design sense to the Pepsi pavilion for the 1964 World's Fair in New York. A paean to international unity featuring a cast of hundreds of audio animatronic children, "it's a small world" was one of the unqualified hits of the fair.

"Did you ever work with Walt Disney himself?" Bill heard himself ask the question. He sounded like a schoolboy. Doll Lady indulged him.

"I saw him once or twice when he would come 'round to check our progress. Mostly, we were an isolated bunch. We often joked that it really was a small world, and it seemed we were the only ones in it." She placed a kindly hand on his shoulder. "That was the beginning — just a bunch of workaholic Imagineers bonding over an impossible deadline and an idealistic dream. You know, when you believe in something, you believe in it all the way," she said, unconsciously paraphrasing the famous Disney quote. "When we were designing it, I think we had all come to believe that it really could change the world. Then, as we got near that deadline, it was such a mad rush. We had less than nine months to build it, you know. It was all black coffee and gin. We started calling ourselves the Small World Society way back then. If you heard someone say it was time for a proper 'society lunch,' you knew it was martini time." She chuckled at memories she dare not share with Bill or anyone.

"Mary, Rolly, and Marc and Alice really outdid themselves on that little boat ride," she reminisced, referring (in addition to Mary Blair) to Imagineers Rolly Crump, and Marc and Alice Davis. "You know more than ten million people rode it at the fair alone?"

"No," Bill said, admiring the old lady more with every word she spoke, "I had no idea." He couldn't bring himself to tell her that millions more people found the ride and its titular song tantamount to torture. Fortunately for him, considering the song was playing without ceasing at that very moment, he had developed a natural immunity to the effects of the Sherman Brothers' melody.

That immunity, in fact, had allowed him to torture friends and family for years. Whenever someone complained about having an earworm (a song stuck in their head), Bill would begin to sing a chorus of "it's a small world." The tune was unfailing in its ability to cure Stuck Song Syndrome — with one small side effect: it would plague the victim for days, even weeks, longer than the song it replaced.

"So, once the fair was over," Doll Lady continued, "and the ride had been moved to its home at Disneyland, the society was no more. That is, until Walt died. With his leadership gone, I think some people felt a need to protect his vision. A handful of us started meeting again after hours for drinks and discussing the future of the company. Since the core group had all worked together on the boat ride, naturally, we revived the society name." She sighed, "I don't think Mary was very comfortable with it, but the boat ride became so associated with her. So the whole society began to revolve around her."

Bill turned into the parking lot of Animal Kingdom Lodge. "I hate to interrupt, but I'm going to cut to the chase here." Bill hesitated for a moment. He was angry with himself for using the phrase "cut to the chase." He despised it, because it violated his rule against talking like self-absorbed 1980s movie producers, as opposed to self-absorbed 2010s movie producers who uttered phrases like "organically relatable." Those he had no problem with ... especially if they were interested in optioning his life story.

"Go ahead," Doll Lady coaxed him.

"What is the society's agenda, exactly?" he asked sheepishly.

"Agenda?" she feigned offense, "What must you think of me, Bill Durmer?"

"Nothing," he attempted to deflect the question, "It's just the Cast of Thousands..." She interrupted him.

"The Princess Brigade?" Her contempt was evident. "Is that what they did? Kidnap you and then give you, the kidnap victim, a list of demands?"

She lowered her voice, speaking more to herself. "Actors. Leave it to them to muck up the proper order of an abduction." Bill snickered under his breath. He really liked this crazy old woman's spirit.

"Their intent seemed good," he offered. She nodded, but seemed to be biting her tongue.

Finally, she declared, "Bill Durmer, know this: the Small World Society only wants to preserve the vision and heritage of Walt Disney for the children of the world. Nothing more. Nothing less."

"Fair enough," Bill shrugged. "Then why did you want to meet me?"

She patted his shoulder. "Simply that, Bill Durmer. I just wanted to meet you." She leaned back. "You can take us back now." Bill nodded and steered the bus back in the direction of her resort. They rode silently, save the looping track of "it's a small world" on the sound system. The hotel staff were ready and waiting for them. They unloaded the dolls as efficiently as they had loaded them earlier.

When they were done, Doll Lady stood up, gathered the two remaining dolls and faced Bill. He stood out of respect. She smiled up at him. She tucked both dolls under one arm and offered him her hand. "Until we meet again, Bill Durmer." Bill pushed her hand aside and leaned down to give her a hug.

"It's been my pleasure," Bill said, smiling at her. "You're a..." There was no other word than the one he was holding back. "Well, you're a doll."

She reached up to touch Bill's face. "When Mary passed her word on to me, I never thought I'd live to see this day. Jennifer was right about you." She smiled at him and stepped off the bus.

"I don't suppose you're going to tell me what any of that means," Bill chided.

"Not a chance," was her playful reply. "You'll know soon enough." To the dolls she said, "Time to go, my little rubberheads." With her parting mystery still lingering unanswered, she turned and walked away.

Chapter Seventeen:
Keep the Home Fish Mounds Burning

"What have you done to my family this time!?" Nancy bellowed as she burst unannounced into Katherine's kitchen. Katherine, accustomed to such displays of incivility from her sister-in-law, continued methodically fixing lunches for the kids.

"Nice to see you, too, Nancy," she said dryly. "Your soothing voice is a light to my otherwise dark and dreary world."

"Don't try to win me over with your words," Nancy replied. Despite her efforts to stay fit, she had neglected to exercise her irony muscle for years. "Why is my brother a bus driver?"

"Is this a riddle? If so, I don't get it." Katherine had learned long ago that indulging Nancy's angry tirades only fed the beast. So she opted for mockery instead. It wasn't the most loving response, but it was fun.

Nancy let out an exasperated sigh as she sat in one of the barstools and flung herself across the countertop in melodramatic anguish. The Durmer family photo albums were filled with photos of Nancy in this exact position at the bar. Christmases and birthdays, funerals and family reunions, no family gathering or special occasion was too big or too small for a signature Nancy hissy fit. Never one to miss an opportunity, Katherine quickly snapped a shot with her phone and sent it to Bill. It wasn't her best work, but she felt it really captured the immediacy of the moment.

"This family is falling apart, and you don't even care," Nancy whined.

Knowing full well it was a pointless exercise, Katherine nonetheless tried to reason with her. "Oh, don't be so melodramatic, Nancy. It's only temporary."

"I don't expect you to understand," Nancy groaned. "It's not like you have siblings yourself."

"I'm the youngest of five." Katherine had to remind Nancy of this at least once a year. Typically, it was at a birthday party. Nancy, after failing to recognize one of Katherine's sisters for the millionth time, would remark that she never knew Katherine had any siblings. She would then admonish Katherine in front of all the party guests, accusing her of being too ashamed of her sisters to even talk about them. The timing of this insult was crucial, so she would wait until everyone was gathered to sing "Happy Birthday." Bill or Kenny would pull her aside to explain how inappropriate her behavior was. Nancy would then fling herself prostrate across the bar ... just in time to be captured in the photo of the birthday boy or girl blowing out the candles. It was a time-honored Durmer tradition.

"I spent all morning calling ladies from the JL to see what they knew." Nancy believed referring to the Junior League by its initials made it sound more hip and egalitarian. It didn't. "Fortunately, no one seems to have gotten wind of our situation just yet."

Katherine, ignoring the melodrama, called the kids into the kitchen. Clay ran in, followed by a speed-crawling Clementine. Once both were in their seats and eating, she turned her attention back to Nancy. "Why would the Junior League even care what Bill was doing? It's not like *I'm* a member."

Nancy laughed at the very notion. "Well that goes without saying," she snipped. "But you don't know these people. They have spies everywhere. They're like the CIA with tea biscuits."

"Speaking of tea." Katherine poured Nancy a tall glass of iced tea.

"Is this sweet?" Nancy asked. "Because I'm so stressed out all I can think about is refined sugar." Katherine nodded, and Nancy downed half the glass in one gulp. "That's gonna cost me another half-hour of KB."

"KB" stood for Kick-Ballates, a fictional exercise regimen Nancy had created that combined kick boxing with ballet and Pilates. Though she had claimed in the Junior League newsletter that her system was sweeping the nation, she remained its only adherent. There had been an initial flurry of interest from hipsters who believed it a Greek form of kickball. But when Nancy told them to take their "tiny fedoras, mangy scarves and 'Jew tatts' back to the juice bar," they savaged the studio with negative reviews on an obscure message board. Fortunately for Nancy, the site's only readers were other hipsters who had no interest in trendy exercise programs anyhow.

One of the reviewers, a semi-pro soccer player with double master's degrees in comparative philosophy and linguistics, managed to parlay the crafty wordplay of his review into a pilot order for a sitcom. It was titled *Kickballay* and was the story of a haughty, down-on-her-luck ballet dancer who returned to her small, Southern hometown to find herself working as a middle school gym coach. Alabama native Courtney Cox was attached to star. Nancy's copyright infringement suit was still pending.

She took another swig of tea. "Totally worth it." Finishing off the tea, she refocused her ire on Katherine. "How could you let him do that? It just sickens me to think of him pumping diesel and telling fat people to 'squeeze in, there's room for everybody.' Please. If fat people could squeeze in, they wouldn't be taking the bus."

Katherine rubbed her forehead trying to make sense of that last bit. She couldn't. Nancy had finally done it. She had taken snootiness into the realm of the abstract and absurd. And who ever said contempt couldn't be an art form?

"He's your brother, Nancy." She didn't even know why she was trying at this point. "Maybe you should be a little more accepting."

"I'm accepting! Darn it, I'm the Jermaine Jackson of tolerance!" (She probably meant Jesse Jackson, but no one could be sure.) "I spent the whole day on that stupid committee of Auggie's working with," she lowered her voice to a whisper as if uttering an obscenity, "Baptists!"

✳✳✳

The so-called stupid committee had been convened to respond to the legal and public relations firestorm created by Mayor August "Auggie" Pomeroy's previous stupid committee, convened to respond to the Black Jubilee. Auggie had sworn the morning after the Jubilee to act "swiftly and decisively" in dealing with the crisis. Swiftly and decisively became recklessly and impulsively when he hired a flotilla of barges to haul the oil-stained seafood out into the Gulf and dump it. The Coast Guard, catching wind of this scheme (not a difficult task, literally or metaphorically — Auggie had bragged about it on national news for days), blockaded the city, preventing the barges from departing.

Proven incompetent and ill-informed of federal environmental protection laws, the mayor delegated his next move to a hand-picked committee of Decent Chancers. The first day of committee meetings had been spent intensely debating a name for their proposal. Auggie had tentatively named it "Project Fishy." One contingent of committee members rallied behind "Operation Breaking Free," while sailing enthusiasts preferred the more poetic "Tacking on Winds of Change." It was finally dubbed, in an unfortunate compromise, "Operation Breaking Fishy Winds."

Their inspired solution was to dump the mounds of rotting fish back onto the city's beaches and set them afire. This was executed under the cover of darkness, because Auggie's assurances that it was "totally legit" didn't inspire much confidence. They also hoped the massive bonfires might attract curious interstate travelers to the town. It did. A convoy of EPA officials was crossing the Bayway at the exact moment the mounds were lit, casting flames hundreds of feet into the sky.

Mayor Auggie's plan of delegating responsibility to the committee worked flawlessly. However, with his first round of scapegoats now awaiting indictments, he needed fresh meat to deal with the crisis caused by his previous attempts at crisis response. The new committee had thus far only achieved one tangible result: paying $90,000 to a Birmingham ad firm for branding their nonexistent plan as "Project Disaspportunity." Nancy had promised they could save money on an animated logo by enlisting Bill to create it. His recent flight from reality was a black eye for her and meant they would have to pay a post-production house full rate — something ad agencies and their clients are loath to do.

✳✳✳

"So what is the plan?" Katherine asked. "I can't even take the kids outside." For nearly a week, a dense fog of acrid, black fish smoke had clung to the town, as the massive mounds of rotting sea death continued to smolder. The town had become a national disgrace and a laughing stock, prompting late-night comedians to refer to it derisively as "Not A Chance."

"There is no plan," Nancy admitted. "If only Bill were here. None of this would have ever happened."

"Actually, he thinks the Black Jubilee was his fault," Katherine confided in her, "because of the store closing."

"That's preposterous," Nancy replied dismissively. She silently hoped

Katherine's lack of society connections would mean she hadn't seen the latest Junior League newsletter. The cover article was titled, "Nancy Durmer Thompson Claims 'It's All My Brother's Fault.'" Nancy had initiated the interview as part of Project Disaspportunity, hoping to shame Bill into taking a more active role in the town's cleanup efforts. But with her brother now employed in a blue-collar profession, she wished she had stuck to her tried and true motto of, "when it's time to talk about family, talk about any family but your own."

Katherine took a seat opposite Nancy and refreshed her own tea glass. She picked at a tuna salad on her plate as she talked. "I think the stress of the store, the whole Jubilee debacle, about to turn forty … it all was too much for him." She sighed and tried to convince herself that what followed was true. "I think a little time away will help him figure out his next move." Nancy disagreed.

"You're being too easy on him." She propped up on her elbows and repeatedly jabbed the countertop with her index finger to emphasize her points. "I know my brother. You have to lead him. He's a dreamer. If left to his own devices, there's no telling what kind of hare-brained vision he'd chase after. It's like I always tell my dancers: creativity is a wild beast. You can't let it run free. You have to cage it to make it useful." Katherine couldn't decide if what Nancy said was incredibly idiotic or incredibly brilliant. And that very fact scared her senseless. A thought occurred to Nancy. "Does this have anything to do with those weird towel people?"

"No! Nothing like that." Katherine was not about to tell her about Gaston and the Council of the Nine. Or the threat from the Powers. Or the mysterious D-notes from an anonymous adviser. Or about pig-napping princesses. Or strange old ladies who traveled with hundreds of dolls. In fact, she chose not to say anything else other than, "No."

Nancy's clutch vibrated across the countertop. She grunted in frustration, "Ugh! What now?" Removing her phone, she read an incoming text. "Wonderful. Emergency committee meeting. There goes another three hours of my life." She stood, finished off her tea and headed toward the door. She stopped just short of it. "Kat?"

Katherine was struck dumb. In the two decades they had known each other, Nancy had never addressed her in such a familiar way. "Yes, Nancy?"

"Talk to Billy." Nancy's icy demeanor thawed just a bit. "The town needs him right now. I…" She couldn't bring herself to finish the thought.

She looked past Katherine to the kitchen table. "Bye kids! Auntsy Nancy loves you!" Clem jumped up and down in her high chair squealing babble, and Clay waved frantically. Nancy turned and darted out the door before her sentimentality could get the better of her.

"Bye, Nance!" Katherine called after her. She hated that their relationship was so contentious. In difficult times, it would have been nice to know she could call on Nancy as a true friend. She wondered if Nancy had any true friends at all. The phone rang. Katherine checked the caller ID. To the kids she said, "It's Daddy and Cleary!" They danced and cheered and chanted the names of their wandering family members. Katherine clamped her free ear shut to hear over the din. "Hello?"

"Hi, honey!" Bill yelled into his phone, half in reaction to the clamor of his children on the other end and half to make sure he was heard over the clamor on his. He was lounging by the pool, watching Cleary play with some other kids her age. All the parents around him were either sunbathing with telltale white cables dangling from their ears or engrossed in their own conversations, so no one even gave notice to his volume. "How is everything?"

Katherine meandered into the family room and plopped on the couch. "Meh. Same ol' same ol'." Then she added, "Your sister just left."

"Just left? You haven't even had time to get the smell of brimstone out of the drapes, yet. I should let you go."

"William Durmer!" Katherine scolded him, "That's your sister you're talking about."

"Yes, I know," he replied, "hence my concern." His sardonic wit was not so easily quenched. "And why are you defending her? What has she done to you? Has she dangled any pocket watches in front of your eyes while having you count backwards from ten?" Whenever Bill thought of his wit as sardonic, he always recalled the etymology of the word. It referred to a Sardinian plant that, when ingested, would cause violent laughter ending only in death. His wit had yet to clear that high bar, but he secretly hoped someday it might.

"Bill, I think she really misses you." Katherine's empathy was in high gear.

"I take it she heard about my job," Bill guessed correctly. "She's just using you to control me. It galls her that I did all this without even consulting her. Listen, I know my sister. You have to fight her. If she wants you to go left, go right as fast as you can."

"Wow, you guys have such a healthy dynamic." Katherine preferred ironic to sardonic. She explained to her husband how he was desperately needed back home and how Project Disaspportunity was, "all disass and no portunity."

"I'm not giving up on my dream just to come home and animate a logo for some lame PR stunt," he argued.

"It's not that. They need some real leadership, Bill," she implored. "The town is foundering. I know you could help. I believe in you. And like it or not, so does your sister."

"Kat, I'm not a leader." Bill didn't care who believed in him. He didn't believe in himself. "I'm a behind-the-scenes kind of guy. And given my recent run of luck, who would listen to me anyway?"

Katherine's best arguments about Bill being a fixture in the community, someone who could unite the town behind a well-reasoned plan and the smartest man she ever knew fell on deaf ears.

"Why not file a claim with the oil company?" Bill asked. Katherine explained that Auggie's second plan, which she derisively called Operation Fish Fry, meant that they were no longer eligible for those claims. "Then find a sponsor," Bill suggested, "a company with ties to the state and in need of an image makeover, maybe a carmaker who's had a string of recalls or something like that. They clean up the town and come out heroes. Everybody wins."

"Bill," she lowered her voice so the kids couldn't hear her concern, "*I* need you. It's horrible here." Her voice began to crack. "We can't even go outside."

"Why don't you bring the kids down here? We've got the room."

"No, it's too small, and..." She hesitated. She was reticent to finish a thought that might wound too deeply. Nevertheless, she felt it had to be said. "I can't run away from this." Bill was silent on the other end. He knew full well her meaning. He took a deep breath.

"I can." He hung up. He sulked in his lounge chair, while back home Katherine sank down into the sofa and wept.

***

Across town, Nancy arrived at One-Eyed Jack's toy store for the last-second committee meeting. She entered, but saw no one.

"Hello? Jack?" Nothing. She continued through the store, past Jungle Land, the Milky Way and Homeland until she arrived in the Barnyard at the back of the store. Still there was no one. "Jack?" she called out again to no avail. She heard the whir of a servo and looked up to see Snooty McOinker tilting his head down to look at her. Nancy was not given to flights of fancy, nor was she easily spooked. But she could swear the pig was staring right at her, and that thoroughly creeped her out. Then the pig snorted, causing a startled Nancy to nearly tumble over a child-sized bench behind her. Righting herself, she looked at the pig again. Its stare had followed her. Then it spoke.

"Hello, Nancy Durmer Thompson," the pig half-snorted in his cartoon voice. Nancy shrieked.

"Jack!" She yelled back toward the storeroom, "This isn't funny! Come out here!" Under her breath, she added, "You little one-eyed freak of nature."

"Jack isn't here, Nancy," Snooty said. Nancy was over it.

"Who are you?" she demanded of the pig. "What kind of sick joke is this?"

"Don't worry about who I am," Snooty replied. "We need to talk about your brother." Well, now she couldn't leave. She sat down on a little bench for a long chat with a talking pig-bot.

Chapter Eighteen:
Nine Words of Nine Words

It had been several days since Bill had last seen Red, and the cast members at Transit were of no help. Likewise, he hadn't experienced any new encounters with the Council of the Nine since Doll Lady bade him farewell two days earlier. If he were honest with himself, he was disappointed by these two uneventful days. Although he had set out for Orlando with every intention of blending in, he found the attention he received from the Nine had become his favored form of entertainment. Without all the subterfuge and intrigue, he was just an ordinary bus driver. Making matters worse, he hadn't spoken to Katherine since he had hung up on her. At first, not calling her was a matter of principal. Now it was a matter of shame.

Toward the end of a slow afternoon of running cast member/VIP routes, Bill found himself driving an empty bus from stop to stop. Just as he was about to pull away from Boardwalk Resort, again with no cast members aboard, a familiar voice called out for him to reopen the door. Bill looked and saw Red trotting toward the bus. Bill thought again how spry the old man was. Red moved as if he were weightless, evidencing no signs of exertion. Bill opened the door for him, and Red hopped aboard with the same carefree ease.

"You a runner, Red?" Bill asked. "Because you don't even seem to be breathing hard."

"Good genes, I suppose," Red shrugged modestly. "Never been much for running, but I was a bit of a sailor at one time." Red gazed into the distance, a wry smile on his face. "But that was a lifetime ago." It occurred to Bill that this detail about sailing might constitute the most revealing piece of Red's story he'd heard to date. Perhaps that was a good thing. Maybe people spent too much time yammering on about their own stories, losing themselves in exposition rather than propelling the action of their lives forward. A person's actions invariably revealed more about their true character than any multitude of words. Still, he could do with some good old-fashioned exposition right about now.

"Where are we headed?" Bill asked.

"Take me where you took the Doll Lady," was Red's cheeky reply.

Bill smirked and replied, "Around in circles it is, then." At Red's urging, he recounted the incident with the Cast of Thousands and summarized the conversation with the Doll Lady. "There were a couple things that she and Snow White said that stood out to me as odd."

"Only a couple?" Red asked, sounding impressed.

"Well," Bill shrugged, "odd is becoming a relative term. Snow White said something about the 'new son,' but she never explained what that meant. And Doll Lady made a reference to Mary, I assume she meant Mary Blair, giving her a 'word.' What does that mean?"

"Giving her word about what?" Red asked, leading him. He was testing the younger man, determining whether he was ready for the mother of all expositions.

"No, not giving her word like that. Giving *a* word. It was like," Bill hesitated to say it, fearing both that he was dead wrong and that he would sound dead foolish, "like a prophecy. She said the word had been passed down to her." Red squeezed his face with his fingers, pulling his mouth downward, wrestling with himself for the right course of action.

"Ahhh, I suppose the rules don't apply to me anymore," he said to himself. "Bill Durmer, my boy, it's high time you got some answers. I hope you're fueled up. This may take a while."

"We're good to go," Bill replied. "Let's go for a drive."

"Well then," Red leaned forward, a mischievous gleam in his eye, "let me tell you the story of the Prophecy of the New Son."

✳✳✳

Red began by explaining that as Walt Disney aged there had been a growing concern that he had not named a successor. Some insiders rued the fact that Walt and his wife, Lillian, had not produced a male heir, their only children being two daughters. To Bill, this supposed concern about an heir sounded more like it belonged in the story notes for a Disney princess film than in the boardroom of a major corporation. Red assured Bill that it was most certainly real, yet Bill still suspected the old man of adding his own dramatic embellishments.

"But his brother took over after his death, right?" Bill countered, "And later his son-in-law?"

"True, but Roy was never the visionary Walt was. He was a business-man first and foremost. He stuck around long enough to see Uncle Walt's vision for this place made real," Red said, waving his hand about to refer-ence the resort, "at least in part. And Ron..." Red hesitated as he began to discuss Ron Miller, Walt's son-in-law and one-time CEO of the compa-ny. "Ron was in there at an unfortunate time. That whole situation was unfortunate." Bill thought he caught a glimpse of Red wiping a tear from his eye. "Anyway, Walt knew, even if he had a son, that no one raised in the spotlight and privilege of Hollywood could ever be what he had been. Everything he was, everything he did was both a reaction to the struggles of his childhood and a reflection of his vision of a better life. He had that unique ability to be both looking forward and looking back at the same time, embracing the best of both."

"That's a good way to put it," Bill noted. He had always found in Walt Disney a fascinating dichotomy between the nostalgist and the futurist, between Main Street, USA and Tomorrowland.

Red continued, explaining that Walt knew anyone who took his place would need to be part artist, part entrepreneur and part engineer with a visionary sensibility and an unwavering sense of "what worked." He quoted Ron Miller as saying that for the genius of one Walt it took 50 geniuses to replace him. The more Red talked, the more Bill suspected the old man might be pulling out all the stops to craft the rumor of the century, with himself, a fellow bus driver, as the willing mark.

"You remember what I told you of the Council of the Nine," Red in-quired of Bill, "how they sort of grew up around the Nine Old Men?" Bill did remember. How could he forget? "Well, that's not the whole truth," Red confessed. "I mean it is true, from a certain point of view."

"And what point of view is that?" Bill asked the question in a joking tone, but he honestly didn't know what to believe anymore. Was Red lying before? Was he lying now? What was truth, and what was a tall tale? The sad fact was he had to trust the old bus driver, because everything that had happened was far too strange to be a fiction.

"I wasn't sure you were ready to hear what I have to tell you then," Red answered in his own defense, "and I couldn't be certain the Nine had set their sights on you as the one." Then he added, "But I knew they eventually would." Bill was growing weary of the obfuscation.

"The one what, Red?" he snapped.

"Patience." Red assured Bill that the answers he wanted were coming, some immediately, others in due course. "On November 30th of sixty-six, Uncle Walt passed out at home and was rushed to the hospital."

"Right," Bill recalled this story from the various Disney biographies he had read. "He died two weeks later, in a hospital room with a view of the studio."

"At St. Joseph. Exactly." Bill had impressed him again. "Very good, Bill Durmer. But all of that is official history. What you don't know, what only a handful of people have ever known, is what happened in those two weeks." Red explained that when Walt awoke in the hospital that final day of November, he claimed he had seen something, a vision. Weak and wracked with pain from the recent removal of his left lung and the growing tumors in his chest, he struggled to scrawl out a sketch of that vision.

Roy brought pencils and animation paper from the studio. For nearly two days, Walt attempted to capture his vision. He hadn't drawn anything in decades. Regardless, the famous Walt Disney quest for perfection was in full sway. Rumor had it Walt told Roy at the time that the vision was clearer and more precise than anything he had ever seen in all of his years as an artist. Never before — not as a boy painting with tar on the side of his family's farmhouse in Marceline, not as a Red Cross driver stationed in Europe adorning German helmets as souvenirs for GIs, not even in the early days of the Disney Brothers Studio when he was animating Oswald the Lucky Rabbit — had he known so precisely what it was he needed to draw.

When he felt he had the best version of the sketch he could draw, Walt sealed it in an envelope and had Roy destroy the multitude of drafts. Over the remaining twelve days of his life, he would drift in and out of consciousness. Each time he came around, he would jot down a few words that had come to him while he was out.

"The prophecy?" Bill guessed. Red nodded.

"Nine words of prophecy, each comprised of nine words. Together they predict the coming of the New Son. The next Walt Disney." Red let the words hang heavy in the air.

Bill sighed, "And they think I'm the one."

"Yes," Red confirmed. "And so do I." The old man squeezed Bill's shoulder like a proud father. Bill shook his head in bemusement and began to laugh. At first it was only a chuckle, but it grew the more he thought about the absurdity of his situation until he laughed so hard he cried.

"You gotta go on with the story, Red," Bill said between peals of laughter, "because I gotta know how they all screwed this up so badly." He took several deep breaths and tried to focus on his driving to calm himself.

Red resumed, "On December 14th, the day before his death, Walt called his brother to the room. There, he gave Roy the nine words of prophecy, each in its own envelope and addressed to one of the Nine Old Men. The envelope containing the sketch he gave to Roy with strict instructions: it was not to be opened until all nine word bearers unanimously agreed on a candidate to be the New Son."

Bill interrupted, "Why 'new son?' What does that mean?"

"They say it refers to a line in the prophecy itself," Red answered, "though there are so many rumors about what exactly the prophecy says, it's hard to say."

"What about Kurt Russell?" Bill asked in a seeming non-sequitur.

"You do know your arcane Disney history, Bill Durmer, I'll give you that." He referred to an old anecdote that the final words Walt wrote prior to his death were "Kurt Russell." The actor was contracted to the Disney studio at the time of Walt's death. "It really happened," Red confirmed. "Roy thought at first that the boy might be the one, but he just didn't fit the prophecy. No one knows why Walt wrote it. There were several false starts over the coming months. But they came to realize that some lines of the prophecy just couldn't be deciphered yet."

"Why is that?"

"Because they hadn't built the means to do so." Red explained that the Nine Old Men determined that certain lines of the prophecy referred specifically to aspects of attractions the Imagineers were working on for the parks. Former animator Marc Davis, one of the Nine Old Men, was then a senior Imagineer with WED. Working with the bearers of the problematic passages, Davis integrated tests into those attractions to help identify the New Son. "At first, the tests were planned for Disneyland, Mineral King and here," Red said, referring to the two extant parks and the planned Mineral King resort that was scrapped shortly after Walt's death. "But they realized it was just good horse sense to have them all in one location." Just as the bus drove through the entrance gate for the Magic Kingdom, Red said, "Unbeknownst to 99.999 percent of the guests, this park is an elaborate test designed specifically to find the New Son."

Bill found himself unable to speak. He thought of the adage: "If you can't say anything nice, let Nancy say it for you." Given that his sister was not there to do his dirty work, he remained silent. While he found Red's story fascinating, he wanted to shake these people out of their obsession. He was as much an admirer of Walt as anyone, but he believed visionaries like Walt Disney rise to that level because of their uniqueness. If their particular combinations of talent, personality and vision could be replicated, they wouldn't be icons. As much as a part of him wished it could be true, he simply didn't believe it.

Red could see the conflict on Bill's face, but chose to continue on his current tack. "When it became clear that a successor might not appear for years, the Nine Old Men realized they might have to pass their words down to new bearers. As the second and third generations of word bearers took over, they began to squabble and fight, distrustful of one another. By then, entire sub-cultures had grown up around them. And everybody had their own agenda. That's when they created the Council of the Nine and wrote the rules."

"What sort of rules?"

"Well," Red scratched his head as if trying to recall a distant memory. Bill suspected this was either a part of the act and that Red knew them by rote or that he was making them up as he went along. "First and foremost, no word bearer may retain their place on the council if they betray the company or the Disney name. Second, after the unanimity of the original Nine Old Men was lost, it was determined that no word bearer should know the words of prophecy given to the others. That's not to say everyone sticks by that rule. In fact, it's almost become a sport to send spies into opposing camps to ferret out their given words." He began to chuckle. "Heck, we've had double agents, triple agents. We even had a nine-way spy once."

"A nonuple spy," Bill commented.

"Nonuple?" Red asked as if Bill were the one talking nonsense.

"Don't dig too deeply in my mind, Red," Bill cautioned. "It's a weird, tangled place full of useless information and bad ideas." Red was amused by Bill's self-mockery. "Alright, rules — keep 'em coming," Bill said. Red obliged.

"Let's see," he began to recite them as if memorized from an official handbook. "A word bearer may pick his or her own successor. If a successor is not named prior to the demise of a word bearer, the remaining Council members must unanimously appoint one. A word bearer may not reveal the identity of other members of the Council or their support organizations, especially to a candidate. When a candidate is identified, the Council must convene to test that candidate and decide his or her fate." Bill raised his hand like a kid in school.

"Point of order," he said, halting Red. "There are more than six billion people in the world, hundreds of millions of adults in the US alone. How do you identify candidates in a world that big?"

"Good question. The Nine Old Men recognized this problem, too. The prophecy itself gives some clues as to geography. But even that was fairly broad. So they created a..." He was careful to use precisely the right word. "A *mechanism* to gauge a candidate's suitability as measured against the entire prophecy."

"Mechanism?" Bill pondered the word choice. To him, it seemed Red's story was falling in on itself.

"I can't really say more than that, but you'll understand soon enough. If one of the word bearers, or someone in their camp, thinks they have found a candidate, they report it back to the Council, and the mechanism is activated."

Bill was determined to learn more or to expose the ruse in the doing. "Okay, the rules prevent a word bearer from revealing one another to the candidate. And we can assume that extends to the groups as well. But there's nothing to prevent an outsider from telling me who the word bearers are." He moved in for the kill. "So tell me."

"Clever, very clever," Red admitted. "You're right in assuming I'm not a word bearer or part of one of the groups. At least I'm not anymore. However, there are some things I think you're just going to have to learn in due time." Bill wasn't giving up.

"Okay, then. I know three groups have already revealed themselves to me: the Powers, the Cast of Thousands and the Small World Society. Doll Lady is clearly the word bearer for the Small Worlders. I'm not sure about the other two. Since they've already come forward, you can tell me about them."

"Yes, I can," Red conceded. He began with the Small World Society. Walt had given their word of prophecy to animation director Woolie Reitherman. He, in turn, had passed it down to Mary Blair for reasons unknown. The prevailing rumor was he was so moved upon seeing Blair's giant mural in the Contemporary Resort that he passed the word down to her on the spot. As Bill already knew, Blair passed it down to the Doll Lady. Red stubbornly refused to give her actual name, but did offer this tantalizing tidbit: "It was the Doll Lady who suggested you as a candidate in the first place." The logical conclusion that someone in Decent Chance had been spying on him for the Small World Society came as no surprise to Bill. The town's penchant for meddling was well known. Bill even suggested the chamber of commerce adopt the slogan, "We're in your business." It was still under consideration. Irony was a lost art in Decent Chance.

To animator Eric Larson, Walt had given the word now represented by the Cast of Thousands. Larson had instituted a training and recruitment program purportedly to bring a new generation of top-flight animators into the studio. His ulterior motive, however, was to use the program to identify potential candidates. When that effort proved fruitless, he passed the word along to his protégé, Don Bluth.

"Bluth, of course, left the studio because he felt they had lost their creative vision," Red recounted. He then shifted into gossip mode, "But I heard he became obsessed with the idea that he was the New Son, and he did everything he could to influence the rest of the Council to choose him. When they refused, he took his crayons and went home." Red added a caveat, "But that's just a rumor. Take it for what it is."

Bluth, in obedience to the first rule of the Council, gave up his word to Henry Selick, the eventual director of *The Nightmare Before Christmas*. Selick didn't believe in the prophecy and passed the word along to friend Tim Burton. Burton only held it for a short time before leaving the studio. Since that time, it had passed from one Cal Arts alum to another. "I can't tell you who has it now," Red said, "but I can tell you that he probably got it by accident. I'm not even sure he remembers that he is a word bearer, to be honest. The Cast of Thousands only came about out of necessity, to compensate for his disinterest."

"And the Powers?" Bill asked. "Who are they?"

"They're not to be trifled with; I'll tell you that much," Red scowled. His disdain for the group seethed through his every word. "Their real name is the Mintz-Powers Group."

"As in Charles Mintz and Pat Powers," Bill groused. "Lovely." Charles Mintz and Pat Powers were fixtures in the early days of animation and had only one thing in common: both had betrayed Walt Disney. Mintz worked for and eventually married Margaret Winkler, the distributor of Disney's Oswald the Lucky Rabbit series. Unfortunately for the Disneys, Universal Pictures, the studio releasing the Oswald shorts, retained ownership of the character. Convinced Walt himself was not instrumental to the creation of the shorts, Mintz hired away most of Walt's key animators and secured the contract to produce the films. He used Walt's own people against him.

Powers, one of the founders of Universal, had sold Disney the sound system used to create "Steamboat Willie" and the studio's other pioneering efforts in sync-sound cartoons. When Disney failed to find a distributor for the Mickey Mouse and Silly Symphonies shorts, Powers stepped in. On one fateful New York trip, Walt confronted Powers about the studio's share of box office receipts, which Powers was behind in paying. In response, Powers hired away Walt's best animator and close friend, Ub Iwerks — the only animator to remain loyal to Walt during the Mintz exodus — to start a new animation studio. Powers had made the same mistake as Mintz: believing Walt Disney inconsequential to the success of his own studio.

"Their only purpose in life is to denigrate, discredit and destroy the Walt Disney name," Red lamented. "I can't say any more. You'll have to learn the rest for yourself. But beware: if the rest of the Council believe you to be the New Son, the Mintz-Powers Group will stop at nothing to get rid of you."

Bill didn't say it, but his only thought was they wouldn't have to do much. Even if everything Red said were true, he had no intention of becoming anyone's savior. He just wanted to blend in.

Chapter Nineteen:
Just Call Me Mommy

The following morning, Bill needed to clear his head from Red's great mythological download. So he and Cleary arose early to be at the gates of the Magic Kingdom for the park's opening. Given that Red claimed the Magic Kingdom to be an elaborate litmus test for finding the second coming of Walt Disney, any of the other parks would have worked much better for cleansing his thoughts. What he wouldn't admit to Cleary was that he was actually acting on the instruction of yet another D-note. He didn't want her to believe he was basing his life's decisions on what were essentially glorified greeting cards. (Because basing his life on a nonexistent coded message in a cartoon was so much more respectable.)

"I can't believe we've been here for two weeks and haven't been in the parks at all," Cleary noted. On edge and half-expecting to be hogtied and suspended from Tinkerbell's zip line by a gang of angry barbershop singers at any moment, Bill became defensive.

"Yeah, well, I've been working," he argued, "and abducted. Anyway, we're here now."

"And we can come back as much as we want," Cleary mistakenly enthused. Actually, only Bill would get unlimited admissions. Cleary could only come back eleven more times. Or maybe it was two more times if the rest of the family joined them. Then again, Clementine may not have counted against the family admissions. Bill was unclear on the specifics, and the math was making his head hurt. So he kept his mouth shut and let Cleary enjoy the dream.

As they walked along Main Street, Bill found himself pointing out the little details on the storefronts as he had on their previous trip. When he realized what he was doing, he feared he was becoming as obsessive as the groups that made up the Council of the Nine.

"I can't do this," he said, more to himself than to Cleary.

"Can't do what?" She had been enjoying herself. Whenever her father became talkative about a topic that fascinated him, she believed he was at his happiest. And she hadn't believed him to be truly happy in months.

"Let's just not talk about Disney trivia or Disney history or any of it. It feels like I'm at work," he rationalized. "Let's just be dumb tourists and enjoy everything on a surface level." At least a dozen dumb tourists around him were savvy enough to think he meant them and took offense. Bill, noticing their angry glares, pulled Cleary away down Main Street. "If I wanted people to look at me that way," he joked, "I wouldn't have broken out of prison."

"What?" Cleary, though mature beyond her years, could be a little slow on the uptake when it came to her parents' sense of humor.

"Nothing." Bill worried she might actually believe him an ex-con. His dark humor had backfired with her before. When she was three, Cleary had gone through a phase of not wanting to eat meat. As his daughter, she would likely have a pale complexion anyhow. If she grew up to be a vegan, the combination of a low-iron diet and genetics might render his daughter completely transparent. So he did what any parent with irrational fears might do: he told his toddler the last time they had a daughter who wouldn't eat her meat, they locked her in the attic. Cleary didn't know he was joking. Because she was three. For several months, Bill and Katherine tried to convince Cleary she didn't actually have a sister living in the attic. Running out of options and fearing she would blurt out the story at preschool, they chose to have another child in the hope of distracting her. Welcome Clay, the child born out of the fear of family court judges with no sense of humor.

"I've got an idea!" he bellowed. Redirection — that would take her mind off prison. Bill introduced Cleary to the time-honored bus driver tradition of creating outlandish rumors. He handled the first few to give her a sense of how the game was played. While admiring the Partners statue of Walt and Mickey, Bill convinced a family from Dubuque that Disney had created the mouse on the advice of a therapist. According to Bill's rumor, Walt was learning to confront a decades-old fear of rodents stemming from a childhood incident in which he fell down a rat-filled well.

As they admired the mosaics in Cinderella Castle, he met a group of local women on a moms' day out at the park. Their matching pink t-shirts proclaimed them "Free at Last." Bill found it mildly offensive that a group of Caucasian and Asian-American women would co-opt a signature slogan from the Civil Rights Movement just because they were happy to abandon their children for the day. But there was no time to admonish them for their poor parenting choices. He was too busy proving to his daughter that he was the better liar.

Seeing the women as easy marks, he told them the Brothers Grimm version of Cinderella had featured beautiful stepsisters rather than ugly ones and a magic, wish-granting bird rather than a fairy godmother. (This part was true.) Then he claimed the Disney studio had based their version on a distant cousin of Walt's who had dissociative personality disorder. According to Bill, her personalities, presumably inspired by her love of the fairy tale, had included ugly stepsisters, a talking mouse and a fairy godmother. And he claimed the glass slipper, differing from the Grimms' gold slipper, represented the fragile nature of sanity. They politely acted interested and excused themselves, giggling like schoolgirls and glancing back at Bill as they walked away. Bill had a sudden and unexpected flashback to his adolescence. He offered Cleary some unsolicited advice: "If a boy shows up on the first day of school in a pinstripe seersucker suit, remember that his mother made him wear it. It's not his fault." Cleary backed away slowly and avoided eye contact.

As they emerged from the castle into Fantasyland, she questioned the ethics of their game. "Isn't this like lying, Daddy?"

"No, we're just telling stories." He lied. Lies to cover up lies. Lies to justify lying, in fact. But, he needed to maintain what little dignity he could. At this point, he feared his other two children would only ever remember him as "that funny man who brought the fish plague." Cleary was his last chance at a legacy.

"It's no different than a girl dressing up in a blue gown and calling herself Cinderella," he said, borrowing Red's argument.

"But, guests know that Cinderella works here," she countered. "They just think you're another guest. And it's not like you're doing it to entertain them. You're actually trying to deceive them." She had a point. She always had a point. But Bill was not so easily swayed. He was an intelligent man, a man who could present a well-reasoned argument based on sound logic and biblical principle:

"Yeah, but it's funny." Bill really needed to get back into church.

Reluctantly accepting her father's poor defense of lying, Cleary tried her hand at the game. Bill quickly learned that his daughter was quite adept at elaborate deceptions, which made him fear for his future. While waiting in line for the Dumbo ride, she convinced two teenage girls the film was created to honor the memory of the herds of flying Indonesian elephants which had gone extinct in the late 1930s. It seemed that the invention of technologies such as sonar and radar had confounded the elephants' innate sense of navigation, and the sole surviving herd had errantly flown directly into a typhoon and were decimated. She convinced them so completely that the girls swore they would write essays on the lost species for summer school. Bill was not at all surprised to hear the girls were in summer school.

After taking in Mickey's Philharmagic, Cleary told a family with twin toddlers that *Fantasia*, upon which the 4D film was based, was inspired by Walt's hallucinatory experiences after being gassed during World War I.

"Yeah," she added nonchalantly, "Walt was always tripping." The family fled from Cleary with great haste. Bill seriously needed to keep better tabs on her TV habits. Over tacos at El Pirata y El Perico, Bill declared Cleary the winner, prematurely ending the game before she could scar every child in the park.

Moments later, the Free at Last mothers took up residence at the tables surrounding them. There were dozens of them now, ranging in age from their 20s to 40s and all sporting matching pink t-shirts. With their increased number came increased diversity, which eased Bill's concerns about their slogan. They were a raucous bunch, their laughter echoing throughout Adventureland. "Hey, it's the Cinderella man!" one of the blondes yelled, pointing at Bill. The ensuing torrent of shouts of "Hey, Cinderella man!" struck Bill as simultaneously belittling and flirty. He had never been able to discern the difference between the two. In fact, in high school he had assumed any attention from a girl was good. He didn't date much.

Now older and wiser and wanting to eat his lunch in peace, he faked an embarrassed grin and waved to the ladies, hoping that would be the end of it. It wasn't.

A tall brunette, who bore a striking resemblance to Katherine, rose and joined Bill and Cleary at their table. "You know we didn't buy that whole

Cinderella story."

Bill stumbled over his words to respond. "We were just trying to—
I was teaching— We were playing a little game. No harm intended." He
hoped that would be enough for her to leave. It wasn't.

"It was a lying game," Cleary announced, excited about her victory. "I
won!"

"Teaching your daughter to lie?" the woman said in mock horror. "If
my son made a game of lying, I don't know what I'd do. Perhaps look for a
new son." Bill got it. It was time to punch his ticket for Crazy Town again.
"We were told you had an odd sense of humor, Bill Durmer."

"Oh," Cleary exclaimed, "they must be one of the groups you told me
about. She doesn't seem like a nut-job." Bill clamped a hand over Cleary's
mouth.

"You'll have to excuse my daughter," he said. "She has a condition."

"Don't apologize. We've been looking forward to meeting Cleary, too."
She offered Cleary her hand. Somehow, the fact that the alleged nut-jobs
knew her made Cleary feel like a celebrity. She enthusiastically shook the
woman's hand. Bill, however, was less impressed.

"So what do you call yourselves," he jeered, "the Free Birds? The Frees
at Last? The Pink Ladies? What?"

"No. These are just our cover," she said, referring to the t-shirts. "We're
the Moms. Call us the Moms."

"Are you the word bearer, then?" he asked. She was taken aback.

"Wow. You know more than I was led to believe." Her suspicion grew.
"Who told you about the prophecy? You know that's against the rules."

"No one," Bill said, then amending that to, "A friend. He's no longer one
of you, so the rules don't really apply." She was confused. Once entrusted
with the secret of the prophecy of the New Son, no one had ever willingly
left the fold. "So whose word do you represent — I mean of the Nine Old
Men?"

"That's complicated. The Moms are sort of a subgroup of the Frankenollies." She explained that when the rules were written to govern the
Council of the Nine, certain word bearers grew worried that Frank Thomas
and Ollie Johnston constituted a voting bloc that could threaten the balance of the Council. Thomas and Johnston were legendary animators who,
because of their talent, longevity and genial spirits, later became icons of
the golden age of Disney animation. They were for many years the only

surviving members of the Nine Old Men and were mentors to many of the new generation of animation masters. They were also lifelong friends. The Council requested they be co-bearers of the word originally given to Johnston. The Council then gave Thomas' word to Card Walker, then president and CEO of the company.

Because they never courted controversy and were so squarely in the mainstream of American animation, Thomas and Johnston never inspired the devotion of radical groups the likes of which revolved around the other word bearers. It was only after the death of Thomas a few years earlier that the Frankenollies were founded to honor them. Johnston had held onto his title as word bearer after the death of his friend, passing it on only in death.

"Our current word bearer prefers to remain anonymous," she said. As she did, she slid a D-note across the table to Bill. He and Cleary were both surprised and intrigued. Bill opened the card and read the message inside as the woman simultaneously recited it. The message, as always, was simple: "Follow her."

"I'm dealing with you, then?" Bill inquired rhetorically. "So what do I call you?"

"Mommy," she said without irony. "Call me Mommy."

"Okay, that's weird." Bill was not entirely comfortable with the idea. "I mean you're my age."

"No, I'm not." She was firm on this. "I'm much younger."

"Oh, come on!" Bill tried to edge the conversation back toward friendly banter, but stubbornly insisted on arguing the point in doing so. "You're a lovely woman, but you can't be that much younger than me."

She, on the other hand, was not opting for a lighter tone. "You are 39, Bill Durmer, soon to be 40. I am nowhere near 40," she declared in a most serious tone.

"But you can see it from where you are." He wouldn't stop. "How old are you? Thirty-eight? Thirty-seven?" It was a question he knew he shouldn't have asked and was somewhat relieved when she refused to answer.

"Just call me Mommy so we can get on with this," she insisted.

"Not gonna happen. How about Mom?" They agreed on terms, and she returned to her table until everyone had finished lunch. Then Mom led Bill, Cleary and her pink-clad gang on a little walk.

They strolled en masse past Pirates of the Caribbean. A cast member, dressed as Captain Jack Sparrow, was training young wannabe pirates in the ways of the sea. The Captain spotted the pink blob of humanity and followed them with his mascara laden eyes as they passed. "I love the *Pirates* movies, don't you?" Mom enthused.

"They're entertaining," Bill replied, trying his best to sound unaffected. Lowering his voice just enough that Cleary couldn't hear, he added "I am concerned, however, that we're sending kids the wrong message by encouraging them to model their behavior after violent criminals." Bill was actually a big fan of the films. The previous Halloween, he had planned to dress as Jack Sparrow only to be told by his family he didn't have the cheekbones to pull it off. Always with the cheekbones. He was loath to discuss the movies ever since.

"Oh, lighten up," Mom said. "It's just creative play. It's not like they're teaching the kids to lie to complete strangers." That hurt. "Besides, the costumes are cute."

They walked to the Swiss Family Treehouse, and both Mom and Bill shared their admiration for the attraction. This surprised Bill, as he half expected her to say it was old-fashioned and boring. The whole group wound their way up the staircase into the giant, fake tree. At the top, they paused to take in the view. Bill surveyed the Kingdom, its skyline punctuated by mountaintops and rocket ships and castle spires. He thought this might be his moment of temptation after a proverbial forty days in the wilderness. Only the forty days was actually a little over two weeks, and the Satan of this scenario looked eerily like his wife. Okay, maybe it was a bad analogy. Either that, or he was going to be hard-pressed to find a marriage counselor he could afford on a bus driver's salary.

"I heard they updated this attraction in California and made it Tarzan's Treehouse," Bill uttered in disgust. "Can you believe that?"

"I've seen it," she replied. "I really like it. It's kinda fun."

"Don't you think that sort of betrays the spirit of what Walt intended?"

"Nope," she answered succinctly. She walked away down the stairs. She elaborated on her answer as she went, and Bill had to struggle to keep up and hear her. "Don't get me wrong. *Swiss Family Robinson* is a cute movie. I like it. Especially the kid racing on the ostrich. That's my favorite." She stopped and turned to Bill. He almost collided with her due to his downward momentum. "Besides, the Tarzan version is really cute. You should go check it out."

Bill couldn't figure this woman. "What exactly is your agenda anyway?"

He suspected there wasn't one. She showed no intention of answering him, instead leading the group toward the Enchanted Tiki Room.

As they stood in the outdoor covered queue for the attraction, she attempted to engage Bill in some small talk by asking what his favorite Disney animated films were. He mistook it for some kind of test and offered more involved answers than she wanted to hear. First he expressed his admiration for *Snow White*, because of what a pioneering achievement it represented and because, even though it was the first animated feature ever, it still held its ground as one of the greatest. He praised the innovation of the multiplane camera system and how it immediately engages the audience in a sophisticated cinematic language, inviting them to lose themselves in the world of the film. He drew allusions to the immersive experience of the parks and postulated that had *Snow White* never happened, the parks would not have followed decades later.

He could have listed his other favorites of the Disney canon and their respective strengths — *One Hundred and One Dalmatians* for its loose, sketchy lines that retained the spirit of the animators' drawings, *Sleeping Beauty* for its bold, angular backgrounds and striking use of color, *The Jungle Book* for its superb character animation, *Aladdin* and *Beauty and the Beast* for their clever combination of hand-drawn animation with computer techniques and for the witty lyrics of the late Howard Ashman — but instead he chose to focus on the ones he disliked most. On and on Bill talked about the lows of Disney animation until everyone was seated inside and the animatronic birds drowned him out.

After the show was over, Mom asked him, "What did you think?"

"I think it was better before they screwed it up with Zazu and what's-his-name," Bill groused. "I don't know why they don't tear those ugly animatronics out of there and return it to the original show. It was much more charming. This is just annoying."

She nodded for a moment, then began to walk away out the door. She led the assembly back to the opposite end of Adventureland and stopped at a snack counter. "Who wants a Dole Whip?" she called out to her group. Her question was met by the excited shrieks and hoots of women who lived every day on calorie-counting diets and were ready for a sinful pineapple indulgence. She ushered Cleary and the other women to the front of the line. Mom gave Cleary a twenty and then pulled Bill aside. Bill recognized the fiery look in her eyes and knew he was in for a world-class excoriating.

He braced himself.

"I was warned that you sometimes like to hear yourself talk and that you have strong opinions about everything," she said, "and I don't have a problem with that. But to listen to you talk, sometimes I wonder if you're a Disney fan at all. All you do is complain about what they get wrong instead of celebrating what they do right." She was right, of course. In trying to sound like he didn't care, in trying to make himself out to be some disaffected critic, he had lost sight of a part of himself: the innocent part.

"I bought every Disney movie on VHS before I even had kids," she continued. "And when they came 'out of the vault' on DVD, I bought them again. And then I bought the special edition DVDs. And now I'm buying the Blu-Ray releases. I see every Disney movie on opening day. I have season passes to this park, and I visit Anaheim at least twice a year. I shop at the Disney Store, and I take Disney cruises." Bill wondered if she were going to have to pay royalties for this conversation if she kept invoking the Disney name. She continued, "I don't care if the plot of *Chicken Little* was uneven and illogical or if the characters in *Home on the Range* were unlikable. If it has the Disney name on it, I buy it, visit it, go see it or ride it, because I know that chances are it will be good entertainment for my family. I trust the name. And you know what? I can always find something I like about it."

Bill wasn't sure if she was dumb, deluded or simply a more positive person than himself. But he knew she scared him. Maybe it was because she didn't handle him with kid gloves. Maybe it was because she looked so much like his wife. But the combination of the two hit a little too close to home.

She jabbed a finger into Bill's chest as she gave him his charge. "You want to know what our agenda is? It's this: if you take this thing on, if you are the one, you have to believe in it. As Walt used to say, 'When you believe in a thing, believe in it all the way, implicitly and unquestionable.' Know that I'm going to share whatever you create with my children. So are the rest of these ladies. Don't let them down."

All Bill could say was, "I won't," adding reluctantly, "Mom." Maybe it was guilt for trying to deceive her at the castle or regret for savaging the company to which she was blindly devoted, but he felt the need to come clean. "I won't let them down, because I have no intention of taking..." What was he not taking? Was it a job? An honorary title? He honestly didn't know. "Whatever it is you people are offering. I'm not your leader or savior or whatever it is you think I am. I'm just not that special."

Mom gave him a patronizing smile and patted his cheek. Although, the pats felt more like slaps. "Oh, but you are." She punched him in the arm. "You big, stubborn idiot." She really did remind him of Katherine. As he watched Mom walk away to join her friends in the drink line, Cleary brought her father a pineapple float.

"How was your talk?" she asked.

"Painful." He took the float and held it against the new bruise on his bicep.

Chapter Twenty:
The Return of the Fishbowl Pajamas

Bill and Cleary bade the women farewell and made a beeline for Tomorrowland, hoping to put as much distance between themselves and the Moms as possible. The midday summer sun baked the pavement until more heat emanated from below their feet than from the sun itself. These were what Bill called the ninety-ninety Days, ninety degrees and ninety percent humidity. The combination was one hundred percent miserable.

"Ugh," Cleary moaned, "it's like walking around in a hot sponge out here." Signs of the oppressive mugginess were abundant: whole families spritzing themselves with spray fans filled with ice cold water, kids lining up at the Coca-Cola-sponsored misting stations, cast members scurrying about to mop up the sticky, milky puddles left behind by splots of wayward ice cream, and the exhibition of acres of sweaty, sun-reddened skin. Bill had a theory that, on days like today, the surface area of tourists' clothing was inversely proportional to the surface area of the person wearing it. The bigger the person, the smaller the clothing ... and the stronger Bill's gag reflex.

Amidst the sea of blotchy, bloated flesh, Cleary spotted an anachronistic misfit. "Daddy, look! It's the man with the fishbowl pajamas!" Bill looked where she was pointing and saw Tomorrow Man, in full costume, walking toward them.

Bill apologized to his daughter. "Honey, I'm afraid this isn't going to be the kind of day off we hoped for." Cleary shrugged it off.

"I'm okay. Anybody can ride rides," she said, "but not every girl has all these people telling her how special her Daddy is."

Tomorrow Man reached them and extended his hand toward Bill. His face was as taciturn as Bill remembered. "Bill Durmer, to you I extend the hand of friendship." Bill shook the man's hand.

"I'd like to say I'm surprised to see you, Tomorrow Man," Bill said smiling, trying to crack the older man's earnest demeanor, "but I really can't."

"And rightly you should not. Mommy phoned ahead to let me know you were aware of the prophecy." And in one sentence, Tomorrow Man had proved Bill was right in refusing to call her Mommy. As if proof were necessary.

"Where do you keep a phone?" Bill quipped. He had a point. Unless there were hidden pockets in Tomorrow Man's neck rings, he wasn't packing so much as a breath mint in that shiny get-up.

Tomorrow Man ignored Bill's sarcasm and crouched before Cleary. Bill thought this a risky gamble. Unless loosening of ligaments was an unadvertised side effect of Brylcreem and Just for Men, Bill worried the old man might not be able to get back up. "Greetings and blessings of peace to you, young Miss Durmer." Cleary smiled at him.

"Hi. My brother's going to be so jealous." Clay had returned from their previous trip as Tomorrow Man's biggest fan. He talked about the man with the "pishbow padamas" for weeks and took to wearing a clear plastic teapot of Cleary's on his head as a helmet.

Tomorrow Man stood to his full height with an ease that surprised Bill, although it shouldn't have. He was wearing a padded space suit (with a 34-inch waist) and a plastic bubble on his head in the Florida heat. And not even breaking a sweat. It should have been obvious this was a supremely fit man. "Bill Durmer, a mission awaits you, young man."

"I had a feeling you might say that," Bill replied. "Well not that exactly, but something, you know, spacey." Tomorrow Man put an arm around Bill's shoulder and steered him toward the tower housing the Astro Orbiters and the Tomorrowland Transit Authority, a leisurely futuristic train ride above the land. They stepped aboard an inclined conveyor known as a Speedramp and rode up to the train's loading area.

"They used to call this the WEDway PeopleMover," Bill informed Cleary. "I liked that name better."

"I know, Daddy. You told me that before," she replied, adding, "and I like it better, too."

Tomorrow Man greeted a female cast member who was assisting guests with loading. He leaned close and whispered to the young woman, "WED-way. Tom sent us." The young woman's eyes widened. She rushed over to a control panel, opened it and entered a numerical code. An indicator inside the box flashed from red to green. She turned to Tomorrow Man, who was boarding the PeopleMover with Bill and Cleary, and saluted him with a fist crossed over her chest.

"God speed, sir," she said in all seriousness. Bill rolled his eyes. He couldn't help himself. Some of these people really needed hobbies. Or therapy. Time to climb aboard the crazy train.

The cast member had made certain no one else got into their train. This was a comfort to Bill, because the curious stares of others would have made him embarrassed for Tomorrow Man, even if the man weren't embarrassed himself. Conversely, the lack of innocent bystanders in their train likely meant they were in for something weird. Yea. The PeopleMover accelerated forward, whipped around a corner, curved around the outer rim of the tower and toward Stitch's Great Escape.

"Tell me, Bill Durmer," Tomorrow Man bellowed over the noise of the park, "have you found that vision, yet?" At that very moment, the PeopleMover plunged into darkness. The only light in the tunnel illuminated Walt's original model for Progress City, an elaborate expansion of his original concept for the Experimental Prototype Community of Tomorrow. EPCOT the city, of course, would never be built. This model was all that remained of Walt's dream of a forward-looking metropolis. Tomorrow Man shook his head in disgust as they passed the model, though Bill scarcely noticed because the old man's bubble remained stationary. "Now *that* is a vision. This is why we need you, young man. The world can no longer suffer under the strain of bureaucracy and dream by committee. We need a singular vision again."

As Tomorrow Man prattled on about visions, Bill just nodded. He was disinterested, but he was already along for the ride and might as well see what was coming next. Whatever it was, he hoped there'd be snacks. Preferably bridge mix or some of those little sausages.

As the little train cruised along on its linear induction motors, Tomorrow Man began to recite, word for word, the same screed (against the cartoon future that never was) he had shared with Bill six months earlier. The train turned and entered a tunnel within the shell of Space Mountain. When they were in complete darkness, the train lurched to a sudden stop.

Tomorrow Man stopped talking mid-sentence. Bill listened intently to the sound of hydraulic pistons activating and the creak of shifting metal. A gust of cold, conditioned air whooshed out of the building from an unseen source ahead and to his left.

"You might want to hold on," Tomorrow Man said blithely in the dark. The train lurched forward again and veered toward the left, plunging them into the colder air. Bill heard a door close behind them and the tracks switching back into their proper position. They plunged rapidly downward, passing just underneath the tracks of the Space Mountain coaster. Guests squealed as the coaster's cars whizzed overhead. Cleary's delighted screams mixed with theirs. The train continued down, deeper into the ride building, until the faint light and roar from the coaster above faded altogether. Bill could see nothing and could hear only Cleary's euphoric screams. The train plunged deeper and deeper into the dark without slowing or turning for what seemed an eternity.

Finally, the train gradually leveled out and slowed to its usual relaxing speed. As they traveled, the light level slowly increased, allowing their eyes time to adjust. The gradually rising illumination revealed a long, windowless, doorless corridor with only the PeopleMover track and a slightly elevated walkway running in parallel. Bill studied the endless passage, his mind darting back and forth between competing calculations of how long the tunnel might be and how deep they had traveled.

The walls and ceiling in the corridor were themed in a retro-futuristic style reminiscent of the original look of Tomorrowland — a design aesthetic first unveiled in the 1967 redesign of Disneyland's Tomorrowland. The corridor's paint scheme graduated from pure black through various shades of grey and into pure white, to correspond with the changing light levels.

"There are those who would complain about every little change we make here," Tomorrow Man said, "and others who would complain that we're too resistant to change. What they don't know is that some changes, and in some cases the lack of changes, are dictated neither by artistic direction nor economic concerns." The car slowed as it entered a circular loading area identical to the public one. Beyond it, the PeopleMover track continued back down a corridor identical to the one they had just traveled. The three stepped out of the car and onto a Speedramp rising from the floor of the circular loading room and leading to the floor above. "Some changes are made specifically to serve the prophecy. The sight you are about to behold is an example of just that."

Cresting the top of the ramp first, Cleary gasped. Her voice echoed through the cavernous space, a hangar-sized windowless warehouse with 40-foot ceilings, hard concrete floors and the odorous perfume of dust, oil and oxidizing metal. The entire space was filled with relics of Walt Disney World's past: a row of submarines from 20,000 Leagues Under the Sea, cars from Mr. Toad's Wild Ride, Skyway gondolas, a huge, scale model of a Saturn V rocket and numerous other props, sets, and ride vehicles. Scattered among them were dozens of discarded animatronic characters.

Tomorrow Man stepped off, beaming at the sight before him. He slapped Bill on the back, "Quite a collection, eh sport?" He doubled back behind the Speedramp to admire a collection of animatronics that included Mickey, Donald and the Three Little Pigs. "Just got these little fellows back from Tokyo." He patted Mickey on the head. "Welcome home, my friends."

"So, all of this," Bill spun around, arms outstretched, "is for the prophecy?" Tomorrow Man chuffed at Bill.

"Nonsense!" He bore a look of disappointment. "Only select bits are here for that purpose. You'll see what I mean soon enough." He led them down a winding path through the various artifacts. Cleary marveled at the sights. Bill, however, didn't seem as enamored of the place. "Your countenance speaks of discomfort, Bill Durmer. What troubles you?" For a moment, Bill was tempted to give Tomorrow Man a list of every little thing that troubled him, beginning with the man's stilted sci-fi dialogue.

"It's just creepy," Bill finally admitted. "Submarines should be in the water. Animatronics should be moving. Gondolas should be flying overhead." Bill had always had an unease about objects existing outside their intended usage. The place felt less museum than mausoleum. "To see them like this, I don't know. It makes me sad." Somehow, Bill's admission eased Tomorrow Man's mind. The old man in the fishbowl smiled at Bill and put an arm around his shoulder.

"Right this way," he said. He led Bill and Cleary to a point in the center of the room where sat a collection of old ride vehicles shaped vaguely like space shuttles. "Do you remember the old Star Jets?" Tomorrow Man asked. Bill shrugged. He knew the old Tomorrowland had featured a different ride where the Astro Orbiters now spun, but he couldn't remember the specifics. Seeing them now, he recalled they had orbited the rocket standing in the far corner. Eleven star jets sat roughly in a circle with the twelfth in the center. As Bill feared, Tomorrow Man instructed him to sit in the center one.

"Can I sit, too?" Cleary was more excited about this prospect than her father. Bill helped her climb inside. Rather than joining her, he perched himself on the nose. Whatever indignities he was soon to suffer, cramming himself into a dusty old space shuttle on the floor so that his knees bracketed his chin and every lipid on his torso was squeezed into an unsightly inner tube of flab around his middle would not be one of them.

Tomorrow Man, however, proudly climbed into one of the shuttles. "My people are scheduled to rendezvous on our coordinates in short order. I urge your patience." Momentarily, "his people" began to arrive. A motley crew of ages and appearances marched toward the ring of shuttles, each wearing a Tomorrowland costume from a different era of the park's history. (They were not costumes in the make-believe sense, but what those outside the Disney world would call uniforms.)

Nine of the newcomers took their places in the remaining empty shuttles. A tenth — a fit, beautiful woman with greying hair and wearing a costume styled similarly to Tomorrow Man's but with a 60s-era miniskirt — took the final shuttle. Tomorrow Man turned to her with a scornful snap in his voice, "I expected you sooner."

"TTA was one-oh-one," she snapped back.

"Strange that it worked fine for us," Tomorrow Man grumbled back. Bill tried to resist grinning. He had no idea what one-oh-one meant, but he recognized the rhythm of their banter. This lady was obviously Mrs. Tomorrow Man.

The influx of people continued until they stood two-deep encircling the shuttles. Bill was getting nervous being, quite literally, the center of their attention. As he was wont to do in such a situation, he attempted a lame joke. "Anybody know where I can see Mickey Mouse?"

Almost in complete unison, over half of the group reflexively answered, "In the Judge's Tent at Mickey's Toontown Fair."

"Sorry, I was just," Bill started to apologize for his joke, but changed course. "Tomorrow Man, could you introduce me?"

Tomorrow Man stood in his star jet and motioned to the group, "Sit, my friends." Those standing in the outer circle shuffled and shifted to seat themselves on the floor. "Bill Durmer, behold the Tomorrowlanders!" Tomorrow Man bellowed in dramatic fashion, his voice bouncing about the room with majestic reverberation. Bill suspected for a moment that the room had been designed so large precisely for that moment, to lend it the grandeur they desired. He pictured Tomorrow Man coming alone to the warehouse over the decades, practicing his line to get the intonation exactly right. "Let the inquiry begin." Tomorrow Man resumed his place in his star jet. Bill waited anxiously to learn what exactly the inquiry would be.

Mrs. Tomorrow Man (Tomorrow Woman?) began. Her voice was considerably more kindly than when she was speaking to her husband. "Bill Durmer, tell us," her eyes twinkled as she spoke, "what would you do with Tomorrowland?" This was a far broader, yet more pointed question than Bill expected. He thought the inquiry might deal more in the esoteric — questions absurd in any context like, "Have you ever dreamt of weasels in petticoats?" or "Do your ears burn when staring at the North Star?" That kind of thing.

He cleared his throat and began to speak without really considering what to say. After all, he didn't want the job. Was it a job? That still hadn't been resolved. He plunged ahead. No goals, no failure. "I would start by getting rid of Stitch. I can tell you that much." His comment about Stitch's Great Escape, the attraction that had replaced a succession of earlier attractions — Alien Encounter, Mission to Mars and Flight to the Moon, in reverse order — brought snickers from his audience.

"And what would you put in its place?" another questioner asked.

Bill thought for a moment. "I would do something akin to the original moon and Mars attractions — something fun, but grounded in adventure and hope for the future. Maybe something like a Mission to Anywhere."

"What would that be?" Tomorrow Man asked.

"Use the existing theater," Bill responded. He was getting excited at the idea now. "But return it to a more film-based attraction. Make it like a 4D experience in the round, but explore technology to create a more holographic experience. Mist screens? Projection spheres? Maybe 3D on a sphere? I'm not sure. But the audience should be able to choose the mission." He was rolling now and starting to have fun. "Equip each seat with a touch screen to allow the guests to vote on which mission to pursue. Have choices like Mars, one of the moons of Saturn, the ocean deep and a Utopian city of the future." Bill studied the faces of his inquisitors and found them, to a person, smiling at his response. Cleary patted him on the leg as if to say, "Good job, Daddy."

Bill went on to describe other changes he would make. Monsters, Inc. Laugh Floor and Buzz Lightyear Space Ranger Spin he would move to Hollywood Studios as part of the growing Pixar area there. Buzz he would replace with a classic dark ride that allowed riders to imagine they were members of the first human colony on a terraformed world far across the galaxy. Though he knew the idea might be sacrilege to the purists, he suggested Carousel of Progress be updated to tell the story of multiple generations of one family, allowing for longer gaps between the decades presented.

Finally, he decried the noise and smell of the Tomorrowland Speedway and proposed that the vehicles there be retrofitted with electric motors, relishing the notion that not only would alternative fuel engines be more fitting with the intent of Tomorrowland, but that the whine of the motors would even sound more futuristic. He would also equip them with self-driving systems (or at least the illusion of them) so that the cars could whip in and out and around each other at higher speeds and create a more exciting, forward-looking ride. Reluctantly, he admitted he had no idea what should take the place of Monsters, Inc. Though Bill believed there was room for a character-based attraction, he felt no Disney film character truly embodied the spirit of Tomorrowland.

Thoughtful glances, hushed whispers and contemplative nods met his suggestions. Bill found himself in an emotional place as unexpected as the warehouse in which he sat. He actually cared about their responses to his ideas. For some reason, this whole business of the prophecy, at first a curiosity, then an annoyance to him, had begun to affect him more deeply. For the first time since he closed the store, he felt alive — a mind active, a heart quickened. He thought about the biblical Parable of the Talents and Jesus saying on another occasion that to whom much is given, much would be required. Whether mastered or not, Bill possessed a great many talents. He began to wonder if his dream of blending in and neglecting his talents was tantamount to heresy.

The next question came from a young woman behind him. "What's wrong with today's popular vision of the future?" Bill spun around to face her. Her youth surprised him. She didn't appear to be more than a teenager, but the question belied a profoundly mature mind. Bill imagined this would be Cleary in a few years.

"*Blade Runner*," was Bill's response. He elaborated, "That film popularized a dystopian view of the future that has influenced untold numbers of writers and filmmakers since. While there are certainly scientists and futurists who still work toward a more hopeful tomorrow, pop culture still embraces that bleaker view. And the fear-mongering politics of today certainly don't help matters." Bill steered clear of casting blame at either political party, knowing that both were equally to blame. Plus, he came dangerously close to breaking his rule of not discussing politics in public. And rule breaking was a slippery slope. If he broke that one, soon he'd be murmuring and drinking yellow liquids.

Another questioner, a thirty-something man in the most current costume, gave Bill the lowdown on a planned Tomorrowland film starring a former professional wrestler as a modern astronaut who finds himself in a Utopian future. He wanted to know Bill's thoughts on the film. "Well," Bill began, scratching his chin, "I'd scrap the whole concept and start over."

"Why?" the man asked.

Bill explained his belief that the drama — or more likely comedy — would arise from the conflict between the protagonist's cynical view of humanity and the idealized future in which he finds himself, making the view of a better future seem a quaint joke, an unattainable pipe dream. "Besides," he added, "Tomorrowland is not about attaining the future. It's about always reaching for it." More nods and whispers.

"What would *you* do?" Tomorrow Man asked.

Bill smiled at the older man's leading question. In deconstructing the announced concept for the film, he had already begun to concoct his own. For a moment, he wondered if any of the Tomorrowlanders worked for the studio and were simply fishing for script ideas. How would he defend himself if they did steal his concept? Somehow he couldn't imagine standing in front of a judge and trying to convince her that his copyrights were infringed upon by a secret group of Disney fans who called themselves the Tomorrowlanders, followed a man in fishbowl pajamas and believed Bill to be the Chosen One. That testimony would end only one way: with Bill in a padded room. But he decided to go for it.

"Well, assuming that the film needs to be created in the first place," Bill began, questioning internally whether it did, "I'd start by changing the setting. Tomorrowland would be a place, but not a place in the future. It would be a community sort of like Walt's idea for Progress City, a place where the best minds could come together to invent and innovate. Maybe a private island. It would be owned by a reclusive scientist and inventor, Dr. Tom Morrow." Bill had evoked the name, because he knew the People-Mover audio once had a reference to a Mr. Tom Morrow, and he liked the cheekiness of it. This choice, however, elicited a chorus of gasps from his audience. He wasn't sure what it meant, and no one bothered to explain. So he continued.

"Then you could borrow a page from the *Pirates* playbook and have two young protagonists, maybe teenage children of scientists who have come to work at Tomorrowland. They discover who Tom Morrow is and the three end up in some kind of an adventure, probably defending one of his inventions from outside forces. It should be something unique from what you see in the parks. Expand the mythology right from the get-go."

"Like what?" The question came from one of the rank-and-file Tomor-rowlanders in the outer circle, clearly a breach of etiquette since those in the inner circle scowled at his audacity.

Bill shrugged, indulging the question, "I don't know... How about The Eden Bubble? A device that creates a bubble of space free from the pur-ported effects of the biblical fall. Essentially a bubble that is free from bro-kenness. Nothing within the bubble will ever break down. Or die. Or decay. He sees it as an opportunity to advance medicine or test theoretical impos-sibilities. Others want to steal it for more nefarious purposes.

"I could see it as a trilogy. The first film ends with Dr. Morrow reveal-ing to the young protagonists his next big thing: a building that houses a wormhole or a space-time bending device, allowing him to travel through-out the universe without ever leaving the building."

"Space Mountain," Tomorrow Man said, beaming at Bill like a proud father.

"Yeah, Space Mountain," Bill confirmed. "The third film would involve Morrow's efforts to take the ideas he and his team have perfected to the wider world and the powers that be trying not only to stop him, but to destroy Tomorrowland for good." He shrugged, "That's right off the top of my head, so it could certainly be developed further." They all seemed quite satisfied.

"Who plays Tom Morrow?" The young girl asked.

"I don't know," Bill said. "Someone unconventional like Alan Cum-ming or David Tennant. Or Tony Hale. He would really give the character an unhinged quality." They all nodded thoughtfully, because most of them had no idea who Tony Hale was.

Tomorrow Man stood in his shuttle again. "I believe we have heard enough. We must vote now on whether he is worthy of the test. My vote is 'worthy.'" Beginning with Tomorrow Woman, each person in the inner circle stood in his or her Star Jet and stated their vote. The vote was unanimous: Bill was worthy, but of what? "We will now proceed with the test to determine if Bill Durmer fulfills the word of the prophecy of the New Son." All save Tomorrow Man settled into their shuttles. He approached and motioned for Bill to stand. "It's all on you, Sport." He spoke louder, for the benefit of all present, "You must select one item in this warehouse. Stand here, take your time, look at everything and choose."

Bill scanned the warehouse. He was unsure what to do here. Would his choice reveal something about his innermost self? He had read Native American mythologies about boys being taken into the forest by sprite-like creatures. The boys would have to choose between several items. The choice would reveal the boy's destiny, whether it be warrior, medicine man or farmer. Perhaps the Tomorrowlanders had something like that in mind. If he chose the animatronic Mickey back beyond the Speedramp, would it reflect a sympathetic connection with Walt Disney himself or simply label him as a product of a consumerist culture that automatically associates Mickey with the larger brand? Would choosing the rocket that once held the star jets reveal him as a traditionalist or a change-resistant conservative?

He peered past a long bank of rack-mounted instruments, control panels and monitors. There, in the shadows, was an animatronic character that intrigued him. It was a figure of a middle-aged man in a scientist's lab coat and thin glasses, sporting a receding hairline. Were he a real person in a crowd, Bill would have never noticed him. But here, amidst the fanciful and futuristic, his ordinariness was what struck Bill as interesting. The figure seemed to be staring back at him. Without pondering his situation any further, Bill raised his hand and pointed to the figure. "Him. That animatronic back there." Bill looked at Tomorrow Man who was smiling widely.

"He has chosen rightly!" Tomorrow Man bellowed. Applause and cheers erupted from those gathered, and all rose to shower Bill with their adulation. "I cannot speak for the other groups, Bill Durmer," Tomorrow Man said to him, "but I have no doubts that you are the one. Then again, I knew that the first time I laid eyes on you in Cosmic Ray's." He winked at

Bill. "By the way, that figure you chose? That's Mr. Tom Morrow, from the old Flight to the Moon." The revelation took Bill's breath away so that he couldn't respond beyond a smile and a nod.

After much back-slapping and congratulations, Bill and Cleary were led back to the loading area below and put aboard a PeopleMover. A long ride through the darkening corridor and up past the Space Mountain coaster brought them back to the dark tunnel where they had veered downward in the first place. A few minutes later, they were unloading from the train and mixing with the thousands of unsuspecting guests who would have thought the events of the last few hours nothing more than another piece of Disney storytelling.

"Since you're the New Son and everything," Cleary said, "can you get us free ice cream?" Bill laughed.

"Was that a not-so-subtle hint?" he asked. Cleary smiled a mischievous smile. "You know, we just had floats not that long ago. I think we should wait for dinner."

Cleary pouted, "Walt Disney would have gotten his daughter an ice cream."

"Maybe so, but I'm not Walt Disney." He took her hand and led her across the park to Frontierland. Feeling the prophecy-related events for the day must have been over, he was now ready to experience attractions that were purely escapist for him. "How about Country Bear Jamboree?"

Cleary shrugged, "I don't know. I don't think I've ever done that one, but if it's as bad as the movie..."

"It's not," her father assured her. Nothing was. As they approached the entrance of Grizzly Hall, they noticed the cast member at the door turning guests away. "Oh well." But the cast member waved them over.

"Right this way," she said, loosening the velvet rope and allowing them inside. As soon as they were through, she secured the rope to its stanchion and continued telling everyone else the attraction was closed. Bill didn't like the looks of this. He felt like one of those beautiful people who gets past the guards and into the hottest club in a big city. Of course, he was guessing at what that feeling actually was, since he had never been one of those people or inside one of those clubs.

He heard a raucous commotion of conversation and laughter, and all of the voices were decidedly female. He led Cleary into the theater to find every seat filled with the pink-shirted Moms. Mom, the Katherine doppelganger, spotted him and stood from the front row. All the other women turned to greet him. "Bill Durmer!" they cried out.

Mom outstretched her arms, "Come to Mommy."

Bill sighed. "Wonderful."

Chapter Twenty-One:
A Melodious Menagerie of Purveyors of Musical Perfection

Bill found himself sitting alone in the Grizzly Hall Theater, his only company being the woman he called Mom. (He was resolute in his refusal to call her Mommy.) Cleary had accompanied the other Moms to grab an early dinner next door at Pecos Bill's. Mom insisted that it be only the two of them present for "the test." She checked her watch regularly. Bill took this to mean she was not fully in control of the test.

"We've got a few minutes," she said, checking her watch again. "I think you'll like the test. I've seen some of it. It's pretty cute. They did a good job with it."

"Did anyone ever point out that you say 'cute' a lot?" Bill asked.

"So?" She stared at Bill, awaiting an answer. This chick really made him nervous.

"It's just that..." he had no idea what to say. "Not everything is cute. Some things are beautiful or stunning or amazing or inspiring."

"I like cute. Cute pretty well sums it up for me." She pointed a finger in his face. "You're the one that has the problem. Either you have an irrational dislike of the word, or you don't think anything is cute. That makes me sad for you." Bill couldn't believe it. She had beaten him at his own game, turning small talk into an uncomfortable conversation. He wasn't giving up without a fight.

"You left out a third option," he noted.

"What's that?"

"Maybe I just don't like you."

She smiled and patted his hand. "Of course you do. I look like your wife." Bill couldn't argue with that. Another nervous flip of the wrist to check her watch. Her dainty wrist was smooth and lightly tanned, her hand long and slender, her nails perfect and red. It all added up to Bill longing for home. "Ever heard of Mineral King?" she asked.

"A little, in passing." Something told him it was better to let her talk. Bill actually knew quite a bit about Mineral King from his research into Disney history. But he didn't tell her that, because he suspected stealing her thunder would only end in him getting punched.

"It was a resort Walt was planning in Mineral King Valley in Northern California. It was going to be a year-round resort — skiing in winter, horseback riding and hiking in summer. There would be hotels, shops, restaurants, a movie theater and," she nodded toward the stage, "an animatronic show featuring a bear band."

"Wow," Bill feigned amazement. "That's fascinating. What ever happened?"

"When Walt died, the project did, too. And the bear show ended up in the parks instead. Before he died, one of the last things he did at the studio was to check in on Marc Davis to see how he was coming on the planning for the bear show and stuff. Pretty soon, maybe the next day, he was in the hospital. While he was in the hospital, he kept sending notes and stuff to the animators and Imagineers. Well, Marc got some notes on the bear show that didn't make any sense to him at all. He was convinced Walt was losing it. After Walt's death Ollie Johnston came to Marc and showed him his word of prophecy, and then," she snapped her fingers, "it all clicked!" Slipping off her shoes, she pulled her feet up onto the seat, wrapping her arms around her knees. "Of course," she continued, "they didn't have the technology to make the test work at first. Then again, I guess it didn't matter since there were no candidates in the early days."

That begged a good question, one Bill simply had to ask, though he didn't expect to get an answer. "How many candidates have there been over the years?"

"That have gotten to this point where the groups are putting them to the test?" A wily grin told Bill the answer before she even spoke it. She held up her index finger. "One." Tilting the finger slowly downward, she pointed it straight at Bill's heart. Bill was taken aback. It had never occurred to him that he might be the first person in more than forty years to fit the prophecy. He had assumed that this was a routine exercise for the Council of the Nine, that every few years they would find some unsuspecting sap and pump him full of grandiose notions of fame and power. Hearing the truth, he had an epiphany of sorts: these people were actually counting on him. Blood pressure rose. Palms grew sweaty. He suddenly felt pressure to succeed, to do more than simply blend in. This was exactly the kind of pressure he had tried to escape back home.

Before Bill could meditate on his own cowardice any further, the lights dimmed. A spotlight shone on mounted trophy heads of a buffalo, a deer and a moose. Tilting his head toward the stage, the buffalo was first to speak, "Hey, Henry! Let's get on with it!"

Melvin, the moose, turned toward the deer, "Buck, you think ol' Buff here is gettin' impatient?"

"Does a bear do his stuff in the woods?" Buck replied.

"Not if he's got his own green room," joked Buff.

"Watch your language, boys," a voice called from the stage. "This here's a family prophecy." A curtain opened to reveal Henry, a country bear in a high collar and tie. Henry appeared to look directly at Bill. "Now if the candidate would so oblige, let's kick into our first number." Bill smiled at the elaborate cleverness of creating an entirely separate version of the show for the sake of the prophecy. Though it all seemed more than a little crazy, he felt privileged to be in what must have been the only audience to ever see the whole thing. Henry kept staring at him. "Well, son?"

Melvin the moose chimed in, "Go ahead and answer him, or he'll keep staring at you for hours."

Buck added, "Yeah, he ain't programmed for nothing else!"

"You better answer," Mom said, smirking at Bill.

He felt foolish but obliged. "Go ahead."

"Well alrighty, then," Henry said. "I give you now a melodious menagerie of purveyors of musical perfection: The Five Bear Rugs, plus Gomer." The center stage curtain opened to reveal The Five Bear Rugs, a hillbilly band comprised of animatronic bears playing instruments that included a little brown jug and a one-stringed "thing." The bandstand supporting the five band members (and the always silent Baby Bear) slid forward. Simultaneously, another bear named Gomer, along with his ragtime piano, rose up just left of center stage. Bill thought he recognized the tune they began to play, but wasn't sure. Mom leaned over and projected her voice above the music.

"If you've ever heard of Disney's Living Character Initiative, this is where it started," she said. "That is, it started with the prophecy of the New Son."

The Initiative was a program to create greater realism in character behaviors. Unseen puppeteers would control the actions of characters, whether computer graphics or advanced animatronics. The goal was to have characters that were not simply puppets or costumed cast members, but ones that interacted with guests in an exceedingly real way. It was the next step in immersive entertainment.

"So someone is backstage controlling the interaction?" Bill asked.

With a coy grin, she answered him, "I said it started with the prophecy," adding with a hint of understatement. "It's a little more advanced now."

Henry began to sing:

> "There once was a bear who lived in the circus,
> Jugglin', tightropin' and swingin' trapeze.
> A high-divin' prize fighter in a big bowler hat,
> He was dandy and fancy as you ever would please.
>
> But he longed to get out and see the whole wide world,
> So one day he busted clean out of his cage.
> Confused and bewildered, he then fell in love,
> Which sent Lumpjaw, that big bruin, into a terrible rage."

The bears stopped their song abruptly. All of the animatronic figures stared in Bill's direction. He shifted nervously in his seat.

"Come on now, son. Even Baby Bear knows that one," Henry said. Baby Bear gave his teddy bear a squeeze and turned his arch expression away from Bill in what appeared to be a display of disdain.

"What am I supposed to do?" Bill whispered to Mom.

"I think this fella's half a metaphor short of an idiom," quipped Melvin.

"Ain't too smart, neither," replied Buck.

"Now, give him time, Melvin," Henry said. "It ain't every day a fella gets prophesied on." To Bill he said, "Take your time, son."

"The song is a clue," Mom explained. "They're waiting for the answer."

This was bad news for Bill. During the song, he had been distracted by the animation of the characters and hadn't really paid attention to the words. He raised his hand, realizing only too late how foolish he must've looked.

"Could you sing it again?" he asked. The bears did nothing for at least a full minute. They were all dead still. Suddenly, Henry blurted out,

"Well alrighty, then. I give you now a melodious menagerie of purveyors of musical perfection: The Five Bear Rugs, plus Gomer." The bear band started into the song as if they had never played it. The illusion of autonomous intelligence was broken, but the show went on.

When they finished the song for the second time, Bill hastily answered, "Bongo!"

"Well now," Henry said, "looks like you know a thing or two about bears. Bongo was the star of a three-reeler in Disney's *Fun and Fancy Free.* Nice shootin'." Gomer cried out in alarm and began to shake. "Now calm down, Gomer, ain't nobody shootin' at us. That is, as long as we keep the show goin.'"

Another curtain opened to reveal Liver Lips McGrowl, a thick-browed bear with absurdly large, pursed lips. He sang the second song of the test, accompanied by Gomer and the band:

> *"He held that pose in a Goofy time,*
> *Selling his auteegraphs for only a dime.*
>
> *He was a beezy bear, bearly asleep,*
> *Likely to grin and bear it.*
> *When that bear was on the screen*
> *A duck was likely to share it.*
>
> *He was gived his own series of shorts,*
> *Unlike many of his furry cohorts,*
>
> *But no sooner'n he was hooked,*
> *The receipts done started to lag.*
> *And when his second title come out,*
> *The whole series was in the bag."*

As the band played the final strains of the song, Bill puzzled. He knew the character the song described, a mischievous, dimwitted bear who had become only the seventh character to receive a titular series of shorts. He couldn't recall the name, though. "Humboldt, Humbug, Hubert," he said to himself, then landing on it. "Humphrey! Humphrey the Bear!" Bill blurted the answer before Liver Lips' curtain could even close.

Mom patted him on the arm. "Good one. I like Humphrey. He's cute."

Two more songs followed, one about Winnie the Pooh and one about Baloo from *Jungle Book*. Though Bill was pleased with himself at deducing the riddles, he wondered, *Is that it?* More than forty years of waiting and planning, countless dollars spent on research and development for this? For Trivial Pursuit: Bear Edition as hosted by robots? As a former member of the Decent Chance High School scholars' bowl team, Bill suspected something more difficult was coming, a bonus round of some type. The bandstand slid back, Gomer descended beneath the stage. That left only Henry.

"Well, I reckon that about does it for us," Henry said. What? This was the great test? No bonus round? As if to answer Bill's unspoken doubts, Henry then asked, "Any requests, son?" Bill froze. He didn't know what to do. The only song title he could recall from the Country Bear Jamboree was "Blood on the Saddle," sung by Big Al, a rotund, slow-moving but determined bear playing an out-of-tune guitar. That didn't seem like the right choice, though. He had an idea.

"How about 'Feed the Birds?'" Bill queried.

"That's not one of their songs," Mom harshly whispered to him. Bill nodded to reassure her he knew what he was doing.

"Well..." Henry said thoughtfully. "I'd a figured you'd pick 'Blood on the Saddle.'" Suddenly, as if interrupting Henry's planned show, a curtain opened to reveal Big Al. Thanks to the recorded voice of Tex Ritter, Al began caterwauling his signature tune.

"Now, Al, we're trying to conduct important business here," Henry said, and the curtain closed on Al again. Bill chuckled at the gag, appreciative of the fact that, even in creating this elaborate test, the Imagineers hadn't forgotten to entertain. "As I was saying, we don't usually play numbers from *Mary Poppins*, but seein' as how it was Uncle Walt's favorite song, I reckon you done made a right smart choice."

Mom beamed. All the curtains opened at once, revealing every bear from the show, even Big Al, the robust Trixie and, descending on a rope swing from the ceiling, the feather boa-wearing Teddi. Henry sang the first stanza of the song to the accompaniment of the band and Gomer. At the chorus, all the other bears and even the trophy heads joined in. Bill cast a glance at Mom to see tears welling up in her eyes, but wasn't sure if it was from the touching song or the weight of the moment. She whispered to him, "Nice job." The bears finished the tune and all returned to their places, save Henry.

"I do believe congratulations are in order," Henry said to Bill. Shifting his attention to Mom, he asked, "Are you the word bearer?"

"No," Mom blushed and smiled widely at being addressed by the bear. "The word bearer prefers to remain anonymous at this time, but I speak for him."

"Fair enough," Henry replied. "Inform the word bearer that the candidate passed the test. And y'all have a lovely evening." The curtain closed. Mom released her breath.

"That was surreal," Bill said.

"Yeah," Mom concurred, "that was good stuff."

They exited and joined Cleary and the Moms next door for a burger. Neither said much to the other. Likewise, Mom didn't discuss the test with her compatriots. Her only indications to them that Bill had passed were a big smile and a hyperactive nod. When they had finished their early dinner, Bill and Cleary agreed they'd had enough for one day. They parted ways with the Moms and left the park.

***

Bill had insisted they take the bus that morning, so they found themselves standing in the heat with about a dozen other guests, waiting for their bus to arrive. When it finally did, Bill and Cleary boarded through the rear door. The bus was largely empty with more vacant seats than occupied ones. Within seconds, everyone was aboard. The driver slowly pulled away from the curb and began to make his way back to the All-Star Resorts.

Bill looked toward the front of the bus, hoping to recognize the driver from shift changes. He hadn't actually met many other drivers, but there was always the chance. Instead, he noticed a familiar face sitting right behind the driver. "Cleary, I'm going up front to talk to somebody," he said. "You okay staying here?"

"Yes, sir," she replied. "I'm fine." A mother with her three children was sitting nearby and overheard the conversation.

"I'll keep her company," the mother said. Bill thanked her and headed up front. He slid into the seat behind the driver and spoke to the old man sitting there gazing out the window.

"Red, how are you?" he asked of his de facto mentor. Red turned at the sound of his voice.

"Well look who it is!" Red exclaimed. "You look tired, my boy. I take it you've been busy."

"You would not believe the day I've had!" Bill replied. At this, the driver of the bus glanced back over his shoulder at Bill.

"I'm sorry. What's that?" the driver asked.

"Nothing. I was just talking to Red here," Bill answered. The driver then glanced back over his left shoulder toward Red.

"Okaaaayyy..." The driver said as if Bill were crazy. The reaction confused Bill. Red only shrugged and smirked at him. Was there something inherently wrong about befriending Red? Had Bill found himself on the wrong side of some bus driver popularity contest? Bill had an irrational need for everyone to like him, so he pursued the driver's approval at the expense of his conversation with Red.

"You know, I'm a driver, too." It seemed a natural place to start. But when the driver heard that Bill was employed at the parks, he was incredulous, having never seen him before. Bill explained that he was new and had been driving mostly VIP and cast member routes. This, too, was met with incredulity.

"Really?" The driver sounded more patronizing by the second. "Because I been driving here for more than six years," he said in what Bill guessed was a New Orleans accent. "And they ain't letting me nowhere near a VIP!" He laughed a hearty guffaw. Bill laughed with him, trying desperately to fit in. Bill introduced himself, learning the driver's name, Gerry, in the process.

"Well it was nice meeting you, Gerry" Bill said. "Gotta get back to my friend."

"Yeah," Gerry said, chuckling, "you get back to your friend." Gerry continued laughing to himself. Clearly the man was losing his grip on sanity. Bill worried that too many years behind the wheel of one of these beasts might drive him crazy, too. Add one more reason to take the prophecy seriously. He began to recount to Red the events of the day, being careful to speak softly so as not to be heard by Gerry.

Meanwhile, Cleary was simply trying to stay awake. The mother sitting near her noticed Cleary's heavy eyelids. "Busy day, honey?" the mother asked.

"Yes, ma'am," Cleary answered. "Weird day."

"Are you here with just your daddy today?" the woman inquired, trying to keep Cleary awake. Cleary nodded. "Is your mom back at the hotel?" The girl shook her head. Then Cleary, bored and wanting to stay awake, decided she might as well have some fun with the situation. No tall tale about Disneyana would do. It was time to raise her game and declare herself the storytelling champion of the family.

She slid over toward the woman and leaned in close. Casting a nervous glance toward her father at the front of the bus, she whispered, "Actually, my mom is at home. My dad came and got me at her house. It was just supposed to be for the weekend, but it's been like two weeks or something." The woman gasped and nervously shifted her glance between Cleary and Bill, all the while pulling her own children closer. Cleary continued, "I asked to call my mom, but he keeps coming up with reasons why we can't. I don't know if she even knows where we are." Cleary did her best to work up some tears.

"Oh, you poor girl," the woman whispered back. "Now you tell me, has your father hurt you?"

"Oh no, ma'am," she answered, wiping her not-so-moist eyes. "My dad hasn't hurt anybody since he got out." The woman clutched her children tightly.

At the front of the bus, Bill and Red were deep into their usual topic of conversation. "If you've got four of the nine on your side, it won't be long now," Red commented. "The Mintz-Powers are going to have a heap of pressure on them to act. It's going to be interesting."

"That goes without saying," Bill noted. "Red, any chance I could call on you the next time one of these groups shows up? I could use your savvy." Red squirmed in his seat and cast his gaze out the window again.

"I'm not gonna be around for that, Bill." His voice cracked as he spoke. "Today's my last day here." Bill was flummoxed.

"What? Were you fired? Are you retiring?" Though he couldn't even explain why, this revelation was a severe blow to Bill's confidence. Knowing he could count on Red's knowledge and counsel had made this bizarre ordeal more manageable for him.

"Something like that," Red replied. "I can't explain, but you won't be seeing me anymore. But listen to me, Bill Durmer. You are the New Son. I know it. And I know you'll do the right thing." The bus pulled into the All-Star Movies Resort. "I believe this is your stop." Bill stood and offered Red his hand.

"Red it has been an absolute honor." The older man shook his hand with a firm grip. "But tell me, really, where'd you learn all this stuff?" Red smiled.

"My father knew a thing or two about this business," he replied. Bill just shook his head in mock frustration.

"Always mysterious," he commented. Cleary approached and took her father's hand. Bill nodded to Red and stepped off the bus with his daughter. Just as Red had predicted, Bill never saw him again.

The Durmers shuffled lazily to their room. Once inside, they both crashed on their beds for a late afternoon nap. The air in the room was thick and muggy. The air conditioner strained to keep pace with the brutal Florida heat. Outside, the shrieks of teenagers in the pool echoed through the courtyards. Families squabbled, and parents scolded exhausted children. Bill's head was drenched with perspiration, and he tossed fitfully. He dreamt he was in a PeopleMover on a track inside an endless tunnel. Another train approached from the opposite direction. As it whizzed past, he noticed Katherine sitting alone in it, calling out for him. He climbed back to the rearmost car of his own train, trying to reach her. But it was too late. Peering down the track ahead, he looked for a stop or a turn-around. There was nothing but endless track.

The tunnel filled with flashing blue and red light, growing brighter and brighter until Bill could no longer see the tunnel beyond. From somewhere inside the light, he heard Cleary cry out, "Daddy!" He snapped awake.

Cleary stood over him smiling. "We got another D-note!" Bill rubbed his eyes and struggled to prop himself up in the bed. "Open it!" she demanded. Bill fumbled with the envelope and finally tore it apart. He opened it and frowned.

"Hold tight. Help will come," he read. "What does that mean?" Just then, the lights went off. "What the?" He handed the card to his daughter. Checking the phone, he noticed that it, too, was dead. He slammed it down and shambled across the bed toward the window. The room was almost entirely dark with the blackout blinds drawn. Reaching the window, he flung the blinds open. The room did not brighten as he expected. Had he slept until after sunset? He hated that. Looking up at the sky, he saw dark storm clouds gathering. "Gonna be a bad one," he said.

He noticed flashing blue and red lights bouncing around in the distance, beyond Buzz Lightyear's legs. A harsh voice pierced the murk of the early evening. "Bill Durmer. We have you surrounded. Surrender now or we will come in after you."

Bill closed the blackout shade and fell back onto the bed. "Wonderful," he sighed.

Cleary noted nonchalantly, "I guess that's what the note meant."

∗∗∗

Two hours later, they found themselves peeking through the curtains out into the black, waiting for something, anything to happen. Bill spoke a little too loudly.

"Hell of a thing."

Chapter Twenty-Two:
A Kiss for the Ages

Jaimee hugged Katherine tightly. "Are you sure you'll be okay here?" she asked. Katherine nodded.

"Thanks for listening, Jaimee." Katherine hugged her one last time. Jaimee climbed back into her cruiser. She and her partner waved goodbye as they pulled away and joined the growing caravan of emergency vehicles exiting the resort. Steam drifted up from the asphalt and was pierced and moulded by the line of headlights. It was part laser show, part holiday display — a slow-rolling strand of Christmas lights stretching toward the rapidly approaching sunrise. The rain had stopped an hour earlier, but lightning still flickered high in the clouds to the Northeast. A continuous, low rolling thunder lingered.

Katherine ambled back to the command vehicle, stepping inside to enjoy the air conditioning. She found it unmanned. Sitting in one of the chairs, she stared at the console which, save a few blinking red LEDs, was now devoid of activity. A voice crackled over the radio, "Eleven-three-fifty-seven at Wilderness Campground," the woman said.

A male voice responded, "Ten-four. I'm on it. Inform the local."

As Katherine pondered what exactly they were discussing, a small voice from behind her said, "Mama?" Katherine spun around to find Cleary standing in the doorway. She leapt to her feet and grabbed hold of her daughter, squeezing her and lifting her as she once had when the girl was a toddler.

"Oh, my baby," Katherine uttered, her voice cracking and tears streaming down her cheeks, "I was so worried." Cleary began to cry, too. "Are you okay?" Cleary wriggled free of her mother's grasp and wiped the tears from her eyes.

"I'm fine," she sniffled. "I'm just really tired." Katherine knelt in front of her. She wiped the remaining tears from the girl's eyes and, with a mother's touch, brushed back the hair from her face.

"Weren't you scared?" she asked.

"A little, maybe," Cleary shrugged. "We just didn't know what was going on. But Daddy took good care of me."

"I'm sure he did," Katherine replied, meaning every word. She felt a rush of guilt for ever believing him responsible for the standoff. Should she apologize for wrongs never committed and thoughts never spoken? She was one of those people who believed life was not a muscle condition, but a heart condition. It was not a question of what people did, for good or for ill, but the thoughts, feelings and intents behind those actions ... or inaction. Though she had not accused Bill of creating the crisis, she had thought it. And that was betrayal enough.

No sooner than she had resolved to confess to Bill her doubts, she spotted him walking with Mortimer toward the vehicle. She stood, straightened her clothes, sidestepped Cleary and walked toward Bill, ready to offer an apology. Bill, for his part, was walking, head low, planning to do exactly the same thing. When they were a few yards apart, Bill offered her a half-hearted grin. He looked awful, his eyes dark and sunken in their sockets, not unlike the haggard look he bore after the night of the Black Jubilee.

"Hey Baby," he said. That was all Katherine needed. She ran the last few steps toward her husband, embraced him and kissed him long and hard. They had long since resigned themselves to the fact that no new kiss would ever crack their top five, the most recent of which had been the day they learned Cleary was on the way. But right then, standing in a steamy hotel parking lot in the shadow of a S.W.A.T. vehicle and under the watchful eye of the battalion chief, they upset the balance of their most legendary kisses. This one was top two, easy. Mortimer stayed back a pace, allowing the two to silently reconcile.

"Oh, get a room!" Cleary called out from the truck. They separated, both laughing heartily.

"Where did she get that?" Katherine asked.

"I've been meaning to talk to you about her TV habits," Bill replied. Katherine kissed him again.

"Praise God you're safe," she said, beginning to cry again. Bill held her gently and allowed her to weep on his shoulder. When she had gotten a good cry out of her system, Mortimer led them into the command vehicle for a debriefing.

Mortimer was apologetic for the confusion and was even a bit confounded himself at how things had gotten out of hand. "We received a tip from a woman who claimed a little girl on the bus told her she had been kidnapped by her father." He asked Cleary, "Now, you wouldn't know anything about that, would you?"

Cleary immediately looked to her mother. "I'm sorry. I was just telling tall tales, and that one went a little too far, I guess." To her father she said, "Sorry, Daddy. I never thought she would believe me." Bill, however, accepted full blame for starting the game in the first place.

Mortimer continued, "According to the bus driver, the girl was with a man who claimed to be a bus driver himself. I can only assume that was you." Bill nodded. Mortimer cleared his throat. He looked away for a split second in what would have looked like shame, if the man had been capable of that emotion. The Chief then stared dead into Bill's eyes, "Mr. Durmer, I've spoken to your wife on this matter, but I think you might want to have yourself checked out by a..." he cocked his head to one side like a curious dog, "...a qualified professional."

"What do you mean?" Bill knew he exactly what he meant: a psychiatrist. But for the life of him, he couldn't infer why.

"The driver told security that the man — that *you* were sitting in the seat behind him, carrying on a conversation with... Well, with no one. Thin air. An imaginary friend, if you will." Mortimer's gaze was unbreakable. "Have you been feeling well, Mr. Durmer?"

"That's preposterous!" Bill replied. "I was talking to Red the whole time. The driver saw me! He saw us both! Red was on the bus before I even got there." Bill was flustered, searching for meaning in this revelation and the right words to express his consternation. "This is a set-up. It has to be. That driver set me up!"

Mortimer tried to calm him down. "Your wife mentioned this Red to us as well. She did. And we did some searching. Mr. Durmer, I don't know how to tell you this, but there's no driver on record that goes by that name. Not even a nickname. Either this Red is setting you up himself, or..." The chief wouldn't finish the sentence. Bill forced his hand.

"Or what?"

"Or he doesn't exist at all," Mortimer replied. Bill was speechless. He looked to Katherine, searching her eyes for a clue to this latest puzzle. She, too, was confused.

"Cleary, you saw me talking to Red, didn't you?" Bill asked.

The girl was reticent to answer, "Daddy, I thought you were talking to the driver. There wasn't anyone else in your seat." She lowered her face, ashamed to be the one to break it to her father that he might be coming unglued.

"I don't understand," Bill said. "I don't..." He trailed off. Sure he had his neuroses, but he had never been given to such flights of fancy. Once, when driving drowsy after a long day and night at the store, he mistook a mailbox for a whitetail deer and swerved to miss it, nearly flipping his car. And there had been the time he thought he saw a leprechaun on the beach while on his Jubilee watch. But the Mobile news stations (and later YouTube) had been all ablaze with reports of a leprechaun sighting across the bay in Crichton.

Bill's leprechaun turned out to be a mangy nutria rat that, for reasons unknown, drunken teenagers had caught and dressed up in a Notre Dame dog sweater. The Gipper, as he came to be known, reappeared on the beaches from time to time and became somewhat of a local legend — but never to the extent of the famed redfish, Louisville Mashgill, God rest his soul. A sighting of the Gipper was a portent of good news, as it typically preceded a Notre Dame defeat on the gridiron. And there are few things dearer to an Alabama fan's heart than the humiliation of the Fighting Irish. As for the sweater, it must have been constructed of the highest grade synthetic fibers, perhaps with a touch of Kevlar, because it rarely showed signs of weathering.

Apart from those two cases, Bill had never been known to hallucinate. So even he found it difficult to believe that he had concocted so elaborate a phantom over so long a period of time. He defaulted to Katherine's memory. "Kat, you saw him. When we were here at Christmas, he was our bus driver the night we had to move to the Grand Floridian. Remember?" Katherine shook her head. "Oh, come on, I talked to him the whole ride over."

"You didn't talk to anyone," she said softly, taking his hand. "You fell asleep, standing up, a few minutes after we got on board."

"No!" Bill demanded. "No, I didn't." Katherine only nodded and squeezed his hand tighter. So this was finally it. He had officially gone 'round the bend, lost his marbles and driven wholly outside the calling area. No, that couldn't be it. That couldn't be the only explanation. Red had imparted so much wisdom and so much knowledge about the prophecy. There was no way Bill could have created that of his own imagination. There was no way he could have known those things. Bill rubbed his forehead as he pondered this. "This doesn't make any sense."

"No, it doesn't," Mortimer remarked. He slid a report across the table toward Bill. Pointing to a specific line item, he said, "This denotes the time when security spoke with the bus driver. You see, the recommendation here to send an officer over for a preliminary interview. Nothing more." He pointed to another line item. "Now this shows where someone ordered an inter-agency response to a hostage situation involving a heavily armed suspect."

"I don't understand," Katherine said. "Who ordered that?"

Pointing again to the report, he replied, "It was a code C-nine. Council of the Nine."

"No," Bill argued, "That doesn't make sense. Wouldn't the Council have to agree unanimously on something like that? And at least four groups are on my side."

"What do you mean 'on your side?'" Katherine asked.

"I'll explain later," Bill replied. "Chief?" Bill tried to get a response out of Mortimer, who just sat there, nodding and trying to piece it all together. Finally, he looked up and pointed a palm-open hand at Bill. (Disney cast members never pointed with a single finger. Not even battalion chiefs.)

"You're the one, aren't you?" he asked Bill. "You're the one they've been talking about." Bill nodded. The chief leaned back in his chair and exhaled strongly. "I never believed in the prophecy myself. But my wife," he whistled, "that woman is obsessed with it." Katherine was growing more confused by this conversation every second. Bill had told her about the groups that made up the Council, but hadn't told her about the prophecy. She only knew that they were interested in him because of a vague expectation that he might rise to some level of power. She decided to let this play out between Mortimer and Bill rather than interrupt with her questions. "You would have seen her yesterday," Mortimer continued. "She's one of those Frankenmommies or whatever they're calling themselves these days."

Bill shrugged, "I met a lot of people yesterday."

"She's sort of barnside broad, big shock of greying hair on top, eyes like a mongoose, voice like a hyena." His description of his wife pushed the limits of both Bill's and Katherine's self-control. There's nothing in this world quite so painful as wanting to laugh and knowing you can't. But they both wanted to laugh so very badly. They avoided one another's glances — just to be sure.

"No," Bill said with as sober a tone as he could manage, "but like I said, I met a lot of people." Mortimer waved it off.

"Doesn't matter. What does matter is that somebody's trying to stop you, maybe hurt you, perhaps kill you." Mortimer backed off, "Okay, probably not kill you," he said. Then pointing a single finger at Bill, proving that he, too, was a rule breaker, he added, "Maybe maim you. These people seem like they sure would enjoy a good maiming." From the wistful sound of his voice, Bill worried that the chief could enjoy a good maiming, too. Mortimer stood, taking the report back, "And they'll go to any length to stop you."

"The Mintz-Powers?" Bill asked, wondering how much the man knew.

"Most likely," he confirmed. So he knew a good bit. Bill prayed the Powers weren't killers — or even maimers — that maybe they were just over-the-top scarers. Surely, if they were of a maiming mind, Red would have told him. What was the point of having a possibly imaginary mentor if Bill couldn't count on him to mention the maiming? Maiming should have been near the top of the agenda: *You may be the chosen one, some people will want to stop you and they're big on the maiming.* New rule: Only allow someone to be a mentor once he has been confirmed to be an actual, corporeal human by at least three other people. And a dog. Dogs know these things.

"What do I do?" Bill asked, already knowing the answer: avoid the maiming.

"Two choices," Mortimer replied. He held his hands up, palms facing Bill, to represent the choices. "Give up and fade away." He waved his right hand to represent a dissipating vapor. "If you do that, they win. And you'll never know what you could have accomplished. Or ... you fight." He balled his left hand into a fist. "You do whatever it is the Council needs you to do. You see this thing through. And they lose." Bill stood and offered the chief his hand. He took it and squeezed so hard Bill could swear he felt a bone crack.

"I will," Bill pledged. The time for blending in was over. He would never be like the baker. He couldn't. Much had been given him. Now much was expected.

The chief personally escorted them back to their room and posted guards outside their door. Over room-service breakfast, Bill (with some help from Cleary) regaled Katherine with the tales of the Prophecy of the New Son. By 7:30, Cleary was sacked out. Her parents continued their conversation in whispers.

"I promised the chief I would do it," Bill said, almost as if he needed to hear the words himself to believe it. "I guess I'm going through with it. You know I have a rule about breaking my promises."

"But what about Decent Chance, Bill?" Katherine asked. "It's so bad at home. You just don't know. They need you. No one there thinks the way you do. No one else can get everyone to listen." Bill knew she was right. He had abandoned his home in its most desperate hour. What was he to do? On the surface, the choice was easy: pack up and go home. His hometown needed him. And what difference would it make to a worldwide media conglomerate if he weren't around? They had done pretty well before he came along. He was quite sure they could manage. But it was more than that. It was more than financial success, hit movies, theme park attendance, spreadsheets and stock values. It was a matter of replacing strategy with dreams, synergy with genuine, personal vision. On a more elemental level, it was about not only providing for his family's needs, but providing them with an example. To whom much is given.

An idea sprang to his mind, as ideas often did, when he was at his most vulnerable and desperate. Inspiration. The breath of God. Though he knew he could never be the baker, he could still pursue the dream of living inside the magic. He could assume the mantle of company visionary. And he could save his home. And he could do it all at the same time. Bill shared his idea with Katherine. She spoke no words in response, but the tears in her eyes said enough. He had proven his quality.

They were up another hour, catching up on lost time. Then they slept until mid-afternoon in each other's arms and would have slept longer if not for a knock at the door. Bill dressed in a rush and cracked the door open, expecting to see one of the guards.

"Bill Durmer, it's good to see you again." The man was in his early sixties, well groomed and dressed in an expensive suit. He looked familiar, but Bill couldn't place him.

"I'm sorry," Bill slurred, "have we met?" The man smiled a comforting smile and plunged his hands in his pants pockets evincing an aw-shucks folksiness.

"You may not recall," he began. "I'm Darren Robinson. We met briefly at the Grand Floridian last December." Then it hit Bill: the Towel Baby Couple! He swung the door open a little wider and leaned against the door jam.

"Right, I remember," he said. The couple had not told him their names. So how could Robinson have expected Bill would recognize it? He had only learned the name from Red, but if Red wasn't real... That line of thinking, he sensed, would only end in futility. Therefore, he chose to focus on the here and now. "What can I do for you?"

"The time has come," Robinson replied. "You and your family get dressed and meet me in the food court." He smiled widely, "Your whole life is about to change." With that, he turned and walked away. Bill closed the door quietly, hoping not to awaken his family.

"That was weird," Katherine groaned.

"Welcome to the party." Bill slid back into the bed next to her. "I guess this is really happening. What if the rest of the groups don't believe it? What if I fail? So much is riding on this now."

"You won't fail," she whispered. "I believe in you." She kissed him. In this kiss, he could feel the full weight and history of their marriage: the frustrations, the heartbreak, the joy, and the hope. He was also pretty sure he could feel a fever blister coming on, and he made a mental note to tell her to take care of that later. But mainly, he felt love. This was easily the best kiss they had ever shared. It was a kiss for the ages.

Chapter Twenty-Three:
Under the Watchful Gaze of Dwarfs

Haunting eyes — giant, carved, dopey, haunting eyes — stared down, unblinking and unrelenting, at Bill. As an animated character, Dopey was charming and sweet. As a nineteen-foot stone carving, he was just plain scary. Statues of the other six dwarfs and one of Oswald the Lucky Rabbit joined Dopey in completing 320 degrees of a massive circle, their hands upturned above their heads, supporting a giant, marble dome. The final figure in the rotunda was Mickey, dressed in his robe and hat from "The Sorcerer's Apprentice." Where the other characters' gazes were fixed down toward the center of the marble floor, Mickey's was cast skyward. And unlike the others, he was not physically connected to the dome. A large gap between his hands and the supporting beams suggested that, while the others were the pillars upon which the company was built, Mickey was its magical heart.

"These are like the ones on the Team Disney Building in Burbank, right?" Bill inquired of Robinson, pointing to the statues. "Were they based on those?"

Robinson smirked, "These were here first." Nine throne-like chairs were arranged in a circle at the center of the room, each one positioned directly in front of one of the statues. And in the very center of the room sat a circular stone bench large enough only for a single person, enabling that person to pivot and face each of the chairs. Beyond the statues, three steps ringed the rotunda, leading to a gallery about twenty feet deep and completely encircling the room. Cleary and Katherine sat on the steps sharing a bottle of water. Bill paced nervously about the rotunda under the watchful eyes of Robinson and his giant, stone compatriots.

"The Council had this place built in the early nineties," Robinson explained, "when we got some exciting news: a prospective new candidate."

"You've been following me for nearly 20 years?" Bill was both offended and impressed. On one hand, it was a serious violation of his privacy. On the other, it demonstrated a level of patience and perseverance he could scarcely fathom. "What? How?"

"All will be made known soon enough," Robinson answered. Bill sat in the chair before Sleepy. Robinson took up the Doc seat opposite him.

"What about you?" Bill asked. "Where do you fit into all this?"

"I'm just fortunate, I suppose," he replied. "I made a little money in industrial solvents." He was self-effacing about his success. "I know, not exactly show business. When we were building a new house, I hired a couple of Disney animators to paint murals for us." So far, Robinson's story was lining up perfectly with what Red had told Bill upon their first meeting. For a figment, Red was well informed. Bill decided to test Red's account further, primarily because he was trying to come to grips with who, or what, Red was.

"Lemme guess," Bill said, "John Musker and Ron Clements?" Robinson was aghast.

"H- h- how did you know that?" he stammered. A giddy smile emerged, "That's amazing. Yes, Clements and Musker." He wagged a finger at Bill. "You're everything you were advertised to be, Bill Durmer. Anyway, it was they who told me about the prophecy. I'm not sure they took it very seriously, but something told me it was real. I got to meet some of the higher-ups and members of the Disney family over time. Next thing you know," he shrugged, "here I am."

Bill hesitated to ask his next question, but he didn't know if he'd ever have the opportunity again. "Tell me, Mr. Robinson," he addressed him formally, knowing he could never call anyone wearing that nice of a suit by his first name, "What about the baby? Is it connected somehow? To all of this?" Robinson sighed, leaned back in his chair and stared at the ceiling of the rotunda.

"Some things," he began, then changed course. "When you love someone — I mean truly love them with all your heart and soul and mind and strength — sometimes you may not understand why they do what they do.

But you love them anyway. The 'baby' represents a dream lost but unforgotten. Maybe one day we will find a new dream." He looked through glistening eyes across at Bill's puzzled expression and smiled, "but I didn't answer your question, did I?" Bill shook his head. "The answer is yes. And no. The prophecy has nothing to do with the baby, but the baby has everything to do with the prophecy." Robinson forced a smile and rose to turn his back toward Bill, before his emotions got the better of him.

Robinson returned to the center of the rotunda. Checking his watch, he said, "Heads up. It's time to care." He directed Bill to the stone seat. Katherine and Cleary he told to stand close to the Mickey statue. A door flung open on the opposite side of the gallery.

"It's Tomorrow Man!" Cleary exclaimed. Sure enough, there he was: the man in the fishbowl pajamas, followed by his league of Tomorrowlanders. He stepped down into the rotunda and stood in front of the Doc chair, giving Bill his customary salute and a slight bow as he did. His cohorts gathered around the statue of Doc, careful to stay at the gallery level. Next came the Doll Lady. Following behind her were a parade of people, young and old, each wearing a costume to match the rubberhead they carried. They, the Small World Society, took up their place around Happy. Doll Lady waved sweetly to Bill as if she were a grandmother watching her favorite grandchild on stage at a school play.

The Moms came next, this time accompanied by the male members of their group, together making up the Frankenollies. They followed the woman Bill refused to call Mommy. Upon seeing her, Katherine leaned over and whispered to Cleary, "She really does look like me. You say she and your Daddy were alone in the Country Bear Jamboree?" Cleary nodded. To herself, she said, "We'll have to have a little talk about that." They gathered at the statue of Grumpy.

"Appropriate," Bill quipped as Mom took her place in front of the Grumpy chair. She playfully snarled at him. Then, noticing Katherine's burning glare, she affected a more dignified look.

Snow White led in the Cast of Thousands, their costumes evoking giggles and moans from the other groups present. They gathered under those big, creepy eyes of Dopey's. Snow White and Bert led a man in business casual attire to the chair. He looked perplexed and distracted. Bill recognized him as Marc Oerlander, the casting executive he'd met on his first day in town. Bill waved to him, but Oerlander only furrowed his brow. He had no idea who Bill was or even why he himself was there.

"Oerlander's a word bearer?" Bill asked Robinson.

"He is," Robinson said, rolling his eyes. "It's Eric Larson's word. Larson passed it to Don Bluth." Bill took over from there.

"Yeah, Bluth to Henry Selick, Selick to Tim Burton. Then it bounced around to other CalArts alumni until it came to Oerlander," Bill said, recalling the story from his conversation with Red.

"That's right," Robinson was taken aback. "How did you know that?"

"My imaginary friend told me," Bill quipped. "I'm confused. I thought Oerlander was a pretty sharp guy when I met him."

"Everybody thinks that at first," Robinson confided. "Most people never get past thinking that. He's so distracted and apathetic that he just agrees to whatever is going on around him. And every bureaucracy loves its yes-men."

"Well, does he know what he's doing?" Bill was concerned that Oerlander might be as significant a hurdle as the Powers.

"Let's find out," Robinson said with a wink. Then he called out to Oerlander, "Marc, glad you could finally join us. It should prove to be a historic day."

"Absolutely," Oerlander replied, nodding vacuously. "Listen, is this going to take long? I've got tickets to *La Nouba*."

To Bill, Robinson whispered, "Not a clue." In fact, Oerlander didn't even have tickets to the Cirque show. He was just craving an Icee, but didn't think that sounded "business-y" enough.

Next through the door came a throng of hipsters, nerds, artists, engineers and eccentrics of every variety. These were the outsiders, the ones who got picked last for kickball in school and had now taken it up as adults to right those perceived wrongs. One glance and Bill felt an affinity to them, although he didn't look the part himself. Bill sometimes thought of himself as a Jordan Almond: boring pastel outside, completely nuts inside.

"The Remagineers," Robinson whispered. "Some current Imagineers, but mostly former. Their word was given to Marc Davis, the only one of the Nine Old Men who worked full-time in Imagineering. He passed it on to Ken Anderson, and he gave it to Marty Sklar. There were some rumors of an uprising in the ranks a few months back. Many in this group were concerned about the direction of Imagineering under Marty's leadership. Not big fans of 'synergy' this lot. So we'll see if Marty turns up."

The Remagineers ambled into the general area of the Bashful statue, but none stepped forward into the inner circle of the rotunda. "Where is your word bearer?" Robinson asked.

"Unavoidably detained," one of the older hipster types replied. "He'll be here, though." Robinson nodded and whispered to Bill, "We must have all nine here to confirm you, but not to worry; there is work to be done in the meantime."

Immediately following the Remagineers entered a mob of pirates. Save one, all were dressed as characters from either the attraction or the films, and most of those were dressed as Jack Sparrow. At least a dozen of those were dead ringers for Johnny Depp as the character. "The Captain Jacks," Robinson said. "They used to be the Devils and Black Sheep, but then the movies came around... Their word was given to Milt Kahl who passed it on to X Atencio, the writer of the 'Yo-Ho' song and the ride script." Bill nodded. He, of course, knew who X Atencio was.

They gathered around Sneezy. The group's representative stepped forward. He was the lone member of their contingent not wearing a pirate costume. Instead, he wore a fedora, horn-rimmed glasses, a weathered black t-shirt, beaten up designer jeans and an old pair of Army boots. Despite the lack of makeup and costume, he resembled Johnny Depp more than did the rest.

"Wow," Bill remarked, "You really look like—"

The man cut him off. "I'm not," he said defensively, "but I get that a lot." He stared at the floor and allowed his longish hair to hide his face from Bill. Even then, he looked remarkably like Depp. Bill noticed Katherine staring at the man, too and was immediately grateful he and the man weren't in the same sightline. So as to avoid direct comparison.

In came a group dressed as ghouls, goblins, ghosts and funeral attendees. A gaunt man led them. He had a long, narrow face and wore a black tie and tail-coat, giving him the appearance of an undead butler or the world's scariest mortician. His makeup affected a more ghastly and gaunt appearance than was normal for his already pale, thin face. In his lapel, he wore a black rose. "The Grim Grinning Ghosts," Robinson commented. "Their word was given to John Lounsbery. When Lounsbery died, Woolie Reitherman recommended it go to Leota Toombs Thomas, the Imagineer."

"Right," Bill replied, "who performed Madame Leota in the Haunted Mansion."

"Precisely. I would have thought Leota would pass her word along to her daughter, a second-generation Imagineer. Instead, she gave it to Reynaldo there," he said pointing with the whole hand toward the gaunt man, who was now leading his group toward Sleepy.

"Who is he?" Bill asked.

"Rank and file cast member," Robinson replied. "He's sort of popular with the guests for plussing the attractions he works, especially Haunted Mansion. Some find him insufferable. They say he's always 'on,' whatever that means. He's never been anything but professional on the Council though, downright grim even." Reynaldo bowed slightly to Bill as he assumed his place, never once breaking his somber expression.

The room grew silent as the final group entered. Bill immediately noticed that each and every member of this group was male. Most were young, the oldest being no more than his age and not a grey hair among them. Some wore impeccably tailored suits, while others wore t-shirts that either promoted competing studios and theme parks or mocked Disney institutions: Mickey making rude hand gestures, a haggard Cinderella in curlers with a cigarette dangling from her lips et al. "I suppose you can guess who these scoundrels are," Robinson said, his disdain oozing through every word.

"Yeah," Bill replied, not even justifying their presence by uttering the words: Mintz-Powers. Hisses and jeers rose from the crowd as the group convened around Oswald.

"Would any of you gentlemen like to admit to last night's maliciousness?" Robinson sneered. "I'm sure Battalion Chief Mortimer would love to hear from you." A large woman in the Frankenollie area cackled, sounding vaguely like a hyena. Bill spotted her and waved.

"Hello back there, Mrs. Chief Mortimer!" he called out. The woman giggled and waved a massive, flabby arm with such velocity as to create a persistence of vision that made the arm look like a giant, fleshy Japanese fan.

Robinson was still focused on the Powers. "I don't suppose your word bearer is present?"

A young man in jeans, a blazer and a faux vintage t-shirt stepped forward. The shirt bore the image of a rabid cartoon rat with the word "Rickets" emblazoned across it. Bill noticed his eyes. They were cool green — impossibly, intensely green — almost luminescent.

"You know as well as I do that he has no interest in taking part in this nonsense," the young man sneered. He flashed a devilish grin, "And you also know that you can't do anything without him. We're just here to watch your golden boy go down in flames." Without a hint of reverence, he plopped down in the chair, throwing one leg over the arm. "There's nothing you rat lovers like more than a good fireworks show." Something about the man's intonation triggered Bill's memory.

"You." He pointed at the man with his index finger. He wasn't an insider, yet. He could point all he wanted. "You called me. You threatened my family."

The man flung his hands out in a nonchalant gesture. "Prove it." Bill wanted desperately to administer a radical nose-ectomy. This guy was testing the very limits of his belief in Philippians 2:3. Relishing the ire he evoked in Bill, the man quipped, "You know, Durmer is an anagram for 'murder.' Do you want to murder me, Golden Boy?"

Yes, he did. Instead of indulging the man, he turned the other cheek ... and turned to face Robinson, "Now what?"

Robinson addressed the group, "As you all know, we lost a word bearer and a dear friend when Roy E. Disney passed away last December." Bill knew that Roy E. was the son of Walt's brother, Roy, and had been a longtime leader within the company. "He did, however, pass on his word of prophecy to a new bearer." He called out loudly toward the door at the back of the gallery, "Would the bearer of the word given to Les Clark please enter the Rotunda?"

The door swung slowly open. In stepped a familiar face: Mrs. Robinson. She walked silently across the room, cradling the towel baby in her arms. She walked directly to the center of the rotunda, past her smiling husband, to Bill. She gently kissed him on the cheek. "I told you it was you."

"Yes, you did," Bill replied, his voice echoing hers in its halcyon sweetness. Mrs. Robinson assumed her place in front of Mickey.

"Wonderful," the Powers man quipped, "This council must be a lovely time for all of you people. A reunion of your talk group from the nut house." His compatriots laughed with him.

Robinson, however, was not amused. He approached and towered over the younger man. "Do you have the word of the prophecy?"

The Powers man fidgeted like a child who'd brought home a bad grade. "No," he pouted.

"Then get out of the chair," Robinson snapped.

The young man was defiant. "Make me." Robinson leaned down close to his face, causing the younger man to fidget and dart his eyes about like a scolded dog.

"See those guys in the pirate suits?" Robinson whispered more as statement than question. The younger man glanced over at the Captain Jacks. "Those aren't toy swords," Robinson said, adding, "and I'm not certain about the guns." No sooner than Robinson turned away, the young man was up and out of the chair, joining his group on the gallery level.

"You will now present your words," Robinson said to the word bearers. He retrieved a wooden box from a hidden panel underneath the stone seat. Using an antique skeleton key, he opened the box. To Bill he said, "They say this key came from the farmhouse in Marceline where Walt spent the best days of his childhood." Opening the box revealed an odd-looking tablet of sorts. It appeared to be hand-carved from a single piece of wood in the shape of Mickey's head, roughly a foot square. Nine semi-circular openings dotted the left side, each slightly different in shape from the others. And each opening lead to a narrow channel that ran nearly the full width of the tablet. A thick, frosted glass covered the channels. Bill couldn't pinpoint why, but the tablet looked both hi-tech and ancient at once, another brilliant piece of Imagineering at the service of the prophecy.

Each word bearer approached in turn and presented a small wooden vessel, semi-cylindrical with a thin glass panel on the flat side and an aged strip of paper sealed within. Bill caught a glimpse of one and immediately recognized the handwriting. It appeared to be written by a weak hand, shaky and scrawled in places, florid and precise in others, but it was undeniably that of Walt Disney. Robinson, upon receiving each word, slid its containing vessel into the tablet. An audible click indicated the vessel was locked in place, and a dim LED would illuminate the written word within.

When Mom approached, Robinson stopped her. "You are not the word bearer. Does he intend to continue this course of anonymity?"

"I am his proxy, yes," she replied. She clicked in her vessel. Mrs. Robinson presented hers last.

"Seven words are present. We must have the final two before the prophecy is read and the vote is taken," Robinson announced.

"Good luck with that!" cried someone in the Mintz-Powers group. Robinson ignored the heckler and continued on.

"I know some of you still have tests to conduct, however. The word bearers and I will take the candidate, Mr. Durmer, to perform the tests. The rest of you will wait here." To the Mintz-Powers and the Remagineers, he said, "Each of you will need to choose a proxy to accompany us." The punk in the Rickets the Rat t-shirt stepped forward. From the Remagineers came a man in a brightly colored Hawaiian shirt with close-cropped greying hair, a Fu Manchu mustache and a collection of exotic earrings dangling from one lobe. But none of those was his defining feature. The man had thick fur covering both arms to the knuckles, as well as his neck and chest. "That's the Yeti," Robinson whispered to Bill, "Former Imagineer, now freelance. He helped designed Expedition Everest. That's why they call him the Yeti."

Yeah, Bill thought, *that's why*. "Is he the word bearer?"

"To be honest, I thought he would be," said Robinson. "If Marty gave his up, and the Yeti's not the new bearer, I have no idea who it could be." Robinson introduced the Yeti to Bill, then huddled with the hairy man in hushed conversation. The Johnny Depp look-alike drew near to Bill.

"I'm rooting for you, mate," he said in his best Jack Sparrow accent. Bill chuckled.

"Right," he replied, "like the movie." He extended his hand. "Bill Durmer."

"Call me Jack," the man said in turn. Up close, the resemblance was uncanny. Bill took a shot in the dark.

"Central Florida. This must be like coming home for you," he said. He recalled that Depp had grown up in Florida. He hoped to catch the man off-guard and get him to admit to his real identity. He added, "Unless you consider Kentucky your real home. You know, that whole 'you're from where you're born' thing."

Jack smirked, "I see what you're doing. Don't think I don't." He slapped Bill on the back as he passed him to give his regards to the Doll Lady.

Meanwhile, Mom warily approached Katherine. "Mrs. Durmer?"

"Please," Katherine answered, "call me Katherine." Ever the genteel Southern lady.

"Okay, Katherine. I saw how you were looking at me from across the room, and I want you to know you have nothing to worry about. I—" Katherine cut her off.

"I'm sorry. Who are you?" she demanded, hoping to get a real name.

"You can call me Mommy."

Katherine burst into incredulous laughter. "I don't think so." She took Cleary by the hand and walked away toward Bill. Mom, crestfallen, stood silently wondering where she had gone wrong.

"Time to go!" Robinson announced. The whole party — Bill, Robinson, Katherine, Cleary and the nine word bearers and proxies — made for the door.

"Let's go ride some rides!' the Yeti exclaimed.

Chapter Twenty-Four:
Fate, as Determined by a Head in a Jar

Following a trek through a maze of warehouses (including those where Bill had met the Tomorrowlanders and the Cast of Thousands), a ride on the secret WEDway and a walk across Tomorrowland and past Cinderella's castle, the fellowship found themselves strolling through Adventureland. Along the way, Bill was interrogated by several of the word bearers.

The Yeti engaged him in conversation about the state of Imagineering, inquiring about Bill's work on Snooty McOinker, his float designs and the media integration system he had proposed for Exclusion by the Bay. Bill, in turn, quizzed him about the planned Beastly Kingdomme, the land of mythical creatures within Animal Kingdom that never came about. Bill felt small and provincial beside such an accomplished and well-traveled man as the Yeti. He wondered whether the wrong one of them was being tested. Then again, the man did call himself 'the Yeti,' so Bill at least had that going for him.

Doll Lady joined when they discussed recent controversial changes to "it's a small world" in Disneyland, incorporating Disney and Pixar characters into the attraction. Bill's take was that he could understand the profit motive. He reminded the others that the Disney brothers had been on the verge of bankruptcy numerous times over the years, largely because Walt preferred taking risks on new ventures or projects — based solely on instinct — over being fiscally conservative. On the other hand, the Disney of today was on far from shaky financial footing. Bill also held that Walt's statement proclaiming that Disneyland was "never finished" to be an endorsement of plussing attractions or replacing those that didn't hold to the highest vision — not just change for change's sake. All that considered, he didn't like it but could live with the change.

"You people are pathetic," the Powers man jeered. "Harry Potter will shut this place down within a year," he said, referring to the wizard-themed attraction across town. "Disney hasn't made a decent movie since Lion King, and don't even get me started on Pixar. Now you think some failed TV salesman is going to save the company? What a joke."

"Troll," Bill said through gritted teeth.

"What was that?" the man asked.

"If this were an internet discussion, that would make you a troll," Bill explained. "But I think the term applies nonetheless." The Powers man snorted dismissively. Bill added, "There's something I think you should memorize: 'whatever is true, whatever is honorable, whatever is just, whatever is pure, whatever is lovely, whatever is commendable, if there is any excellence, if there is anything worthy of praise, think about these things.'" The little man in the rat shirt sulked to the back of the group, his pride wounded. Bill had scarcely gone a day in his life without failing to live up to that himself. In fact, he couldn't even explain how he had recalled the verse in full at that moment. But he was certain it was something the angry young man needed to hear ... as did Bill himself.

As they approached Pirates of the Caribbean, Jack came alongside Bill. "Nice work with the malcontent," he said.

"Thanks." Bill thought he'd give it another go. "You know, my kids prefer your Willy Wonka, but I'm a Wilder man myself. I guess I'm old school that way."

"Nice try," Jack replied. Guests stopped in their tracks at the sight of the man, many posing for photos with him in the background as he passed. The other word bearers, noticing this, formed a barrier around him. "When we get inside," Jack said, "you and I will need to ride alone. The others can wait outside."

At the entrance to the queue line, Robinson gave the two men special golden Fastpasses, and they were off. They weaved their way down through the belly of the dimly lit, faux Caribbean fort. Jack allowed his hair to hang down, ducking his head the whole way, doing his best to hide his face from onlookers. Bill stood between the shorter man and others whenever possible, using his own height to aid in Jack's attempt at stealth. "For someone who claims not to be famous," Bill said at one point, "you sure have perfected hiding in plain sight."

Channeling Captain Sparrow again, he replied, "Matter of survival, mate. Savvy?" They reached the head of the line, and Jack withdrew a trinket from his pocket. He handed it to a young, female cast member in the load area and the girl's eyes widened. Bill saw that it was one of the Aztec coins from the first Pirates film. If he were a betting man, he would have laid odds that it was pure gold. "WEDway. Captain Jack sent me," Jack said. The girl whispered to her fellow cast member, a boy no older than she. He swiftly roped off the queue line and announced that the ride was undergoing routine maintenance and would re-open in a matter of minutes. The girl entered a code in the ride controls and then deposited the gold coin into a slot in the control panel.

Jack and Bill climbed aboard one of the ride boats and began their journey through the heart of the Caribbean. Ahead of them, a vision of Davy Jones in all his tentacled glory appeared, a projection on a falling mist of the character played by Bill Nighy. Jones laughed, staring at the boat. "You may think ye be taking the WED way, but by my eyes, ye be going the dead way."

Jack smirked, "Nighy could never figure out why they had him read that." Noticing Bill's suspicious glance, he added, "So I've heard."

A haunting voice came over the sound system. "WED men tell no tales," the voice said, not exactly a portent of certain doom.

"I can't believe the work that went into tailoring these things to the prophecy," Bill said with a sense of wonder. "Talk about work that wasn't driven by a profit motive."

"Well," Jack replied, "maybe prophet with a P-H."

They passed pirate skeletons defending cursed treasure and fighting to hold the course of a shipwreck in a hurricane. Passing into darkness, they braced themselves for the downward plunge both knew was coming. At the bottom of the fall, as the course leveled out, they encountered a scene of a pirate ship swapping cannon fire with a Caribbean fort. As their boat floated into the scene, the pirate captain, updated to resemble Hector Barbossa from the films, cried out, "Hold yer fire, you bloomin' cockroaches! Ye shant be harming those under the protection of parlay."

"Cease fire, men!" The commander of the fort yelled to his troops. "They are carrying letters of marque bearing the king's seal!" They sailed past the scene of the mayor being interrogated by marauding pirates dunking him in the town's well. An animatronic Jack Sparrow, who under normal ride conditions hid from the marauders around a corner, now stopped and stared at the boat in which Jack and Bill traveled. The live Jack placed his palms together and bowed to his animatronic likeness. They came next to the infamous auction scene, in which captive women are sold off to the highest bidder. Bill laughed out loud as he considered the irony of Walt Disney, the man whose critics accused him of sanitizing the world beyond recognition, approving a scene involving human trafficking as folly.

Suddenly the boat slowed to a stop. All music quieted, as did all of the dialogue and sound effects except the drunken pirates yelling, "We wants the redhead! We wants the redhead!" The voluptuous animatronic figure they so desired broke from her usual come-hither pose. She blinked and shook her head as if waking from a long sleep. Holding a finger to her pursed lips, she silenced the pirates. The only sounds in the room now were the gentle lapping and swishing of the water past their boat and the whir and whine of the redhead's servos as she turned and looked directly at Bill and Jack.

She slowly lifted her arm, pointed directly at Bill and said, "And the redhead wants that tall one there. He's the one." A loud cheer went up from the sound system, accompanied by the appropriate arms raised and heads thrown back in raucous celebration from all of the characters. The music resumed, and every character bowed low as the boat slowly accelerated forward. For the remainder of the ride, this was the scene: characters that neither man suspected could assume any positions other than those seen by millions of guests over the decades ceased their routines and stood (or sat) silently and bowed. Bill and Jack rode in a simpatico silence.

In the final scene, a jaunty Jack Sparrow, dripping with swag in a trea-sure-filled room, stopped singing and stood up from his chair and bowed to Bill. "I had no idea they built him to do that," Jack noted with wonder.

Climbing off of the boat, something about the experience didn't sit well with Bill. While it was a dramatic variation on the normal ride, it didn't feel as conclusive as what he had seen at Grizzly Hall. Without even thinking it through, he blurted out to Jack, "I don't buy it."

"Buy what?"

"You could have put anybody in that boat, and it would have done the same thing," Bill said, still working it out in his head. "You had the ride operator change the programming. It didn't matter who was in the boat, or probably even if anyone was in the boat at all. The same things would have happened."

"But they wouldn't," Jack countered. "Look, I didn't know what to expect when we got here tonight, so I rode it alone before opening this morning. Until we got to the auction, everything was the same as we saw it tonight. But the redhead didn't react. She didn't look at me. She didn't say anything. From there on out, the ride was exactly the same as it always is." He stopped Bill with a firm hand on the shoulder. "What happened tonight was special. I hope you see that."

"But you could just be saying that to convince me. I wasn't there, so I don't know what you saw."

"What does it matter?" Jack argued. "The test is designed to determine if a candidate is the one, so the word bearer will know how to vote." He smiled at Bill. "You got my vote. Case closed."

"But is it really? If the ride is rigged, how do you know if you're voting the right way?" This was more than a simple debate to Bill. He wanted answers. He wanted certainty. Jack took hold of both of his shoulders now and stared him down.

"Are you looking for a sign to convince me?" Jack asked, "Or do you need a sign to convince yourself?" Bill hung his head and nodded. Point taken. His emotional journey had taken him from mockery to disinterest through stubborn refusal and now to hopeful anticipation. But with that wishful thinking had come a counterpoint of nagging anxiety that he wasn't worthy of the honor. No animatronic bear, no aging futurist in a space suit, no number of eccentrics could vanquish his enemy of self-doubt.

They exited through the gift shop where Jack bought a pirate bandana with Goofy ears, which he wore under his fedora the rest of the evening, in an effort to go incognito. Bill waited for Jack and followed him out to the plaza where the others were waiting. Allowing Jack to get a few paces ahead, Bill called to him, "Hey, Johnny." Jack looked back without suspicion.

"Yes?" Jack replied.

"It's nothing. Never mind." Bill smirked. Victory was his.

Reynaldo came near. In sonorous tones, he groaned, "Master Gracey bids us come."

"Right. Haunted Mansion," Bill replied. "Here we go." Robinson corralled the others. The Yeti had to be pulled away from a group of hardcore

Disney-ites who had recognized him and demanded photos and auto-graphs. Tomorrow Man had attracted an even longer line of autograph seekers. The first few were old timers who remembered the costume from the early days of Disneyland. Of the others, all that could be said was they were followers, blindly conditioned to fall in line, autograph books and cameras at the ready, without questioning why. And one confused soul was trying to get Reynaldo to give him advice on a casket purchase.

Amid the disbelieving gawks of the Walt Disney World guests, the off-beat troupe began their pilgrimage from Adventureland to Liberty Square. The space man and the reluctant, flop-eared pirate. The dapper millionaire, his potentially delusional wife and their terry cloth baby. The bejeweled man-beast and the clueless mid-level manager. The little old lady talking to her dolls. The mom, the undertaker and the jerk. And amidst them all, what appeared to be a traditional American family, perhaps the strangest sight of all. Too bad none of them thought to bring a camera.

Bill drifted to the back of the group, coming alongside the Powers man. "You never told me your name," Bill said, offering the man his hand.

"I thought it best not to." He shook Bill's hand anyway, recognizing the peace offering for what it was. "Just call me Powers, I guess."

"Fair enough." Bill was feeling a twinge of guilt in his gut over his anger toward the man. Either that or the jalapeños on his burger were a mistake. Still, he couldn't take the chance. "I'm sorry," he began, "for calling you out in front of the others. It was a classless move on my part."

"I didn't give you much of a choice," Powers replied.

"There's always a choice," Bill said. Powers grabbed Bill's arm, halting him and allowing the group to go on without them.

"Why are you doing this?" Powers asked. "These people are using you. You know that, right?"

"Why do you want to stop them so badly?" Bill rebutted. "And that stuff about me not being able to save the company? The last time I checked, the company didn't need saving. I mean, ABC, ESPN, the parks, a cruise line?" With each item he listed, he felt he was strengthening his case. "Pix-ar, for God's sake!"

Powers responded rhetorically, "What do you think it needs saving from?"

"If you believe that, why fight the process? Why not do something to save it?"

Powers' freakishly green eyes went steely cold, and a devilish grin crept across his face. "Because it's more fun to watch it burn." He gave Bill a playful punch to the chest and walked off. Bill was left speechless by the man's shameless display of schadenfreude. When Powers had gone a few yards, he stopped and looked back at Bill. "For what it's worth, Bill," he called back, "I like you. You're a good guy."

Moments later, Bill caught up with the group. "Where were you?" Katherine asked. "I turned around, and you were gone." Bill feigned confusion.

"You mean..." he stammered. "I thought... Then who was that I was kissing back there?" He winked at her and kissed her on the forehead.

"You're not funny, Durmer." She slapped him on the rear as he passed by.

"Yes, I am, and you know it!" he yelled back. He joined Robinson and Reynaldo at the queue. To Reynaldo he said, "I guess it's you and me then." Reynaldo slowly shook his head, never breaking character.

Robinson explained, "This test is a little different. We can all ride if we want to."

They made their way to the head of the line. Here, Reynaldo was the star, especially among the cast members working the attraction. Upon seeing him, they would whisper his name amongst themselves or come and shake his hand, confessing humbly what fans they were of his work. Always in character, Reynaldo would answer them, "I am tickled to *death* that you feel that way," overemphasizing the word "death" by dragging it out and lowering his voice even more than usual.

After they had passed through the stretch room and progressed along the queue to the loading area, they paired up into the Omnimover "Doom Buggies." The Robinsons went first, followed by Bill and Reynaldo, then Cleary and Katherine followed by the others.

"So no special version of the ride? No crazy code words?" Bill asked.

Reynaldo turned his head in what seemed to be slow motion and answered simply, "No." He pivoted his head away just as slowly.

"So, what," Bill asked Reynaldo, "are the ghosts gonna ask me questions or something?"

Again, Reynaldo answered, "No," as slowly as before.

"Maybe the guy in the casket," Bill tried again, "he'll pop up and say 'Oy! You're the one!'"

"No."

"I got it! All three hitchhiking ghosts will get in our buggy." Reynaldo had heard enough and finally broke character.

"Look, it's Madame Leota, okay?" he snapped. "She's the one who will confirm it. Or not confirm it. But we won't be able to hear her if you keep talking! God!" Reynaldo huffed. Bill suspected he had hit a nerve. Just to be sure, he followed up with one more question.

"What will she say?"

"I. Don't. Know!" Reynaldo barked, then slumped in his chair and began muttering to himself. Yep, nerve. Bill didn't listen too closely for fear of hearing something that might permanently shatter his fragile self-esteem.

"Great," Bill sighed. "Redheads, talking bears and now a head in a jar." It seemed to Bill a strange way to decide a man's (and a company's) fate, but then again, this was his first prophecy.

Soon, their Doom Buggies delivered them to the Séance Room, eternal haunt of one Madame Leota. The Robinsons, Reynaldo and Bill, the only ones privy to the nature of the test, listened intently.

"Bearers of word and doers of deed," they heard her say well before they could see the mesmerizing effect of the woman's head inside a floating crystal ball. The effect was achieved by projecting footage inside the ball, in this case, footage of the late Imagineer and word bearer Leota Toombs Thomas. "Be not motivated by pow'r or greed," she continued. "Heed the call of prophetic writ. From my ball shall I witness it, the rise of a New Son long foreseen, And longer still the wait has seemed."

Reynaldo and Bill were now directly facing the crystal ball, and Leota seemed to be staring directly at them. "Now I declare the prophecy true, for there is an air of destiny about you ...William Durmer." Bill felt chills run down his spine, and his hair stood on end. Reynaldo and the Robinsons all sat wide-eyed, motionless. Bill locked eyes with Katherine, who looked ashen.

She mouthed, "That was weird." Bill nodded in agreement. He held up his arm to show her the goose bumps.

"That's not right," Reynaldo said. "That was just a line from *Dead Man's Chest*. It can't be right." He grabbed Bill by the sleeve, practically imploring him, "We have to ride it again. There is a special version of the ride script just for the test, but it's supposed to work without it. We've got to do it again to be sure."

Upon unloading, an ad hoc conference confirmed it: they would ride again. None of Leota's poem was part of the normal ride script, so clearly the test protocol had activated as planned. But everyone's concern was over her final line. Several of the party heard it not as saying Bill's name, but "William Turner." If that were the case, the line was lifted directly from the second *Pirates of the Caribbean* film, a suspicion heightened by some hearing a change in Leota's voice on the last line. Powers argued that, if the line were lifted from the film, it would prove someone had tampered with test, thus invalidating it.

They reentered by going backward up the "chicken exit" — for those riders who chickened out prior to boarding the Doom Buggies. Just as a cast member was about to reprimand them, he froze. "Reynaldo," he whispered to himself. Reynaldo removed the rose from his lapel and handed it to the man.

"WEDway. Master Gracey sent me," he said. As had happened on Pirates, the cast member closed the queue line and activated an altered ride experience expressly for the Council. All boarded again. This time, Jack joined Reynaldo, due to his knowledge of *Pirates* lore, and Bill squeezed in with his wife and daughter.

"Will it always be this strange?" Katherine asked.

"We can only hope," Bill answered with a wink.

The ride the second time was far from normal. No sound effects or music. No motion from the animatronics. Silence and stillness. What was usually a playfully macabre experience became genuinely frightening. Again, they entered the Séance Room, this time with even more anxiety than before. Madame Leota was silent this time — that is until Bill was directly in front of the crystal ball. Then she said as before, "There's an air of destiny about you, William Durmer."

"How did they do that?" Katherine whispered. "I mean, has it always been recorded with your name? How did they know? And if so, why didn't they just find all the William Durmers in the world and test them? There can't be that many." All good points, and none to which Bill had answers.

Toward the end of the silent ride, Cleary said, "I don't like this. I want to get off." Bill held her closer.

"It'll be over soon," he said to her. "It'll all be over soon."

Upon disembarking, Reynaldo approached Bill in deference. "You are the one, Bill Durmer." He stood there awkwardly staring at Bill for a moment. Bill was unsure what he expected.

"Thanks?" Bill replied warily. Reynaldo nodded and walked away, his head hung low.

"I don't think he likes you." Bill spun about to see Powers ambling toward him. "But you got his vote."

"Apparently so," Bill replied diffidently.

"Remember, you're at least one vote short," Powers reminded him. "And you always will be." Powers shoved his hands in his pocket and shrugged as if to say, "There's nothing I can do about it."

As they emerged into the muggy night air, Tomorrow Man called out to no one in particular, "A little help here!?" Everyone turned to find that the man's fishbowl helmet had fogged up so completely that he couldn't see at all, eliciting a much-needed collective laugh. Mom took Tomorrow Man by the arm and led him until he could see.

"Back to the rotunda," Robinson said. And off they went. Off to decide Bill's fate.

Chapter Twenty-Five:
Ontological Issues Ignored by a Hack Writer

"Who says a motley band of freaks can't be civilized?" Robinson's self-deprecating humor had been one of the hallmarks of his entrepreneurial career. He lost count of how many multi-million dollar sales he had made with his aw-shucks, "I don't even know what this stuff does" pitch. From a briefcase, he produced a scroll with elaborately carved handles and bearing even more artfully crafted text and drawings. Nodding to Yeti, he said, "Leave it to Imagineering, huh?" The quip was greeted by a few nervous laughs.

Tension in the room was palpable, and the man who was the focus of all that anxiety was feeling it more than anyone. Bill fidgeted and bounced his legs. Sweat beaded around his hairline. His throat was coarse and dry. He flicked his fingernails as he watched Robinson open the scroll.

"Can you believe this thing?" Robinson said to Bill.

"I just wish someone would have put a back on this seat," Bill replied. His remark elicited more genuine laughter. "I know I need to be able to face everyone, but jeez, haven't you people ever heard of swivels?" Even more laughter. Bill was feeling it now. He had them eating out of his hand. He could feel the rush of their adulation. Or maybe it was the sting of their scorn, and the laughter was in fact mockery. They were an inscrutable bunch.

Robinson cleared his throat and began the ceremony. "According to the rules of the Council of the Nine, candidate confirmation can only begin after his discoverer has come forth." He looked to the Doll Lady, "You are Mr. Durmer's sponsor, Doll Lady. Have you brought the discoverer?"

Rising from her chair with her usual placid smile, she said, "I have." Behind her, the Small Worlders parted, creating an aisle. Emerging from the back of their contingent, wearing a solid white dress and carrying a matching doll, came a tall, leggy brunette. Bill gasped.

"Sweet mother of Christmas," Powers blurted out upon spotting her. "It's Jen Tillman." As with any room the supermodel entered, men tried to convince themselves she would fall for them if given the chance, and women developed eating disorders on the spot.

Bill was dumbfounded. He stood as she entered the rotunda, and the two old friends locked wide eyes. Jenny gave him a wink. A supermodel was winking at him, and again, no camera.

She sidled up to Doll Lady, towering over her. The old woman beamed with pride. "Have you prepared a statement?" Robinson asked Jenny.

"I have," she replied. She handed her rubberhead to Doll Lady and unfolded a piece of paper tucked in its dress. She read it with the practiced ease of one who had been in front of many a TV camera. "My name is Jen Tillman, but growing up, I was known as Jenny. I'm from a small town called Decent Chance, Alabama, on the Eastern shore of Mobile Bay. Growing up, I would often spend summers with my maternal aunt in California. She was," Jenny glanced down at Doll Lady, then corrected herself, "*is* an amazingly talented woman." Her aunt! Bill couldn't believe it. He wanted to butt in, to ask her how long she had known, how and why she had kept the secret for so long.

"She would regale me with stories about Mary Blair and Walt Disney and the World's Fair. She would tell me stories until she had none left to tell, but I would always beg her for more. One time I went to visit her, and she was fraught with sadness. Mary Blair had recently died. Over the course of my visit, she discovered that she would become the new word bearer. As usual, I asked for a new story. It was then she told me about the Prophecy of the New Son. I was only seven, but from the moment she told me, I could hear but one name in my head: Billy Durmer. And I continued to believe Bill to be the one," she hesitated and looked at Bill, "even as an eleven-year-old, when my mother found a note in church where he and his best friend had been making fun of my appearance. I was crushed, but my belief was not diminished." Her eyes filled with tears as she recounted the story, as did Bill's.

"I'm sorry," he mouthed to her. He may have learned the verse that would become his personal code that morning in church, but it was nothing compared to the lesson in forgiveness he had just learned from Jenny Tillman.

"When I heard about Bill's loss — of his father and grandfather — it was an epiphany for me. I'm not sure why, but I knew I had to tell my aunt about Bill right then. Fortunately, she didn't think I was completely crazy. A majority of the Council agreed with her, and the mechanism was activated." She folded up the paper. There was that word again: mechanism. Bill had no idea what that could mean, but one thing was certain: whoever or whatever Red was, he had yet to steer Bill wrong.

"That's my story," Jenny said, "but I want to add one more thing." Robinson was about to admonish her for the breach of protocol, but Bill held him back with a touch. He wanted to hear. "Yes, Bill is creative, brilliant, a visionary — all of that. But more importantly, he is good, he is kind." She scanned the room, looking each word bearer in the eye, landing finally on Powers. "He is the kind of person you want guiding you." Jenny smiled at Bill, and the two old friends each pondered the road not taken. Then she added, "Adolescent teasing not withstanding, of course." The crowd laughed and applauded. Bill noticed more than a few moist eyes. Jenny drew near to Bill and kissed him gently on the cheek. Between that kiss and the whole Mom thing, Bill expected to have a rough night sleeping on the floor of the hotel room.

"Anything to add, Doll Lady?" Robinson inquired.

"No," she said. "Jenny summed it up nicely." Doll Lady returned to her seat and Jenny to the back of the crowd.

"Then let us proceed," Robinson replied. To his wife, he said, "I believe one final test is due." She nodded, rose to her feet, the towel baby cradled as ever in her arms. She approached and kneeled before Bill sitting on his stone seat. She grabbed his hand.

"Now, William..." Bill was moved by her choice to call him by his proper name; it reminded him of his mother. She continued, "I need you to tell me how you got here. What specific chain of events brought you to this moment?" She cautioned him, "Tell me everything, every seemingly insignificant detail. It's important that you do."

"Everything?" Bill was incredulous. All he had to do was give a complete explanation of a life he only barely understood himself, the summation of which would determine the future of his career, his family and, if all went according to plan, his hometown. So ... no pressure. He took a deep breath. "In a world," he said in his best movie trailer voice. The resulting laughter eased his nerves. He then began his account with the closing of the family store, sparing no excruciating detail in describing his own failure or heartbreak. Explaining the Decent Chance myth regarding the relationship between Durmer's and Jubilees then called for a primer on the nature of Jubilees themselves. Then came the story of that fateful night.

Bill recounted his despair as he trod the beach in the still, warm air. Baring his soul, he described how desperately he needed a Jubilee that evening. "I sat on the dock, and I prayed. I don't recall what I said, but in my heart I prayed for a sign, some indication of what path my life's journey should take." He shifted in his seat and ran his hands nervously through his hair. Recollection had made him feel the pain of that night afresh, and the wounds were far from healed. "The winds shifted, and the Jubilee began. I guess you all know how that worked out." He continued, recalling the email from Gaston and the resulting inspiration from watching *Beauty*. "So I packed up and came here. And I had every intention of just blending into the background, too. I just wanted to..." What was the right word? There was none. He settled on, "Disappear. But all of this, all of you have made me realize I have something to offer the world. To whom much is given..." He didn't finish the thought, allowing those who knew it to fill in the rest for themselves.

Any feeling of catharsis gained from telling his story, any illusion of crossing a proverbial threshold soon faded as he saw Mrs. Robinson's face. Her eyes were dull, and her head hung low — sheer disappointment. "Is there anything else?" she pleaded with him. "Anything at all?" Bill shook his head. "Think, William!" she cried desperately, demanding of him some elusive memory.

What did she want from him? He had passed the tests of rocket men and bears, pirates and floating heads. He'd been kidnapped and threatened and apparently spied upon for years. He had spent a sleepless night with countless gun sights trained upon him. He'd done all they had asked, no matter how ridiculous, and now he would be denied because he'd failed to tell his own story to her satisfaction? His own story?

It reminded him of a teacher in high school whose final exams consisted of broad essay questions like, "Write everything you know about Chapter Nine." Once, in a fit of anti-authoritarian fervor, he had penned the response, "I know nothing about Chapter Nine." He argued all the way to the county school board that, given the specific language of the question, his answer was correct. If he knew nothing of the chapter, he had successfully written all he knew. His vindication made him a folk hero amongst his classmates. Nancy, of course, saw his rabble rousing as a blight upon her own character. For the better part of a year, she told everyone Bill was adopted. From carnies.

Bill wracked his brain, searching for some nugget that would satisfy her. Thinking out loud, he said, "I was there, on the dock. I prayed, and then..." It came to him. "And then there was," he looked at Mrs. Robinson, his eyes widening, "there was a mouse." Her face brightened with curiosity and anticipation. "It crawled onto the beach out of the shallows. Then it stopped and stood up. On its hind legs like a man. And it stared at me, right into my eyes, and squeaked something. Then it ran away as the Jubilee began." He breathed a sigh of relief. "How did I not remember that?" Mrs. Robinson squeezed his hand, rose and returned to her seat without another word.

Bill didn't know why, but without giving it a single thought, he called to her, "You would have made a wonderful mother."

The Robinsons smiled adoringly at Bill, and one needn't have been a psychic to know what they were both thinking: that Bill would have made a wonderful son.

"Mr. Yeti," Robinson called to the furry man, "any word from your word bearer?"

"Within the hour, sir," the Yeti replied. Robinson grunted with disapproval.

"And you, Powers?" Robinson inquired. Powers, perhaps inspired by Bill's transparency, was lost in thought.

"I'm sorry, what?"

Robinson grew impatient. "Any contact from your word bearer?" he barked in a condescending staccato. The humble manner of Powers' reply stunned all present, especially his own contingent.

"No, sir," he answered. "I regret to inform you there is not." Robinson, sensing a change in the man, kindly asked that he try again. He then called for a recess until the Remagineer's new word bearer arrived. Cleary found a camera to borrow and busied herself taking photos with the various costumed characters. Katherine sat in Bill's lap as they huddled with the Robinsons.

"What's the story with the Mintz-Powers?" she asked. "Who is there word bearer anyhow?"

"Oh, Lord," Mrs. Robinson groaned. "How much time have you got?"

"It started well enough with Frank," her husband explained, saying — as Bill already knew — that the word was originally given to Frank Thomas. Thomas gave it up to then-CEO and President Card Walker when he and Ollie Johnston became co-bearers. The word stayed with the presidents of the company through Frank Wells. "When Frank died in a helicopter crash—"

"God rest his soul," Mrs. Robinson added.

"When Frank died, he willed the word to another executive, but the CEO at the time wanted it for himself." He added as an aside, "Understand I'm leaving their names out of this out of respect, but I think you know who I'm talking about." Bill did. "Anyhow, when the new word bearer refused to relinquish it, he was forced to resign. When he joined a competing studio, he disregarded the rule about passing his word on. None of us have had any contact with him for nearly two decades now. At first, I believed he was holding onto it simply out of spite for his old boss. Then I thought he was afraid certain rivals of his might be named the New Son. Now... I just don't know."

Katherine stared at Robinson. She sighed, "I'm more than a little concerned about how seriously I'm taking this stuff." She asked Bill, "Does this make me a fan girl?"

Bill nodded. "Fly your geek flag high and proud, Honey." A peculiar smell struck Bill's nose. He sniffed the air around them. "Anybody else smell wet dog?" Just then, Yeti ran up to them. The furry man-beast breathlessly whispered something into Robinson's ear. Robinson listened intently, and when Yeti had finished, they shared a celebratory laugh.

Robinson patted Bill on the shoulder. "Showtime." He shepherded the groups back into position and the word bearers to their seats. Once everyone was in place, Robinson bellowed out toward the door, "Would the word bearer please enter?" Every eye fixed on the door as it opened. Who was this mysterious new word bearer?

A small man entered, walking with a precise, mechanical gait. In the shadows at the far end of the gallery, his head hanging low, no one could yet identify him. Necks craned, and feet shuffled as every last person tried to get a better look. Drawing closer to the light of the rotunda, the petite man lifted his head. He had one steely grey eye, and the other was covered with a black, leather patch.

"Jack?" Bill and Katherine exclaimed in unison. This caused no end of confusion as at least a dozen pirates responded to the name. "We've got Jacks of too many trades," Bill announced while smirking at his own cleverness. He awaited the crowd's laughter and growing adulation, but no one else could manage so much as a smile. It was over. He'd proven himself an idiot. He resolved that, should he be confirmed, his first act as New Son would be to make all on the council use their real names. Unless the name was Jack. His second act would be to require everyone to laugh at his jokes no matter how lame. It was for their own good, really. What good is a megalomaniacal despot with low self-esteem?

However, they hadn't laughed because none of them had even heard Bill's quip. They were, to a person, fixated on One-Eyed Jack. As the initial shock wore off, everyone began murmuring with wild abandon. Bill envied them. The Yeti rose and relinquished his seat to Jack. But before he sat, Jack approached Robinson with the vessel bearing his word of the prophecy. Powers rose quickly to his feet. "I object!"

Robinson worked hard to suppress laughter. "This is not a courtroom, *counselor*. To what exactly are you objecting?"

"To it," he said pointing at One-Eyed Jack. "To him. The mechanism cannot be a word bearer." Bill puzzled at this.

"Actually," Robinson said, "there is no such rule. If the previous word bearer felt Jack the most suitable successor, then that should suffice." Powers shrugged at his compatriots and slumped back into his chair. Retrieving the Mickey tablet, Robinson beckoned One-Eyed Jack step forward. Jack inserted the vessel. Click. Light. Jack took a step back and faced Bill.

"There's something I've been meaning to tell you," he said to Bill, "for quite some time." He reached behind his head and untied the strap holding the patch in place. Slowly, deliberately, he removed the patch. Underneath was not another eye, not an empty fleshy cavity, but a metal socket. Katherine and Cleary gasped upon seeing it.

"What is that, Jack?" Bill asked.

"You know every year when I go on vacation?" he asked. Bill nodded. "I'm not going on vacation. I'm going for upgrades. Re-programming."

"Reprogramming? Like a cult?"

"No," Jack answered with a mischievous grin, "like a machine." He pointed to the socket. "This is where they connect me for the upgrades."

Bill was speechless. The hack writers of his life's story were back, because he had a million questions and couldn't verbalize a single one.

"What is the mechanism, Jack?" Katherine asked from the gallery.

Jack spotted her and waved. "Hello, Katherine. So lovely to see you. And you, too, Cleary." He then began to answer Katherine's question but looked at Bill to do so. He explained that the Council recognized early on they needed a way to observe potential candidates, to evaluate them. But they realized that people, by their very nature, were not objective. "That's why they built me," Jack said reticently.

"Built you?" Bill asked.

Jack smiled, swung his arms open wide, and said, "meet Imagineering's crowning achievement: animatronics, the Living Character Initiative and artificial intelligence all in one package. Though I often wish they had built the package a little taller." Bill stared at him, looking for some hint that he was joking. But Jack had never been known for his sense of humor.

"This just can't be," Bill said. "You can't be a ... uh ... a robot. You're my friend. I've known you for *seventeen* years. There's no way that kind of technology exists today, much less back then." He shook his head repeatedly. "It just can't be."

Jack squatted down in front of his friend and tried to explain. In the early days, he had been more like the figures in the Living Character Initiative, sensitive to certain stimuli, but largely controlled by a team of puppeteers hiding in a control room at the back of the store. "Why do you think I never left the shop?" he asked rhetorically. The personality created for him by the puppeteers became the foundation for his programming, and the growing database of recorded stimuli his memories. Once technology had progressed to the point where Jack could move, react and analyze data autonomously, only one thing was missing: thought.

"But they couldn't crack that one, Bill," Jack said. "It's funny, I can remember everything from the day they first put me in place — faces, voices, everything — and I can recall running comparative analyses of your life against the prophecy. But I don't recall having my own thoughts. I don't recall feeling alive." He placed the patch back over his eye and tied it in place. "Funny thing is, it was Walt himself who cracked the code — posthumously, of course. He often talked about dreams, about pursuing them and how, even if you don't achieve them, you'll know you've been alive. So ... they gave me dreams. They gave me goals.

"Once I had dreams, I began to feel. And once I began to feel, I began to truly think. It was overwhelming. I didn't know how to balance it all at first, but I had a good teacher." Jack stood and addressed the crowd. "Everything I have learned about being a man, I have learned from my friend, Bill Durmer. And I know, I *feel*, he is the New Son." Jack reached up and patted Bill on the shoulder and retreated to his seat.

A flood of conflicting thoughts and feelings swirled inside Bill. He felt betrayed and violated. He questioned the nature of friendship and his own identity. More than that, he questioned the ethics of a group that would create a man only to serve their own purposes. Deeper still were the theological and philosophical issues raised by Jack's very existence. What was he? If he could feel and think and dream as he claimed, did that make him alive? Was he a man, a simulacrum or a mechanical animal, living but lacking an eternal soul? The thing that nagged at him most was the suspicion that if anyone ever wrote the story of his life, which was beginning to seem inevitable, they would give these questions about Jack's nature short shrift, favoring instead the more sensational story of the prophecy. Hack writers.

Bill had always been fascinated by the word "ontology," not necessarily for its meaning but for the way it sounded. He would throw it out in conversation, never knowing if he was using it correctly, but wondering if anyone would challenge him on his usage. They never did. In this case, its meaning was pertinent. Ontology dealt with issues of the very nature of being. The nature of Jack's being was one that demanded considerable scrutiny.

But there was no time to deal with the ontological issue of One-Eyed Jack. There was a prophecy to fulfill.

"The time has come for a vote of confirmation," Robinson proclaimed.

"I hate to always be the voice of condescension," Powers said.

"I think you mean 'dissension,'" Robinson corrected him. "I believe your Freudian slip is showing." Stifled snickers from the crowd. Bill almost tried his "Jacks and trades" joke again, seeing as how the audience was more responsive, but thought better of it.

Powers attempted to continue despite the joke at his expense. "Anyway, as I was saying — as I have said I don't know how many times — you're still short one word bearer and, therefore, one vote."

Robinson smiled slyly, "Actually, we're not." He yelled toward the door, "You may come in now!" It was a rerun of the anticipation prior to One-Eyed Jack's introduction. The door opened. A tall, elegant woman entered.

From the shadows, she cried in a shrill, Southern drawl, "Billy, why did a talking pig make me drive all the way to Orlando?"

Chapter Twenty-Six:
The Last Drawing of Walt Disney

"Billy, have you seen these people?" Nancy implored. She edged closer to the door, her shoulders drawn up defensively. The din of the crowd reverberated through the gallery. Across the way, the Mintz-Powers argued with Robinson, some pointing furiously at Nancy. Bill could make out a word here and there, most of them so coarse they were only suited to sailors, bikers or film producers. Nearby, Cleary was nonplussed, as Katherine stood behind her, plugging her ears. It was a routine occurrence when Nancy was near. It wasn't that Nancy was given to the use of profanities herself, but something about her very presence inspired it in others. The Yeti stared at the thirty-something debutante and waved. Nancy recoiled in disgust. "What is he wearing anyway?"

"It's nothing," Bill answered. "Probably glandular."

"Ugh..." Nancy grunted. "Reminds me of my mother-in-law." Bill would have argued the point if it weren't established fact in Decent Chance that the McAdamses, Kenny's mother's family, came from hairy stock. Kenny's great-grandfather, Abraham McAdams, answered to the nickname Ape his entire life. For the better part of four decades, the children of Decent Chance looked forward to the culmination of the annual Christmas parade, but not for the appearance of Santa Claus. No, the jolly old elf was merely the warm-up act for the real star: Abraham "The Ape Man" McAdams, swinging shirtless from a wood and papier-mâché tree in the cold night air.

"I know they're eccentric, Nance, but..." Bill surveyed the room, noticing the anxious glances of the disparate groups, wondering if his sister was talking him out of the whole thing. "But they are well-meaning."

"Hitler was well-meaning, too, you know," she retorted. Bill didn't even justify her comment with a response.

"They just want someone to lead with vision. Think about what this could mean. For our families. For Decent Chance." He searched her atypically inscrutable expression for some sign. "Just give it a chance," he said.

"A decent chance?" she asked playfully.

"Not even that," Bill replied. She nodded her agreement. Bill hugged her tight. "It's good to see you, baby sister."

Soon thereafter, Nancy found herself standing at the center of the room, all eyes on her as Robinson spoke. "You have received a portion of the Prophecy of the New Son, a word of prophecy spoken by Walt Disney himself as he lay dying and written in his own hand. This word was given originally to Frank Thomas, one of Walt's Nine Old Men, a master of the animation arts. By accepting this word, you bear the responsibility of helping to discover the New Son, in essence the next Walt Disney. Do you accept?" Nancy nodded. "Do you have the vessel?" She dug in her clutch and retrieved it.

"You mean this wooden cigar thingy?" she asked. Robinson confirmed it and showed her how to insert the vessel into the tablet. Nancy was delighted with the device.

"Can I get one of these at the Disney Store?" she asked before proceeding to her chair.

"Would the candidate please stand?" Robinson requested. Bill complied, standing just to the right and behind him. Robinson read from the scroll, "At the time of the vote, the names of the nine original word bearers shall be called. As each is called, the current bearer of that word will come forward and read aloud the word of prophecy. Once the bearer has read the word, they will cast their vote for or against the candidate." Robinson rolled up the scroll. "Seems straightforward enough." He inserted a small key into the base of the tablet. The first vessel lit up, and the frosted glass cleared so that only the one vessel was readable. The glass itself seemed to illuminate from within and came to life as a type of computer screen, with the name Wolfgang Reitherman on it in the classic Disney font.

Robinson read the name, and Doll Lady came forward. He held the tablet low for her to read, "A new son shall rise on the Eastern shore." She removed the lei from around the Hawaiian doll's neck. From it hung a small key like the one Robinson had used. She inserted it into a slot on the right side of the tablet and turned. This action caused the light inside her vessel to change to a dim green. The glass screen frosted over her vessel and cleared over the second. Doll Lady hugged Bill and returned to her seat.

"Eric Larson," Robinson read. Oerlander, busy with the ever-important task of counting the marble tiles on the floor, had to be told by Snow White to step forward. Robinson handed him the tablet.

"No, I'm not Eric Larson," he said. "You've got the wrong person." Robinson sighed. Assuming the older man hard of hearing, Oerlander shouted, "Eric Larson is dead!"

"I know that," Robinson curtly replied. "Just read that right there," he snapped, pointing at the vessel.

Oerlander read without a hint of ceremony or gravitas, like a third grader who hadn't learned to recognize or respect punctuation, "On his heart the mark of our kingdom lore." He furrowed his brow. "Is this like a riddle or something?"

"Just put the key in here and vote yes or no," Robinson explained. Oerlander inserted the key. Most in the room held their breath, wondering if the clueless man would do the right thing. Snow White and the rest of the Cast of Thousands were motioning frantically to get his attention, nodding and mouthing the word "yes." Oerlander thought for a moment, then went with the strategy that had gotten him this far in his career. He turned the key and his vessel glowed a soft green. Robinson exhaled with relief.

"Is there bonus pay in this?" Oerlander asked. "Because I don't recall anything about secret committees in my contract."

"Please sit down!" Robinson barked. Oerlander happily complied as he was dangerously close to finishing his count of the tiles before being so rudely interrupted. Then it occurred to him he'd forgotten where he left off. Anything worth doing is worth doing twice, so he started over.

Robinson called the next name, "Marc Davis." One-Eyed Jack stepped up, practically sprinting to get to the tablet.

"Of a swifter mind and with WEDway hands," he read through a wide smile. He entered his vote and handed the tablet back to Robinson. To Bill, he quipped, "The Monocular Bionic Man to the rescue, huh Bill?"

"Indeed," Bill replied. Jack offered Bill a knuckle bump, a move that amused Bill to no end. As Jack neared his chair, Bill said, "Hey Jack!" The Lilliputian man-machine looked back. "You're a good man, my friend."

Ontological issues be damned. Jack nodded and smiled proudly.

"Ward Kimball." Tomorrow Man stood at the reading of the name. He approached Robinson with a heroic gait.

His booming voice echoed throughout the chamber as he read, "With an eye toward past on Tom Morrow lands." Inserting his key, he paused before turning it. "For the future!" he bellowed.

At the reading of John Lounsbery's name, Reynaldo stepped forward. In his grim, sonorous tone, he slowly read, "At the ball of Toombs will his fortunes rise." Once his vessel glowed green, Reynaldo nodded to Bill, letting the slightest hint of a grin slip past his morbid visage. He began his funereal creep back to Sleepy's chair.

Captain Jack rose at the reading of Milt Kahl's name. Eschewing the boozy delivery of his namesake character, he read the line soberly, in his own voice, "And his face shall call forth the redhead's eyes." He cast his vote.

"His face, huh?" Bill asked. "I must really be the one, if she picked my face over yours."

Captain Jack smirked and said, "Look me up the next time you're at Disneyland Paris." He sauntered back to his place.

"Ollie Johnston," Robinson called. Mom stood. "Are you sure he doesn't want to do this himself?" Robinson asked, referring to the actual word bearer. Mom only shrugged.

Taking the tablet from Robinson, she read, "If the King's will bear him in open house." Once she had cast her vote, she brushed past Robinson and grabbed Bill by the back of his neck. She kissed him softly on his cheek, lingering a little too long. Katherine cleared her throat loudly from the gallery trying break it up. Dodging Katherine's burning stare, she whispered to Bill, "Congratulations. You big, stubborn idiot." Feeling the woman hadn't gotten her point, Katherine cleared her throat again, louder and more forcefully this time.

"Get her, Kat," Nancy quipped under her breath. Mom pulled away.

Robinson stared at Nancy soberly. "Frank Thomas," he said. Nancy nodded and stood. Slowly, but gracefully, she made her way to the spot where Robinson and Bill stood. She took the tablet.

"Read this," Robinson said to her.

"Then so shall his home, child, sister and spouse," she read. Her brow furrowed. "I don't understand."

"It means," Robinson explained, "that you have a say. Your family has a say in this. I suppose that's why you received this word."

"So what do I do?" she asked. Bill knew his sister. She wasn't asking about the method of the vote, but advice on which choice to make.

"Vote yes, Aunt Nancy," Cleary said. Katherine nodded in agreement. Nancy hesitated.

"It's okay, Sis," Bill said. She put the key in and started to slowly turn it.

"I can't!" She jerked the key back out. "Bill, I can't do this. It doesn't make any sense. I mean, a prophecy by Walt Disney? Really? This is what you want to base your life on?"

"I'm not basing my life on it," he argued. "I'm just..." Just what? Did he even know what he was doing anymore, or had he just gotten caught up in the fervor? "I'm just trying to use my ... gifts. To make the world a little better," he explained. She shook her head.

"No. I'm sorry." She put the key back in.

"Why?" Bill demanded angrily. "Why won't you, just this once, do something for me? You know, I've blamed luck. I've blamed fate. I've blamed boats and storms and the bay. I've blamed the whole damn town. I've blamed myself. I've even blamed God. But now I realize, the one person I should be blaming is you."

Nancy retorted sharply, "Blame me for what, Bill?"

"For my life!" He paced back and forth, running his hands nervously through his hair as he was wont to do. "For wasting the last two decades in a little shop in a little town. All because you begged me to take over." He stood toe to toe with her. "You knew Mom was ready to sell it. Or turn it over to one of Dad's brothers. But no, you changed her mind. You convinced her that it just had to be me. Why is that, Nancy?" He answered his own question, which was just as well, because Nancy was using all her energy to hold back tears. "I'll tell you why: because you had to be in control. Because you wanted to walk into the store every day, just like you always had, and be the little princess." The tears came now, freely and heavily. "You just had to keep me from my dreams!"

She punched her brother in the chest. "No!" She hit him over and over. Bill only stood and accepted the blows. "No! No! No!" Nancy withdrew from him and wiped her eyes. She spotted Katherine and Cleary in the gallery. Katherine held the crying girl close, consoling her. "You want to know why I insisted you take over the store? Or does it really matter? You seem to have formed your opinion of me, and it's not going to change."

"Tell me," Bill said, softly seething.

Nancy placed herself directly before him and grabbed his shirt sleeves, forcing him to look at her. "I was nineteen. I had just lost two of the three most important men in my life. I was not going to lose the third. I couldn't! You don't know what it was like when you left for college. I cried for a week!" She let go of him and backed away a step, reeling from her own vulnerability. Tears streamed down Bill's cheeks. "No, I'm not a saint. I'm not as perfect as 'the great Bill Durmer.' But if I've ever hurt you, it's only because I didn't want to lose you. But now you just resent me for it, so I guess it doesn't matter what I do." She snatched the tablet from Robinson, inserted the key and turned so violently that the key broke off. A collective gasp filled the room. Katherine was apoplectic, staring at the broken key in shame and disbelief. "I'm sorry," she said to Robinson. "Did it work?"

Robinson took the tablet from her and examined it carefully. The screen had become completely translucent. All the lights were extinguished. Nancy panicked, "I'm sorry. I didn't... You don't really need it, right? Just do it verbally," she pleaded with Robinson. "I'll start. I vote yes. Do you hear me?" Robinson was unresponsive. She took her brother's hand. "I voted yes. I promise. It was yes."

Turning the tablet sideways, Robinson touched the lock where the key had broken off. Suddenly, the lock began to turn. It turned back to a neutral position, and the broken piece of the key fell out into his palm. The frosted glass flickered and flashed. One by one, the first eight vessels became visible for a brief moment, then glowed green and frosted over again. The glass cleared, revealing the ninth vessel. On the screen, were the words, "Les Clark." Robinson breathed a sigh of relief.

Nancy asked, "What happened?"

"It's okay," Robinson replied, then announcing to everyone. "Everything's okay." A smattering of applause broke out among the crowd. Bill squeezed Nancy's hand.

"You will never lose me," he said. "Do you understand that?" She nodded and returned to her seat.

Robinson turned to his wife. "Les Clark." Mrs. Robinson rose and took the tablet to read the final line of the prophecy. Bill could feel his heart thumping in his throat. Katherine and Cleary clenched hands tightly. A deafening silence filled the room.

It occurred to Bill that he still didn't know which way she would vote.

She had never confirmed to him whether his recounting of his story was what she was looking for. The only thing to do was hold his breath and wait.

Mrs. Robinson read the line as loudly as her sweet, little voice could muster. "Now as then, it starts ... with a mouse." She winked at Bill. "You passed," she whispered to him. Bill released his breath. Mrs. Robinson inserted her key and turned. The vessel flashed green for a moment, then the tablet went blank. The screen's frosting disappeared, and all of the lights flashed brightly and went out. A small, but audible click echoed through the room. Mrs. Robinson gave the tablet to her husband, puzzled by what had happened. He turned the tablet over to find that a hidden hatch had popped open on the underside. Reaching inside, he pulled out an old, weathered envelope.

"Thank you. You can sit now, Dear," he said to his wife. As Mrs. Robinson carried the towel baby back to her seat, her husband turned the tablet over to find that the entire prophecy was now visible and brightly lit. He began to read the prophecy in full:

> "A New Son shall rise on the Eastern Shore,
> On his heart the mark of our kingdom lore,
> Of a swifter mind and with WEDway hands,
> With an eye toward past on Tom Morrow lands.
> At the ball of Toombs will his fortunes rise,
> And his face shall call forth the redhead's eyes.
> If the King's will bear him in open house,
> Then so shall his home, child, sister and spouse.
> Now as then, it starts with a mouse."

Robinson placed the tablet down, trading it off for the scroll. Unrolling it, he read, "If a unanimous vote of confirmation is given, the candidate must pass the final test. The item will determine conclusively if the candidate is truly the New Son." Robinson tucked the scroll under his arm and held the old envelope out for Bill. "It's your fate."

Bill couldn't move. He stared at the envelope as if it were an alien thing. A collage of memories flooded his mind: the storm clouds over the bay, Claymoor spinning yarns in his rocking chair, his father casting a net on a Sunday morning, Red driving a bus, turning over the Closed sign for the last time at the store.

"I need a moment," he said and retreated to the back of the gallery. The crowd parted to make a path for him. No one said a word.

Bill searched for a dark corner, a difficult task in a round room. Finding the darkest spot he could, as far away from everyone as he could get, he fell down to his knees. For the first time since that fateful night on the pier, since his life had turned upside down, Bill Durmer prayed.

"Father," he whispered, "I don't know what to do here. I'm sorry I haven't talked to you in a while, but I was a little confused. The last time I asked you for a sign, you gave me an apocalypse. Or maybe that was just a kick in the butt, I don't know. But I'm asking you again. I'm here on my knees, begging you to show me the way." He sat silently for a moment, debating with himself whether to continue, knowing there was no point in lying. Searching his heart, he knew what he was about to say was the truth. "Not my will, but yours be done."

When he returned to the stone seat, Robinson inquired, "Everything okay?" Bill nodded and took the envelope. His fingers slid underneath the flap. The glue on the seal had become brittle over time and gave way easily. Lifting the flap, he could swear he smelled the stale, sanitized air of a hospital room. Inside, he found a folded piece of animation paper. He began to unfold it, letting the envelope fall to the floor.

Robinson leaned over his shoulder to catch a glimpse. His wife nervously rocked the towel baby. Tomorrow Man removed his fishbowl helmet and wiped sweat from his brow. Captain Jack chewed on the arm of his horn rimmed glasses. Jenny squatted beside her aunt's chair, gripping the older woman's arm tightly. Reynaldo rubbed his upper lip, removing the makeup there and revealing skin even paler underneath. Mom unconsciously twirled her hair between her fingers. Powers chewed his fingernails. Oerlander discovered his own reflection in the shiny marble floor and stared downward, trying to curl his tongue into a U-shape. One-Eyed Jack sat bolt upright, coolly observing the nervous actions of others, alternately trying some of them on for himself. Katherine and Cleary tiptoed over to Nancy's chair, one on each side, and the three of them clutched hands

Bill opened the last fold of the paper. What he saw upon opening it caught his breath. "Oh, my God." There in the shaky, hand drawn stylings of a dying man, was a sketch of a landscape. The face of the moon peeked out from behind clouds, looking down on the scene of stairs descending a bluff to a narrow beach. On the stairs was a man, sitting, looking at something on the sand below. And on the beach was a mouse, standing upright and staring back up at him. The last drawing of Walt Disney. William Eugene Durmer, Jr. was the New Son.

Robinson looked at the word bearers and cried out, "The prophecy has been fulfilled!" One person in the back of the crowd clapped, then another and another until the room was brimming with cheers and applause. The word bearers rose and converged on Bill to see the drawing. But Katherine and Cleary ran over, getting to him first. Cleary wrapped her arms around her father's waist. Katherine kissed him and stood behind him, caressing his hair as the others gathered around.

Through the crowd, Bill saw Mrs. Robinson still sitting in her chair. She kissed the towel baby, then loosed her grip. Gravity tugged at the swaddling, unraveling the blankets and towels until the towel baby was no more than a heap of linens on the floor. Mrs. Robinson only sat and wept. Bill handed off the sketch to Katherine. "I'll be right back." Bill gingerly approached Mrs. Robinson. He knelt and began to pick up the remains of the towel baby. He felt a hand on his shoulder.

"Leave it," Mrs. Robinson said.

Maybe it was that he couldn't stand to see a woman cry. Maybe it was that she reminded him a little of his own mother, but he was compelled to help. "But your baby."

"It's okay," she smiled through streams of tears, "I don't need it anymore." Bill helped her to her feet and led her to her husband. Backslaps and handshakes propelled them along. Tomorrow Man crowned Bill with the fishbowl helmet and shouted, "It's a great, big beautiful tomorrow!"

***

That evening, following the closing of the Magic Kingdom, the Council of the Nine enjoyed a parade and a fireworks show all their own. Sitting on a blanket at the base of the statue of Walt and Mickey, Katherine rested against Bill's shoulder, his arm wrapped tight around her. "What now?" she asked.

"I don't know," Bill said. "I guess it's time to start dreaming." Just then, Mom stepped in front of them, eliciting an exasperated sigh from Katherine.

"I have something for you from my word bearer," she said.

"So I still don't get to know who he is?" asked Bill. Mom shook her head and tossed a small envelope at his feet.

"See you around," she said as she walked away.

"Don't count on it!" Katherine called after her. Bill glared at his wife. "What? I don't like her."

He ribbed her, "You could try being nice." Katherine watched the woman walk away.

"She is devastatingly beautiful, though," she joked. She reached for the envelope. Opening it, they found a D-note that read, "Congratulations. Have a Nescafé on me." They puzzled at its meaning for a moment, then tossed the note aside. It was not the time for mysteries.

In the shadows away to Bill's right, a large man in a business suit smiled and walked away.

Chapter Twenty-Seven:
Closing the Book on Bill Durmer

"We honor and respect the trust people place in us.
Our fun is about laughing at our experiences and ourselves."
- Walt Disney Company values -

"And I hate chapters that start with quotes," Bill ranted. "It's just lazy writing. Be original." He had been on edge for months about the pending publication of *Midlife Mouse*, a book about his tumble down the mouse-hole to Wonderland. He had every right to be nervous as the author was a first-timer, a failed Birmingham filmmaker who lost his business when an ad agency client refused to pay him for the animated logo he created for Project Disappportunity.

"If you're so nervous, why didn't you hire a better writer?" Katherine asked. Bill shook his head. The book had been the least of his concerns in the six months since his confirmation. First he had a battle royale with the company's board. Whereas many senior executives in the past had been word bearers or at least privy to the prophecy, the modern board was skeptical at best. But company archivists were soon to confirm the authenticity of the drawing. They also learned Roy O. Disney had altered the company's charter shortly after Walt's death to ensure the New Son's ascent to power. Bill was given the new title Chief Visionary Officer. While he had veto power over projects in all the company's divisions, his primary purpose was innovation — innovation of content, method and form.

With the corporate battles behind him, Bill set about performing his new job with gusto, determined to prove to the board his worth. Despite the charter, they didn't trust him for some reason. Just because he had risen to power through the efforts of a robot, a bunch of outsiders and an imaginary bus driver, they failed to take him seriously. Skeptics.

Fulfilling his promise, he began his era by defining a new direction for Tomorrowland. Work had already begun at Imagineering on creating a unified look for the land at all Disney parks worldwide. Rather than going with a retro-futuristic feel, they consulted visionary architects of the day to create the most optimistic view of tomorrow possible. Tomorrow Man came out of retirement to oversee the project. Bill had already begun to work with a number of private spaceflight and deep-sea exploration companies as consultants and potential sponsors of his Mission: Anywhere attraction.

Even before he had won his battle with the board, Bill had pitched his *Tomorrowland* film trilogy to producer Jerry Bruckheimer. The first film was scheduled to begin principal photography the following Spring, with Tony Hale set to star. Tomorrow Man still didn't know who the actor was. (Bill feared the author of his biography wouldn't know either and would only mention the actor by name without ever bothering to elaborate. He was right.)

Bill's story had become a media sensation. Before the biography was even complete, the company green-lighted a film adaptation. Johnny Depp was attached to play Bill. An unknown cast member from Disneyland Paris, known for his uncanny resemblance to Depp, was signed to portray Captain Jack. Bill could never get either of them to admit to being on the Council of the Nine.

His extraordinary journey was even slated to become an experience at the Magic Kingdom. Titled Mickey's Magical Prophecy Party, the after-hours, separately ticketed event allowed guests to experience the prophecy test versions of Country Bear Jamboree, Haunted Mansion and Pirates of the Caribbean and to ride the secret PeopleMover to the retired attraction warehouse. Each night of the event, several guests would be randomly chosen to be the new Bill Durmer. Cast members portraying the Council would lead them through the evening. When they rode the attractions, the characters reacted accordingly; Madame Leota would even say the names of the chosen guests. They were tested in the warehouse by cast members portraying the Tomorrowlanders, "kidnapped" by the Cast of Thousands and taken on a boat ride through "it's a small world" with their own matching rubberhead. At the end of the experience, they then proceeded to the rotunda for confirmation. Other guests would step into the roles of the various groups supporting the Council. When the final yes vote was cast (and they were all yes votes), the winning guests would be presented with a highly stylized version of Walt's drawing featuring themselves in Bill's place. The event was booked at least a year in advance.

At all of the Disney parks, visiting in costume as One-Eyed Jack, Tomorrow Man, the Yeti or any of the other eccentric characters from Bill's story had become commonplace. There was even talk of an annual Convention of the Nine, or NineCon, at which the enthusiasts could gather. The company was quick to capitalize on the craze by issuing official Council of the Nine merchandise, including costumes and memorabilia. In fact, a week out from Christmas, current estimates held that at least one out of every three homes would have at least one prophecy-related gift.

Also as promised, Bill had used the power of his new position to help his hometown. First, he had convinced the company to spearhead the cleanup of the fish mounds and the restoration of the coastline. He used the media coverage of his story to boost tourism in Decent Chance to unprecedented levels. Finally, he created an unprecedented public-private partnership between the company and his hometown to create a new initiative, named Disney Villages.

The goal was to promote and preserve the character of small-town America by setting architectural and beautification standards, investing in arts education and supporting locally-owned businesses. Disney would build resorts in the towns and offer entire vacation experiences to guests. They would also offer franchises of Disney-owned retail stores, allowing the franchisee to share the brand identity. Durmer's Tomorrowland was the pilot store of this effort, opening in the old Durmer's Electronics storefront. It offered cutting-edge electronics and other forward-looking merchandise consistent with the new Tomorrowland theme.

One-Eyed Jack's toy store was another matter entirely. Rather than attempting to find the right partner in each village to run such a unique franchise, the company chose to simply build more Jacks. The original Jack, for his part, was excited at the possibility of having "siblings." This choice led to more ontological issues that would be ignored for years. Bill once joked that Jack was only biding his time until there were enough duplicates of himself to overthrow mankind. Jack's cool reaction to the comment unnerved Bill — even though he knew the man-machine was still refining his humor programming. For Christmas, Bill gave Jack a framed print of Asimov's Three Laws of Robotics. Just in case.

Decent Chance and Walt's boyhood home of Marceline were the first Disney Villages. Based on initial interest in the planned resorts, Bill spurred the creation of an entire division to begin identifying and planning additional villages, with the goal of having at least one in each state. Following the groundbreaking for the new Disney Chance Bayfront resort, Cleary pointed out the irony to her father that the same people who tried to keep Walmart out of the town were now embracing a much more aggressive presence — a near takeover — by another large corporation. Bill, unable to counter her argument, suggested they just sit quietly and enjoy the sound of the bay.

Bill's cousin, Auggie, attempted to take the lion's share of the credit for the Disney Villages concept, but he was fighting an uphill battle making that argument from behind prison bars. The new mayor, however, could legitimately claim a share of the credit, especially considering she cast the swing vote in Bill's confirmation. In a fit of hometown pride and inspired by Bill's goal to use his talents for the betterment of the world, Nancy put her name on the ballot for the special election following Auggie's indictment. If image-conscious control freakery were a talent, she had found a natural outlet for hers. Her first official act as mayor was to establish a council on physical fitness, admitting in private that she just didn't want a bunch of fatties ruining her new office furniture. Maybe a tiger could change its stripes, as Bill would say, but it was still going to maul you at the first opportunity.

As for the Council, they evolved into a sort of brain trust supporting Bill in his efforts. He even created an honorary position for Powers, reasoning that a little dissension is a good thing. They didn't meet regularly, but when they did, Katherine was always present — just to keep an eye on Mom.

To ensure that he spent ample time with his family, Bill encouraged Katherine to begin home schooling the children. In only a few months, they had spent as many weeks on the road as at home, splitting time between Florida and California, with trips planned to New York, Paris, Shanghai, Hong Kong and Tokyo. Clay had finally worked through his speech issues and took great pride in reciting the names of the cities he was soon to visit. Screams of "Shanghai!" became a battle cry of sorts for him and often preceded a sneak attack from the pirate sword-wielding five-year-old in fishbowl pajamas.

Bill became concerned early on that his initiatives were out of reach for most Americans. He was determined to find a way for those of limited means to experience "the magic." One idea he had in mind was to create a more luxurious experience at the value resorts. Which is why, almost exactly a year to the day from their last real family vacation, Bill found himself shuffling sleepily toward the food court of the All-Star Movies Resort.

Taking a cue from Captain Jack, he wore a Goofy pirate bandana and allowed the ears to dangle down to hide his face. He had become such a celebrity, especially on Disney property, that it was nearly impossible for him to walk unmolested through the parks. With his head hanging low, his flip-flops scuffing the concrete, he made his way out of Andy's bedroom, past RC, weaving between umbrella-shaded patio tables and inside to the drink stand.

As he stood waiting for his turn at the coffee dispenser, a familiar voice bellowed from behind him, "Well, look who it is!" Bill couldn't place it at first, but one glance over his shoulder was all he needed to recognize Christmas Tree Head. "So we meet again."

"So we do," Bill replied. After months in the media spotlight, Bill had become slightly more adept at meeting strangers. "How have you been? Good year?"

Christmas Tree Head bobbed his big head up and down, causing the ornaments on his hat to sway violently. "Can't complain. Slow up top, a little crazy in the middle and full in the bottom," he said, "kind of like my ex-wife." He guffawed. Bill politely laughed along. "Say, didn't I see you on the news about something?"

"I was mistakenly wanted for kidnapping back in June," Bill kidded. "Maybe it was that."

"Tell me something," Christmas Tree Head said seriously, "you don't like small talk much do you?" Bill was busted.

"No, I really don't," Bill confessed. "I'm sorry."

The big man was gracious. "No harm done. You're a nice enough fellow anyhow."

Then Bill did something he would have never done a year earlier: he introduced himself. "Name's Bill, Bill Durmer," he said, trying to keep his voice low enough to avoid drawing a crowd. Bill recalled that Christmas Tree Head had called him by name the night they were shuffled off to the Grand Floridian, but the big man showed no hint of recognition. That in itself was a relief to Bill.

Christmas Tree Head grabbed Bill's hand and squeezed it nearly in two. "Pleasure to meet you, Bill Durmer," he said. "Or meet you again, I suppose."

"I suppose so. What was your name again?" Bill wondered at that particular idiom, ending a question with "again" when it had never been answered before. It seemed almost snide, like thanking a cheapskate for a minuscule tip.

Christmas Tree Head demurred, "You wouldn't believe me if I told you."

Bill took his newfound extroversion a step further and grabbed the big man's shoulder. "I have specialized in the unbelievable since we last met. Try me."

"Walter," he said. "Walter Disney." Bill was taken aback.

"Seriously? Are you—" Bill's unfinished question was met with a hearty, well-rehearsed laugh.

"Nope. No relation," he said. "There's a handful of us around the country. Makes life interesting, I tell you that much. It's tougher for some than for others. It's not an easy thing to walk around every day of your life being compared to Uncle Walt." Bill could relate more than the man knew.

It was Bill's turn at the coffee. He stepped up to the machine and realized, much to his chagrin, that he had left his cups back in the room. Christmas Tree Head offered up one of his. "Here's a brand new one. Never used." Bill tried to refuse, but the big man wouldn't have it. "This Nescafé's on me," he said. Bill flinched. His hair stood on end. There was something in his words that was familiar yet out of his memory's reach.

"What did you say?" Bill asked, trying to determine where he had heard that phrase before.

"I said coffee's on me," Christmas Tree Head replied. Bill brushed his suspicions aside. He had grown accustomed to expecting a new revelation or mystery around every corner at the parks. He supposed no one ever quite got over "being prophesied on." Bill humbly accepted the coffee mug. The big man spied an opening at the next coffee machine and excused himself. Bill was still working out the perfect creamer-to-sugar ratio when

Christmas Tree Head came back.

"You have a good day, Bill Durmer," he said. Bill, holding stirrers in his mouth, couldn't reply but nodded. Christmas Tree Head reached a meaty paw into his shirt pocket. "Don't know why you would need it, but here's my card." He laid it on the counter beside Bill's cup and was gone. Bill snapped the lid on his coffee and then noticed the card. It was glossy red with an embossed, gold script D on the front. Bill slowly picked it up and looked around for the unrelated Walter Disney to no avail. He opened the card. It was blank.

"Unbelievable." Bill rushed back to the room to tell Cleary and Kat the news. He didn't get the chance. No sooner than he had opened the door, Cleary held something up within an inch of his face. Bill recoiled, fearing he would be hit.

"*Midlife Mouse*," she chirped excitedly, "The incredible true story of the next Walt Disney." Bill pushed the book away just enough that his forty-year-old eyes could see the cover. He took it from her.

"Advance copy," Katherine said. "There's supposedly a whole box at home." Bill scanned the front and back covers. His pulse raced as he did.

"How is it?" he asked nervously. Katherine shrugged.

"We've just been looking at the pictures," Cleary explained.

"I'm in the book, Daddy!" Clay yelled, followed by, "Shanghai!" He attacked the bed with his sword.

"Book. Book. Book," Clementine repeated as she toddled around the room.

Bill plopped on the bed between Katherine and Cleary, who opened the book to a photo section in the center. There were archival photos of Claymoor, the store, Bill's parents, and the Decent Chance public pier. Another section was dedicated to Disney history, including a pictorial history of all the word bearers. As Cleary flipped through those, pointing out the faces she recognized, Bill saw something familiar in one of the photos she skipped over.

"Turn that back," he said. When she did, he couldn't believe his eyes. He saw the face of a kindly, but energetic old man with thin grey hair, a sloped nose and prominent ears.

"That's Roy E. Disney," Katherine said to Clay, who was now draped over her shoulder. "He was Walt's nephew." Noticing the caption, she commented, "Awww... He died just a few days before our trip last year. A few more months, and we could have met him." Bill pictured the man in a bus driver's costume.

"I think I did," he said. He touched the man's face on the page. "Thanks, Red." Katherine and Cleary didn't comment. They had long since stopped questioning Bill's sanity on these things. They'd seen too much. Taking a deep breath and trying to brighten the mood, Bill said, "Okay, let's read this thing!"

He picked up the book and turned to the beginning. "Chapter One. Bill Durmer was in over his head. Lightning crashed in the night sky outside." Bill frowned. "The night sky outside?" he asked rhetorically. "Where else would the night sky be?"

"Bill," Katherine pleaded, "Just give it a chance."

He acquiesced and continued reading. "He peered through a crack in the curtains to spot the small army that had him surrounded like a rat in a rat cage. A thousand questions raced through his mind, but he would never ask any of them. Durmer didn't like questions, only answers. He was a master of small talk, but this night called for harsher words. 'They'll never take me alive,' Durmer murmured."

He stared at the book in disbelief. "Murmured," he repeated. How could this happen? An entire lifetime spent speaking loudly and distinctly, never experiencing the full breadth of verbal expression, all for naught.

Throwing caution to the wind, Bill took a shallow breath and with the least strength he could possibly muster, he murmured for the first time in his life. For a brief, dull moment, Bill Durmer murmured like many men had murmured before.

"Hack writers." And he slammed the book shut.

Acknowledgments

First, I wish to thank my wife, Kelli, and my children, Savannah and Cooper, for putting up with me during the years of gestation for this project. I promise that on our next Disney World trip I won't think about the sequel … much. I love you all.

Thanks to my friend, Kimberly Poiroux Brewer, for her initiative to start a Facebook group dedicated to encouraging me to write my first novel. Thanks for the push I needed, Kim!

Thanks to my documentary collaborator and dear friend, Kris Wheeler, for helping me realize how much I love the written word.

My beta readers were a huge help: Deborah Krauss, Lee Meadows, Nicklaus Louis, Jerrod Brown, Kristin Heptinstall, Hyrum Rhodes and Kimberly Torchia. Thank you all for believing!

Thanks to fellow authors and self-publishing gurus Rob Kroese, Stant Litore and Leonard Kinsey for their great advice, great humor and great (virtual) friendship. You make me glad Al Gore built the Internet.

For superb editorial advice and unflagging encouragement, I owe a huge debt of thanks to the kind and talented Tom Wofford.

Thanks to Chris Garrison for bringing "The Last Drawing of Walt Disney" to life. You are a time machine of cartooning talent, my friend.

Thanks to Nicklaus Louis, for his help in making this look like a real book.

Thanks to my pastor, Bob Flayhart, for his instruction and inspiration.

Huge thank-yous go to Shea Bowles and Chris Tomberlin, my best friends for more than two decades, for unwavering support of my career(s).

Finally, thanks to my parents, Terry and Alice Franklin. You have always believed in me and never once told me to "get a real job." I love you both.

About the Author
Wayne Franklin

Wayne Franklin grew up in the suburbs of Mobile, Alabama, the son of a mechanic from rural Escambia County and an office manager from Fairhope – the inspiration for Decent Chance. Despite this very Southern background, and the fact that he is the creator of the blog real-southern. com, Wayne still has no discernible accent. A career commercial director and editor, Wayne co-founded the Sidewalk Film Festival in Birmingham and is the co-producer/director of the award-winning documentary *Duke & The King*. When not writing, blogging, producing, directing or editing, Wayne does his best to be a Bill Durmer to his wife and two kids. Minus the running away to a theme park thing. Despite rumors to the contrary, he never worked on Project Disaspportunity.

www.ingramcontent.com/pod-product-compliance
Lightning Source LLC
Chambersburg PA
CBHW050021180626
46810CB00002B/515